# CHICAGO SIN

*Omnibus*

## ALTA HENSLEY

## RENEE ROSE

 Formatted with Vellum

# CONTENTS



## DEN OF SINS

## ROOTED IN SIN

## TASTE OF SIN

# WANT FREE RENEE ROSE BOOKS?

**Go to http://subscribepage.com/alphastemp** to sign up for Renee Rose's newsletter and receive a free copy of *Alpha's Temptation*, *Theirs to*

*Protect, Owned by the Marine* and more. In addition to the free stories, you will also get bonus epilogues, special pricing, exclusive previews and news of new releases.

# DEN OF SINS

A Dark Mafia Romance

# CHAPTER ONE

*Armando*

Is a sinner ever free?

Regardless of the answer, I'm as close as you can get. I'm no longer trapped in a cage.

The prison gates open, and I walk out with nothing but a paper bag that contains the few belongings I came in with.

My cousin, Marco, waits for me, standing in front of his SUV with an overly expressive smile on his face. I know him well enough to see right through it. Sure, he's happy to see me, but he's obviously uncomfortable.

Can't say I blame him.

Marco visited me here on occasion. He would drive up from Chicago, our hometown an hour away, to spend an hour updating me on what was going on with the Outfit. He, and sometimes his brother Leo, are the only ones who visited out of the *La Famiglia*.

Again, something I understood.

Prison could be contagious. No one wants to catch it.

It's a plague that once transmitted is hard to treat.

Even my mother didn't visit—not being able to handle seeing her son treated like an animal. Her words, not mine.

As I hesitate outside of the prison gates, Marco eventually steps forward, breaking the silence. "It's good to see you," he says, finally giving up his painted smile.

"Yeah." I'm not sure I'm up for small talk yet.

Marco seems to understand and moves on quickly, motioning to the car. "Come on, let's get you out of here."

We both climb into the vehicle, and Marco starts the drive back to the city.

I stare out the window, seeing nothing. Apparently hearing nothing until I realize Marco has been talking the whole time.

"...when you hit Rocco's for a haircut and shave Friday. It's the same old crew, of course, but I'll bet they give you priority in the barber's chair.... The florist shop is still next door, but Mary Alice sold the place to her apprentice, Hannah. Remember her? She was just a kid when you left, but she's hot as fuck now...."

I tune him out. The places he's talking about—our old familiar haunts—seem so far away and removed right now. I guess I'll have to go there to feel anything.

"Some shit's changed since you've been away," Marco observes.

I don't answer, waiting for him to go on.

"The Outfit's getting more and more powerful, but it's losing its soul. A lot of the Made men are getting complacent. There's no more progress, you know? No old soul wisdom, as the don calls it."

I absorb his words without comment. Marco is a smart guy. There's no one whose opinion I respect more, especially when it comes to Family business. He came into the Outfit about the same time I did, but he has good insight into it. He is far wiser than his age or experience.

He definitely possesses the old soul wisdom. Marco seems to be able to look at the organization objectively and notice what's really going on.

I try to focus on his words, on work, and on what will be my reality again now that I'm back in the fold of the family, but I fight an overwhelming tightness in my chest.

The sides of the SUV feel suffocating, reminding me of the prison cell.

I take a deep breath and crack the window. It's been a long time since I've been around anyone who hasn't been jaded by the system. People in prison speak differently than people who are free.

Getting used to Marco—getting used to anyone—is going to be a challenge.

Fifty-four months. That's how long I served in the state pen. My colorless existence between four concrete walls.

Longer than some members of the Outfit served. Shorter than others. I kept my mouth shut and did the time like I was supposed to. I also earned a business degree.

"Out on good behavior," Marco huffs, as if he's reading my mind. "Who would have thought?"

I don't answer but think how ironic that is since I literally shanked a man in prison. Thankfully, I'm a Made Man, and the don kept me protected and out of trouble. Amazing how the mafia has the ability to make things simply disappear on the inside. The power inside the system may even be stronger than outside the concrete walls.

Noticing the white knuckles of Marco's hands as he grips the steering wheel, I see I'm making him uncomfortable. I know why. I got pinched, and he didn't. I served time while he remained free. I've felt the same way before. A survivor's guilt of sorts when one of your own goes down for a family crime. It's hard to face, and there is always a part of you that wonders when you'll be next. It's cliche to say that prison changes a man, but it's fucking true.

Now, riding passenger in my cousin Marco's car back in Chicago, I don't experience the big joy of freedom. I note the sky. Tall buildings. The traffic. The noise and energy of the city that ate me up and shit me out. It elicits nothing. The familiar streets, familiar places evoke nothing of my old self. Of the young man I was before I did time. I've been numb the whole ride, having some kind of out-of-body experience with being on the outside. I've thought of this day since the day I went in, but now that it's here, now that I'm out... I feel nothing at all. I'm dead to the experience.

"Hey, let's stop for dinner. My treat, obviously." He maneuvers his SUV to parallel park in front of Lorenzo's Italian restaurant, one of the Outfit's favorite haunts.

"Sure, yeah." I don't want to. The silent car ride was excruciating enough. I appreciate Marco's loyalty to me, but I'd rather not have to spend another hour with him. I don't want to see anyone I used to know.

But I always did love eating at Lorenzo's. The food is served in large portions, and everyone is treated like a guest of the house, especially if you're part of the Outfit. The waiters and staff used to know me by name, greeting me with enthusiastic handshakes and hugs. It'll be interesting to see if anything has changed.

An explosion of voices assaults me as I step inside.

I have no weapon. I have no way to fight.

# CHAPTER TWO

*Armando*

My whole body goes rigid, my instinct to fight for my life activated before I can turn it off.

*"Bentornato!"* Welcome back. Cheers of celebration follow.

Fuck.

*Bentornato, Mando*, the giant banner spanning the private room reads.

Everyone shouts and claps around me as I struggle to exhale the breath lodged under my ribs. They're focused on me with welcoming faces, but I can't make my face crack even the semblance of a smile for the assholes.

*"Cristo*, you coulda warned me," I mutter to Marco. We're six months apart, me and him. Raised together. Fought together. We became Made Men together. We're tighter than brothers.

And for a split moment... I thought we were going to die together.

He cuts a look at me, taking in my balled fists. The muscle ticking at my jaw. "Surprise," he says sardonically. "Sorry. I'll get you a drink."

My ma throws herself at me, her thin arms strangling my neck. I have to force my fingers open to hold her. I feel too many ribs on her back. Adrenaline's still pumping from the unwelcome fucking surprise.

Seriously. Who gives a new prison-release a *surprise* party? I coulda killed one of them if they were within swinging distance. Thank God Marco didn't give me a gun when he picked me up.

I scan the room filled with familiar faces.

Don Pachino sits in the back, chewing on a cigar and sipping whiskey, his capos and son-in-law beside him. I lift my chin to him across the room to show respect, and he raises his glass.

It's a soldier's welcome: the hero's return.

Except only the people in this room will treat me like a hero. To the rest of the world, I'm forever marked by my felony conviction.

A criminal.

"You're too thin, Mando," my mother chides when I finally get her to loosen her hold on me.

"So are you, Ma." I kiss her cheek. She's much more bony than when I left. Her hair's going grey, too. It kills me to see how much my stint in prison aged her.

I stare down at the cross around her neck and wonder what she must think of me. It's not often that the son of a devout Catholic ends up in prison. I know I've disappointed her in a way that can never be made right again.

The cross around her neck only serves as a further reminder of how far I have fallen from the altar boy with dreams of one day becoming a priest like my childhood hero, Father Fantoni. The faith he had always preached to me about seemed to have no power in saving me from my own demons and family ties.

My mother stares at me with a mix of love and uncertainty. I can see the fear in her eyes that I could end up back where I just came from, but still she welcomes me with open arms. She loves me despite what I do and who I surround myself with, and for that I am grateful. She's a mother in the mafia, and that comes with a certain amount of baggage but also understanding. But no mother wants to see her son go to prison. I'm supposed to keep what I do secret from her church and the ladies she does lunch with. I'm not supposed to mess up.

I do want to tell her that I'm sorry for letting her down and that I will try to do better, but it's hard to find the words.

I don't know why stepping into the old place feels like a punch in the gut. This party is for me. I should be celebrating. But I don't remember what joy feels like.

I don't even remember what it means to feel.

Father Fantoni approaches, and though I'm surprised to see him at the party, I know he's no stranger to the Outfit. He's seen us all grow from children and is just as much family as anyone else in this room.

"I hope to see you at Sunday Service now," he says as he places a welcoming hand on my shoulder. "Welcome home."

There is no judgment in his eyes. No condemnation.

"Yes, Father. As soon as I get... settled."

Seemingly satisfied with my answer, he nods and continues making his rounds in the room.

"Good to see you, Mando." A sweet feminine voice murmurs at my shoulder.

I turn to take in the practiced beauty of my ex. Her perfect makeup, straightened hair. Big green doe-eyes.

Fucking Grace.

Oddly, I feel nothing. Not rage. Not pain. Not betrayal.

I flatline on any response, so I turn and hit her with full eye contact. "You didn't have to come."

"Course I did." Her fingers tangle and fight each other in front of her waist. She's in high heels and a blue polka-dot wrap-around that shows off her perfect tits, with a diamond heart necklace dangling above them. A necklace I sure as hell didn't give her. Ten feet behind her stands Emilio, her new conquest. Or maybe he conquered her—what do I know?

All I know is she didn't even bother showing up in person to return my engagement ring.

"No. You really didn't." I say it pointed-like, and color leeches from her face.

"If you want me to leave, I will," she whispers, lips trembling.

There was a time seeing those green eyes shining with tears would make me move mountains to comfort her. Now, I feel nothing at her distress. I just shrug. "I don't give a shit either way, doll."

I push past her and make my way to the don. His salt and pepper hair has also grown more salty, but he still looks every inch the reigning king. The godfather of the Outfit, if you will.

He's the only one I have to respect here. The one I owe my loyalty to. The rest of these *stronzos* can fuck themselves.

Aside from my cousins, no one in this room bothered to visit me during my stay in the pen. Why are they acting like they care now?

"Mando. Sit." Don Pachino pats the barstool beside him. I'm not sure if I should be offended that he didn't stand up to embrace me. I drop into the seat and offer my hand. He tucks the cigar between his teeth and squeezes my palm too hard, like he used to when I was a teen. Showing me who's boss.

Alex, his son-in-law, moves away to give us privacy.

"Care for one?" He slides the cigar box in my direction. I should take it. I should light up and smoke with the don. Show I'm still his trusted lieutenant. Prove my loyalties haven't changed.

But the smell turns my stomach. "No thanks." I rub my nose like that will clear the stench. "Too early."

Marco presses a high-ball glass of Maker's Mark into my hand and disappears again, slick-like, before I remember to thank him. I throw it back, relishing the burn as it slides down my throat.

"So, you're out."

"*Si signore.* Glad to be back."

It's not true. I'm not glad to be anything. *Glad* isn't an emotion I've known for a very long time. But it's what I'm supposed to say.

Don Pachino pulls a thick envelope from the inner pocket of his five-thousand-dollar suit and hands it to me. "This is to get you on your feet again."

I tuck it in the pocket of the jacket Marco brought me when he picked me up. The one that feels so foreign on me, even though it was my favorite.

"Thank you, Don Pachino."

He takes a puff of the cigar. "I got you a no-work construction job. Pays six grand a month. You're taken care of, Mando."

I bow my head, the gratitude I should show not surfacing. I have to fake it. "Thank you. I'm so grateful."

He claps me on the shoulder. "I told you I'd take care of you, didn't I? You're family, Mando."

"I appreciate that. So much." Jesus, I hope my tone doesn't sound as flat to his ears as it does to mine.

I don't mean to look, but somehow, I find myself staring across the room at Grace, rubbing her tits over Emilio's chest.

"You were gone," Don Pachino says with finality. He's making it clear where he stands on the issue in case I'm gonna make waves.

I don't answer because what the fuck am I going to say? *Yeah, it's cool he stole my fucking fiancé while I was doing time like a good soldier.* Sorry if I don't go kiss his cheeks and let him fuck me in the ass some more while he's at it.

Don Pachino doesn't take kindly to my silence. His casual air evaporates, and he looks me square in the eye. "There will be no retribution for it. *Capisce?*"

I only hesitate a moment before I nod. One thing I always respected about Don Pachino—he's damn clear about his expectations. "Understood."

"Do not test me on this."

"I won't."

"We're Family. All of us." He gestures around the room with his cigar. I wait for him to finish his point, but all he mutters is, "And you were gone."

Yeah.

Got the memo.

I was gone. My girl was fair game.

Now I know how things get played.

I definitely feel disrespected by both of them, but the truth is, no hearts were broken.

I may have thought I loved Grace when I left, but that shriveled and died long before I got the news about her new engagement. It died that first year in prison when she stopped writing and never came to see me.

"I want you to stay clean while you're on parole. You ride that no-work job and build your life again. Don't carry a piece or drive a car or violate the other terms of parole. I don't want you getting sent back for something stupid."

"I'm not going back," I agree.

No fucking way.

Not because I'm so goddamn happy to be out. I still can't dredge up a single lick of emotion.

But I'm damn sure I won't go back.

I'd rather take a bullet to the head.

# CHAPTER THREE

*Hannah*

*Hannah Munn, Florist to the mob.*

That's me.

Say what you will about the mafia, but there are a few perks to having your business in their building. One is the regular customers—which I desperately need.

My shop, *Garden of Eden,* is a place that allows the sins of the mafia to grow.

And if I don't sell five more bouquets by the time I close tonight, I won't be able to make my payment to the don.

And the simmering anxiety that brings would be the downside to being owned by the mafia.

"I need two bouquets. A big one for my wife, and—"

"And a smaller one for the girlfriend," I finish for Lorenzo, the cheating bastard. It's the same every week. "Some beautiful lavender roses came in yesterday. I made you a stunning bouquet for the wife." I walk to the cooler and pull out the arrangement—a dozen fat lavender roses with pink and purple freesia and greens.

Because I believe flowers mean something, I put a lot of effort into Lorenzo's wife's bouquets. Like, if I get the arrangement right, if I really wow her, it will make up for her husband's infidelity. Although maybe she's off with her own side piece—what do I know? She could have some hot pool boy or sexy yoga teacher licking her from toes to clit right now. I shouldn't care about someone I know nothing about, and yet I do. I take on other's emotions to a crippling degree sometimes. Always a people pleaser.

"And this one is for the girl *du jour*." I hand him a bouquet of brightly colored gerbera daisies.

Lorenzo cocks a half-smile like he's not sure what *du jour* means. Or maybe he's wondering if I'm being disrespectful. Hope not. I flash a bright smile to assure him I'm trying for cute.

I head back to the cash register and ring him up. Lorenzo's been coming here since before Mary Alice hired me as an apprentice ten years ago when I was just a teenager.

Every Friday, he and a half dozen of the Pachino men go see Rocco, the barber next door, for a straight razor shave, then hit *Garden of Eden* to get blooms for their ladies. Another crew comes through on Thursdays. And the older, retired generation usually stops in on Saturdays. One thing about these mafia men I've noticed is they like their structure and routine.

"Keep the change, doll." All these years, and he never bothered to learn my name. Or if he has, he never uses it. He pushes the six dollars and coins back across the counter. "It's your hush money." He winks. Same joke, every time. Every. Single. Time.

"Thank you, Lorenzo." I drop the money back in the till. Lord knows I'll need it to cover the checks I've already written that may already be bouncing me straight to bankruptcy. Or worse, getting my kneecaps busted by one of the very same customers I'm giving thanks for.

"You heard from Mary Alice?"

I smile, indulgently. I suspect Mary Alice was Lorenzo's girl *du jour* a few times over the years, but my former boss would never tell. Florists are excellent secret-keepers.

"Yeah." I spin one of the roses in his bouquet to set it at a better angle. "She texts photos of her grandbaby pretty much every day. She's in seventh heaven out there." Mary Alice moved to Green Bay when her daughter had a baby last year, forcing me to choose between continuing my studies to become a nurse like my mom or buying the business from her.

My parents definitely think I made the wrong choice. They don't say that outright—they're more the type to let me make my own mistakes, but I sense their worry every time the topic comes up.

I'm starting to wonder if I made a mistake too.

"Well, you tell her I said hello." He tucks the two bouquets under his arm and pushes his wallet back into his pocket.

"I'll do that. Have a great weekend."

He starts to leave then turns back. "Everything okay around here? Anybody bothering you?"

I shoot a glance at Josie, my BFF-slash-slacker employee who's putting a chrysanthemum arrangement in the cooler. She smirks because we just had this conversation. These guys like to play hero.

"Everything's fine. But thanks for asking." My smile is genuine because as much as I like to roll my eyes and snark about my customers, I'm secretly fond of them. Probably because when I was fifteen, their five-dollar tips made me feel rich. And the romantic florist in me still appreciates their chivalry.

I like the safety of being on their watch. Knowing if something did go wrong—if I got held up or I had a stalker situation—I'd know exactly who to see to exact justice.

Lorenzo tips an invisible hat and leaves, and Josie snorts. "You're right."

I laugh. "Did I not tell you? At least one of them will offer to slay dragons for me every week. It's kind of endearing."

"Of course." Josie nearly knocks an arrangement over as she pushes vases around on the cooler shelf. "The idea of roughing up some asshole for the pretty, defenseless florist gets them hard."

"Mmm hmm. Cute, right?"

"Yeah, I guess you can't complain about having your own private security team. And at least he wasn't creepy about it. One dumbass yesterday bought flowers and then pulled out a rose and gave it to me. I was like, dude, if you're going to ask for my number at least give me the whole bouquet."

I snort. "Yeah, they're players." When I was in high school, I used to get all fluttery and nervous when the younger guys came in, thinking one might ask me out. I had this whole mafia-guy crush. They exuded confidence and power. They flashed their money, and they had swagger. I wasn't naive enough to believe all the bluster, but it turned me on just the same. My secret fantasy.

But while they flirted up a storm with Mary Alice, they were only polite with me. I don't know, maybe they don't date Black women. Or maybe I was just a kid in their eyes and forever would be.

"Well, maybe not all of them, but at least half are players," I amend.

Josie comes over and leans her elbows on the counter. Her gold hoop earrings swing. They're giant—big enough to balance her poofy blonde curls.

Anxiety coils in the pit of my stomach as we get physically close to each other. It happens every time. Probably because I need to talk to her about her crappy work ethic but keep putting it off. I ignore the feeling, like always.

"Tell me you haven't thought about taking one of them up on it. Not as a permanent thing but just to let him treat you to a nice dinner once in a while," she says.

"Nah."

"Uh huh." Her tone implies disbelief.

"Okay, there was one, but he had a girlfriend. He never asked me out, but he charmed the socks off me every time he came in. And so good looking. He lectured me once when I was closing up about walking home alone at night and how it wasn't safe. He insisted he escort me the couple of blocks. I found his protectiveness so freaking hot."

"Which one?" Josie asks.

"I don't know. I can't remember his name," I lie. I totally remember. *Armando.* Sexy smooth-talking Armando with that panty-melting smile.

But I was almost grateful he was engaged. Because as much as I crushed on him, I never, ever, want to date a mafia man. They cheat on their wives. They're misogynists—they think women belong barefoot, home in the kitchen. They are dangerous. Extremely so. They commit crimes, they hurt people, even kill people. Yes, they are men, but there's a thick undertone of villain in every single one of them.

And Armando—he felt the most unsafe. Not like he'd hurt me physically.

But emotionally. I'd fall way too hard for a guy like him. It was good he disappeared.

"He doesn't come in anymore. I haven't seen him in a long time—like, years," I tell Josie.

"Maybe he got whacked. You never know with these guys, right?"

I'm way too empathetic because that thought makes my stomach tighten up into a knot. I hardly knew the guy apart from selling him flowers for his fiancé every week. "Hope not. He seemed like he was going places."

"Yep. Illegal places that landed him in Lake Michigan with cement shoes," Josie jokes.

I refuse to entertain that idea. "Maybe he moved away. He and his girlfriend were engaged." I know because he filled her apartment with every color of rose after she said yes. Mary Alice had to call for an extra shipment because he ordered so many.

"I'll bet he's dead. Or witness protection." She shrugs and pushes an unfinished bouquet off to the side. "I'm going to take off, okay?"

My anxiety flutters again. It's forty minutes until her shift ends. She hasn't even finished what she was working on, and her work area is a mess. I definitely need the help in case a bunch of the guys next door stop in to buy bouquets before they go home.

*Please, God, let there be a closing time rush.*

I should tell her that, but instead, I bite back my sigh. I love her too much to create strife between us. I know—hiring a friend was a mistake. One I'm going to keep paying for if I don't figure out pretty quickly how to be a boss bitch. But Josie got laid off from her dream job as an interior decorator apprentice, so I invited her to work here with me, thinking how fun it would be to run a business with my best friend at my side.

Except it's not always fun. And lately, it's more stressful when she's around than when she's not. It doesn't take a psychotherapist to figure out that's why I get anxious when she's here. My subconscious wants me to clarify things with her, but my heart can't stand the thought of alienating my best friend.

But that's kind of the least of my worries about running this business at this point. And I may not even have a business past next month if things don't turn around.

"Okay thanks."

*Ugh.* Why am I thanking her? I'm *paying* her. And she's leaving early.

Without asking.

And I now have *her* mess to clean up.

Still, if I had it to do over, I'd probably hire her again because the thought of hiring a stranger makes me way too nervous.

I am so not cut out to be Boss Bitch.

Instead of saying anything more, I look to the door and try to will someone to walk in and order all the flowers I have to offer.

# CHAPTER FOUR

*Armando*

"It's not a big apartment," Marco says as he puts the keys into the door and opens it. "But it's down the hall from me, and the building is centrally located."

I take a look around the small apartment. It's simple and cozy, but there are no decorations or any other personal touches. The bedroom is furnished with just a bed, dresser, and a small nightstand. There's a black, leather couch in the living room and a kitchen table in the corner of the room. The only window is in the living room, but there's a balcony outside with a great view of the Chicago skyline.

"You can decorate it however you want, put up whatever pictures you want," Marco says, gesturing to the blank walls. "The landlord is cool here. Also, my lady friend says that she knows a few people who can do interior design for you if you want. I can hook you up with them if you're interested."

I look around the apartment, feeling a bit overwhelmed. I've been in jail with a cellmate for long enough that the idea of actually being alone for a night is bizarre.

"I know it's not much, but it's a start," Marco says, apparently trying to be encouraging. "Soon you'll be back on your feet, and you can do whatever the fuck you want."

I nod and take a deep breath. "Thanks, Marco." I should show more enthusiasm, but I can't muster it.

Luckily, Leo enters the apartment, his dominance filling the room. During my time in prison, my cousin has grown. He's no longer the scrawny, young, arrogant kid trying to prove himself to the Outfit. He's nearly tripled in size and reminds me of a brick wall. Nothing but brawn strides into the room. I don't think Marco and I combined could take this man down if we tried.

His eyes dart to the balcony. "What the fuck? A balcony? A ladder escape? Are you just inviting someone to come up here and jump him?"

"He's laying low right now," Marco retorts. "It's not like there's a hit on him or anything. Let the man enjoy a view and some fresh air after having gone so long without it."

Leo grunts in hesitant approval, his eyes still scanning the apartment for any threats. He finally turns to me. "Welcome back, cuz. I've missed you." He claps me on the shoulder, his grip strong and comforting. He then narrows his eyes at his brother. "Balconies only bring pigeons. Pigeons bring shit."

"I put beer in the fridge," Marco says as he walks toward the kitchen with an eye roll. "Anyone?"

"Yeah." I need one. I feel completely out of place in what is supposed to be my home.

Leo takes a beer from Marco and tips it toward me. "Cheers, cuz. To a new start."

I take the beer, wanting to savor the taste of freedom, but it tastes as flat as my emotions. Is this freedom?

It's all so strange. I'm out of prison, but I'm not really free. I'm living a life dependent on the generosity and connections of others.

Leo sits on the couch and stretches his legs. "So, Mando," he begins. "You cool with Grace and Emilio? Truly cool?"

"Fuck no." I can actually be honest with my cousins.

Marco grunts his agreement.

"The don says to be cool, so I'm cool. But truth between us, the situation is fucked." I cross over to an armchair next to the couch and sit with my beer as I take a long swig.

"I never liked Grace," Marco offers, leaning up against the kitchen counter. "I wasn't surprised when she went searching for her next meal ticket."

"I don't give a fuck about Grace." Or at least not anymore. "It's fucked that what was mine wasn't protected while I was inside. Emilio stepped in when he should have been watching out. He broke the fucking code, man."

"Yeah, it's bullshit," Leo agrees. "He broke the code for sure. No way to defend that."

"I didn't see it coming," Marco says. "I would have squashed that shit fast if I had."

"Same." Leo's jaw tightens. "Emilio kept that under lock and key. By the time word got out, the don was aware and seemed to give his approval. So..."

"If the don says no retribution..." Marco begins.

"There won't be retribution," I finish.

But that doesn't mean I have to like it. That doesn't mean I have to forget. I take another swig of beer and shake my head.

"Besides. Grace always took me as a lazy fuck. I can't see her giving good head." Marco smirks, clearly trying to lighten the mood.

Personally I don't agree with knocking a guy's ex because you're basically insulting his taste in the first place, but whatever.

"Yeah, you definitely need to find yourself someone who can meet your sexual appetite. Because after your drought... you gotta be one ravenous motherfucker," Leo adds.

I remember when I used to see men come out of prison and think the same thing. Like the worst thing in the world for these ex-convicts was how long they'd have to go without sex. I'm sure I'd think the same thing as Marco and Leo. Sex is the first priority because how could it not be?

But, shit... I'm not even sure how to start. My entire body feels fucking numb. Including my dick.

"The don gave me some bullshit construction job. It's just for appearances," I tell them. "I show up and collect a check."

"Yeah, I heard that," Marco says.

"Not a bad gig." Leo finishes his beer in one last swig and then motions for Marco to pass him another one.

"It feels as if I've been put to pasture," I admit. "I was in my prime before all this shit. Now, I'm practically retired."

"Temporarily, right?" Marco asks. "Until parole is over?"

I shrug. "My entire life feels temporary. A big fucking pause button was hit when I got pinched. Now what?"

"You need money?" Leo asks.

"Nah." I shake my head. "The don took care of that. And this job puts me in a good spot. But thanks."

The last thing I'd do is take money from my cousins. I feel like a burden as it is.

"You did your time. You didn't snitch. And now you're back. You've earned some retirement life. Enjoy it while you can. I'm sure that once parole is over, the don will have you working full time, earning again."

"We'll get your life back in order," Marco adds. "It will take some time, but you'll rise from the fucking ashes. I promise."

# CHAPTER FIVE

*Armando*

"Armando." Rocco pats the barber chair. "Right here, sir." I disengage from the gathering of Made men who fill the old-time barber shop with cigar smoke while they talk over each other in loud voices.

The walls are a drab off-white and crammed floor to ceiling with framed photographs from the days when the shop was a speakeasy. Wood paneling, a bay window, old fold out chairs and a magazine rack brings me back to a time I cherished. Each man is dressed in a tailored suit and tie, his hair slicked back, mustache and beard perfectly trimmed and groomed.

Rocco's barbershop is an oasis of the familiar in a world that has become otherwise unfamiliar.

My body's stiff and jerky as I drop into the seat. Every step I take in my old shoes is like a goddamn out-of-body experience.

Coming to this place is an out-of-body experience.

Everything's exactly the same, yet it feels so fucking different. I used to love Friday afternoons in this little shop. The pleasure of Rocco's warm towels wrapped around my face. Feeling like a king while the old man attended to me with the guys all hanging around shooting the shit. I loved hanging with the big boys. So proud I'd made lieutenant and got to play with the heavy hitters. I was on the top of the world then. Top of my game.

I had the girl. The money. And a glorified position in the Outfit.

I felt alive. Powerful. There was so much possibility dancing before me.

Only thing different now is the girl. But I got over Grace the day she called and told me she was moving in with Emilio. So why the fuck can't I find any pleasure?

Arturo, Don Pachino's right hand man, gives me a scrutinizing look through a billow of smoke. "You don't look comfortable, Mando. Hard to trust someone with a blade close to your throat after sleeping behind bars?"

Flashbacks of when someone actually was foolish enough to try to attack me in prison come flooding in. I had pissed off the wrong person, but he didn't know how lethal I could be. He made the mistake of underestimating me, and he paid for it.

"Don Pachino's been in the business for a long time, Mando. He knows how to pick his men. You have a reputation for being loyal and careful, which is why he trusts you." He pauses and then continues with, "But more than that, he knows you won't hesitate to do whatever it takes to make sure the job gets done. You just need to keep your head in the game. Don't fuck it up again because you allow that darkness in. You know what I mean. Fight it off, son."

I nod and force a smile. "I'm good Arturo. Nothing to worry about."

I take a moment to survey the room. It's still filled with the same faces. Familiar ones. Ones who have seen me through thick and thin.

But something is off. I feel it in the air. Tension. Skepticism. A lack of trust that never seemed to be there before.

I understand why. I was in prison for a long time, and while I had the support of the Outfit on the inside, there was still some distance kept. Regardless of what they said, I know they viewed me as a liability. There was always a chance I'd rat to save my ass. They also knew I couldn't help them if I was behind bars, so they acted as though I didn't exist.

Now I'm back, and I feel the sizzle of awkwardness in my veins.

They don't know me anymore, and I don't know them. We are strangers to one another.

"You know," Arturo begins, "It's not too late to try and make things right again."

I furrow my brow in confusion. Make what right? What the hell was he talking about? Make Grace come back? Make the don forget I ever went to prison? Make my incarceration disappear?

Arturo continues, "The don loves you. We all do. You were born for this, Mando. You're the best of the best. And you should never forget that. You're still young, you can make it back to the top. Everyone knows it."

I close my eyes, feeling the warmth from the hot towels against my face. I feel the sharpness of the blades against my throat, a reminder that I'm still here. Alive and breathing. As much as it pains me to admit it, I know Arturo is right. I clawed my way back from the bottom and am still standing. As long as I'm alive, I can make it to the top. But at the same time, I've been grounded by the don himself. Ordered to keep my nose clean.

The pull of good and evil is strong. The devil on one shoulder and the angel on the other is now my reality.

It takes all my effort to twist a smile onto my face. It's probably more of a grimace.

Arturo's statement brings an awkward pause in conversation. It's mostly the oldtimers today with only me, Marco and Leo representing the younger generation. I suspect someone told Emilio to stay away out of respect for me today. Probably Marco. He looks after me like a second brother. I'd do the same for him if the tables were turned.

"I'll bet that shave is gonna feel good, right kid?" one of them says.

"You wet your dick yet?" Angel, another oldtimer, asks. "*Madonna*, when I got out, I picked up a girl at the strip club and banged her all night long. *For three nights!*" His boom of laughter is joined by several of the other guys'.

I go tense although I don't know why I'm defensive. Because the thought of fucking doesn't get the slightest rise out of me? Because *life* gets zero rise out of me?

Arturo's still watching me, though. Whatever he sees, I try to hide it.

"You're not broken up over that girl of yours, are you? The one who's with Emilio now?"

"Nah," I say immediately.

Even if I were, I wouldn't let it show.

Don Pachino warned me: no bullshit with Emilio. Guess I know who ranks higher these days.

Emilio is his sister's kid. I'm just his *wife's* sister's kid.

Rocco slathers me with more shaving cream. The smell triggers all the old memories but none of the pleasure I used to feel sitting in this chair.

I'm a fucking ghost back to haunt his former life. I can't actually touch it. Can't actually taste it. Definitely can't feel a goddamn thing. My life's turned to shades of grey. Or maybe it's still in color but with one of those grainy filters that makes the images dull and cold.

Rocco moves the razor across my skin expertly. I wish Arturo hadn't brought it up because now all I can think about is how easy it would be for him to slice my jugular.

Would he do it? I used to be so secure in my bond with *La Famiglia*. The guys in this room could be trusted with my life. We were loyal to each other, to the Outfit. Everyone else, we locked out.

Now I don't trust any of them. And Rocco's not in the family. He's just an Italian small business owner who benefits from our patronage. He might hate all our guts. I used to think he treated us like royalty because he loved having us here. He liked the tips and the business. But who knows? Maybe he's just scared like everybody else.

Maybe he's collecting information, waiting for a moment to rat us all out.

Or maybe I'm in a paranoid mind-fuck I need to escape from.

The shave ends, and I view my image in the mirror. My jaw is smooth, but I look like a fucking corpse. Stone-faced. Dead eyes. Rotted out heart.

I stand and pay.

Arturo calls out when I head straight for the door. "You're not gonna hang around? What? You got something better to do?"

"Damn straight. He's gotta find a girl to exercise that dick of his," Angel chortles.

"Yeah," I agree. "That."

Marco and Leo watch me, seeing more than I wanna show. "You don't need a ride?" Marco asks. He drove me here.

"Nah, I'm good." I just want to be alone. Get the hell outta here. I lift my hand to them all and walk out.

*Fanculo*, that was painful. Even the simplest acts of living are like kneeling on sand now.

I gotta figure out how to wake the fuck up.

# CHAPTER SIX

*Armando*

I walk out of Rocco's.

It feels foreign to be able to do so. To be able to simply walk outside and breathe in fresh air of my own free will. No prison guard standing nearby while I enjoy my scheduled yard time. No fencing and barbed wire. Nothing but pure freedom.

It's a strange sensation. After so many years of confinement, the wide-open world has become like another planet. It's like I'm a stranger in a foreign land, with no idea of where to go or what to do now that I'm free. Surrounded by bustling people, their conversations and laughter filling the air, it all seems almost out of body.

"Hey," I hear Marco's voice from behind me.

I glance over my shoulder and see Marco and Leo following me out the door.

"I'm fine. Really," I say, actually meaning what I said that I want to be alone.

"I know you're going through shit," Leo begins, "But Arturo is right. You're going to rebuild your life. It will start feeling like normal soon."

Marco places his hand on my shoulder. "Let's go get a drink or something."

"Nah, I know you guys have work to do today. I'm not a charity case." I take the time to look each of my cousins in the eyes. "I'm fine. I just need to go for a walk and get my shit in order. I appreciate it though."

I can tell by the way they both side eye each other that they don't want to leave me, but I'm right in the fact that they do need to get to work. *La Famiglia* is calling.

"Fine," Marco finally says. "But later. Drinks on me."

I nod and watch them both hop into Leo's car without another word. Grateful that they didn't put up too much of a fight, I decide to get out of the line of fire of Rocco's. I don't want another person to come out and feel pity for me and feel like they need to entertain me or something, so I begin to walk.

I know this neighborhood so well. Rocco's and then the florist, *Garden of Eden*, next door used to be part of my usual routine. A shave and then buy flowers for Grace. It was a comfortable routine. And now that I just had my shave, I realize I have no reason to walk next door to the florist. Who would I buy flowers for now?

Shaking my head, I know I need to give up this fucking pity party. I'm a free man. I should stop moping around. But the shackles of my past still cling to my wrists and ankles, dragging on my limbs. It's hard for me to feel happy or optimistic about the future when I am constantly reminded of the darkness of my past.

There's coldness inside, and I doubt it will be replaced with warmth.

And that's when something living surges in me—something primitive and instinctual. If I were a caveman, I'd raise my fucking spear. Because the guy in a grey sweatshirt leaning against the building moves in my direction. His hand reaches into his pocket.

I reach behind me before I remember I don't have a piece. It's illegal for a felon to carry, and I'm trying to keep my nose clean.

I'm instantly reminded of when I was jumped back in prison. Able to fight only with what little prison resources I had. Survival at all costs but nothing to rely on other than wit and brawn.

It all happens in a matter of seconds. I bum-rush the asshole, grabbing his wrist before he can point the pistol. The force of my attack launches us both off the stoop and into the gutter. My shoulder rams into the place where his collarbones meet, sending an explosion of pain across my chest.

We're tangled in a mess of limbs, struggling against each other as I try to get ahold of the weapon. He's stronger than I am; his face is twisted in a snarl.

Prison has dulled some of my physical prowess. I'm no longer the sharp knife I once was. My reflexes are faster, but my body isn't fine-tuned.

The guy is clearly out for blood, but I'm ready to fight to the death because I know if he gets that pistol free, I'm a dead man.

The struggle intensifies, and I feel my strength waning. He pries my grip from his wrist, and the gun creeps closer to his own hand. I know I'm outmatched. I'm not strong enough—not fast enough. I already feel the cold, hard steel of the gun against my skin. But I don't let go. I know that this is a fight for my life, and I won't back down. I twist his wrist, forcing him to drop the gun, and then I press my knee into his throat, so he can't scream for help.

I see the fear in his eyes as he struggles to break free from my grip, realizing I now have the upper hand. There's a moment of stillness as we stare each other down, and I feel the tension between us. It's a fight for dominance, for power, for our very lives. We are two predators in the wild, locked in a deadly battle.

The momentary pause on my behalf gives the man just enough time to free himself and attack me again with even more force, pushing us both against the doorway of the closest building, where we topple into the door of the florist. I use it, opening the door to trap his wrist and slamming it closed to dislodge the gun.

The weapon clatters to the floor inside the flower shop, and we both follow the movement. It's a mad scramble as we thrust the door open and tumble through. I land on the gun first.

I have to squelch my desire to shoot him point blank in the head.

I'm not going back to prison. Besides, I need to know who he's working for.

Because this is obviously a hit.

I empty the chamber of ammo and use the gun to smack him in the temple. He stumbles back but doesn't black out. Instead, he tackles me to the floor, and the gun goes sliding again.

# CHAPTER SEVEN

*Hannah*

It's him. *Armando*. The one I used to lust after. This is not how I envisioned him reentering my store.

The scream gets stuck in my throat the moment reality sets in on what is actually happening before me. I'm too shocked to even move. For five long seconds, I just stand here like an idiot staring at the brutal fight.

Then I realize—I should do something.

Call someone.

I pick up my phone, not taking my eyes off the two men struggling on the floor. Both appear to be fighting for their lives. Armando is efficient and calm. He doesn't make a sound as he grapples with the other guy, rolling until he gets on top. Pummeling him into the ground. But then he loses his advantage and gets knocked backward into a shelf of plants.

I cover my mouth to keep in the cry of dismay at seeing my sweet inventory mauled. It's not like I have the money to replace even a single pot if they break one.

Armando catches sight of me. "End the call," he grits as he wrestles the guy to the floor in a headlock. The command in his voice is deadly. Scary enough to make me drop my phone to the counter with a clatter.

"I said *end it*," he snarls. They're on the floor still, a writhing mass. This is not the nice man I remember who came into the store to buy flowers for his woman. This is a beast before me.

"I never dialed!" I protest, picking the phone up to flash him the screen.

He's not watching because the other guy produced a pocket knife. Armando narrowly misses getting sliced. There's a practiced precision to his movements like instead of being a mobster, he's actually a secret agent, a James Bond style superspy. Maybe it's the total lack of panic. He doesn't appear to be a man fighting for his life. He comes at his opponent like some angel of death sent to finish this guy.

Armando punches him hard in the face, follows to punch him again. The guy slashes with the knife at the same time, causing Armando to skirt to the side. Plants clatter from the table, pots crashing.

I whimper my dismay.

Armando picks one up and smashes it over the guy's head. The guy goes down, and Armando follows, his fingers around the guy's throat with one hand while he holds down the knife-wielding arm with the other. "Who sent you?" he demands.

The guy makes a gurgling sound but gets his arm away.

I scream when he stabs in the direction of Armando's face. Armando shifts in time but loses his advantage. The other guy scrambles up and smashes a pot from my metal plant stand into Armando's temple. He goes down hard, the crack of his skull against my tile floor making me cry out again.

I dial 9-1-1 on the phone but forget to press send because the guy launches himself at Armando with the knife.

In a gasp-worthy move, Armando somehow makes it back up just in time, swinging the heavy metal plant stand at the guy's head. The guy goes down hard and stays there.

In case you ever wondered, there's no mistaking death when you see it.

The shape his body takes is so completely askew. His neck is clearly broken.

Armando's hands tremble as he takes in the sight of the man lying motionless before him. I feel a chill go down my spine as shock paralyzes me in place.

Armando looks around the room, as if expecting to see more enemies coming for him, and I do the same.

What's coming next? What was that? What the fuck was that?

This can't be happening. Is this really happening?

Is there a bloody man lying dead in the middle of my florist shop?

The room is silent but for the sound of a ticking clock and the ringing in my ears.

Armando curses and drops to his knees, checking the guy's pulse.

Then he moves quickly—all efficiency and practice. He locks my door, closes the blinds and turns the sign to closed. He picks up the gun then drags the body past the counter toward the back. "Don't move," he tells me as he passes.

*Don't move.*

I don't know why, but until that moment, I hadn't considered *my* life might be in danger.

I was an observer, and I was rooting for one side to win.

My pick won the round.

But now it sets in that we're not going to be slapping high fives here. A guy *just got killed* in my shop, and I witnessed it.

I'm the *only* witness.

And the killer told me not to move. Which means I should definitely move.

Armando drags the body into my cooler. He's going to come out here and deal with me next.

That's a problem. I grab my purse and quietly, quickly walk past the cooler.

I sense Armando near, but I don't stop. I know if I do, it will be my last mistake. My heart pounds, and I can feel the sweat on my palms. I'm almost halfway to freedom when I hear a noise from the back of the shop. I spin to see Armando walking slowly towards me, gun in hand and a menacing look on his face. He's not going to let me go this easily. He takes a few more steps towards me, and I know I'm not going to make it out alive. I turn back towards the door, but it's too late. He's almost at me now, and there's no escape.

"Stop. I said don't fucking move!" That voice. He does command so well, every cell in my body wants to obey.

But that would be stupid, so I break into a run.

*"Hannah."*

Surprise that he remembered my name makes me falter. The hesitation costs me. He's on me in a flash, grabbing my elbow and whipping me around.

"I said, *don't move.*"

God, he's still devastatingly handsome. Square jaw. Aquiline nose. Hazel eyes with long lashes. He's so close, I smell the scent of Rocco's shaving cream on him. He's in a crisp, expensive blue button-down, open at the throat to reveal a clean white undershirt.

"I'm on your side," I say on exhale.

I'm not sure if it's self-preservation that makes me say the words or if it's the actual truth. I know Armando. I actually always liked the man... maybe a little too much.

I am on his side. I am.

He pivots me to face the wall, tugging one of my hands to pin there.

"I told you not to move." This is the voice of a mad man. Of the mafia. A killer. I need to remember that.

"I'm not going to say a thing." The famous last words of people before they are killed.

This is it. I'm dead.

I expect the knife to come to my throat. Instead, he smacks my ass.

I squeak in surprise. It was a hard smack—punitive, not playful—and for some reason, it turns me on.

I turn my head to look over my shoulder at him. An ass-smack isn't a real threat. It's something hot. Sexual. The cold in my veins evaporates.

He smacks my ass again, the other cheek this time.

*Hello.*

I don't have a clue what we're doing here, but I'm getting more excited than scared.

I must be confusing adrenaline for lust. Yes, that must be it.

Or is this insanity kicking in? Am I so terrified of dying that my body is confused by the foreign sensation, and—

He slaps my ass one more time, harder than the last.

My body responds. Warmth radiates from my core, and I can't help but moan in pleasure. It's embarrassing that I can't control emotions that I should keep hidden from him. I feel my heart racing, my skin tingling, and I'm growing wetter by the second.

He slides his hands down my sides, tracing a path of heat as he goes. He then grabs a roll of floral tape from my apron pocket. "Here's what's going to happen." He twists my arms behind my back and ties my wrists together with the floral tape. It's flexible, but he wraps it a dozen times and makes it tight, so I can't twist enough to get it off. "You're going to stay right here, facing this wall, until I get back. You're not going to move. You're not going to make a sound. *Capisce?*"

I nod my head quickly. "Yeah, okay." I sound breathless.

I'm scared. Scared shitless. But there's also something crazy churning inside me. Some spiraling heat, a tingling awareness.

I don't know if it's because I had a crush on this guy before or because he slapped my ass and woke up an erogenous area, but liquid heat pools between my legs.

He steps in front of me, and I feel his breath on my skin. He leans close and whispers in my ear. "Follow the rules, Flowers. Follow them or else." His voice is low, possessive. His hot breath tickles my skin, sending pleasure coursing through me.

He takes my chin in his hand and turns my face up to his. He pulls away slightly, and I gasp for breath, my heart thudding in my chest.

He traces his finger along my jaw and down my throat. "I'll be back soon. Don't move."

Armando then takes a step back and looks me up and down, his gaze burning with what I hope is desire. His eyes linger for a moment on the tightness of the floral tape binding my wrists, and then he gives a faint smirk. "Be a good girl," he warns, before turning and walking away.

Am I reading him wrong? And have I lost my fucking mind? I shouldn't be feeling anything but the overwhelming need to run and run fast. I should be fighting, screaming, and most definitely be terrified.

And yet, I stand here with my heart pounding and... my body on fire with desire. The heat between my legs grows stronger with each passing second, and a strange thrill of excitement shoots through me.

My body aches with anticipation. I'm still bound and helpless, but this time my fear has been replaced by something else. Something exciting. I can't help but wonder—maybe even fantasize—what will happen when Armando returns.

I listen as he steps back into my cooler. I hear the sound of his voice speaking in short, clipped sentences. He must be on the phone.

Who is he talking to?

What is he saying?

Oh Jesus, is he calling more of the mafia to come and help him with this... *situation*? Is Garden of Eden about to become even more of a blood bath than it already is but with my blood?

If I were smart, I wouldn't stick around to figure out what he's going to do with me. I'd somehow find a way to escape. I'm not the stupid girl who falls for the bad boy. I've never been weak. I've never been the damsel in distress. So why in the hell am I even standing here?

And just as I'm starting to think about inching toward the back door, he returns and spins me around. With my wrists bound behind my back, my double D's thrust forward and spread. "All right, Flowers. What am I going to do with you?"

Maybe it's self-preservation. Maybe it's the crush. Or the way my ass still tingles where he slapped it, but I do the only thing I can think of, which is to lean forward and kiss his mouth.

His lips press against mine, stealing my breath away. His tongue slips inside, coaxing mine into a slow, dizzying dance. I moan into his mouth, my hips shifting against his mass, like some new north star.

Armando's hands slide lower, over my hips and down my thighs.

His fingers brush against the fabric of my clothes, and I shudder. He cups my ass in his hands, kneading and squeezing, sending fire into every nerve ending. This kiss...

# CHAPTER EIGHT

*Armando*

I rear back from the kiss in surprise. It's unexpected and juicy and Fahrenheit 451-level hot.

And just like defib paddles applied to my chest, a jolt of energy surges through me.

The lights come on. My body comes back to life.

It's been almost five years since I've tasted a woman, and there's suddenly so much lost time to make up for.

I'm on her in a second, kissing the fuck out of that lush mouth, sliding one hand up her shirt. I just killed a guy and hid the body in Flower's freezer. That's what I should be dealing with. But the moment she kissed me, color bled back into my world. I need to explore it like I need my next breath. She's in a short skirt, and I'm suddenly way up it with my other hand, cupping her pussy.

The soft silky fabric of her panties is damp.

That's all the information my brain needs to go full steam ahead. I'm an animal, incapable of pulling back. Raw instinct propels my actions more than any coherent thought.

I shove her shirt up and lower my head to feast on her nipple, her gasps filling my ears. "Tell me, Flowers." I slide my fingers under the gusset of her panties to drag through her damp folds. "What got you so wet?" I screw one finger into her, and she gasps and goes up on her toes.

My body is on fire, my need so sharp I can taste it. I'm going to take her right here, until all the darkness inside of me has been driven out. Until I can breathe again.

Her head falls back as I thrust my finger deeper, stealing a moan from her parted lips. Whether she wants to or not, she grinds her hips, pushing down onto my hand. I'm buried so deep inside of her, I'm touching her core.

"Please," she whispers.

Is she begging for me to continue, or for me to free her and walk out that door? The line between right and wrong is too blurred for me to know.

My heart pounds in my ears, and my cock feels like steel. Our mouths crash together in a desperate kiss, exploring, tasting, teasing. My free hand curls around her body as I tease her lips with my tongue. I feel her tremble beneath me as I press another finger into her pussy.

Her fervent whimpers drive me on until I'm so hard, so ready to devour every inch of her that I'm trembling like a weak man. My hand snakes up to cup the back of her neck as we breathe each other in. The heat from our bodies entwining is almost too much for me to take.

If she begged and pleaded for me to stop, there'd be no way I could.

I know she can't be comfortable pressed up against the wall with her hands bound behind her back, but I can't seem to dial back my attention.

Yes, there is a dead man in her cooler, and I have her here as my captive.

But the world around us seems to disappear, leaving only us two enclosed by sexual heat and frenzied desire. Nothing else matters except this moment when she is all mine.

And that's what she is. *Mine*.

As adrenaline from my fight flows through my body, I can't control the demon from coming out and claiming her fully.

I scissor my fingers, spreading her tight little hole, driving them inside harder and faster, pounding into her with an intensity that has her gasping for air as her body quivers beneath me. I don't stop until I feel her muscles clenching around me as she cries out in pleasure.

"You like being tied up? Or was it your spanking?" I ask.

She stares at me with gold-flecked brown eyes. Her wild mane of curls tumble all around her head like a halo, falling over her right eye. She's gorgeous—pure femininity embodied in a small, curvy, dark-skinned package. I haven't been with a Black woman before, but after living with guys of every color in prison, the racism I grew up around has long since disappeared from my thoughts. But even more importantly, I've never been with a more beautiful woman. Breathtaking would be an understatement. A true goddess who can't be matched by another.

"Or was it—" I frown, remembering the shit show I'm in. "Was it the violence—what you saw out there? What had you moaning out my name, Flowers? What has this pussy so wet? Does death turn you on?"

"I-I don't know."

For a moment, my rational brain tries to break in. Slow my roll. Remind me that this isn't the time or the place. But her pussy clenching around my fingers and the flush in her cheeks brings me back to the only thing I care about—seeing this thing through.

"You need me to alleviate the ache down here?"

I stop moving, waiting for her consent. We're both breathing hard, our faces just an inch apart. She holds my gaze and gives a tiny nod, just before she attacks me with another kiss.

I go nuts on her.

I've never had a female as the aggressor before, and it fucking drives me wild. I shove my fingers deep inside her again and squeeze her ass with my other hand. She moans and whimpers her pleasure, squirming against me, her lips still pulling on mine, tongue lashing into my mouth.

I screw a third finger inside her, prepping her for what's to come. I don't mean to be so raw and dirty, but my body moves of its own accord. My other hand strokes between her ass cheeks, seeking the tight bud of her anus.

She cries out in surprise when I find it, contracting and falling against me.

I push her back against the wall and finger-fuck her with my left hand while my right alternates between rubbing her anus and squeezing her plump asscheeks.

Her pink Converse shuffle and dance beneath her. My dick isn't even out, but I experience her pleasure as my own. It's been a long time, but I don't remember ever having a girl go off like this. Not so easy. Not so fast. Never so welcoming. The mixture of eroticism and tension between us makes it seem like my life depends on getting her off.

But maybe that's the adrenaline from almost getting killed.

From—

But I'm not thinking about that now. Right now, I'm watching Hannah, the beautiful young florist, fly over the crest of her orgasm.

She screams when it hits hard, and I smother her mouth with mine, swallowing her cries.

I keep my body pressed against hers and slow-pump my fingers until her channel stops milking them. "Fuck, Flowers." I ease my fingers out, then hold her gaze with heavy lids as I put them in my mouth. "Tastes like heaven." My voice sounds guttural and rough. "I could spend all night eating your pussy."

She blinks at me, her eyes unfocused and glassy, her cheeks flushed with color.

I remembered her as gorgeous, but she was so young when I went away. Barely out of high school. Now she's all grown up. She pierced her nose. Grew her hair out into wild, golden-tipped ringlets that fall nearly to her ass. She's gloriously beautiful.

I can't help myself. I need more. Like I'm going to fucking die on this spot if I don't get my dick wet *right now*.

"I want to be inside you," I find myself saying out loud. It's wrong. So wrong. I have the girl tied up with florist tape, for fuck's sake. But something about the way she looks at me makes me think I have a chance. "You gonna let me bend you over that counter and fuck that sweet pussy hard?"

Christ. I'm so fucking depraved. What girl would say yes to that?

But unbelievably, she wets her lips and says, "Do you have a condom?"

Fuck, yeah, I have a condom. I may not have had the urge to use one until now, but I sure as hell prepared for the opportunity in case I did.

I have her bent over in said position in about two seconds flat. I shove her short skirt up and slap her ass cheeks again several times, then yank down her panties. I love the pink blush on her ass, my handprints starting to show.

I find the condom. The pistol I'd stowed in my waistband falls to the floor when I release my cock, but I ignore it, too blinded with desire to even think straight.

Somehow, I get the condom on.

Drag my cock through her juices.

She's still wonderfully wet. Gloriously, miraculously wet. I sink into her heat, and my entire body shudders with pleasure.

"Fuck. You feel so good." I'm not chatty, but one touch from this girl, and I'm babbling like a brook. I have her face pressed down on the workbench, her glorious dark brown and honey-colored curls spread in a wild curtain. I push it back from her face, then gather a fistful at the back of her head. "You like having your hair pulled?"

She makes a little whimpering sound like, "Uhn." Might be a no, but her pussy gushes with fresh lubricant, so I take it as a yes.

I take a firmer grip on her hair and begin to thrust in time with her pants of pleasure. I can feel every twitch and spasm of her pussy as I push my way deeper into her depths. Her body shakes as if electric currents are coursing through her. I quicken my pace, driving harder into her with each thrust.

I reach down to caress her breasts, kneading and massaging them as I continue to drive relentlessly into her. Her moans become more intense as I reach around to stroke and tease her clit. I feel her tightening around me, pushing me closer and closer to the edge. As she shudders and cries out in pleasure, I thrust as deep as I can.

And then I lose all control. I fuck her fast and hard. Fireworks dance before my eyes. My body explodes into pleasure. Heat spikes at the base of my spine. My blood sizzles.

I've been dead for years. Who knew all I needed was a good fuck to come back to life? And it is the *best* of fucks.

Nothing compares. Every stroke I take inside her makes me jerk with pleasure. I'm riding her too hard, but I can't dial it back. My loins slap against her ass. Her bound wrists bounce on her lower back.

"My hips," she gasps. "It hurts."

Oh shit. I'm banging them against the hard wooden workbench.

I wrap my arm around the front of her to provide padding, and then keep slamming the hell out of her. I don't give a shit that I'm bruising my arm. In fact, I sort of relish the sensation. Pleasure and pain mingle together into a symphony of sensory feedback. Her scent gets up in my nostrils, along with the smell of roses and lilies and whatever other flowers she has in the place.

She gasps as I drive hard and deeper, feeling the pressure inside her building to an unbearable degree. Her hips begin to quiver in response, begging for more. I reach down and slide one hand between us, my fingers finding her clit and rubbing in circles. She moans as she arches her back and grinds against me, her body shaking and writhing. My thrusts become faster and more powerful as I drive toward the edge.

I'm too far gone to wait for her to come, definitely too lost to figure out how to make her orgasm. I mutter a curse and shove deep, pulling her head and torso back up against the front of me as I finish.

I bite her ear, flick it with my tongue. "I'm sorry I hurt you," I murmur against the soft skin of her jaw.

She whimpers slightly, and a pang of regret wavers through me.

Funny.

I just ended a guy on her floor and felt nothing. I was the Terminator doing a job. Now I suddenly have a conscience. And I *should* be sorry. I just fucked a girl I trussed like a chicken and took as my prisoner. And her asking if I had a condom probably did not constitute consent. It was a plea for some measure of safety.

Fuck. What kind of *stronzo* am I?

# CHAPTER NINE

*Hannah*

Oh my *gawd.*

I'm dizzy, my body buzzes. I'd forgotten to be afraid while we were having sex, but now, awareness creeps back. I'm pinned against my workbench with my panties down and my wrists tied behind my back, a semi-stranger's cock still stretching me.

What in the hell am I doing?

It may not seem like it now, but I'm usually cautious about who I have sex with.

I don't know how I lost my head like that. It was just so hot. So animalistic. Feral. That teenage crush on Armando made it feel so necessary. I didn't come, but I was so close.

Now I'm tingling and hot and needy as hell. Which doesn't help the tolling bells for foreboding.

I could be in real trouble here. Life or death stuff.

*I'm sorry I hurt you.*

I cling to that one piece of evidence that this man is not a psychopath. That he didn't just rape me. That I'm going to walk out of here alive.

A knock pounds on my back door, and Armando pulls out of me

with a curse. He yanks my panties up and drops the condom in the wastebasket.

The taut urgency returns to his movements as he spins me around, his gaze darting around the premises. I stiffen when he pulls a roll of duct tape from my shelf and rips off a small piece.

"No—"

He slaps it over my mouth.

I scream behind the tape, terror suddenly ripping through me.

*Ohmygodohmygodohmygod.*

What's happening? What's he going to do with me?

The knock sounds again, and Armando grabs my arm, propelling me toward the storage closet.

"Shh." He puts his finger over my taped lips as he pushes me backward into the crowded dark space.

I try to scream *no*, but it comes out as nothing more than a muffled sound.

"Quiet, Hannah." There's a warning to his tone.

The door shuts.

Panic sets in. I'm afraid of the dark. I don't like small spaces. And I definitely don't want to be tied up and left in here to rot.

I want to slam my head against the door to make noise, except he was expecting whomever showed up at my back door. So it's someone he knows.

Which means I can't hope for a rescue from them.

In fact, if he's hiding me in here from his associates out there, it could be for my own safety. Like they might insist on killing me.

Oh fuck.

My entire body starts to shake. Not a slight tremble, but a terrible shuddering that makes my knees knock together and my ribs lock down in a painful cinching.

I hear male voices and footsteps tromping past the closet. The sound of a body being dragged.

Tears drip down my cheeks and over the duct tape on my mouth. My breath rasps harshly in and out of my nose.

"What about the florist?" a male asks just outside the closet. "Need me to clean that up?"

"I got rid of her," Armando says.

"Yeah?"

"Yeah. She didn't see anything. It's cool."

I was right. He's protecting me. That's why I'm in the closet. Because if his buddies out there knew I saw something, I might have to die.

But then... how do I know he's not going to kill me anyway? Maybe he just wants to make me his fuck toy first. Keep me tied up in his closet for months and months and *then* throw me dead in a ditch.

Oh my God.

This is bad.

"I'll finish the clean up here. I owe you. Don't tell anyone about this. I'll tell the don myself, yeah?"

"Yeah, as long as you do."

"Swear to Christ. Hey—get rid of his gun, too. I can't carry one."

"Are you fucking nuts? Someone's trying to kill you. You need a piece."

"I can take care of myself."

He definitely can. I just saw him take care of an armed man without ever firing. In fact, he'd purposely emptied the gun chamber. I don't think he meant to kill that guy at all. It was definitely self-defense.

"I fucking hope so."

The back door shuts. I wait, my shaking intensifying as the possibilities fly through my mind.

*What'shappeningwhat'shappeningwhat'shappening?*

The closet door flies open, and I blink at the sudden light. Armando's face comes into focus. His brows lower when he looks at me. "Aw, baby. Did you think I was going to leave you in here?" He thumbs away the tears under my left eye.

Did I? Not really. I just didn't like being tied up and standing in a dark closet. Feeling helpless.

He drags me forward, out of the closet and works the corner of tape free over my upper lip. "I'm sorry for this." He yanks it all off in one pull. A strangled cry erupts as the tape leaves my lips.

"You okay?"

"No," I snap. "Let me go." My demand sounds way more watery than firm.

"Sorry, Flowers. That's not possible." He pulls me into my workshop. "Here's what's going to happen. I'm going to clean up your shop, and you're going to stay where I put you and not make a sound. Can you do that, or do I need to put you back in the closet?"

I'm tempted—so tempted—to knee him in the balls. Except I just saw what this man is capable of. He fought a man armed with a gun *and* a knife, and he won. There's no way it would go well for me.

He thumbs away the tears under my right eye. "Be cool, Flowers, and we won't have any problems. Okay?"

"I don't want you here." It's a dumb thing to say, but it's true. I want him to leave. I want him out of my shop. My life. My reality.

I think I'm going to puke.

I wish this evening never happened.

"Feeling's mutual, Flowers." He pulls back the stool at my desk, which is essentially in the hallway where he can see me from the front room and pushes me into it.

"It's Hannah." I turn to face him as he gets a broom and dustpan out of the closet and moves swiftly into the shop. "But you know that."

I'm a little bitter that his speaking my name was my downfall. If I hadn't hesitated when he called my name, I would've made it out the back door.

"Hannah." His back is to me. He sweeps up the broken pots and soil with swift, deft movements. "You own the place now."

I watch the muscles in his back ripple each sure stroke of the broom. I shouldn't be flattered that he knows things about me. And really, it's not like he knows something earth-shattering. It's a basic fact everyone in his organization knows. Yet it makes my pulse quicken.

"Armando."

The sound of his name makes his head snap up and brings his gaze to mine. My stomach drops away. He's as breathtaking as I remembered him, except so very serious now. There's no hint of a smile on his face anymore. None of the charm and ease. And the eyes...

Compassion weasels in.

Because his eyes look ancient.

"You remembered."

I shrug like he never starred in a hundred of my darkest fantasies. "You remembered mine, too. Where have you been?" My voice sounds rusty.

Shutters close behind his eyes, and he turns back to his work. "Prison. Just out."

A shiver runs through me. *Prison.* Josie and I didn't think of that possibility.

"Was that your... first time since getting out?" It would explain why he was an animal when I kissed him.

At first, I think he's not going to answer. He ignores me, dumping the contents of the dustpan into the garbage. Then he mutters, "Yeah."

I'm simultaneously pleased and destroyed by that. I guess I wanted to believe he was just that attracted to me. I mean, he did remember my name.

I am such a fool.

Then I realize he's watching me, and I try to school my face. Keep on a blank mask like he wears.

"You okay? I was... rough."

Oh shit, I'm blushing. I sense the heat crawl up my neck and spread to my ears and cheeks.

He *was* rough. And it was hot. I never knew I'd like having my hair pulled or my butt slapped, but I did. I'm still needy for more like a glutton. Almost painfully needy.

"I'd buy you flowers, but I'm guessing that's not your thing." He gives me the barest hint of a smile, and stupid me, I reward him with one in return.

"Only if you get them here," I say, which is dumb because I wouldn't really want a guy to buy flowers from me to give to me. I only said it because I need the money so badly, I'd be offended if he shopped anywhere else.

And why in the hell am I even examining this line of thought? I'm being held captive in my own shop. *By a murderer.*

It's not time for roses and romance.

So I poke. "What happened to the fiancée?"

He grimaces, his expression going harder. "Lotta questions, Flowers."

I arrange the pieces of the puzzle in my mind. "She didn't wait," I answer for him.

He straightens the toppled table and rearranges the remaining plants on it.

"I'm sorry." It slips out before I can bite back my offering of compassion.

He ignores my sympathy, walking past me to fill the mop bucket in my large utility sink. I smell the scent of bleach. Well, at least he cleans up his own mess. He could've ordered me to do it.

I twist my hands behind my back. "These hurt."

"Stop moving."

"Thanks. Great suggestion. I hadn't thought of that."

He cuts a look at me while he dumps a generous helping of bleach in with the water. "You're tied up because you gave me trouble. Maybe rethink the attitude if you want me to let out the leash."

"Leash?"

He wheels the mop bucket into the shop. There was a smattering of blood on the floor, but not much, thankfully. He swabs the entire floor.

"Why didn't you use the gun? Too loud?"

He shakes his head. "Shut up, Flowers."

"You didn't want him dead."

Armando makes a tsking sound as he mops the hall, then wheels past me and dumps the dirty water into the sink. "Keep out of this. You saw nothing. If anyone asks, there was a struggle, but we both left to finish things outside. You locked the place up and left early."

My stool is a spinning one, and I use my feet to whirl around on it like a kid. "No offense, but that story would not hold up under questioning."

Armando stalks over to me.

The part of me bold enough to talk back shrivels, especially when I remember this man is a brutal killer.

He stops when he reaches me, indecision flickering in his expression. Maybe he sees the fear on my face. He reaches for me, and I flinch. He slows his touch. Burrows his fingers through my hair at the side of my head then curls them up to tug it tight.

"Listen. Hannah. I'd rather not say the shit I'm supposed to say right now. Not to you."

My stomach flip flops as I try to decode the meaning of his words. I keep getting caught on the *not to you.*

Like he *does* think I'm something special. But maybe, I'm looking too hard for meaning, so I won't regret what I just let him do to me.

Like I want to believe that crazy rough sex meant something to him.

I know I still feel it all over. And if I stop looking for meaning or wondering if I just degraded myself, I might believe experiencing a man like Armando was worth it. I'm pretty sure he just ruined me for vanilla sex. Ruined me for kinder, gentler men. I should've known there was a reason those mafia assholes always appealed to me. I prefer an alpha male. I'm sure it's a purely biological weakness many women share with me.

I try to swallow around the invisible band choking me.

"I won't tell anyone what I saw," I manage to say. My voice sounds strained.

"Good girl. Then we won't have any problems."

Oh, we'll still have problems. Individually and together.

I screw up my courage because making demands isn't my strong suit, especially not in a crazy situation like this. I lift my chin. "But you're paying for the damages here." I don't take my gaze off his face as I flutter my hand in the direction where the pots had been broken.

"Yeah. Of course."

Whew. That was easier than expected.

I sit forward on the stool, as much as I can with his grip on my hair holding me immobile. It only has the effect of pushing my tits out. His gaze drops to my cleavage and hunger creeps into his expression.

I lick my lips, and his gaze lifts to my mouth. "A-are you going to let me go?"

The hunger drops away, replaced by that hardened mask he wears. "We'll see, Flowers." He releases my hair and turns away.

A chill creeps across my skin.

All the horrific doubts crowd into my brain and cut off intelligent thought.

I surge to my feet. He whirls, his hand around my throat in seconds, not squeezing, but guiding me back to my seat. His voice is even when he shakes his head and says, "I didn't say you could move."

And it's that cold hardness more than anything that freaks me the hell out.

He must see the panic in my expression because he puts his finger lightly over my lips, trailing it downward. "Shh. Take it easy. You do what I say, you won't get hurt. *Capisce?*"

I stare back at him and nod quickly.

"Good girl."

# CHAPTER TEN

*Armando*

Fuck.

I don't know what I'm going to do with the girl. I can't keep her tied up forever.

She is a witness to a murder, but I don't harm the innocent.

That guy I killed today? He was a professional. Not a good one but definitely a guy who took money for the hit. Probably sent by the Hermanos.

*Cazzo.*

I went straight from my first confession out of the joint back to hell. Don Pachino told me to keep my nose clean. What a fucking laugh. I finish wiping the shop, trying to erase all evidence of the struggle. I owe her for a couple pots, but the damage isn't too bad. Luckily, there wasn't much blood.

Marco is a prince for taking care of the body for me. He's the only guy I trusted enough to call. There are soldiers. I used to have my own crew, and I coulda called one of them, but something told me not to.

I stand in front of Hannah and slide my palm around the meat of her arm to lift her to her feet. She glares up at me.

"Where are the keys to that van out back?"

Her eyes widen. "Why? You can't put a body in it—"

"There's no body," I cut her off. "But we need to leave—now. And I don't have a car."

I don't have a license, either, but that's sort of the least of my problems. I probably should've kept that gun, too. At this point, I'm in for murder and kidnapping. The five years for a felon in possession of a firearm is minor in comparison.

"I-it's a piece of shit. I don't even use it because half the time it stalls on me."

Fuck.

"I'll take the risk. *Where are the goddamn keys?*"

"In my purse—*Jesus.*" She lifts her chin toward the purse tucked under the counter.

I like that she's offended by my tone and gives a little shit back to me. It means she's not scared out of her mind. She still believes I ought to treat her better, which, of course, is true. I'm just out of fucking practice with having manners.

I rifle through her purse and find the keys then check her driver's license for an address. "You live alone?"

She pales. "W-why?"

"'Cause someone's trying to kill me. I don't think I should bring you to my place. Is your place cool?"

Relief flickers over her face, and she gives me a shaky nod. "Yeah. I live alone. I mean, it's small."

"Yeah, I just got out of a seven by twelve foot cell. I think we're good."

She gets more words out of me than I've spared for anyone since I got out, my mother and Don Pachino included. I tug her to the door, but she balks, looking back toward the register.

I tried to read her resistance. "You don't leave cash in the register at night?"

"I need to make a deposit—tonight. Or your boss won't get his money when he cashes my check." A sheen of tears fills her eyes, and it does something weird to my chest.

I've felt nothing since they locked me up.

*Nada.*

No heart beating in my fucking chest.

But now empathy suddenly rears its pansy head.

I don't know. I guess I'm surprised how little she's fussed over my treatment of her, but here she's tearing up about the money.

She must be in dire financial straits.

Buying the business might have been a shit move for her.

I bring her back to the register and flip through the keys on her ring until I find the small one that fits. There's not that much money in it. I'd say less than three hundred bucks.

"There's an envelope in that drawer." She indicates it with her chin.

I find the zippered pouch and tuck the money inside. "That it?"

The sheen of tears appears again, and she nods.

Definitely money trouble.

Well, if she keeps my secret, I'll owe her. I shove my hand in my pocket. "How short are you?"

"What?" She searches my face in surprise. "Oh, um, at least a hundred, maybe more."

I flip through my cash the don set me up with when I renewed my oaths to him and the Outfit, or as the don likes to call it, *la Cosa Nostra*. I shove another six hundred in her money pouch. "That cover it?"

Her eyes round, and she nods, breath erratic.

"Good. Here's what's going to happen. You play it cool—real cool— and I'll untie you and let you ride up front in the passenger seat. We'll make your deposit." I smack her ass with the money pouch. "Then we'll go to your place. *Capisce?*"

She nods quickly. "I'll be cool. I promise."

When she licks her lips, I'm overcome with the sudden urge to claim that mouth again. Because I have never kissed a girl like I just kissed her. So full of passion and heat and raw desperate need. I want to get another taste.

And then I want to see those lips stretched around my cock. Working my length with the same receptivity she showed me bent over her workbench earlier. I want to see the pleasure in her eyes when I make her come, feel her body tremble and shake with a pleasure that only I can give her. I move closer to her, my hands sliding up her arms as I press my hips against hers, not leaving any room for doubts as to what I want or where I want it.

I swear to Christ, she must read my thoughts because when I look down, I see her nipples protruding beneath her layers.

And I've lost my mind because all I can think is maybe I should fuck her again before we leave.

Instead, I tug her toward the back and out the door to the alley where Marco and I loaded the body into his trunk forty-five minutes ago. I stop at the back door and use the teeth of one of her keys to rip the tape off her wrists.

Before I release her, I wrap my hand in her hair and tug her head back. "Don't make me sorry, Hannah." My body's right up against hers. Her chest rises and falls rapidly, drawing my gaze to her delectable cleavage. I trace my thumb across the line of her jaw.

"I won't. I'll be cool. Promise."

"Good girl." I release her in degrees, not wanting to separate my body from hers. Not sure I can trust her outside this shop. She could scream. Or run. Or grab for her phone.

But I guess this is how I find out. If she misbehaves, I'll deal with it. And then I'll know I can't trust her.

Which means...fuck, I don't want to think what that would mean because I don't hurt women. And I definitely don't hurt the innocent.

And she's both.

# CHAPTER ELEVEN

*Armando*

I open the back door and push her out then pull it shut behind us and test the lock. "Show me you can be trusted." I smack her ass again.

I'm not usually the ass-smacking type. At least I wasn't before prison. Sure, I gave my fiancée a spank or two during sex, but Hannah is a different story altogether.

Her ass is juicy. Round, plump. Firm. I don't just want to bend her over and fuck her again, I want to spank her brown cheeks rosy and own that ass with my cock.

Jesus, fuck.

I'm a feral animal.

A wild beast rutting.

And Hannah is my prey.

I want to throw her in the back of the van and have another go at that lush body of hers right here, right now.

I almost wish she'd give me a reason to keep manhandling her, but she behaves herself, strutting straight to the passenger side of the beat up, rust-covered, 1970s Dodge Ram van with a flower decal on the side and waiting for me to unlock it. The paint of the aging van is peeling and chipping off, the rust eating at the edges. The lettering of *Garden of Eden Florists* on the side is blistered, peeled, faded and flaking, leaving yellow paint behind.

"Does this heap even run?" I say the words out loud as I open the door for her. I don't mean to shame the girl, but Jesus, this tin can is a dinosaur that has truly seen its day.

"Are you even allowed to drive?" she snarks back as she climbs in.

"No." I slam her door and walk around, keeping an eye on her through the windows. She sits down and folds her hands in her lap, perfectly behaved.

Almost too perfectly. Either she's more worried about getting this money in the bank than she is her safety with me, or she's planning something.

I hope it's the former.

I get in and start the van. Correction—*try* to start the van. It takes a couple attempts before it sputters to life. I don't know how the fuck she handles flower deliveries with a van that needs work. Which I guess speaks to her money problems.

The van smells of lilac and gasoline, and there is a large crack in the windshield. Though the engine is now running, it's not exactly humming like a well-oiled machine. It'll be a miracle if we even make it out of this alley.

I glance at her hands in her lap. Her wrists still wear the mark of the tape I bound them with, and there's an angry red scrape down her arm.

The fuck?

My hand shoots out to snatch up her wrist before I can dial back the aggression. I'm pissed at myself for hurting her. I don't even know when it happened. My body goes into full rage mode like I'm going to defend her against myself. The aggression is different from how I was back there with the hitman. Not so clean and clinical. There's emotion this time.

She gasps and tries to pull away. I force myself to gentle my hold because I'm scaring the hell out of her. "Did I do that?" I manage to choke, running my thumb over the long thick red line.

She looks at me like I've lost my mind.

Maybe I have.

"What? The scratch?" A shaky laugh tumbles from her lips. "No. My kitten did that last night. He fell in the bathtub while I was in it. Turns out, cats can fly." Another nervous laugh.

*Kitten.*

*Kitten.* It takes a moment for the word to even process. Cute furry thing with claws. Right. Her cat scratched her.

Not me.

I relax my hold and sit back in my seat, forcing myself to exhale. I want to ask if I hurt her, but I already know I did. The skin around her wrists and bruises on her hips. Hopefully nothing worse. Nothing deep and psychological that will haunt her for the rest of her life.

Yeah, right. Guy comes in, kills a man in front of her, then ties her up and fucks her. She's definitely scarred for life.

"My thighs are all scratched up, too."

My eyes drop to the hemline of her short skirt. Fuck if I don't want to see those scratches for myself now.

I wrench my gaze back to the windshield. I need to get my head back in the game. I dip my cock in a chick once, and suddenly every-thing's haywire for me.

Hannah's got some kind of magic pussy or something. Like that doesn't sound insane.

"Which bank?" I ask roughly. "They'd better have a drive-thru."

"Chicago City Bank on Lincoln. Um...hopefully." She sounds doubtful like she knows they don't but just isn't telling me.

"Do they or don't they, Flowers?" I snap.

She reaches over and touches my forearm. "Please? I *have* to make this deposit."

It's so fucked that I'm even considering this. She's my hostage until I figure out what the hell I'm going to do with her, and I'm going to go run her errands?

Give her at least a dozen opportunities to signal for help or run away?

On the other hand, the vague plan in the back of my head is to sit on her until I get a feel for her. Figure out if she's gonna squeal or not. Ignoring her needs isn't going to win trust. And since I seem reluctant to make the kind of threats that will keep her quiet out of fear, I'm probably gonna have to go on trust if I don't want to get rid of her.

And I definitely don't.

I grind my molars, trying to come to a decision. Stopping at the bank is a really, really bad one. I can't send her in alone. I can't leave her in the van unless I tie her up in the back, and doing that in public would be risky.

"Please."

I glance over and curse. "You try anything, Flowers, I will make you sorry."

That's the closest I can come to threatening her.

Would I hurt a woman? No fucking way. We may be criminals, but goodfellas swear an oath to respect women and our elders. I nearly punched myself in the face when I thought I'd scraped her arm.

Doesn't mean I wouldn't smack her ass and tie her up. Show her who's boss.

"I won't."

I growl but find a spot to park near the bank. "Don't open your fucking door until I come around." I glare at her.

She pales slightly. "Chill, Armando. I'm not going to try anything. I just have to deposit this money." She picks up the money pouch I set between our seats and waves it. Her hand's trembling like crazy, and I feel bad about scaring her, but I don't apologize. I just give her the hairy eyeball as I shut the door and stalk around to her side.

She waits until I open it, like I instructed.

"Good girl." I offer a hand to help her out.

She clutches the bag to her chest. "Can I get my purse? In case they need I.D.?"

I already pocketed her phone, but I still don't like it. I reach for the purse and pull the I.D. out of her wallet. "Let's go." I take her hand but fold it behind her back, like she's under arrest. It's symbolic—her other hand is free, but she'll get my meaning.

I start sweating the moment we walk inside the bank. The air is thick with the smell of polished wood, antiseptic, and body odor. There are people everywhere. A security guard by the door with a gun. He's a big, lumbering guy, with a mustache and an ill-fitting uniform. The eyes that look at you from behind his glasses are tired and bored.

All Hannah has to do is scream for help, and it's over.

"Armando," Hannah murmurs. I like it when she says my name. I like that she remembered me. She wriggles her hand in mine, and I realize I'm squeezing too tightly.

I loosen my grip slightly and pull her hand out from behind her back to swing between us. We walk up to the teller, and I swear to Christ my heart's beating so loud I think the teller will hear it. She'll probably think I'm trying to rob the bank and sound the silent alarm.

Hannah quickly fills out a deposit slip and pushes the cash across the counter.

"You had an overdraft charge today," the teller informs her.

Hannah tenses. "I did? I thought I had until the end of the day to make the deposit."

The teller looks at her screen. "No, it's real time. The check came through around two p.m."

Okay, so she wasn't playing me. She really does have money trouble. I tap the stack of cash with the deposit slip. "Will this cover it?"

The teller counts the money and types into her computer. "The overdraft charge was $35, so you're twenty-two short."

I shove my hand in my pocket to pull out another five hundred Benjamins. "Put that in the account, too."

She nods, counts it and types some more. "Will that be all?"

I close my fingers around Hannah's hand again. "Yes." I start to pull her away when the teller calls back to me.

"Hang on."

I freeze, a tight cord of tension running between my shoulder blades.

"Here's your receipt."

Jesus, I just want to get out of this place. But I turn and grab the receipt then pull my little captive with me.

"You were short by a lot," I say as we walk out of the building.

Again, I'm not trying to shame her, I'm just wondering what the fuck her plan was.

She stiffens, tucking her curls behind her left ear. "Better to be short with the bank than short with the don, right?"

"Yeah," I agree. "You behind on rent?"

I don't know why I'm worried for her now, but I am. If she owes Don Pachino money and doesn't pay it, he'll swallow her business up in a heartbeat. That flower shop will become a money-laundering machine. Every delivery van will be driven by a soldier on Family business between making the flower rounds. It's actually such a perfect setup, I'm surprised he hasn't already moved on it.

She shakes her head, sending her golden-tipped curls rippling like a waterfall, but there's still an ocean of worry in the set of her shoulders. I get it. She made the rent today, but she's still worried about tomorrow and the next day and the one after that.

I put her back in the van. Considering what a shit show today was, I'm somewhat amazed this stop actually turned out okay.

I drive to her neighborhood, which isn't that far from her shop in Little Italy. Parking is a bitch, so I circle around a half dozen times. I don't want to park too far from her place because it gives her a better chance to scream for help or run or... whatever.

The stupid thing is that I know exactly how to stop any hint of that behavior. I know how to issue threats. I've perfected mean and cruel.

I could easily make her piss herself with fear without ever laying a hand on her.

But I can't bring myself to do it. Even though it would make things simpler.

Make my job at her place clearer. All I'd have to do would be solidify the threat. Put the fear of the devil in her. Then do intermittent check-ins to make sure she's still scared.

Intimidation is an easy game, really.

But that's not tonight's show.

I don't know what the fuck I'm going to do with her, but everything in me rebels at the thought of scaring her even more than I have.

And honestly? She's a tough cookie because so far, the only thing that broke her was the closet and the risk of not making her deposit.

So she trusts me against her better judgment, or she trusts herself to be able to handle me.

I don't mind either of those scenarios.

We pass a motor cop giving tickets out. Hannah's head jerks up.

I tense, a million ugly scenarios running through my head, the primary one involves her trying to open her door and jump out. But she immediately looks over at me. Nothing surreptitious about it. Not hiding what she just saw. More like she's questioning me—did *I* see that cop?

I cock a brow. I really don't understand this girl.

"What happens if you get pulled over?"

My brain scrambles to follow. Is she for real?

"You worried about me?"

She shrugs. "You don't have a license."

I throw on the brakes when I see someone pulling out and put on my blinker behind them. While we wait, I give her a total stare-down, trying to get into her head. "You scared of me at all, Flowers?"

I should want her answer to be yes. It would mean I've done what needs to be done to keep her quiet. Ensure she doesn't talk. But for whatever dumbass reason, I love that she's not all that scared. Because she's into me.

Her eyes widen slightly like I just reminded her that she should be. "Yeah." She sounds breathless.

"Not enough to want me busted."

She's still holding her breath when she gives her head a little shake.

Huh. Not sure what I did to win her allegiance, but I like it.

I park and throw my door open, walking around swiftly in case she runs.

She doesn't. She hops out and tugs down her short skirt, which rides tight over those shapely thighs. Her mess of curls falls over one eye as she contemplates me.

I hold out my hand like we're on a date and she invited me in instead of whatever the hell I'm doing with her.

"I've had enough of hand-holding with you." She flounces past me without taking it.

Something foreign and buoyant stirs within me. Something I haven't felt in years. What is it?

Amusement.

The girl amuses me.

That's my lips trying to curve, but they don't remember how.

I ignore the urge and follow her.

# CHAPTER TWELVE

*Hannah*

We walk up the stairs to my apartment, and I try to remember if I cleaned out Shadow's kitty litter this morning. My place is tiny, and it can easily start to stink.

But that's stupid—am I really worried about what he thinks?

It's not like he's some guy I invited to come up to Netflix and chill. He's a mobster who killed a guy in my shop today. He's taken me, my van and my apartment hostage, and I have absolutely no clue how this thing ends.

The only thing that keeps me from totally freaking out is his obvious attraction to me. Even now, walking up the stairs, I sense his gaze on my ass.

I turn around to verify. Yep.

"Like what you see?" I say dryly.

"Oh, Flowers," he says. "I am *all about* your ass."

I turn away before he can see the satisfaction on my face. This guy hasn't been with a woman in years, and I'm his first lay, so, of course, he's going to think I'm all that. Even so, his lusty reaction to my kiss back at the shop forever changed me. I don't ever want to be with a guy who gives me less of a response.

It's not that I don't usually get attention. I do. I get plenty of it. Men all over my thing. But it never lasts because I'm the idiot who always gets attached too quickly. I'm an emotional sponge, and I get into their worlds. I feel their emotions for them. Try to fix their problems. Forget about my own. And then suddenly, I'm all in, and they're walking away. Like clockwork.

Seriously, I've dated too many man-babies. Immature players who are more interested in themselves than anything else.

Armando is...

He's extremely capable. And very dangerous, yes. I'm sure in some twisted way that's part of the attraction.

And I remember once upon a time, he used to be charming.

Now he's damaged.

He's been in prison, just killed a guy in front of me and then tied me up and fucked me immediately after. He's probably very damaged.

I'm crazy to be so turned on by him. What is it about the bad boy that makes a woman think she can reform him? It's a losing proposition, I'm sure. He may be sexier and more capable than the usual guys I date, but my pattern of wanting to fix is the same.

Some secret instinct in me wants to heal him.

I think that's what made me give myself over to him. Made me kiss him. Offer my body up to quench his desperate need.

I wait for him at the door because Armando has my purse. He fishes out my keys and hands them to me. When my fingers shake trying to slide the right one in the lock, he takes over, opening the door and ushering me in with a hand at my back.

My apartment is just a studio and a bathroom. Fortunately, it doesn't smell.

The front door is painted the color of a bumblebee, something my landlord would shit over if he knew I painted it. But I needed color in all the drab.

Inside, my apartment is simple and small. The one room is furnished with a small two-man purple sofa, a coffee table with a colorful tapestry flung over it, and a TV I bought at a thrift store for thirty bucks. The kitchenette has four cabinets and a small refrigerator. I'm lucky enough that this unit also has a two-burner stove unlike some of my neighbors. There is barely enough room for a tiny table and two chairs, but I was able to cram them into the space.

My bed is up against the far wall in order to give me as much room as possible. I have colors of the rainbow splattered in pillows across a bright blue comforter to make it appear as a lounge area rather than what it is—a bed crammed in a small room with a sofa.

Twinkle lights are strung from one side of the room to the other, casting a warm hue on the space. It might not be much to most, but it's mine, and I feel comfortable inside.

The kitten mews from the bed, standing up and arching his back in a shivery stretch. "Hi Shadow." He runs to me on tiny paws and twines around my ankles.

I watch Armando as he moves around my space, unsure of how to read his expression.

Eyes usually give away the feelings that hide behind people's masks, but when I look into Armando's eyes, all I see is a void. His entire being seems to have built a wall between us that I can't penetrate. A sensation of unease and unfamiliarity crawls up my spine as I try to connect with him.

Still, there is something oddly comforting about his presence that makes me feel safe. Ironic considering...

"So what happens now?" I demand, pretending I'm not scared of the hulking man beside me.

Armando rubs his face. "Now?"

I'm pretty sure he doesn't know. There's no script for the I-killed-a-guy-in-your-florist-shop scenario.

"Now I'm going to sit on you until I'm sure you're cool."

"I'm cool," I assure him immediately. I guess I've been waiting for him to ask me. Or demand it or... whatever. I've already decided—if I hadn't from the very beginning—that I'm not going to rat on him. "I'm not going to tell anyone what I saw. I won't say a word, I promise."

He nods. "Good."

"So... we're cool. Right?"

"Not yet."

I huff out a sigh. "So what are you going to do?"

He leans his back against the door and scans my apartment. When his gaze dances over the bed in the corner, his lids droop, but he gives his head a shake and pulls out his phone. "First I gotta make a call. Then I'll order us some food. What do you like?"

I shrug. Don't mind a free meal, considering there's nothing but a couple cans of flavored seltzer water and a bag of potato chips in my kitchen. "Anything."

He arcs a brow. "You eat calzones? I know a great place."

"Sounds good. I'll have whatever you're having."

He dials a number, and I hear a short, clipped conversation. Mostly *yeah* and *thanks*. I head to the bathroom. While I'm there, I hear him order two calzones, a salad, and a bottle of wine, rattling off my address, which apparently, he's already memorized.

I use the opportunity in the bathroom to quickly clean out the kitty litter although why I'm working so hard is beyond me.

*This is not a date.*

I hustle out of the bathroom with the tied trash bag of cat poop and run smack into Armando's big chest.

He catches my wrists then wrinkles his nose and pushes the one with the trash bag away from our bodies. "Do you want it to be a date?"

What?

Oh crap, did I mutter that out loud? I thought he was on the phone!

I pull out of his grasp, practically dashing for the door.

He catches me around the waist right before I get there. "Where are you going?"

I hold the bag up. "To the dumpster. I'm not leaving this in here." I use my best *duh* voice.

He doesn't release me. Instead, he holds me even tighter, his mouth coming to the outer shell of my ear. "Keep up the sass, Flowers. I'd love to spank that ass again."

My knees buckle.

Dammit. That was not swoon worthy, but for some reason, my body thought it was. My pussy clenched when he said it, and now all I feel is a hot, slow pulse. The throbbing complaint of that missed orgasm. Maybe one more time with him, just to finish, just to feel if all this heat lives up to its hype would be worth it.

"*You* take it then." I know—I sass. It's not even subconscious.

Luckily—or maybe unluckily—I'm not certain, he doesn't take the bait. Instead, he slowly releases me. "Can't do that, either."

"Looks like we're going to have that date, after all. I always wanted a guy to take me to the dumpster." I toss my hair as I look over my shoulder at him.

He lets me go, and when I turn, I glimpse an echo of the old Armando. His lips quirk like he might smile if I keep it up. He takes the knotted trash bag from my hand and interlaces his fingers with mine. "Nothing's too good for my girl."

I hide a grin as he opens the door and hooks his index finger through the loop on my keys as we leave.

Shadow darts out, and I stoop and pick him up and rub my face in his fur and kiss his sweet head before I drop him back inside and shut the door.

I want to keep up the flirting, but an awkward silence descends between us. At least, it's awkward for me. Armando's as tense as ever. Same hard blank face he wore cleaning up a dead guy. Driving my van.

We walk down the three flights of stairs and outside to the dumpsters then back again without saying a word to each other. Armando glances around outside, doing his badass secret agent impression again.

I wonder who he's worried about.

"So who's trying to kill you?"

Nothing changes on Armando's face. He doesn't look at me. But I see a muscle flex in his jaw like he's grinding his teeth.

He ignores my question and quickens the pace back into the building.

I think through the facts. He just got out of prison, and someone's trying to kill him. So it's either something unresolved from when he went in. Or maybe something that happened on the inside.

"You kill someone first?"

His gaze cuts to me then away.

So that's it. Someone wants revenge.

"Is it someone from within the mafia?"

"Seriously, Hannah." His tone is all business. "Ask another question, and I'll tape your mouth. I mean it."

I'm more offended by the threat than I should be. We're both pretending I'm not his prisoner. I guess I prefer that fantasy to the terror that goes with the harsher picture of what's happening here. Or how this might end.

"You're a dick," I mutter.

Nice comeback.

"I'm trying to protect you." Does he sound slightly defensive?

I scoff. "Yeah, you're a real knight in shining armor, aren't you?"

His own scoff is soft and bitter. "Definitely not that. And you don't want to know all the depraved things I'd like to do to you, so don't tempt me."

Now I do want to know.

About the depraved things.

I want to know so badly... I might ask him. We bump shoulders as we climb the stairs side by side.

"What depraved things?" Apparently, I have no self-control.

He gives me that heavy-lidded look that makes my panties damp. He makes a sound in his throat and then says, "I might tie you to that bed."

*And?* I desperately want him to go on.

# CHAPTER THIRTEEN

*Hannah*

My nipples are tight beads. My pussy's wet and slick. I'm hungry for a re-do, so I can come. I also realize how insane this is. Me, seducing my captor. Or was he seducing me?

What in the hell are we doing?

We step inside my apartment, and he closes the door behind us.

"I'd spread your legs wide and lick that pussy until you screamed." His voice is rough and raw.

I remember again how much passion he brought to our hookup back at the shop. How he's fresh out of prison, and I'm the first woman he's been with.

"W-what do I have to do"—I swallow—"to get that treatment?"

Armando grabs me by the hair and claims my mouth as he walks me backward until my knees hit the bed. I fall back onto it, and he follows, climbing over me, lips twisting over mine.

I would've said the kiss we shared back at my shop was the best of my life, but this one might be even better. It doesn't carry as much desperation, but now I get some finesse. Like a violent kiss followed by a quick nip. A trail of kisses that run down the side of my throat.

"Now you're in trouble," he murmurs as he pins my wrists above my head. "Big trouble."

I writhe beneath him, lust blasting through me. I swear I've never had this kind of reaction to a guy before. I've been excited, especially if I've had a drink or two, but the way my body reacts to Armando now is off the charts.

Our first hook up was a lightning strike. This time, he goes slow. He bites through the layers of my crop top and the camisole beneath it to scrape his teeth over my nipple. My legs wrap around his waist, pulling him in tighter. I twist my hips, trying to find satisfaction rubbing against him. He reaches down and pulls something out of his pocket. I think it's going to be a condom, but it's the roll of floral tape.

Like he *planned* on tying me up again.

And that thought should scare me way more than it does. But with the way his mouth is on mine, I can only interpret his actions one way: the tape is for sexy times.

He winds it around my wrists—not nearly so tightly as he did back at the shop—and pushes my wrists back over my head. He leans up on one hand, gazing down at me. His pupils are blown, eyes full of dark intent, but his face is expressionless. Like he's forgotten how to smile.

He traces his thumb lightly down the inside of my arm. I squirm when it covers the most ticklish part.

"You didn't answer me before."

He sounds so gruff. So serious. If it weren't for the light touch, I would think he was pissed.

"About what?"

"What part turned you on—being tied up or spanked? Or the other thing?"

*The other thing.* I guess that's him grappling with a guy in a fight to the death.

It definitely shouldn't have turned me on. Except I always had a thing for those Jason Bourne movies, and Armando looked every inch as badass as Matt Damon. Or Chris Hemsworth in that Netflix movie *Extraction.* So yeah, up until the actual death part, it tweaked the most primitive part of my brain. The part that seeks to reproduce with the fiercest warrior in the land.

"All of it," I murmur.

He stares a moment longer, without saying anything. Like he's trying to read into the depths of my soul. Then he asks, "You like it rough?"

My face grows warm. I'd be a fool to admit such a thing with a guy I can't trust. Besides, I don't know if it's true. Before today, I hadn't tried it.

"I liked it rough with you." That's the truth—and all I know, really.

Something shutters behind his eyes, and he reaches for my wrists, pulling my arms long over my head and attaching them to the bedpost.

Shivers of excitement run through me at my helplessness. The thrill of being completely at his mercy focalizes every sensation to a sharp point. He shoves my two shirts up and tugs down the front of my bra roughly. I gasp a little, my belly shuddering in and out with my breath, my nipples bead up into stiff peaks. He pinches my right nipple between his thumb and forefinger and squeezes. Hard. Then he slaps the side of my breast.

I croak in surprise. I'm scared—definitely scared—because it hurt a little, and no one's ever touched me that way before. There's a disrespect to it, too, that I'm not sure I like.

Except he watches my face intently.

And that steady regard calms me.

He pinches my nipple again then drops his head to suck it. He laves it with his tongue, scrapes his teeth lightly over the taut bud, pulls it into his mouth and releases it with a pop.

My lips part. Brain fries and scrambles.

He gives the treatment to the left nipple, only he starts with his mouth and ends with a slap.

I cry out, startled once more. I'm a little frightened, a lot turned on. He pinches both nipples at the same time, rolling them between his fingers and thumbs and pinching before he expands his grip to encompass all of the breast.

I drop my head back and arch, filling his hands with my breasts, begging for more.

Armando moves lower, his large palms sliding up my skirt, skating lightly up my thighs to my hips, then hooking under the waistband of my panties and dragging them down.

"I didn't make you come enough before, did I?" His voice is a rusty rumble. "You're a greedy, greedy girl."

I shake my head.

"I'm gonna make it up to you this time."

My breath comes out in a low moan.

He tosses the panties to the side and runs the pad of his thumb over my dewy slit. "Juicy," he observes.

I'd be embarrassed, except he brings his thumb to his mouth and sucks my fluid like it's honey. "Spread."

I stare for a moment, taken aback by the command. He grips behind my knees and pushes them up toward my chest, then slaps the inside of my thigh. It smarts, and I don't like it, but then I forget because he lowers his head between my legs.

The first lick makes my hips jump off the bed. He slides his hands under them and grips my ass, squeezing and releasing as he strokes his tongue up and down my slit.

Crazy sounds come out of my mouth. Strangled sobs. Little *uhn*s. Choked breathing.

I moan and arch and thrash my legs around his shoulders.

He takes his time. The tip of his tongue traces all around my inner lips, then flicks over my clit. He uses it to penetrate me, then puts his lips over my nubbin and sucks.

I scream, yanking on my bound hands, my knees crashing around his ears. He sinks his thumb into my entrance without releasing the suction on my clit, and I start to shake and shudder. I'm close—so close—to release. I just need him to pump that thumb in and out, and I'll get there.

Only he doesn't.

He slides his thumb out. Breaks the seal on the suction.

"No-o," I moan. "Please."

"You want to come?" His voice is so rough and deep I scarcely recognize it.

"Yes. Please. Do it again, Armando. Oh God, please?"

"You gonna be a good girl?"

"Yes!" I don't have any clue what he's talking about, but I will definitely be a good girl. I would do anything he wanted me to at this point.

"If I say *spread*, what do you do?" He brings his fingers down in a light slap over my clit, and my knees snap closed and flap open like wild butterfly wings.

"Spread. Oh God, I'll spread. I'm sorry—I was slow before."

He sinks his thumb into my entrance again, and I moan with satisfaction. I can tell how swollen and wet I've gotten. How much I need this.

"Please," I plead again.

I've never begged for it before. Never needed it like this.

If he would just pump that thumb, I'd be there. Or suck my clit again. I flap my knee-wings some more, trying to take his thumb deeper.

I'm shocked by the sensation of a finger at my anus, and I tighten against it, whining.

"Nuh uh." He shakes his head. "Open for it."

Oh God. Really?

I don't want it. Except I do. Because as that digit works against my back hole, my temperature rises at least eight degrees, and I start moaning like a porn star. It's taboo and wrong, but it feels so good.

He pumps, alternating between his thumb and other finger, then pumping them both at the same time. The moment he leans over and rides my clit with his tongue, I come—*hard*.

So incredibly hard.

Like so hard fireworks dance before my eyes, and I close my mouth around a full-on scream.

The room spins. Lights continue to flash and pop behind my lids. My pussy and anus squeeze around his digits, and I sob out every last bit of pleasure I have in me.

I don't know how long it lasts. I get lost somewhere on another plane.

I open my eyes when he starts easing out, and it feels like I've been gone forever.

Armando's expression is inscrutable as usual.

And that's when the doorbell rings.

# CHAPTER FOURTEEN

*Armando*

I'm hungry, and the timing worked out the way I'd planned, but I'm still pissed to have to answer the door.

I reach up and break the tape holding her wrists and pull her up to sitting, tugging her shirt back down over her rumpled bra. I don't want the delivery guy to see her like this.

I don't want the delivery guy to see her, period.

I'm feeling extremely fucking possessive of her right now. I help her to stand and steer her toward the bathroom. "You go get cleaned up. I'll get the door," I give her ass a slap.

I swear to Christ, that ass was made for slapping. I could seriously punctuate every sentence with a slap to that ass and never get tired of it.

She scoots off to the bathroom, and something shifts in my chest.

Her surrender does something to me. She's not weak or stupid or even scared. At least not too scared. I think she's genuinely submissive. It explains her sexual response to getting tied up and handled. I haven't experienced a woman like her before. Her trust feels like a gift. One that makes me feel strong and weak at once. Humbled.

Highly protective.

I wait until the bathroom door is closed before I open the front door and pay the delivery guy. I drop the food on the tiny two-person table by the window and look for plates and wine glasses. Her place is tiny, but it's cute. She has plants in colorful pots everywhere. Some are flowering, some are wrapped in bright bows. Her furnishings are rustic —white washed shit. Probably flea market finds, but it has the look of purposeful design. Rich people pay a lot of money for this kind of look. She's definitely artistic. She has a real eye for this stuff.

I was going to put the calzones on plates and open the wine, but the sound of the shower running makes my dick throb. My balls are so fucking blue from licking her pussy, I can barely walk.

I should leave her alone. Let her shower.

Instead, I find myself testing the bathroom door. And when I find it open, I take it as an invitation. My clothes drop to her floor before the thought to strip even forms. I pull back the shower curtain and step in.

Her eyes widen, but she doesn't recoil. She stares at my body. I look down. I've been so damn disconnected from it, I don't even know what I look like anymore. My chest is hairy, and I lack any color from the sun. I was bigger when I went into prison. The extra layer of meat has hardened into sinew and muscle.

She doesn't seem to mind what she sees because her lips part like she wants to taste me. I take my time running my gaze all over her luscious form.

It's perfect. She's short but curvy, with a narrow waist, round breasts and heart-shaped ass. A chain of flowers is tattooed around her upper arm with a small, winged fairy sitting on the top of one of the buds. Her skin is a smooth brown. She's nothing like the kind of girls I've been with before. She's real. Beautiful.

I watch the rivulets of water stream over her dark nipples. I want to lick the droplets from them. Scratch that. I'm *going to* lick the droplets from her skin. I pull the curtain closed behind me and pin her against the tile wall, my mouth moving over hers with all the force of pent-up aggression.

I don't know if it's going nearly five years without sex or because Hannah does something special to me, but I can't seem to dial back my sexual aggression with her. Fortunately, she's willing. Her arms loop around my shoulders, and she lifts one leg around my waist to give me the angle I need to get inside her.

"Condom," she gasps between kisses.

Condom. Fuck. How could I forget it?

"Don't fucking move," I growl, pinning her back against the wall with my hand between her tits and waiting a beat for my order to set in.

Then I yank back the shower curtain and fish in my pants pocket for a condom out of my wallet. I rip it open and stand, rolling it over my length.

"Good girl," I say because she hasn't moved an inch from where I left her. "Come here." I pick up her thigh and find her entrance with the sheathed head of my cock, prodding it until I find the sweet spot where it starts to slide in. "That's right," I murmur as I feed the head in slowly. "Take it."

She grips my shoulders, pulling me closer.

"Take every inch." I keep pushing forward, all the way, until I'm fully seated. Then I prop one foot on the tub, her thigh draped over the top of mine, and start thrusting.

It's pure heaven. The last time I fucked her, I was out of my mind with need. This time, I savor every sweet thrust. The slick of our skin sliding together, the heat of her tight welcoming channel.

I take her hands from my shoulders and pin them up against the tile. Not for me—I like the feel of her nails scoring my skin—but for her. Because I'm testing what she likes. How she likes it. It works— maybe too well because her eyes roll back, foot slips. I hold her wrists with one hand and use the other to hoist her ass up, holding her in place.

I should say something—praise her. Tell her how much I like it. I used to know how to dirty talk up one side of a building and down the other. Now I'm so fucking rusty at speaking to another human being. I force my lips to move. "So good, Hannah." It comes out like gravel. Or sandpaper. Deep and ragged. "You feel so good."

She moans softly, and I take it as encouragement.

I don't want it to end, but my hips have a mind of their own, snapping hard, pumping deeper.

She starts making those sexy noises again, and my brain short-circuits. I get too hot from the warm water and steam and my blood pumping straight to my cock. My head's getting light, which isn't good, since I'm the one holding us up.

I pull the shower curtain open by a foot to let in some air and fuck her harder. I forget to hold her wrists because my hands are roaming her body, squeezing her breast, gripping her waist, kneading her ass.

"God, you feel so fucking good," I moan, my voice breathy and hoarse. She arches her back, pressing her chest against my own, and I swear I feel her heart beating in rhythm with mine.

I'm lost in the sensation of our slick skin sliding against each other and the warmth and pressure from her tight grip around me. I'm so close... just a few more thrusts, and I'll go over the edge.

But before I do, I reach one hand around and slip my fingers between us, finding her clit and circling it softly. She gasps, and I feel her walls quiver around me as she comes.

I brush my lips against her neck, sending trails of tingling sensation down her spine as I continue to thrust into her.

My breathing gets faster as I feel my climax approaching, and I grab onto her hips tightly as I plunge deeper and deeper into her, wanting to savor every moment. She cries out as her body convulses around mine.

My balls draw up and pump. I shout and grip her ass with both hands and then bury myself deep as I come. She tips her pelvis to take me deeper, rubbing her clit over my root until she comes, too. Her muscles squeeze my dick in quick pulses, and I come even harder, filling the condom.

I lean my forehead against hers, breathing with her, my dick pulsing and twitching inside her. Our mingled breaths slow. The water's turning cold. I don't want to ever pull out, but I do. I ease out and turn off the water, then step out of the shower to dispose of the condom. The water ran all over the floor because I opened the curtain, so I drop the hand towel down on it and wrap Hannah in the other one. She's still leaning up against the tile looking dazed, so I help her out of the tub, supporting her in case her legs don't work.

She points shakily at the cabinet, murmuring something unintelligible. I open it and find another towel, which I use to dry off.

"Wow," she murmurs.

I turn to face her as I towel off my hair. "Yeah. Thanks."

"So... Are you going to let me go now? Are we cool?"

I go still. Blink. The room swoops around me. I drop the towel on the floor. What the fuck is she saying?

A rushing sound starts up in my ears.

Did I just... *rape a girl?*

Did she think she had to do that for me to set her free?

"Is that what this was?" I choke, not even realizing I'm advancing on her. Not conscious of my hand caging her throat and pushing her back. "Is that why...is that...*fuck!*" I roar and punch the wall beside her. The plaster caves, and my knuckles go through it.

"Fuck." I release her and turn away.

Did she just offer herself up to me in hopes I'll set her free? What kind of monster am I?

I can't even tell when a girl wants me or not. I've gotten so confused, stuck in the modes of violence and survival, I don't even know what's real.

I thought I could manage this situation with Hannah. Had some vague idea about how to keep her from getting hurt by me or the organization, and instead I did the most unforgivable thing.

I pick up my clothes from the floor and pull them on, my chest cracking open as Hannah opens the bathroom door and makes her escape from me.

I follow only because the steam in the bathroom's making me dizzy, and I really fucking need to think.

I hear a stifled sob, and bombs explode in my chest, down my arms, in my gut. Hannah's got her back to me at her dresser, trying to get her second foot in a pair of panties and missing. I should give her space. I definitely shouldn't go to her.

But I do.

In a second, I have an arm banded around her waist to support her wobble, and I reach down to hold the waistband of the panties for her. I slide them up when she gets her leg in and just hold her from behind.

"I'm sorry," I murmur against her hair.

Her chest shudders on a sob. She stands still for a moment, like she's listening. "Sorry for what?" There's a quietness to the question.

It's some kind of test, but I don't know what it means. Like there's some answer I need to give that will make this all better. All I fucking know is the sound of her stuttered breath kills me.

Because all emotional intelligence I once had—if I ever had any—is long gone, I mutter, "Whatever made you cry."

It's the wrong answer. I know as soon as I say it. I know it even better when she squirms away from me, whirls and slaps my face. It's a wimpy slap and half-misses me. It clearly didn't give her the satisfaction she was going for because she curls her fingers into a fist and throws a punch instead.

I dodge it, catch her wrist and wrap her arm in front of her waist. With my other arm, I scoop under her knees and lift her into a baby-carry.

She gasps and struggles. "What are you doing?"

I don't know what I'm doing—why I picked her up or what I'm going to do with her now. All I know is that I don't like the chaos in my chest. In my head.

I carry her to the bed and set her on it, yanking the sheet off the corners to cover her bare breasts. I sit beside her on the bed. I want to hold her, but my touch is obviously not welcome. "I just—" I try to unravel what just happened. She's more pissed now than she has been throughout this whole thing. Which must mean it was something I said... I review what just transpired between us and... *ah*.

I'm an idiot. I asked if she had sex with me, so I'd let her go.

She glares at me, lower lip trembling with obvious offense.

"Hang on, Hannah. Let's straighten this out. I wasn't calling you a whore. I didn't mean any disrespect. Not at all. I was—" I draw a breath, trying to find words to explain the rage inside me. "I was pissed at myself."

The rage settles. Like identifying its source was what it needed.

"Did you feel like you...had to? With me? I didn't—did I force you?"

"No, asshole." She shoves my chest.

I welcome the touch. It's still a connection—something I've lacked for ages. And she didn't try to punch me this time. I catch her hand and hold it there. "Talk to me." I'm practically begging. The words are rusty in my mouth, but I keep pushing them out. "I'm so outta touch with this shit, Hannah."

I watch a tear track down her smooth, flawless brown skin. "I'm trying to stay on this ride with you and not freak out, but...." She takes a shuddering breath and holds it then releases it slowly. "You can't touch me when you're angry like that."

White horror blankets through me. *Cristo*, did I hurt her? I reach out to tip her chin back, examining her neck for bruising, but I see nothing—no fingerprints, no marks. I swear I didn't hurt her—I wouldn't. Not even out of my mind as I was. It's just not in me to hurt a woman. "I didn't hurt you—did I, Hannah?"

She shakes her head.

"I scared you," I guess. Of course, I fucking scared her. I held her by the throat and broke the wall beside her head.

"No." She pushes my hand off her neck and looks away. "It's not that." Her voice is tight. Frustrated.

I am so fucking lost here.

"I don't know if I can explain. Just don't do that again."

My heart beats faster like my body knows this conversation is gonna be important if I can just figure out what the hell we're talking about. "Try me. Try to explain."

She turns her gold-flecked brown eyes back on me, considering. "I'm one of those people who..." Her eyelids flutter down like she's embarrassed. "I don't know—it's like I sense everybody else's emotions. In my body." She gestures with her hand up and down the center of her trunk.

I cock my head. "An empath." Like from *Star Trek*. Is it a real thing? Apparently.

The flicker of hope that sparks in her expression tells me I finally said something right. "Yeah, I guess. If someone in the room cries, I cry. If someone's upset, I get upset. So just... don't touch me when you're mad. It's too much for me."

Shit.

I finally get it. I channeled the shame and anger I felt straight into her body. Or she experienced it that way.

"Fuck." I reach for her, and she doesn't flinch away. I pull her closer to me and lift her onto my lap, adjusting the sheet to keep her covered. "Okay, Flowers. I won't touch you when I'm mad. Swear to Christ."

She tucks her face against my neck. After a moment, her lips move, kissing me softly.

I can't explain what happens in my body. It's like all my organs sort of lift a half-inch. Like I've been in a pressure cooker, and it pushed everything down. And now my insides regained form.

I resist the urge to tighten my arms around her. The need to stand up and shake off all these foreign emotions is too strong. "Let's eat," I say gruffly, lifting her from my lap to her feet and squeezing her ass.

# CHAPTER FIFTEEN

*Hannah*

I pull on a camisole and pajama shorts. Dang it. I *hate* when I cry in front of people. It's so damn embarrassing. Me and my overblown emotions. This is how I scared off every guy I've ever dated.

Armando seems to move past it quickly, though, which is a relief. He unwraps the calzones and drops them onto plates then pours red wine into my juice glasses.

"Sorry, I don't have wine glasses." I slide into the wicker chair I found at a flea market and painted a cheery yellow.

Armando's gaze drops from my face to my braless chest and lingers there as he settles into a chair that matches mine in paint color only.

My nipples bead up at his attention. I swear it's like I've just been mega-dosed with breeding hormones because no matter how many times we do it, I seem to want more.

"It doesn't look like you have a lot of things," he says. "What were you going to eat for dinner if I wasn't here? Your refrigerator doesn't have any food."

I shrug. "I'd figure something out."

Armando scowls. "You should be taking better care of yourself."

I roll my eyes. His protectiveness is sweet, but I'm a grown woman, and I'm not sure I like the idea of being lectured.

"I am taking care of myself," I say. "Just because I don't have a fancy refrigerator stocked with all the latest and greatest doesn't mean I'm not taking care of myself." I smirk. "But thanks, *Daddy,* for caring."

"Maybe that's exactly what you need. A daddy to take care of that ass of yours." He slides closer, his dark eyes full of promise.

My breath catches in my throat. I should push him away and tell him that I'm not interested. But I can't. I want him, even though I know it's dangerous. I take a deep breath, trying to steady my pounding heart, and whisper, "Maybe I do." I flutter my eyelashes. I'm trying to play this game of seduction but I'm probably failing.

"A daddy to spank you when you've been bad," he continues.

My face heats as my eyes meet his. I want to look away, but his gaze holds me. I'm rooted in place, mesmerized.

"I think you'd like that, wouldn't you?"

I open my mouth to protest, but I'm too flustered to respond. I just shrug, not trusting my voice. I don't want to give away just how much he's turning me on—again.

Heat rushes to my cheeks. Armando smirks, his gaze dropping to my lips then back to my eyes. His intense stare says that he's not just being playful. He's serious.

"Do you want a daddy? Do you want a man to take you in hand and tell you what to do?" His voice low and husky.

I swallow hard and shake my head. "Please. Like you could." My fake resistance is obvious, I'm sure, but no way can I admit just how much that question sent shivers down my spine.

Armando moves closer and reaches out to stroke my hair. His touch sends electricity through me, and I close my eyes, savoring the sensation. "Maybe I need to change your mind."

"Good luck trying." I wonder if my feelings are written all over my face. "Besides, you're just a guy who semi-kidnapped me. I mean, is this a kidnapping or a date? Can we have some clarity here?"

He gives me one of those unfathomable looks and takes a huge bite of his calzone and chews. "Kidnapping with benefits?"

I hide a smile with my own bite. "Oh God. This is so good." A long line of cheese trails out of my mouth, and I go out wide to break it.

"Right? Missed the fuck out of Gio's."

I study him. He's coarse-mannered but gentlemanly all at once. A tough guy, for sure, built of taut deadly muscle but no tattoos. That surprised me. "Are you staying the night?"

He gives a single nod. "Definitely."

"What happens tomorrow?" I'm halfway through the calzone already. I didn't realize how hungry I was until now. That granola bar I had for lunch was a long time ago.

Armando wolfs his food down too. "I'm still sitting on you. Until I'm sure."

"What would make you sure?" I press.

He shakes his head. "Stop. Just stop."

I wait, thinking he's going to say something more, but he doesn't. He just takes a swig of wine.

"Fuck this." I stand and wrap up my remaining calzone. If I eat any more, I'll get a stomachache. "You're getting the benefits. I'm the one who's kidnapped. I think you owe me a little more information."

He doesn't move, but his gaze on me is intent. "You're benefiting too." It's not a question, but I sense that he's asking again. He's careful about this. It's what upset him in the bathroom, when he thought I was trading sex for my freedom.

I have to appreciate this code he's operating under. He'll kidnap me, but he won't harm me. I know because of the way he freaked out when he thought he gave me the cat scratches. He'll dominate, but he won't coerce me into sex.

Weariness suddenly sets in. Maybe it's the wine or just the intense stress of the day, but I suddenly want to fall down on the floor in a heap. Or cry some more.

I turn away from him, blinking back sudden tears.

Screw this. I'm going to bed. I head to the bathroom to brush my teeth.

I hear him washing the wine glasses. Putting things away.

I remake the bed, which he screwed up when he pulled the sheet out to cover me. Another gentlemanly gesture.

*Stop making lemonade out of lemons.* I am the definition of Stockholm Syndrome right now.

I climb in and pull the covers up to my waist. "Can I have my phone back? If someone called or texted, they're going to think it's weird if I don't answer."

Armando scrubs a hand across his face. "I'll check it."

I'm deflated, not because I need my phone but because I'm not getting anywhere with him trusting me. I watch him retrieve my purse from one of the cabinets—I guess he hid it from me there—and pull out my phone. He looks at it. "What's your passcode?"

I hold out my hand for it, but he doesn't move. Damn him. I'm going to lose any battle of wills here—I'm way too flexible a person. "Five-five-five-five."

"Lucky fives, huh?" He punches it in and looks at the screen. "No messages."

His phone rings. He pulls it out of his back pocket and looks at the screen. "Hey."

He listens. "Tonight? Fuck." His shoulders sag, and he looks across the apartment at me. "I'm trying to lay low." He listens some more. "Yeah, I gotcha. No, no, I'll do it. I'll be there. In an hour. 'Kay." He ends the call and shoves the phone back in his pocket, then he gives me a long, appraising look.

The hairs stand up on my arms. "What?"

He marches over to my dresser and starts pulling open drawers.

"What are you doing? What do you need? Just *tell* me, asshole."

He looks over at me and shakes his head. "Don't call me names, Flowers." He opens my sock drawer and pulls out a pair of tights.

"What are you doing?" Alarms are going off like crazy, but stupid me, I'm still playing like this guy's my date. Later I will wonder why I didn't fight him. Didn't run.

He crosses swiftly to the side of the bed and picks up my wrists and starts wrapping the tights around them. "I have to go out. I can't take you with me."

"What? No!" Even now, I don't fight much. I'm still relying on my ability to persuade him to change his mind. The guy has a conscience, I know that much.

He knots the tights and wraps the end around the bedpost.

"No! You can't leave me here like this. What if there's a fire? I will die because I can't get out. *Armando!*"

He ignores me and goes back to the kitchen area rummaging through the drawers. When he returns with a roll of duct tape I really freak out.

I kick out at him in a panic, yanking at my wrists to get free. "No! You're not putting that on me!"

Shadow, picking up the energy, races around the room and then under the bed.

Armando rips off a piece. I turn my face away.

"Don't!" I shout. "I am never having sex with you again. I swear to God."

"I understand." He slaps the tape over my mouth. I scream against the constraint. I have to take crazy snorting breaths through my nose because I'm crying.

"Shhh." He caresses the side of my head.

I yank away.

He crouches beside the bed face level with me. I'm hyperventilating through my nose. "Take it easy, Flowers. I'll be back as soon as I can."

I shake my head frantically.

"I'm sorry. The other options would be worse, I promise."

Tears flood my eyes. I'm so pissed, I want to headbutt him. Too bad he's out of reach.

"I'm gonna take your van, so I can get back quickly. Just go to sleep. I'll be here when you wake up."

I scream in my throat and shake my head, but he catches the side of my face, plants a quick kiss on the tape over my mouth and straightens.

Dammit. I missed the chance to headbutt him!

Asshole.

And then he's gone. And I'm tied to my own bed with a pair of tights.

# CHAPTER SIXTEEN

*Armando*

Marco says Don G is out at his strip club Lollipops, so I'd better get my ass over there and report.

The fact that you just whacked a guy is not the kind of thing you say over the phone, and Don G wouldn't want me coming to his house with that shit, either. We don't talk business around the women in the family. We leave them and all the innocent out of it. It's part of the code.

It makes me sick that Hannah didn't get left out of the pile of shit I'm in because tarnishing her might become the thing I regret most.

And here I thought I'd lost my conscience altogether.

I drive her van to Lollipops but park it a few blocks away. I don't want anyone making a connection between me and my little florist. Someone's still trying to kill me, and I can't have her caught in the crossfire any more than she's already been.

I stalk into Lollipops, and the whole gang is there. It's the old crew—Don G's inner circle, minus Alex, his son-in-law. He'd already been like a son to Don G, and he ended up marrying his daughter while I was in the pen, so I'm guessing he's permanently banned from Lollipops out of respect to Jenna.

Funny, at this moment, I wouldn't mind the same. The girls twirling around their poles do nothing for me. Neither does the male company.

Lollipops is a reputed strip club in the city. It has an old-school vibe to it, with neon signs on the walls and velvet-covered furniture. There are two stages at the back of the room, each with its own pole, where two dancers will perform simultaneously. Two large bar sections fill the main area of the club and a few smaller tables littered around for more intimate conversations. The music blasts from speakers set up around the club and seems to fill every corner of the room with booming bass.

The walls are adorned with black and white photographs of former dancers as well as signed photos from other celebrities who have visited over time. While there is a decent selection of drinks available, it is mainly focused on beer, wine, and whisky since those are mostly what people come here for; there aren't many cocktails or mixed drinks on offer.

The girls who work here wear costumes that range from barely skimpier than lingerie to some quite daring outfits—often leaving very little to imagination when they take center stage on one of the poles to show off their skills. They move gracefully around their poles in time with the music, quickly shifting between different dance moves such as pirouettes, splits and twerks while they seductively gyrate their hips or flick their hair around like silky ribbons in mesmerizing displays which usually draws loud cheers from their audiences.

At either end of both stages stand two large LED screens displaying clips from movies—usually action flicks —that serve as background distraction for those not captivated by what is happening onstage at any given moment. Occasionally special performances are put on where the dancers will use props and interact with the crowd—usually met with a lot of enthusiasm from everyone in attendance.

Overall, Lollipops has an air of old-school glamour infused with sin and debauchery.

But I sure as fuck don't want to be here. Especially because I keep seeing Hannah's teary face and picturing her trapped in flames. *I will die because I can't get out.*

I know the chances of her apartment building going up in flames are slim, but dammit, now I can't stop thinking about it.

I should have called someone to watch over her while I was taking care of business. Have someone sit outside her door. What the fuck was I thinking leaving her alone? I know better than that. I protect what is mi—

"Hey, there he is! Mando, come over here." Angel beckons me over. I shoot a glance at Don Pachino chewing his cigar, but he's got a guy on each side vying for his attention. I'll have to wait my turn.

"Everybody buys Mando a lap dance tonight," Angel announces. "Make up for lost time."

*Lost time.*

There was never a better descriptor for my years in prison. Not the way he means, like I lost out on part of my life—which is accurate. But for me, the time is also semi-lost. I shut down in the pen. I mean, physically I was still alive. I slept and ate and walked around. I fought for my life. Killed a man with my bare hands. But I don't remember anything. Correction—I don't *want* to remember any of it. So it's definitely lost time.

"Nah, I'm good. I just came to have a word with—"

"Bullshit." Angel pulls me down into the chair beside him, already signaling one of the dancers with a twenty between his fingers. "Give my friend here a dance, sweetheart. He just got out of prison."

I definitely don't want the dance, but I do what I'm supposed to do—slump down in my chair with my arms loose by my sides and my thighs wide, making myself a jungle gym for the girl to rub her cheap fruity perfume all over.

"Don't say that again," I tell Angel. I know I'm an asshole. It's disrespectful as hell. He's from the older generation and a capo, and the organization is all about respecting our elders. I sense him bristle, so I add "Please."

"Yeah, all right." There's a grudging tone to his voice, but he's going to let my bad behavior slide, since I'm fresh out. I got this one free pass. "I get it."

He doesn't say sorry—of course, I don't expect him to—but we're *simpatico*.

The dancer does her thing, pushing her breasts in my face, straddling me, then turning around and grinding her bikini-clad ass against my dick.

She's wearing a tiny red thong and eight-inch stiletto heels that she uses to keep me in place. Her back is arched, her head thrown back, her long blonde hair cascading down across her shoulders. She gyrates against me like a slow-motion wave, and between the sheer desperation of her act and the fact that I'm stone cold sober and not even trying to hide my discomfort—it feels like I'm stuck in some awful time warp. She looks over at me every few seconds with sad eyes as if begging for mercy, but all I can do is just sit there motionless, waiting for it to be over.

I work to wait for the shit to be over. I seriously don't have the patience for this tonight.

It's hard to imagine I ever will again. Did I really used to enjoy nights like this down at the don's club? Playing the big man. Working hard to fit in, to play the role.

Now I just want to walk away.

From it all.

But that's not an option. You don't get out of *La Cosa Nostra*. Not when you're a Made man. Don Pachino owns me now, for the rest of my life.

Arturo waves another girl over with a bill. "Your turn. On him." He points at me.

Fucking Christ on a clamshell. How long will I have to endure this?

But I know if I don't, everyone's gonna read it the wrong way—especially the Don. I gotta show my gratitude, be good natured here. Yeah, I did time, but it's part of the game. Now I'm out, and they treat me to lap dances and help me set up my life again. I gotta prove I'm worth the effort they're putting in. Also, that I haven't rolled over or gone sour.

That's always the fear when someone's fresh out of the pen. Especially when they're out a year early. But I know better than that. That's a line I would never cross. Not outta fear, either. I *am* still loyal. This *is* still my family.

I'm just not feeling it right now.

But I'm not feeling much of anything, so that's not unusual.

Fucking Emilio sends over another girl, and instead of waiting her turn, they give me two-on-one, a girl's tongue in each ear, their hands all over my fucking clothes.

My cock is semi-hard because, yeah. Tits in my face. But I'm more low-level disgusted by them than I am turned on.

And honestly? If I'd come here last night—before Hannah—I don't know if I would've even sprouted a chub. Hannah woke my dick from the dead.

And—fuck—she's tied up and gagged right now in her own bed. That's the way I repay her.

*I am never having sex with you again. I swear to God.*

I deserve that. But I'm also asshole enough to hope she'll get over it. Because right now, she's my fucking lifeline. She's the only thing that even seems to make sense—and considering how fucked up our interactions have been up to this point—that's saying something.

"I got your next one," Marco calls out to me.

"No, I got it," Leo offers.

I shake my head and Marco nods, grinning like there's nothing going on. "All right. Next time, then."

The dances finish, and I stand up before anyone else can send over a girl. Fuck this. I know I'm being rude. I should stay a few hours, drink a few drinks. Prove my loyalty and work my way back into the inner circle.

But that's not happening. I walk over to Don Pachino and stand in front of him, giving Emilio the death glare until he says, "What?"

Of course, the guy's too much of a prick to take a hint. "I need to talk to the don," I say.

"Give him your seat," Don G mutters, and only then does Emilio get up, purposely bumping my chest as he passes by.

Johnny, the guy on Don Pachino's other side, also gets up, presumably to give us privacy.

"What's wrong?" Don G says immediately.

I sink a little lower in my chair, keeping my gaze trained on the dancing girls on the stage. "Someone has a hit out on me. A cleaner showed up this afternoon outside Rocco's. I took care of him. Just thought you should know."

"Who sent him—someone from prison?"

"Yeah. Probably. I iced a gang member on the inside. Might be revenge for that. I don't know. I'm staying low until I figure shit out. I won't let it affect the job you gave me or any Family shit. *Lo prometo*."

"Call in sick to that job for a few days. You get paid time off. Let things settle. Figure this shit out."

I nod my head and stretch out my hand to shake the don's. "All right. Will do. Thank you, Don Pachino."

"Don G," he corrects, clasping my hand and letting me know I'm still inner circle. Only his closest soldiers called him by the more informal moniker Don G, for his given name, Giovanni.

I stand and nod at the rest of the group.

"Hey, Mando, want another dance?" Arturo calls.

"Not tonight. Thank you. 'Preciate it. All of you." Jesus fuck. I have to force the niceties over my dry lips, and they all sink like ashen lies.

I can't play this game anymore.

I remember I used to be so good at it. The best. Now it's like I'm playing a stranger's part. It all feels so foreign and wrong.

I beeline it out of there and to Hannah's van.

Fuck—*Hannah*.

I sure as hell hope she fell asleep.

# CHAPTER SEVENTEEN

*Hannah*

I jerk awake when I hear Armando come in, and Shadow, who was curled up in front of my chest, jumps off the bed and stretches. I blink at the digital bedside clock. It's been two hours since he left. I slept fitfully for the last hour after I finally calmed myself down with slow breathing. Now all the adrenaline of the stressful day rushes back, so I'm wide awake. And still very pissed.

He comes straight to my side and crouches in front of me. "You're awake." He peels the duct tape off my mouth.

"You're an asshole."

He ignores that and unties my bound wrists from the bedpost. The moment they're free, I swing them at his face. His reflexes are way faster than mine. He snaps them up in an iron grip. "Hey." He modulates the grip, loosening slightly. "You want to spend the night tied up?"

"Go to hell."

He stops work on the knot on my tights and arches a stern brow. It's tragically sexy, which pisses me off even more. I shouldn't find any of this hot. He's confused me with sex, blurring lines, so I can't tell what's what. Actually, I guess I'm the one who started it with that kiss back at the shop. But now, I'm a jumbled mess. It's like I just willingly dove headfirst into an abusive relationship where I'm bonded to my abuser, craving his affection and ignoring the fact that he's holding me prisoner.

It's way worse than all the misguided relationships I've been in. Worse than Jarod, who cheated on me three times before I stopped believing he was sorry. Worse than Eric, the guy it took me six months to realize only thought of me as his booty-call. This is the definition of a toxic relationship. It's not even a relationship. It's Stockholm Syndrome.

Ragey tears fill my eyes again, and I fight some more, wrestling to get my bound hands free.

He tightens his grip, dropping a knee on the bed to hover over me, pushing my hands closer to my chest to trap me. "Hannah."

"You stink of cigar smoke," I hurl at him, like he's a lover come home late from a night of partying with the boys. Then I catch another cloying scent on top of it, and my stomach drops out. "Oh my God! You're covered in shitty perfume! You fucking dick!" I'm unprepared for the flood of betrayal that fills my lungs.

"Hey, hey, hey, hey." He straddles me. Somehow, he worked the knot loose on the tights while I flail at him, and he pins my wrists down beside my head. One wrist is still wrapped in the fabric. I keep fighting him, the pain of my stupidity for screwing this guy gushing like blood between us. "I was at a *strip club,*" he says like that makes it all better. When my mouth elongates in horror, he adds quickly, "For a *meeting.*"

Right. Apparently when you're in the mob, that's where meetings take place. On second thought, I'm inclined to believe that part.

"Everyone bought me dances because I'm fresh out. I wasn't into it, Flowers."

"Oh, I'm sure you weren't." My voice drips with hurt and sarcasm.

His face contorts into scorn. He normally shows so little in his expression that it takes me aback. "You think I needed that shit? After what you gave me?"

I go still.

*After what you gave me.*

Armando's face hovers inches from me, his hazel eyes sparking. There's frustration in him. Passion. I feel it through his skin, but it doesn't harm my body this time—it feeds it.

"If you fucked another woman tonight, I'd cut off your dick." I may be his prisoner at the moment, but I'm still going to make myself clear. I'm not stupid enough to believe our sex today meant anything—I didn't take it as a promise or a commitment. It just happened. But I would take huge offense to him dipping his wick elsewhere after what we did.

"I didn't, Hannah. I didn't even want to be there. I swear to Christ." He suddenly looks so weary. His eyes, ancient. "And you had me worrying about a fucking fire the whole time."

Well.

That's sort of satisfying, too.

I'm still pissed but growing mollified.

He pulls the wrist with the tights still wound around it to the bedpost and starts retying it.

Fresh alarm rings through me. "What are you doing?"

"Rinsing the smell off." He pulls my other wrist up and secures it, too.

*For me,* a little voice whispers.

"You are such an asshole."

He's back to cool and indifferent, his face the brutal mask. "Been told that." He heads to the bathroom and leaves the door open while he strips out of his clothes.

I watch. He's not putting on a show for me. He probably left the door open to make sure I don't scream or try anything, but it's a show worth watching, nonetheless. I saw him naked earlier, but that was up close, and I was half out of my mind with lust. Now, I can observe him clinically. And he's even more impressive the second time. He's solid muscle. Six-pack abs, the kind you could climb. He's not shiny. Not tanned and waxed and all-American. He's hairy, brutal, and strong. He's grit and manliness.

My dad is a kind, working-class man whom I deeply respect and love. He's a big, strong guy who can fix anything with his hands. He works in construction as an electrician. Union guy.

Even though Armando is more of the slick Italian suit type, there's something about him that resonates for me. Some similarity between them that hits me on a biological level. My brain imprinted my father as the archetypal man. Armando fits the archetype. He's strong. Take charge. He gets shit done.

Armando steps into the shower. He's quick about it, soaping everywhere and rinsing off in no more than two minutes.

He pulls on his boxer briefs after he dries off and returns to the side of the bed. He doesn't speak as he unwinds my tights from the bedpost. He doesn't untie my wrists, though.

Maybe he thinks I'll try to punch him again.

I still might.

He climbs in the bed beside me. I keep my back to him, my shoulders hunched. I'm still nursing my piss-off.

When he molds his body to mine and wraps an arm around my waist, I swing my bound arms back to elbow him. He's too fast. He catches my wrists and ties the loose end of the tights to his own wrist. Ah. Now I understand. He wasn't trying to spoon me. He's attaching himself to me.

I imagine he considers it to be kinder than keeping me tied to the bedpost. I guess it is. This position's better, anyway.

And I secretly enjoy the feel of his arm draped over me, the weight of it. It's centering. Comforting in ways it shouldn't be. It's been a long time since I've been held by a man, and I forgot how much I love it. The scent of soap and clean skin enters my nostrils.

His cock twitches against my ass.

"We're not having sex again," I say firmly. Maybe I'm trying to convince myself.

"Understood," he rumbles.

"I mean, ever."

"Shh, Flowers. Go to sleep." He wraps his big hand over the top of my bound ones, almost like we're holding hands.

Because I hate how much I like it, I say, "I still think you're an asshole."

He doesn't answer, and I start feeling guilty, like I should worry about hurting his feelings.

Then he speaks. "Listen, I know you're pissed, Hannah. But trust me, tying you up and leaving you here was the best option I had."

I turn my head in his direction, staring angrily at the ceiling. "That is such bullshit."

"Would you rather I left you tied in the van in the strip club parking lot? Or—fuck. I'm not even going to tell you the other possibilities." Frustration laces his words.

A shiver runs up my spine because I suspect they involve getting rid of me—the only witness to his crime—permanently.

And I'm suddenly as weary as he looks. Maybe I'm just soaking in his state, but it's a crushing weight. Tears pool in the corners of my eyes, and one slides down my nose. "What about the option where you just trust me? I told you I won't talk. When will you believe that?"

Armando is silent behind me, but his body is stiff and tense. His arm has tightened around me and so has his grip on my hands. Finally he exhales loudly into my hair. "I do trust you, Hannah. It's just that the stakes are too high here to go on trust. If I make a mistake, it will cost me my life."

Okay, those *are* high stakes.

"I'm sorry you got caught in the crossfire. I really am. But shit went down that I didn't plan, and now I'm just trying to manage the mess."

"And I'm part of that mess."

"You're the only good part," he says. I think I feel his lips brushing the back of my neck, and I try to stifle the shiver of pleasure that runs through me. Try to steel myself against his words, even though I believe him. I know they're true.

"Don't leave me tied up again." Tears clog my voice.

He pulls my body back against his snugly. "I'm sorry, Flowers."

Earlier I was sure sleeping with my wrists bound would be impossible, but I already find myself sinking into a deep relaxation, the heat and weight of Armando's body like one of those weighted blankets that are supposed to be so soothing.

"I don't want to hurt you, Hannah," he rasps into the darkness.

He already has. But I think he knows that.

I'm an emotional sponge, and that makes me soak in all his feelings.

So I believe him. I have compassion for his situation. But it doesn't mean we're not speeding toward a brick wall. Or that it won't hurt like hell when we crash.

# CHAPTER EIGHTEEN

*Armando*

I jerk awake several times during the night, my heart pounding, the instinct to kill sharp as a knife edge, but each time, when I find my body wrapped around Hannah's soft, warm form, my pulse slows. Each time, I bury my face in her hair—her incredible curtain of tight curls—and breathe in her scent, and I'm home.

Being near Hannah is like opening a trap door and discovering a whole different world exists on the other side. She's not wild, not crazy, but she functions in a way that's so outside of the norm—so far from what I've known—that it's slowly waking me up from the stupor I've been in.

All the emotions, all the passion and flexibility and kindness. Soft strength. Every minute with her changes me. I'm coming back to life.

Except it's not my old life. Not a life I've known before.

It's something so different and bizarre, I don't even know how to think about it.

I untie our wrists and free her hands while she sleeps, tracing a fingertip over the vines tattooed on her shoulder and down her arm. She's so fucking beautiful. So unlike any woman I've dated before. The polar opposite of Grace. Her beauty is so natural. The wild mane of hair that falls to her ass, her short, curvy but muscular body. The tiny gold nose ring. Her smooth brown skin. She's unpretentious and down-to-Earth.

I sift her wild mane of hair, letting the golden-tipped curls wrap around my fingers.

I want to trust her. I do.

But I can't be stupid and reckless. I can't think with my dick.

Still, I've treated her like shit, and for the most part, she's taken it. I need to do something nice.

I pull out my phone and go online shopping. It's a stupid gift. Definitely not something she needs, considering she doesn't even have food in the refrigerator or a van she can rely on. But then, aren't the best kinds of gifts the ones you wouldn't buy for yourself? I enter the Garden of Eden address for delivery and complete the transaction.

Sleeping beauty still hasn't woken up.

Hunger finally gets me out of bed, but when I get up to rummage, I find nothing in her kitchen. I'd leave to go get something, but I don't want to tie her up again. And I don't want to wake her, either.

I find a nearby cafe connected to one of those food delivery companies and order an egg sandwich and latte for each of us.

And then I start looking through her shit.

I open her drawers and look inside. Check out the art on the walls, which mostly consists of photographs or paintings of flowers.

I don't know what I'm looking for—clues about who she is, I guess. Nah, that's a fucking lie. I'm looking for signs of a boyfriend.

I know she doesn't have one, or she wouldn't have fucked me, but I want to know if she dates. Who she's dated. What her history is.

Did she fuck other guys the way we fucked?

Or was that special?

Because it sure as hell wasn't normal for me.

Course, I've never gone five years without sex before.

But I think our connection is more than that. Our chemistry is off the charts. The way she gives herself over to me brings out the fucking dominant in me, which I didn't even know was a thing.

I mean, yeah, I like to lead. I'm an alpha male and need to be the guy in charge. But I was always respectful. I didn't bend women over, smack their asses and get nasty with them. I never tied a girl up before.

Course, that wasn't for fun, it was a necessity.

The first time.

And the last.

But not the time in between. That time, we both liked it.

Hannah brings out the fucking savage in me. It's crazy the things I want to do to her. Even now, when I'm thinking about buying her shit, I want to semi-force myself on her again.

Not real force. Not in a way that pisses her off. But play force. Or half-force. Like at the flower shop when she was scared but turned on. That's how I want her every time.

Trembly. Nervous. Surrendered.

Of course, right now, sex is off the table. She's pissed at me, and I won't push it. I owe her my respect.

Hannah wakes up when the delivery guy rings the buzzer. I'm rooting through her underwear drawer, checking out all her panties.

"What the hell, Armando? Are you perving on my panties?"

Definitely, *amore*. I drop the pink lacy pair I'm holding back into the drawer. My cock's pressed up against my zipper from me picturing her in those panties, picturing pulling them off her—with my teeth.

I don't answer as I buzz the delivery guy up.

Hannah wraps her arms around herself like she's scared. Or feeling vulnerable. "Who's coming?"

"Just food, Flowers. You hungry?"

Some of the tension drops away from her posture. "Yeah." She doesn't leave the bed, though, so I just open the door a crack to accept the food then bring it over to her. She eyes me warily as I hand her the coffee and set mine down on the nightstand.

I completely lost her trust last night. It's probably better this way. She should be scared of me.

I climb on the bed and sit with my back against the wall beside her while she takes a tentative sip of the coffee and then moans softly.

"It's good?" I ask.

"So good. What is it?"

"Just a latte." I look at her curiously.

"It's stronger than I usually get. Or, less sweet. I usually get the kind with all the sugar and syrups and stuff. I didn't think I'd like it this way."

She's talking to me like everything's normal. It eases some of the chaos in my chest that's been there since I made her cry last night.

I open the paper bag of food and hand her the wrapped breakfast sandwich then take out mine. Her kitten, Shadow, jumps onto the bed and pads over, purring. I eat my sandwich, careful not to let any crumbs fall onto the bed and ignore the little thing, but he chooses my lap to curl up in, his little paws playing the piano on my thighs.

I finish eating and push the wrapper back into the paper bag. The kitten stands up to investigate, putting his little nose in the bag then reaching a paw in to touch the crinkly paper.

He's still purring.

I open the mouth of the bag and change the angle, so he can get in, and he crouches down and slips inside, turning around and making the bag bump and move as he does.

Hannah makes a small sound of amusement beside me.

It's cute. I *know* it is, but I don't quite feel it. It's like the centers in my brain where all that shit takes place got turned off. I picked up that kitten last night when we first got here. Looked right in its face, knowing intellectually it was cute as hell, *trying* to feel something, but I hadn't. Same as how I didn't feel anything when I hugged my mom at that welcome home party. And a mom-hug is usually the thing that brings on all the emotions, even if they're mostly shame and regret.

But Hannah's tears did something to me last night. She makes me feel.

That's something.

She's still eating, her bites delicate, and her chewing slow. I climb out of bed and pick up my coffee, carrying it to the bathroom where I search for a razor and shave my face.

When I come out, Hannah's getting dressed. She's wearing a grey t-shirt dress that hugs her every curve, with a white lace midriff top layered over it. She has on an artsy pair of chunky sandals in turquoise, tan and orange. Her toes peek out, toenails painted hot pink with tiny white flowers. I want to suck on those toes.

She turns to face me, her face taut. She's nervous.

Fuck. Is she afraid of me now? I should be glad, but it's like getting kicked in the gut.

"I have to go to the shop." There's a challenge in her words, but a slight twitch in her lips belies her bravado. "I have flowers to sell, and if I don't sell them, I can't pay the bills." She lifts her chin, her nostrils flaring slightly as she pins me with her demanding gaze.

"What time?" I ask mildly. I'd kinda figured she had to work. I'd seen the hours posted in her window.

She blinks a moment, like she's surprised I didn't say no. "I open at noon."

I glance at the clock. It's already ten. "You ready?"

Her body springs to life, and she takes a quick step toward the bathroom then stops. "Um... what's happening, Armando?"

"I'm staying on you, Hannah—until I'm sure. So we're both going to the shop."

"This is crazy." She mutters and pushes past me to enter the bathroom, but the tension's gone out of her. Like before, it seems she's more worried about her business than she is about me. And for some reason, that lightens my mood, too.

I pull her purse out of the cupboard where I stowed it and grab her charger from the desk. I put her phone in my back pocket.

She comes out of the bathroom with makeup on and a colorful piece of fabric wrapped around her head, keeping her curls out of her face. She's wearing mascara, and her lips have a sheer color on them. I want to kiss it off, but I know better than to try.

"Let's go." There's another challenge in her posture.

I hand her the purse and take the keys.

"This is so weird," she says when I lock her door behind us. "I am trying to roll with this situation, but if I think about it too hard, I'm pretty sure I will flip out," she says as we walk down the stairs.

I put my hand lightly on her back. I shouldn't touch her—not after last night—but her body's irresistible. I want to have my hands all over her, all the time. "I'm amazed you haven't, Flowers." I rub my forehead. "You've shot straight to the top of my list." I stop myself because

I don't even know what the fuck I'm saying. Only that it's true. She is way at the top of my list. Of everything.

"What list?" she asks. Because, yeah, that was a weird thing to say.

I shake my head. "Nothing. Nevermind."

She slides me a sidelong glance, curiosity brewing under those thick, curled lashes.

It hits me then: she likes me. That's why she kissed me. It's the reason she hasn't freaked out about me marauding her life. Invading her space. I mean, I knew there was mutual attraction. Off-the-charts chemistry. But I see something else now. It's the good old-fashioned girl-likes-boy current running from her to me. A desire that's more than sexual.

And fuck if it doesn't make me almost want to laugh.

Not *at* her. Definitely not. No, it just lifts so much weight off my chest, I could soar.

I thread my fingers through hers. She may be pissed at me, but she still likes me. I'll earn back the right to touch her.

When she doesn't shake me off, I revel in the small victory. I walk her to the van and open the passenger side door for her.

The van sputters, taking four times to start. Fuck. This needs to get fixed. Today.

# CHAPTER NINETEEN

*Hannah*

I definitely didn't expect Armando to let me go to work. I thought we were going to have another throw-down that I would lose. And I also didn't guess he would come with me.

It's weird and wrong that I'm semi-excited by the idea. Like my boyfriend is coming to hang out at work with me.

I keep reminding myself I'm his prisoner not his date, but then he holds my hand and opens my door, which sends my body into a riot of flutters and thrills.

I wasn't totally paying attention to the route he took, but when he turns into a car repair shop, I sit up straighter.

"What are we doing?"

"Getting a new alternator in this thing. Come on."

I grab my purse, open the door and hop out, noting he's not snarling orders at me not to move any more. Trust is growing.

"I don't have money for an alternator," I tell him when I walk around. I figure he already knows, but it's best to be clear.

"I got you covered," he says.

"I can't let you do that," I say.

His face morphs to one of an authoritarian. "I'm not asking. I'm telling you that the van isn't safe or reliable. So, I'm fixing it. This isn't open for discussion."

It shouldn't be swoon-worthy, but there's something about the way he says it that makes my nipples go hard. It's a flash of the old Armando—the slick, smooth-talking guy who used to come into the shop when Mary Alice owned it and flash huge wads of cash. It's that confidence and ease, a bit of swagger. Like money is no problem, and he's happy to provide. Definitely sexy to me.

He talks to a mechanic, telling him what he thinks is wrong with the van, and then we step inside to fill out paperwork. He has them fill it out in my name but gives his phone number and name as the contact then asks for a shuttle ride to the shop.

It's not that hard, but I've been overwhelmed by the idea of even bringing the van anywhere since the problems started. Mostly because I knew I couldn't afford any repairs. But also because I was afraid they'd take one look at me—a young Black woman who knows nothing about cars—and try to screw me over.

Nobody would ever try to screw Armando over. At least not anyone in his right mind.

He's silent on the ride to the shop, sitting beside me but actually somewhere far away.

I nudge his leg with mine. "Thanks."

He turns his head and looks at me, no hint of a smile, his face that dangerous, blank mask. I don't think he even heard me. "What?"

"I said thanks."

He blinks at me for a moment more, like it takes a while to come back to the present and process my words. Then his gaze drops back away. "My pleasure, Flowers," he mutters.

I think about slipping my hand into his, but I resist. I can't even imagine what he's going through—fresh out of prison with someone trying to kill him. He committed murder and took the witness as his prisoner. A squeeze of his hand isn't going to fix this.

I'm lucky my problems are fixable, and he's willing to help me solve them. If he hadn't bailed me out with the rent yesterday, I don't know what I would've done. And getting the van fixed will be huge for my goals of getting the business profitable. Starting deliveries again.

The shuttle drops us off at the shop, and Armando unlocks the door, looking left and right down the street, secret agent style. His gaze travels over and lands on the place where the body fell.

"Are you all right?" I touch his elbow.

Armando jerks and turns, lifting his brows. A puff of air escapes his lips in a *tuh*. "You're asking *me?*" He settles his palm at the back of my head and brings his mouth down to my temple. "Are you?" His voice is deep and quiet. There's an intense intimacy to the question, like we share a deep secret, which I guess we do. He smells clean, his freshly-shaven skin is smooth against mine.

My heart picks up speed. I become conscious of how close his lips are to my skin. How comfortable his grasp on me is. "Yeah, I'm okay. I didn't know the guy, and it was... sort of unreal to me. Like watching a movie, you know?"

Armando nods. Behind my head, his thumb massages my skull. "Yeah. Same for me. But my whole fucking life feels like I'm watching a movie right now. Everything except—" He stops.

I pull back to look at him. "Except what?"

His fingers slide in the back of my hair and tighten into a fist, capturing a section of hair. He uses it to tip my head back. "Except for you. You feel real to me."

I stop breathing.

He moves slowly, like he's giving me time to protest, and lowers his mouth. He slides his lips over mine. It's an elegant kiss. An experienced one. Not like that mad, hot claiming when we kissed yesterday.

This is different. This is seduction.

And seduction is definitely not playing fair. Because Armando isn't the kind of guy I can fall for. This isn't love. I may have played dirty when I first kissed him, but he's definitely the one playing dirty now.

I manage to get my hands between us, and I push on his chest at the same moment I pull away. He allows it, rubbing his lips together like he's savoring the taste of me.

I stumble backward then turn and hurry into the back, turning on lights and getting things ready to open shop.

Crap. I need some distance from this guy. Because, right now, he's so up in my world, he's in every pore. Which makes it very hard to put up any lasting defenses.

My hands shake as I move around the shop, my mind and body still overwhelmed by his kiss. I can't deny the heat that still lingers between us, and I know it won't go away anytime soon.

I try to focus on work, but my thoughts drift back to Armando and the way his lips felt against mine. A deep warmth spreads through me as I remember the electricity that passed between us.

I pause and look up, only to find him standing in the doorway, watching me with a smoldering look. I hold his gaze, and for a moment, neither of us move. Then, he steps closer and reaches out, running a finger along my cheek. His touch is gentle but firm, sending a wave of pleasure through my body.

His eyes scan me up and down, and my skin heats up under his gaze. "You're so beautiful," he murmurs, leaning in to whisper against my ear.

I shiver, my heart racing as I try to find my voice.

"You're trying to distract me," I say. "From work."

"Is it working?"

"I open soon, and I'm not ready." Jesus Christ the man is danger-ous. The power he has over my body is undeniable.

Armando takes a step closer. "You look ready to me."

"Armando..." I begin, but I'm cut off by his lips pressing against mine. This kiss is different from the first, more intense and passionate. And I can feel the tension between us rising with every passing moment.

Finally, he pulls away and looks at me with a heavy-lidded gaze.

"I understand if you don't want this." His voice low and husky. "But I can't deny what I'm feeling right now."

I nod, my heart pounding in my chest. I want this, too. But I'm scared. Scared of what will happen if I let him in.

"I... I want this," I whisper, my voice barely audible.

He pushes me in front of a tall shelf that I use to store ribbons and decorative items for my arrangements. Pinning me against it, trapping me between the hard surface and his body. His hands move up my sides, and I can't help but arch my back, pushing my body closer to his.

He leans forward and presses his lips against mine, his tongue slipping inside my mouth, exploring and tasting me.

My breathing becomes shallow, and all I can feel is his hard cock promising me of what's to come. His hands slide down my back and cup my ass, lifting me up and pressing our bodies together even more. I wrap my legs around his waist, and he reaches down and effortlessly rips my panties off.

Armando kneels down before me and begins to kiss my inner thighs, slowly working his way up until he finds my clit. His expert tongue caresses it, and pleasure spreads through my body. He moves his tongue up and down, teasing me until I'm panting with desire. His hands slide around to my ass, and he pulls me closer, thrusting his tongue deep inside me. I moan in pleasure, my body trembling. I arch my back, pushing myself closer to him, urging him to go even deeper.

He responds by slipping a finger inside me, his thumb finding and rubbing my tight bud. His thrusts become more urgent, and I can feel myself reaching the point of no return.

My moans grow louder, and my body is shaking as I reach my climax. His hands slide up my sides, and he slowly stands to meet my eyes again.

"Ready for more?" His voice is low and husky.

I nod, my body still trembling from the pleasure he just gave me. He kisses me deeply and turns me around, pushing me against the shelf once more. I hear the sound of a condom wrapper being torn open—or at least I hope that is what I hear, but I'm too far gone to care.

"You said you would never have sex with me again." His husky words caress my flesh and send a shiver down my spine.

"I changed my mind," I somehow reply.

He drags the head of his cock over my slit, then enters me from behind, filling me up with each thrust, and I let out a loud moan.

He moves faster and faster, and soon I'm screaming out his name, grateful I haven't opened for business yet.

His hard thrusts become more and more intense, and I sense another orgasm building up inside me. As I reach my peak, I feel his body tense, and he releases a deep moan as he thrusts. He pushes even deeper, and I can feel his warm cum filling me up as he finally reaches his own climax.

We stay like that for a few moments, panting and trying to catch our breath. He pulls out of me and wraps his arms around my waist, resting his head on my shoulder.

Signs of my completion coat my inner thigh, and I glance to my panties cast to the floor.

He spins me around and kisses me deeply, his hands lingering on my body. His touch is electric, and my arousal quickly rises again in response. He moves his lips from my mouth and trails down my neck, sending shivers over my skin.

He slides his hand lower and presses two fingers inside me, circling them around until I'm quivering with pleasure.

"I like feeling your juices. I like how they coat my finger," he says.

I moan in response, desire and need coursing through me. He continues to flick and tease, his thumb now brushing against my sensitive bud and sending waves of pleasure through me. I arch my back and push against his hand, wanting more.

He moves his other hand to my hips and holds me firmly in place as he caresses my core still trembling from my climax. My legs tremble beneath me, and I'm left gasping for air as he slowly withdraws his hand.

He wraps his arms around me again and whispers in my ear, "I owe you a new pair of panties."

# CHAPTER TWENTY

*Armando*

I sit in the workshop area to stay out of Hannah's way. On one wall is a long workbench with shelves above it that have all her materials like vases and baskets and the green foam things that you stick the stems of flowers in. This is where she puts together her designs. On the narrow half-wall is her desk, covered in stacks of invoices and old school ledger books dating back thirty years. Mary Alice's shit.

Hannah moves quickly through the place, arranging things in the cooler, tidying up. Then she turns the open sign around and props the door open.

I start sifting through the invoices and paperwork, making a quick mental tally of the totals as I go. She's done three weddings in the last three months—those pay big. But the rest of the stuff is all small- time bouquets and arrangements. Looks like deliveries stopped four months ago. That must've been when the van started acting up.

For kicks, I pull down the most recent ledger and open it. I used my time in prison to get a degree in business. I guess I was thinking I'd impress the don when I came out. I haven't even told him about it yet.

Despite my lack of enthusiasm for much of anything right now, business still interests me. I open the ledger and look through the receipts and payments. Arturo had me use an old-fashioned ledger like this to record our car heist income and payouts, so I'm familiar with the layout. I pull out the next ledger and the next. The entries I see reflect the strain Hannah's under. Mary Alice's income hadn't grown in years. It had only maintained. And her profit margin hadn't been huge to begin with. The major expenses were employees and rent. The flowers and other materials are next.

Hannah walks back and jerks to a stop. "What are you doing?"

I don't answer—instead I ask, "You paying the same expenses Mary Alice paid?"

She steps closer, her body rigid. "More or less. The rent went up by two hundred when I took over, and I also have to make monthly payments to Mary Alice for the business."

"How much?"

"Fifteen hundred."

I give a low whistle.

"What?" There's a mountain of defensiveness in her voice.

I shouldn't push, but I want to dig into this. Figure out what went wrong. "You run the numbers first before you entered that deal?"

She goes a little pale. "What do you mean?" When she pushes her hair over her shoulder, I see her hand shaking. She may be perfectly capable of handling me—a legit killer who's taken her prisoner—but she's over her head when it comes to running her business, and she knows it.

I catch her trembling fingers and hold them. "Ah, I just mean, I can see why you're hurting. There wasn't much wiggle room to begin with."

She stares down at our joined hands like they're foreign objects. Christ, she looks like she's going to pass out. She pulls out of my grasp to hold onto the edge of the desk and blinks rapidly.

"Hey—don't freak out. It's workable. It just means you can't do the same thing Mary Alice did and expect to make any money. You gotta make changes."

She leans heavily on the desk, like her legs aren't holding her up. I want to pull her into my lap and tell her everything's gonna be okay, but I'm not her hero. And I'm too cynical to believe it's gonna work out unless she changes strategy.

"What changes?"

I stand up and fold my arms across my chest. "I don't know. You gotta drum up new business. Make new connections. Work new angles. You're paying Mary Alice for her good will—the steady business she had—but you might be overpaying. And that business has dwindled."

Hannah's eyes fill with tears, but she blinks them back. Someone walks in, and she hurries out to the shop floor, throwing a death glare at me over her shoulder when she arrives.

I keep an eye on her. She's within earshot, so I could hear if she asked the customer to help her and see if she tried to slip them a note or something. Honestly, I don't expect her to try anything, but I'd be stupid to blindly trust. No one does that, especially not when it comes to a beautiful woman.

Hannah rings up a cheap bouquet for the woman, sending me another angry glance over her shoulder.

I crack my neck. Why do I feel like such a dick?

I was only honest, and I was trying to help.

Still, I don't like seeing her pissed. Same as last night—when I left her tied up—something uncomfortable slithers in my gut.

Feelings.

Fuck.

Do I even *want* to feel again?

Maybe life is fucking easier when you're numb and can't make yourself give a shit about anything.

I should stay and keep a close eye on Hannah, but I'm itchy to solve my own shit and end this fucked-up situation with her, so I pull out my phone and walk to the back of the shop to call Luis, a guy I used to know. He owns a pawnshop and is happy to move things off the books, too. He's a fence of all things big and small. He's connected with most everything underground in Chicago—including the gangs.

He picks up with a "Hey."

"Hey, it's Armando, from the Pachino Family. Been a while."

"Armando. You out?"

"Yeah, just got out."

"Whatcha got for me?"

"Nah, nothing. I'm staying legit, but I wondered if you could help me with some information."

He pauses. I know nothing in this world comes free. There will be a price for anything I get from Luis. "What info?"

"There's a hit on me. Wondered if you'd heard about it?"

"Nah, I don't know anything about that. Who do you think it is?"

"I'm guessing the Hermanos. I had a run-in with one of their members on the inside. Could you find out if I'm right?"

"Yeah, I'll ask around. This your new number?"

"For the time being."

"'Kay. Be in touch."

I hang up and open the back door to the alley, feeling restless. Something got me thinking this morning that it might not be the Hermanos at all. Seems like they'd do a drive-by with a bunch of guys and automatic weapons. That was more their style. Sending a single guy to plug me on the corner screams hired hit. And why would they hire a hit when they're all perfectly capable of killing me themselves?

Only two reasons you hire a hit: you aren't a killer yourself, or you don't want it known you're responsible. And when I say don't want it known, I don't mean proven. I'm not talking about cops knowing. I mean known on the street.

Say Don Pachino puts a hit out on someone. He's sending a message. He wants everyone on the street to know he's responsible for it. I would think the same goes for the Hermanos. The message would be *don't fuck with our guys in prison or on the outside.*

So a hired mercenary coming after me seems strange.

I don't like it. And it gets me thinking maybe I have more to worry about than I thought.

And now I'm getting fucking paranoid.

Like thinking I shouldn't have ordered from Gio's last night. People know me there. The owner would know my name. And I used a debit card, which means now they have me connected to Hannah's address. So I might've ruined my plan of laying low at her place.

It's the reason I took her van to a random mechanic this morning. I know mechanics. Guys who would give me a great deal on it or even do the work for free. But there is no way I'm gonna link Hannah and her business to my name. She's already in this shit deep enough. If something happened to her because of me, I wouldn't be able to live with myself.

I watch her at her workbench, putting together new arrangements. She's talented. And in over her head.

I want to help her.

It's the first thing I've been clear on—apart from wanting to fuck her—since I got out. First thing that's generated even a spark of interest.

Too bad me getting involved with her business is the worst idea. If I really did care about her business, I'd stay way the hell away.

# CHAPTER TWENTY-ONE

*Hannah*

My stomach is in a knot up under my ribs. Or maybe that's my diaphragm on lock-down. Must be because I can't really breathe. My stress level shot to freak-out mode when Armando was asking me about the business.

Tears prick my eyes as I make up bouquets I don't need. Working with the flowers is the only thing that makes me happy here, though. I mean, it makes me happy in general—that's why I gave up my scholarship to nursing school—my mom's plan for me—to buy the flower shop. Flowers make me happy. I like their colors, their delicate textures, their smells. I love that I get to work with such a beautiful medium and use my eye and creativity in the arrangements.

College didn't suit me. I may have been a straight-A student, but that didn't mean I enjoyed it. No, when Mary Alice approached me to take over, I wanted this more than anything in the world.

But now it seems like I made a huge mistake.

Armando walks in from the back door, and I frown at him. There's a little bit of hate rattling around in me toward him right now.

I know it's not his fault, but he told me the thing I've been hiding from myself for the last six months. I made a huge mistake buying

Garden of Eden. I gave up my education and sure-thing career, and now I am going to lose everything.

"Hey." He leans a hip against the bench and watches me. "I wasn't trying to piss you off."

"I'm not pissed," I lie in a tight voice. What I really mean is I don't want to be pissed because it isn't his fault I'm drowning here.

"I wasn't criticizing your decision or your business, Hannah."

Sure as hell isn't how it feels.

"Look at me."

I ignore his command.

*"Hannah."* He plays Mr. Forceful very well. I'll bet he makes guys pee their pants when he wants to.

I turn to him with lips tight. Pressure bottlenecks in my throat, threatening to explode.

"You're not totally fucked. And you didn't fuck up, either."

I blink at him. Interesting summary. Oddly, his words settle around me with a comforting sort of thud.

He cocks his head. "You wanna make this work, right?"

I open my mouth, taken aback by the redirect on my angst. It's all still sitting there in my chest, but it stopped simmering. Stopped churning. *"Yes,"* I snap, even though he doesn't deserve my anger.

"Hey." He brings one hand to settle on my waist. It does jumpy things to my insides, especially considering how on edge I am. "You're worried. I get it. But you have choices."

I find myself drifting closer to him, like the strength in that rock-solid body or his cock-sure attitude will magically transmit to me. "What choices?"

He shrugs. "You can keep worrying and do the same thing you've been doing."

I scowl, my lungs tightening again.

"Or you can start trying new things to grow your business. Because that's what you want, right? To grow it?"

I nod. Yeah. That's what I'd imagined when I decided to buy. I didn't picture myself just maintaining things the way Mary Alice had done them for years, and I definitely didn't think I'd have even less business than she had.

"I can't grow it when I have no money to invest. I mean, I couldn't even get the van fixed to keep deliveries going. That's why I've just been stuck treading water since I bought it."

"Then you figure something out."

I blink up at him. "Seriously? That's your advice?"

"Not every idea costs money. And money doesn't only come from one source."

I shake my head. I don't know why I thought he had some magic answers for me here. "What do you know, anyway?" I mutter, turning away.

He catches my arm and pulls me back. "Either give it up or fight for it, Flowers. Don't hold your breath and pretend it's not sinking when it is."

I'm not the type to get physical with anyone, but I give his chest a hard shove. "Fuck you, Armando."

I know, not a really profound comeback. But I—

I lose my train of thought when he captures my wrists and backs me into the wall, his hard body pressed against mine. "Watch it, Flowers."

I don't know why I get wet every time he manhandles me. Or threatens me. It's like my body can't distinguish his abuse from foreplay. Not that it feels like abuse. His actions definitely read more as foreplay—it's not just me.

"Get off me," I whisper, but I clearly don't mean it.

"Breathe, Flowers."

I attempt to pull my wrists free, but he tightens his hold. "Breathe, or I'll make you."

"How will you do that?" I challenge. I'm way more turned on than afraid. I want all of his attention on me. On my body.

Maybe even on my business, even though he pissed me off.

He moves quickly, covering my mouth and nose with his free hand, blocking my air.

Surprise and fear leap to the surface, and I fight him, my survival instincts all kicking in.

He releases my wrists and shifts his other hand between my legs, cupping my mons firmly. He lets me take a quick breath, then smothers me again. Shock, terror and pleasure mingle in a rage of sensations. Blood rushes to my clit, tingles start up everywhere. He rubs firmly between my legs the whole time I freak out about not being able to draw a breath.

Just when I'm frantic, he pulls his hand away from my mouth and closes it around my throat instead. I suck in gasps of breath. It's only been thirty seconds, and I'm on the cusp of an orgasm. He doesn't choke me, he just uses his hand at my throat to hold me pinned against the wall while he works his fingers over my folds. He's not even inside me, and I'm ready to go. I reach down and cover his hand with my own, pushing his fingers more firmly against my clit, my entrance, my anus.

He grins and nods, his eyes glittering with pleasure as my breathing grows more shallow. His other hand slides up my body, tracing a path up my neck and sending shivers through me, before coming to rest on my jaw. He looks into my eyes, and I can see the intensity in his gaze.

"I could fuck you all day, every day," he whispers, and I can feel his breath tickle my skin. I nod, unable to find the words.

He tightens his grip around my throat and leans in, pressing his lips to mine hungrily. His tongue explores my mouth, tasting and teasing, and my arousal grows.

With a growl, he slides two fingers inside me. I gasp at the sudden pleasure as he strokes, pushing his wrist against my clit as he does. He starts to move faster and harder, stimulating me in ways I didn't know could happen so closely to sex and being more than satisfied.

*We just had sex.*

Not being able to get enough of this man, I writhe and squirm against him, desperate for more. He takes up my challenge, alternating between hard thrusts and gentle caresses, driving me closer and closer to the brink of ecstasy.

He responds to my moans, pushing deeper and faster with each stroke. I can feel his breathing hitch as I mewl and pant against him, my body trembling with pleasure. His other hand slides around my waist, pulling me closer, and his tongue finds its way into my mouth, tasting and exploring me as his fingers move faster and faster over my sensitive skin.

The sensations are overwhelming. Every nerve is on fire, and I'm close to the edge, my hips bucking against his hand in a desperate attempt to reach climax—again. He must feel it too, and his tongue moves more fiercely against my own, his fingers working harder and harder until I can't take it anymore, and I scream out my release, my body shaking and shuddering.

As I come, choking and gasping for my breath, Armando keeps rubbing between my legs. Stars dance before my eyes, and I close them, shuttled away in some other universe.

When I come back to reality, when my breath slows, and I open my eyes, I find Armando leaning his forehead against the wall beside my head, stroking my jaw with his thumb. His fingers still wrap around my neck and stroke between my legs.

A full-body shudder runs through me, another release.

"Don't give up, Flowers. Stop holding your breath. You can fix this."

I sag against his body. "How?" I warble. I sound pathetic. I should be pissed over what he just did to me. Even if I liked it, it was high-handed and scary. I should push him away and tell him never to touch me again, especially in my place of business.

Instead, I fall into his arms and let him hold me up.

"You try every idea you have until something takes hold. Ask for help. Keep working it. You can do this. You're good at what you do. Trust in that."

As far as motivational speeches go, it's pretty flimsy, but I do strangely feel better. That's probably just the orgasm talking.

I push away from him, even though I'm not sure my legs will hold me. "You're still an asshole," I mutter.

"Believe it," he confirms as I walk away on shaky legs but *breathing* much better than before.

Looking over my shoulder, I catch the way his eyes watch every single move I make. He's hunting, and I'm an easy prey.

I could run. I should run. But with the way he watches over me, I'd surely trip on my lust and desire for this man and fall flat on my face. But then knowing Armando, he'd simply pick me up, smack my ass for trying to flee and fuck me all over again.

# CHAPTER TWENTY-TWO

*Armando*

Hannah's all discombobulated. I can't decide if she's still mad at me or just in a post-orgasmic brain-fuck. She moves restlessly around the shop, randomly stopping to stare at her products but not getting anything done. I suppose it could be a business-related brain-fuck.

The door opens, and a tall young woman with bleach-blonde ringlets and freckles across her nose breezes in. "Sorry I'm late." She heads straight past the counter into the area where I'm lounging and drops her purse on the desk beside me. "Hi."

Whatever softening effect Hannah's had on me doesn't apply to her. I'm suddenly cold and hard again, showing nothing, ready for anything. I don't answer, other than to flick my brow in question.

It makes her nervous, and she backs out and cozies right up to Hannah. "What's with Guido?" I hear her murmur.

Hannah shoots a frightened glance at me, and I instantly prickle with irritation although I can't put my finger on why. I guess I don't like seeing that look on Hannah's face, even when I'm the cause of it. "That's, ah, Armando," Hannah answers. "He's hanging out today."

"Why?" the woman demands. I can't tell if she works here or is just a friend. Possibly both.

"Armando, this is Josie," Hannah says in a louder voice. "She works here."

I glance at the clock. The shop opened at noon. It's 1:45 now. What time was she supposed to be here?

"Oh my God, were you not able to make the rent?" Josie whispers.

Hannah flicks another worried glance my way. "Not quite, but it's okay, I have things worked out for this month."

"What does that mean?"

Hannah just shakes her head. "Can you handle the counter?"

Josie gives her a searching look, but when Hannah ignores it, she says, "Of course."

Hannah buzzes past me and goes to her workbench. She pulls out a vase and two spools of ribbon. Now, she finally has focus. I realize she was waiting for someone to run the front desk, so she could get busy with the arrangements. I probably could have kept an eye on things. It's telling that she didn't ask me. I think she pretends to be more comfortable with me than she really is.

A stab of guilt shoots through me. The same shame I felt last night thinking she might believe she has to fuck me to stay alive.

Is she that good of an actress?

No. I don't think so. She's into it. Her body can't lie. She's not resisting me. Although...am I giving her much of a choice?

Hannah looks calm and confident, assembling buckets of flowers at her feet from the cooler. Where she might be a deer in the headlights when it comes to her books, here at the workbench, she's a goddamn wizard. Her movements are swift and sure as she fills it with a perky bouquet of colorful flowers and wraps a red and white ribbon around a vase. I don't even know what kind they are—orchids maybe? Something exotic and surprising. There's nothing cliche about the arrangement.

And then it hits me. "Is that supposed to be a barber's pole?"

She steps back, examining her work with a critical eye. "Yes."

Genius. Her talent as a designer is fucking off the charts.

"Did Rocco ask for flowers?" Funny, I can't see it.

"No. But he's getting them. I was thinking about what you said. About making new connections. You're right—I don't have any. And the only one Mary Alice had that still works for me is Rocco's. So I figure I should keep that wheel greased. From now on, Rocco's going to have fresh flowers at his place with a stack of my cards beside them."

"Smart thinking." I want to go over with her—watch how it goes down. I don't know if it's to protect her from the guys who might be over there or to stake my claim, but it doesn't matter because I can't.

Best way to protect Hannah is to never connect the two of us.

I gotta sit in the back of her shop like a fucking pansy, hiding from God knows who.

This is bullshit.

"You didn't tell me you had a staff person coming in today." I glance over at Josie who doesn't seem to be doing anything other than picking at her manicured nail and yawning as she does so.

"Her schedule can be...fluid," Hannah says, still focused on arranging.

She pulls another vase down and makes a bigger, showier arrangement in it. It's two feet tall and stunning.

"Who's that for?" I ask.

She nibbles her lip. "There's a hotel a couple blocks from here." She shrugs. "Maybe I'll go introduce myself. You know, in case they need flowers for events. Or could recommend me to the event-planners."

"That's good."

Maybe she will turn this place around.

"I'll drive you after we get the van back. Circle around the block, so you don't have to do valet."

She gives me a withering look. "I wasn't going to do valet. I've never done valet in my life. I was going to walk."

I look at her wedge sandals. "Nah. I'll drive you. You wouldn't want the flowers to wilt. Just wait for the van...it'll be done in a couple hours."

She draws in a breath and lets it out slowly, like she's nervous about this.

"You're gonna be great. They'll love you."

"You think?"

I nod. "Positive."

She steps a little closer to me, into my personal space. I only resist touching her until I realize that's what she wants, and then I band an arm around her waist and draw her right up against me.

She tips her lovely face up. "I'm nervous."

"Flowers, a woman who looks like you? With crazy talent and no diva bullshit? There's no one in this city who *wouldn't* want to work with you. I guarantee it. It's just gonna be about who they currently do business with and what their needs are. Some connections may take longer to germinate, but they eventually will."

She blinks those curled lashes at me. "I want to believe you."

"Don't believe me, Flowers. Believe in *you*. That's the only thing that will get you there."

She draws herself up and squares her shoulders. "Who do you believe in?"

It's a simple question. Should be an easy answer, but I feel like I've swallowed lead. "Nobody, Flowers. Not a Goddamn soul."

# CHAPTER TWENTY-THREE

*Hannah*

Josie keeps trying to get me alone, but Armando won't let it happen. He appears deceptively relaxed, lounging around in the back, but he picked a spot where he can keep an eye on everything—front door, back door. Workshop. Coolers. Kitchenette. It's not like the shop is that big, but there's nowhere I go I don't feel the weight of his gaze.

And every time Josie tries to follow me somewhere with a million questions in her eyes, Armando's suddenly standing there, warning me without saying a word.

Right now, I'm in the cooler, but when Josie came in after me, Armando propped the door open, so he could hear.

It's freaky. It shouldn't get me wet. I'm not sure why his brand of intimidation turns me on so much. I must be wired wrong.

But Josie's concern makes my stomach knot up. I should've been more freaked out about Armando and my situation, but until now, when I see it through her eyes, I didn't realize how fucked up it is.

And of course, I can't tell her the situation. Even if Armando wasn't watching, I wouldn't tell.

I don't know, I'm one of those hopelessly loyal people who takes my friends' secrets to the grave. And I guess Armando falls into the friend category. He was already in it when the situation went down. I was rooting for him from the beginning.

I believed in him. He just doesn't believe in me yet.

I wish that didn't hurt as much as it does.

But I have to cut him slack. He probably has PTSD from prison. Someone's trying to kill him, and he doesn't know who to trust.

Why would he have any faith in me? He shouldn't.

I hear the sound of my phone chiming like I got a text. Repeatedly.

Where is my damn phone? Armando has it somewhere. He's kept it on him the whole time although I appreciate the fact that he made sure to charge it.

I look through the glass and see Josie behind the counter holding her phone and craning her neck to look over her shoulder at me. We've been besties since middle school when she stood up for me against Erica Bane, one of the popular girls, on the third day of school. She knows me through and through. I am stupid to think I can fool her about anything.

She's texting me. And she just realized I'm not in possession of my own phone.

This could be a problem.

I breeze out of the cooler like I own the place, which, funnily enough, I do. Too bad I never feel like it. "Have you seen my phone?" I ask Armando sweetly.

"Uh huh. You left it here." He hands it over, cool as a cucumber. I am slightly disturbed at how convincing he is. How smoothly he covers the lie. But he is a member of an organized crime family after all. And probably grew up in it.

I check the messages, which are all from Josie asking if I'm okay, whether she should go get help and WTF is going on.

*Everything's fine,* I text back. *I hooked up with him, and now he's hanging out. He helped pay the rent.* I make a point of letting Armando read over my shoulder before I send it.

All of that is true. Except maybe not the *everything's fine.*

I haven't forgiven him for tying me up last night. That piss-off still lingers, but otherwise...I am fine. Armando makes me nervous, but half that is the excitement of having him near. Watching me. Not knowing what he's going to do next.

Do I think he'll bury me in Lake Michigan when it's all done? No. I can't see it.

I may be shitty at business, but I'm empathic. I can't help but understand people because I feel their emotions as my own. At least that's how it feels. Josie thinks I'm nuts every time I tell her that, but I swear it's true.

I don't sense menace from Armando toward me. He gives off very little emotionally unless I count lust. But he's not evil. He's not planning my demise.

Josie: *You hooked up with him? Who is he? A complete stranger!!! I've never seen him inside the store before.*

Me: *He's that man I was telling you about from when I worked under Mary Alice. He came back into the store yesterday near closing time.*

Josie: *To buy flowers for his fiancée? Please tell me you aren't fucking a taken man. Hannah!!*

Me: *He's not with her anymore. They broke up years ago.*

I almost add that he just got out of prison, but don't feel it's any of Josie's business. Plus, I think she'd judge not only him but me for hooking up with a criminal. I'm not in the mood to defend my actions.

Josie: *Well... was the sex hot? Did it live up to the fantasy?*

I feel my face heat and steal a peak at Armando who is watching me but no longer trying to read my texts. I seem to have at least earned that small level of trust from him.

I keep trying to prove he can trust me, so he'll set me free, but if I were totally honest with myself, I'd have to admit I'm not ready for it to be over. I like the tingle of excitement I get knowing he's watching my every move. Remembering how much he appreciates my body. I might even be addicted already to the way he touches me.

Me: *So hot.*

Josie: *But why is he here?*

Me: *He's protective, I guess...*

Josie: *Okay, that is super hot. Protective, possessive...yes!*

Me: *You have no idea.*

# CHAPTER TWENTY-FOUR

*Armando*

After Hannah brings the flowers by the hotel and leaves her card, I pull in at a grocery store. I need a razor, toothbrush, and some other odds and ends. Plus, she has no food at her place.

"What are we doing?" Hannah asks.

"Getting groceries." I turn off the van and climb out, looking around to make sure no one's watching us. I haven't seen anything suspicious today, but I'd be stupid to get complacent. "Let's go."

She hops down and comes around.

"Stay close. Follow directions. Show me I can trust you."

She lets out a little huff of indignation. If she was going to try something, she would've done it a long time ago. I know that. But I don't trust anything anymore.

"Get a cart."

She shoots me a withering look. "Are you going to tie me to it, too?"

My dick twitches at the thought. "Don't tempt me, Curls."

"Oh, is it Curls now? I thought I was Flowers."

I ignore her, mostly because I'm way over my daily quotient on words. My throat is literally scratchy from talking so much today.

Hooking my fingers around the front of the cart, I lead her toward the toiletries aisle. I find a toothbrush and toothpaste and a bag of razors. When I toss the box of condoms in the cart, she takes notice.

"You're just assuming we are going to have sex again? What if I want to go back to my no sex rule?"

"Okay."

"Why do you say *okay* like you don't believe me?"

I stop the cart and turn to face her. She's so damn beautiful, even when she's snippy. "Take it easy, Flowers. I'm gonna respect your decision on whatever you want in that regard."

That doesn't calm her down. In fact, she gives the cart a push, forcing me to move out of the way or get hit. I walk beside the cart as she marches down the aisle. "So, what are the condoms for? Are you going back to your strip club? Hmm? Going to pick up some girls there?"

Aw, fuck. I swear my face is breaking because I sense a smile coming on. Is she jealous? She's fucking adorable when she's jealous.

I stifle the smile and keep my face blank. "No. Not going back to the strip club, Flowers. They're in case you do decide you want to continue having sex with me."

She stops the cart and looks at me, considering. Her lips are in a pout, but her posture has softened. "I'll think about it."

I shrug. "Okay."

A blush spreads across her cheeks, and she starts pushing the cart again at a determined speed. "What else are you getting?"

"Food."

"I need kitty litter," she mutters.

"Let's get some." We head to the pet aisle. She picks out the kitty litter. I throw in some Kitten Chow, and catnip treats and one of those poles with feathers attached to the end for the kitten to play with.

"I didn't think you liked cats." Hannah eyes me from under a swath of curls.

For some reason, it hurts that she noticed. That I can't hide my lack of humanity. "I don't," I say gruffly.

It's not true. I don't like or dislike cats. I don't give a shit about them. But I know it's fucked up that I can look a kitten in the face right now and feel nothing. There's definitely something wrong with me. All mammals are wired to think baby animals are cute. I learned that in middle school science class.

I stalk through the store. I picked up a few things at the grocery store before I moved into the apartment Marco rented for me, but I was in culture shock then. Just being in the grocery store had been an out of body experience—like most everything this past week. Now, I'm determined to find something I like or want. I drag Hannah through every aisle filling the cart with all kinds of food. Steak. Ice cream. Potato chips. Fresh fruit and vegetables. Oreo cookies.

"You'd better be paying for all this because I'm not," Hannah mutters when the cart gets full.

"Yeah, I got it."

After a few moments, she says, "I'm sorry—that was bitchy."

Seriously. This girl. Who does that? Who apologizes for an offhanded dig?

"Nah, you earned it."

"Well, I don't like the way it feels."

She doesn't like the way it feels. Hannah Munn is so pure, it makes my head spin. She's not innocent or naive. Not a mouse. She's just... kind. Good. Honest.

And she feels bad now because bitchiness is not her natural state. Grace could pull a cunt all day long and would never apologize for it. Hannah didn't even come close to offending me, and she can't let it ride.

"It was uncalled for. You helped me with money at the bank and with the van." Her voice breaks a little.

Aw, shit, is she crumpling? Over this?

"Come here, Flowers." I pull her against my chest and wrap my arms around her. "It's all right. It's just money. You gotta get over your fear of it."

"I'm not afraid of money," she says, sounding even more upset. She pushes out of my embrace, and I let her go.

"You might not be afraid, but it's your sore spot, for sure. You get more upset about money than you do about anything. Even what happened yesterday."

"Well, it's a big deal," she snaps.

"It's not. You've made it a big deal. It's just money."

"Have you ever not had enough?" she demands.

My memory flashes back to my teen years. My first job for Don G., providing security at Lollipops at age sixteen. Flexing my muscles and pretending to play hero to a bunch of naked girls. I got a taste for cash. Seeing the guys flash it around, going home with a wad of it in my pocket. Buying groceries and gas for my mom. Telling her to quit her second job. "I always wanted more," I admit. "That's how I got into the organization."

Her eyes widen, and she goes quiet, chewing on that. "Are you ever sorry?"

I let out a snort. Am I? I'm not even allowed to think it. I can't think it because if I do, there's no reason to go on living.

Once you're in, you don't get out, except in a body bag.

"Officially, no."

"Unofficially?" she asks softly.

"I have some regrets," I admit. "But there's no exit ticket. I'm in it for life now." I shrug. "I gotta make it work."

She blinks those curled lashes at me, seeing so much more than I want to show.

I gotta change the topic. "Come on, Flowers. Groceries are on me, so finish filling up this cart. I don't know what you like."

"Lobster and caviar, it is." She tosses her hair and swishes her hips as she pushes the cart down the aisle.

That twitchy feeling returns around my mouth.

A smile. Hannah makes me want to smile.

"If my princess wants lobster, then lobster it is," I say.

She pauses, nibbles her bottom lip, and then reaches for a box of plug-in air fresheners. "I'd prefer these over lobster. Help with the kitty smell. They're just super expensive for some oil you plug into the wall. But—"

I snatch them from her hand, not even looking at the price. "You're a cheap date."

She smiles again—a smile I could look at all day every day—and continues toward the check out.

We walk outside, and the thump of bass assaults us from a Chevy Impala low-rider. I whirl to face Hannah, catching the cart to stop it and her.

"What?" Her eyes widen. She's smart enough to recognize my urgency and scans the street, following the vehicle with her gaze. "You know them?"

I don't turn, even though I want to. I fucking hate having my back to danger. "I don't know," I mutter. The pounding music fades.

"It's gone," Hannah tells me.

I turn back to the van and tug the cart, resuming like nothing happened.

Fuck.

That could've been the Hermanos. They could've had assault weapons and fired from the car. Hannah would've been killed.

I'm still ice-cold and emotionless when I picture myself getting gunned down, but the thought of Hannah dying because of me brings bile to my mouth.

I shouldn't be hiding out with her. It would be better to expose myself to danger than to use her as my shield.

I need to get out of her life.

Fucking soon.

Ushering her to the passenger side of the van, I open the door and assist her inside, feeling as if eyes are still on me. Watching my every move. I notice that Hannah is examining my face, obviously picking up on my discomfort. Not saying anything to explain, I close her door and walk around the van pissed that I let my guard down. My eyes dart from side to side, scanning the parking lot, and finally acting like the man I was trained to be.

No more playing house. Our fucking lives are on the line.

# CHAPTER TWENTY-FIVE

*Hannah*

Shadow races to greet us when we get home, climbing Armando's pant leg.

"What the fuck?" He rears away to stare down his leg at my tiny sharp-clawed nuisance.

"I'm sorry." I rush over to extricate the kitten's claws from his thigh. "He's a menace."

"Let me see him." Armando holds out his hand. I hesitate a moment before I hand him over. I'm not sure where Armando falls with treatment of animals although he did buy toys for Shadow.

He takes Shadow from me and holds him up face-level. "Listen, little man. My leg? Not your scratching post. Got it?"

I giggle and reach to take him back.

"Give him one of those treats," Armando says, and my heart does this weird squeezing thing. Like we're pet parents together or something stupid like that. It's ridiculous and weird and *God*—this whole situation exhausts me.

I retrieve the treats and feed Shadow one while Armando puts away the groceries and sets the table.

*I'm mad at him*, I remind my ovaries, which drop eggs every thirty seconds. *Mad at him*. He tied me up in my own bed last night. He's taken my phone, which *I need*. He's still standing guard over me like I'm a prisoner.

Technically, I am a prisoner. Or am I? It's hard to feel like a prisoner when I keep fucking my jailer. I'm struggling to keep my hands off him right now.

We sit down and eat one of those pre-cooked rotisserie chickens and a Caesar salad that Armando made. Armando eats fast, head down, not saying a word. I picture him eating like that in prison, and my chest gets tight. I want to ask about it, but he's so closed off, I don't dare.

He finally looks up, pauses mid-chew, and swallows hard. As if it's just dawned on him that we've sat here in silence as he shoveled food into his mouth like a guard is waiting to take his tray away.

"So tell me something about you," he says.

"Um... like what?"

He pauses, his eyes dart around the room and then center back on me. "What is your favorite flower? I know you are around them all day and know the preferences of your clients. But what is yours?"

"Do I have to have one?"

"Yes. Everyone has a favorite."

"I guess... I like roses," I say. "Red ones." I'm not sure if I would have said that answer if I wasn't put on the spot.

"I would have guessed that," he says. "You have the personality of a rose."

My breath catches in my throat. "And what's that?"

"Strong, beautiful and demands attention."

"I don't demand attention," I say, surprised by his words.

"You should." He pins me with a gaze that makes my tummy flutter. "Never settle for anything else."

"What about you?" I ask. "Do you have a favorite flower?"

"Whatever one makes you happy. That would be mine."

He doesn't smile. He doesn't say the words in a way meant to charm me or woo me. They are simple, direct, and silencing. I don't know how to respond to this man.

So instead, I continue eating, as does he. Though we say very little,

I'm comforted by his presence and the sound of his knife and fork against the plate. I shouldn't be reading into his words or his actions, and yet, I can't help myself.

When we finish, he helps me clean up just as efficiently as he does everything. It's like we're playing house, standing side by side washing dishes and putting them away. The only sound in the room is the running water and the meows of Shadow begging for chicken scraps.

I'm surprised when Armando kneels down and gives the cat a bite from his fingers. "That's it for now. It's rich," he says to the kitten as Shadow licks every last bit of juice from Armondo's beefy fingers.

He then takes his toothbrush and other toiletries off the counter and heads to the bathroom. I'm left feeling... odd. I don't know how to process everything going on and the rush of emotions both good and bad flowing through me. But I need to find my phone. I might have messages that need answering. I can't stand that he won't give it to me.

I search the high cupboards because that's where he stowed my purse last night. No dice.

Then I see it. It's on top of the refrigerator, pushed way to the back behind the floral baskets I have stacked there. It amuses me that he hides it up high. Like I'm some little girl who can't reach.

Okay, actually, I can't reach because I'm short, but I put one knee up on the counter and reach. I fish out my phone and check the texts.

There's two. One from my mom, asking if I'm coming to dinner tomorrow, and one from Josie, telling me she'll be late Monday.

Not asking. *Telling.*

Sigh. Another problem I'm sticking my head in the sand about.

I start to reply when I hear Armando curse.

He storms at me, but I don't flinch. Yes, he's capable of hurting me. He's violent. Dangerous. But there's thought and control behind the violence. And I'm fairly certain he has rules about hurting women. As in, he won't. And frankly, if he was going to hurt me, he would have done it by now.

"What the fuck, Hannah?" he snatches the phone out of my hand, his brows in a deep V as he scrolls over my screens. "Who did you message?"

*"Nobody."* I let my irritation show. I lift my chin at the phone. "Check it yourself."

His thumb flies over the screen as he checks my phone log, too. "You could've sent one and erased it."

"I need my fucking phone, Armando." I let myself sound bitchy because it's a better alternative to allowing him to bully me or showing fear.

He shakes his head and shoves the phone in his back pocket. "That's not how this works, and you know it, Flowers." He catches my wrists and pins me with a dark gaze. "I trust you and leave for one minute... And now you're in big trouble with me."

*Big trouble.*

Why does that make my belly flip flop with excitement?

Because I already know I like his punishments. He spins me around and slaps my hands on the refrigerator, then pulls my hips back to bend me at the waist. My wrists are manacled under one of his meaty palms.

I'm prepared for the slap when it comes, but it's harder than I expect, and I gasp. He smacks my other butt cheek just as hard, then yanks my minidress up to my armpits. He spanks my ass some more over my panties.

"Ow, okay," I snap because it really does hurt.

He brings his mouth close to my ear—close enough that his warm breath feathers across my jaw when he speaks. "You keep your hands glued to that fridge, Hannah," he warns. "If you move, I will make you sorry."

He doesn't wait for my agreement but releases my wrists to yank my panties down my thighs.

Oh God.

It's so hot but also borderline humiliating. Especially because they tangle around my thighs and stay there. I wiggle and shake my legs until they fall down.

"Good girl," Armando says, and everything shifts.

Maybe I had been a little afraid up to that moment. He was a little rougher than he's been in the past. Spanked a little harder. Now I'm sure of him again.

"I'm not having sex with you," I say, trying to maintain the one level of control he's given me.

Sex is the only leverage I have—not that he couldn't just force me. But I know he won't.

"Understood, but that's not gonna stop your punishment." His voice is deep and gruff.

Well, good. I didn't particularly want to stop my punishment. Except he picks up spanking me again, and it's still too hard.

"Ouch!" I jerk and wince as he peppers my ass with five more hard spanks.

"And there is so much I can do to you besides just fucking you."

He continues to spank me more. My ass getting warmer with each swat of his hand. What hurts also feels so fucking good.

"Are you going to be a good girl and follow my rules? Or do I need to keep spanking you?" His voice is deep, authoritative, and my pussy pulsates with each syllable of his question.

"I'll be a good girl." Even though I'm saying the words, they seem to vanish, drowning between my gasps and mewls.

"Do you want Daddy to punish you like a naughty girl or punish you like the bad girl you are?"

Holy. Fucking. Christ. His one question is like a bolt of electricity zipped through me. So fucking intense.

"I want both, *Daddy*." I inhale deeply. "Both."

Then he drops to his knees behind me and pinches my asscheeks with his thumbs. He pulls them apart and licks up my crack.

I let out a warble of pleasure. God, yes. Wherever this man learned to fuck, he learned it right.

He rims my anus with his tongue, then pushes my thighs wider to open me to him. Face buried in my ass, he licks up to my clit and back again. The sting of his spanks morphs into a warm tingle, bringing added heat to the region, as if my core weren't already molten.

He slaps my ass intermittently as he works my folds with his tongue, then screws one finger into me. His thumb rubs over my anus.

"Good thing we're not having sex, Flowers. Or I'd bend you over, put my cock in your ass and fuck you hard."

Oh. My. *Gawd.*

Armando shifts to dip his thumb in my pussy, then returns to my anus with it coated with my juices and pushes like he's trying to get in. He puts three—fuck, maybe four—fingers in my pussy at the same time.

I do scream—a loud, "Oh my God!" I lose my balance, my knees buckling. Armando grips my pelvis to hold me up and removes his fingers. "No," I whimper. Dammit. I was so close to coming.

He grabs me around the waist and pulls back. I shriek as I free-fall into his lap, but he doesn't miss a beat. He hooks his hand behind my left knee and pulls it up and open, spreading me wide. With his right palm, he starts *spanking my pussy.*

Quick firm slaps. He slaps everything—my clit, my entrance, my labia. I wriggle in his lap, trying to push him away at the same time I pull him closer. It's crazy intense. Like lose-my-mind intense in a really good-bad way. Hurty but really freaking satisfying.

I shriek and grab the hand spanking me, cup it around my mons, so I can come. He curls his fingers and dips them in—two, maybe three— and I come, a spasm of release rippling through me.

"Oh fuck," I pant. "Oh my God."

I come some more.

He undulates his hand, so the heel of it pulses against my clit. I come again.

"Jesus." I fling myself back into his arms, my head lolling over his shoulder.

He pulls his fingers out of me, and I moan, but he gives my pussy three more quick slaps, and I come again.

"Holy freaking shit," I pant. "What in the hell did you just do to me?" My whole body is abuzz, ass tingling, pussy raw and sore from the spanking, anus still pulsing from being breeched.

I turn my face into his neck because my eyes suddenly burn with the release. I know if I don't make anything of it, the emotions will pass through me, but I don't want him to see. It's so weird how easily I cry.

He shifts my ass to hold me better, and I feel his rock-hard erection prod my butt. I don't feel guilty. Not really.

But the truth is, I'm still revved up. I don't know, maybe my body's not quite satisfied until I go the whole way. Until I actually ride his cock.

"The only way I'd have sex with you would be if I tied you up this time," I tell him.

"Not gonna happen," he answers without hesitation, but I feel his cock lurch against my backside. He brings his fingers to my clit and rubs a slow circle.

Shit!

This man's touch is my kryptonite. I swear he could make me do anything if he just made me come this hard every day.

I put my face back in the crook of his neck and whimper. I may have just come, but the need is still there. And he's amping it up with every rub of my clit.

"I'd let you ride me no-hands," he offers.

I bite his neck because I'm frustrated. "What is that?"

"You know. Like at a strip club. You can climb all over me, but I can't touch you."

He had to bring up strip clubs and remind me of last night. "No, I don't know. I've never been," I say tartly.

"You wanna ride my cock?" He massages a handful of my ass.

Unfortunately, it seems my body wants nothing more. It holds no grudges.

When I hesitate, he moves, lifting me off his lap and pulling me to my feet as he stands. Then he swings me up into a baby carry. I gasp, worried I'm too heavy, but he doesn't appear to be straining.

And being carried is a delicious feeling. One I don't want to indulge in because there are already way too many things about the way Armando touches me I like. I don't want to get used to any of it because it's not a relationship. It's not permanent. It's this weird high-stress shared experience that forged intimacy. Like people who band together during the zombie apocalypse and are forced to develop bonds that would never exist otherwise.

And yeah, it says something that I'm comparing our situation to the one faced by the characters in *The Walking Dead*.

He sets me on my feet near the bed and pulls my dress, which is still tangled up around my armpits, over my head.

I give his chest a light push, which of course, doesn't move him at all. "No touching," I remind him.

# CHAPTER TWENTY-SIX

*Armando*

*Mary, Queen of Peace.* I'm harder than stone for Hannah. What kind of magical creature is she to transform every conflict into explosive sex? She just fucking surrenders to me. Even when she wants to hold back, her body melts with my touch, all the dirty things I do to her. I don't plan to do them, but she makes me. She brings it out in me. Her body receives, and mine wants to give. It's impossible for me not to deliver every caress, every spank, every orgasm she seems to crave.

And right now she wants to pretend she has control, so I'll give it to her. I strip out of my clothes and grab a condom out of my wallet. I flop onto the bed on my back and roll the condom on my erection.

Hannah's ditched all her clothing. She's freaking glorious—all soft curves and dark skin with that insane mane of hair tumbling over her shoulders and down her back. She climbs onto the bed.

I tuck one hand behind my head but hold the base of my cock with the other until she takes over. A shudder of pleasure runs through me the moment she fists it.

"I'll bet you want me to suck it," she says, pupils blown.

The erection punches out harder. "Fuck!"

"I'm not sure you deserve that." She's playing cock-tease, but I don't give a shit because she climbs over me and lines up that sweet pussy of hers with the head of my shaft. She rubs her juices over it, then sinks down.

I growl, barely stopping myself from reaching for her hips to help. It's fucking hard not to use my hands. Because she's not some stripper-stranger. She's Hannah, and I can't fucking wait to see her come all over my cock.

She rocks slowly over me, her pelvis undulating, her tits shifting. It's goddess worthy. I want to touch those juicy tits. I want to rub her clit. I want to yank her down on me so hard she sees stars. But she's got the control now. And I'm grateful as hell to be inside her.

I roll my hips in time with hers, shifting up to thrust into her when she rocks down. It quickly becomes too much for her. She braces her hands on my shoulders and starts riding me faster, her breasts swinging, hair falling in a curtain around my head.

I fist the pillow behind my head—tear at it—to keep from breaking my word not to touch. When she sees my dilemma, she pins my wrists down on the bed like I'm her prisoner and slides that magic pussy faster and faster over my cock. She works it and works it like a fucking Energizer Bunny until she runs out of breath from the exertion and stops moving, panting.

I lift my hips to meet her every downward thrust. It feels incredible. She's so wet and so tight. And when I look up, I see her tits bouncing and her nipples stiffening. There's no way I can keep my hands still for a few more seconds. They're itching to touch her. To squeeze the ripe mounds. To circle her stiff nipples with my thumb and forefinger. To slide to her clit and make her come.

I'm on the edge. Balls-deep in that slick cunt, backed up against her cervix, I work my hips to get even deeper. My fingers twitch.

She arches backward and clamps down hard on my cock. The shock of her pussy muscles contracting around me is almost enough to send me over. She's panting now, her tits bouncing as she grinds her pelvis forward and back.

I stretch my arms up and slide my hands up her body until they cup her breasts, squeezing and kneading them. Her eyes go wide, and she swallows. I drop one hand to rub her clit. I can't stop myself. I'm too close. Her hips buck against mine, fucking me. I move my thumb in a figure eight over her clit until she's moaning and begging for release.

I let go of her tit and grab her ass to bury myself in her as far as I can. Watching her arch back to meet me as she releases a raspy moan.

Fuck.

"Let me touch you," I start begging. "Let me drive, doll. I'll make you feel so good, I promise."

Her eyes are smoky, rose flushes her skin. She blinks those curled lashes at me as she considers. I thrust my hips up to get deeper and she moans.

The moment she gives me a minuscule nod, I wrap my fingers around her hips and start controlling the movement. I lift and lower her over me, thrusting my hips in time to meet hers. It feels like heaven, but I'm also getting desperate to finish. I've been hard for her all day and just watched her come on the kitchen floor.

She moans like she's getting close with the short, sharp cries that fall like music in the room.

We're both close, but it doesn't happen, and I think a change of position would help. "Let me put you on your back."

I'm not usually one to ask for permission for anything, but she's holding this power over me now, and I'm gonna let her. It's my penance. Better than the ones Father Fantoni assigns.

"Okay," she gasps.

I flip her around in one second flat, keeping our hips glued together. As soon as I'm on the top, I start thrusting with force. Hannah's eyes roll back in her head, her lips fall open with pleasure. She cups her own breasts. I hold the place where shoulder meets neck to keep her head from banging into the wall and fuck the living daylights out of her.

When I decide I need to be deeper, still, I lift one of her thighs up and pound into her in that position.

I kiss her hard again, one more time. This time, my tongue is forceful and dominant. I take her tongue and suck it hard into my own mouth, forcing her to submit. She's mine. She's going to remember that. I want to leave a mark on her. I want her to be able to smell me on her, feel me deep within her. I want her to think of me every time she touches herself or remembers this night.

"You taste so fucking good, Hannah. I'm going to make you come so hard. I'm going to make you scream."

I watch as she falls apart around me, her legs shaking and her back curling, her whole body holding the weight of an orgasm that is too intense. She breathes deeply and hard from her core, writhing against me, her hands holding on tightly to my forearms. Each time her body wraps around mine, I feel my own orgasm build.

"I'm going to come, baby," I growl. "I'm going to fill you up...."

She starts screaming, filling the room with ecstatic needy shrieks. My balls draw up tight, thighs shaking.

"Fuck, Hannah, I'm gonna come," I tell her as stars start to explode behind my eyes.

"Yes!" she cries. "Me too!"

Hannah's orgasm is so powerful, she's shaking even while mine rips through my body, taking over and shaking me to my core. I don't want to stop. I want to stay inside her forever, feel her body pull me deeper, keeping me here, connected.

I continue to come, still banging her hard, and she bites her lip, arches her back and screams some more. Her pussy contracts around my dick, pulsing and squeezing with her climax.

Christ, she's everything.

She really is.

I slow down and stroke slowly for a while, taking it down to a caress then finally stopping and feeling my cock pulse and twitch inside her with the aftershocks.

"*Bella.*"

She frowns and lifts her head from the pillow. "What?"

"You're beautiful."

"Did you just call me by another woman's name?" Her voice is sharp and offended.

A snort of laughter surprises me. Jesus. When's the last time I laughed?

"No, I said *bella*. It means *beautiful* in Italian." I ease out and pull off the condom, reaching behind me to drop it in the trash by the bed.

"Oh." She goes soft and receptive again. Fuck, I love how receptive she is. I'm also loving her jealousy. "Do you speak Italian?"

I settle beside her and stroke my palm over her hip. "A little. I understand it better than I speak it. I'm second generation American, so my grandparents speak it."

"Wow." She turns into me, her palm coming to rest on my chest. "Are you always... like this?"

I push a swatch of curls over her shoulder, so I can see her gorgeous breast. "Like what?"

She chews her lip. "Like this in bed."

I only partially manage to hide my surprise. I learned a long time ago that any time you get a woman to talk about sex, you don't do anything to shut that communication down. Hannah wants to talk—I'm in. Even if I am so far out of touch with my emotions, I'm a robot.

I consider. "No, I don't think so. I used to have more game. My techniques were... more stylized. I even thought sophisticated. But with you..." I close my eyes letting pleasure of what we just did wash over me. "It's more raw. Hungry. Almost desperate."

She blinks at me. There's vulnerability shining in those sultry brown eyes, but I'm not sure what she needs me to say. Or if I already fucked this up.

"Every time we do it, something in me thaws," I admit.

More vulnerability washes over her face, and her breath quickens. Is her lower lip trembling?

I come out with it—all the honesty I know how to give. "You're healing me."

Her eyes fill with tears, and she lets out a puff of air. I cup her face, trying not to react to the tears. A couple spill down her cheek, and I thumb one away.

"You're *destroying* me." Her voice chokes with tears.

I freeze. Stop breathing.

What is she saying? What is she telling me here? Fuck.

That shifty thing happens again in my chest.

"How?" My whole body's tense for her answer.

She sits up, and I follow. "Armando, what is this? I don't even know what we're doing, but I know it's a bad idea."

Aw, shit. My heart stops beating. My chest goes stiff.

"I don't have the answers you're looking for," I admit.

"Everything is happening so fast. Like a raging storm."

"It is."

"So what is this? Is it just sex... a lot of it?"

I shake my head. "No, Flowers. It's not just sex. I can tell you that much." Although I can't keep my damn hands off this woman.

"But it's dangerous," she adds.

A fist clenches in my gut.

"I don't keep feelings locked up in a box. My emotions are big, and they bleed into everything. And I don't want to fall in the deep end when I know there will be no one around to pull me out."

I digest that metaphor. Does *the deep end* mean love?

Fuck.

I want to tell her I won't hurt her. But she's right. Someone wants me dead. I don't know if I'll live through the week. And even if I do, Hannah and I are worlds apart. She's color and light and delicate flowers.

I'm darkness.

Death.

Destruction.

I live and breathe in a den of sin.

I have zero to offer her.

In fact, my continued presence in her life is only a grave danger to her.

As soon as I stop pretending I believe she's actually a problem for me, I should walk.

Walk away and never look back.

If I had any decency, I'd do it right now.

But I don't. I grip her face and claim her mouth like she just professed her love to me. Which, in a way, she did.

"We're both in the deep end, Flowers," I tell her when we break apart.

I've never been in so deep.

She bleeds.... I bleed.

# CHAPTER TWENTY-SEVEN

*Hannah*

Armando's phone rings in the middle of the night. The way he rips out of bed on a gasp tells me he's used to waking up fighting. Another sharp inhale through his nose, and the light from his phone comes on. His expression is hard. Warrior-like. "Yeah?"

I hear a clipped male voice on the other line, the tone just as sharp as Armando's. I hear the words *shot up* and *cops*.

Armando swears and starts pulling on his clothes like he's going to battle. "'Kay. I'm coming down... No, I'll Uber... Yeah."

I turn on the bedside lamp and climb out of bed, too. My heart pounds, even though I don't know what the emergency is.

Armando ends the call and buttons his pants, then slides the phone in his pocket.

"What's the matter? Who was that?" I ask. Maybe I'm being too forward, but he is in my apartment and in *my bed*. I think I've earned the right.

He turns to look at me. His face is hard. Unforgiving. His expression is lethal.

"I need to leave." His eyes dart around the room. "You're going to have to stay—"

"Don't even think about tying me up." I'm proud of myself for keeping my voice low and threatening, instead of hysterical, like last time.

He *is* thinking about it. I can tell because he doesn't move. He's still standing there, looking at me.

"Don't. Armando, when are you going to trust me? I'm not going anywhere. I'm just going back to sleep."

He yanks open my drawer and pulls out a pair of my tights again. "I don't trust you, okay? *I don't. Trust.* Believe me when I say tying you up is better than what I'd have to do to just leave my message and walk away. There'd be no coming back from that."

His words sting. He can *fuck* me but not *trust* me.

"You won't come back from tying me up again either," I warn. I look around for a weapon. When I don't see a good one, I pick up the lamp. "I will fight you." I lift it up like I'm going to bash him with it. I probably couldn't bring myself to use it, especially because after seeing him fight in my shop, I know my chances of winning any battle with him are miniscule. And I'd probably get hurt— *ah.*

I remember his weak spot. "You'd have to hurt me." That would bother him. It's against his personal code.

Nothing changes in his face, and yet I somehow know I've won because he moves again, dropping the tights into the drawer and looking around for his keys. "Put the lamp down. Get in that bed." It's a sharp command.

I don't move.

His phone rings again. He looks at the screen, expression grim. "This is Armando....Yes, sir. Yeah, I already heard... No, I'm not in the vicinity, but I can be there in twenty minutes.... Okay, I'm coming now."

When he hangs up, he points a finger at me. "In the bed before I change my mind. I'm taking your phone and your iPad. If you open that front door, I will know, and there will be hell to pay when I get back. I'm saying this for your safety. *Capisce?*"

My heart pounds, but my ridiculous body is turned on by his bossiness. I climb in the bed, pleased with myself for successfully negotiating my freedom. If you count the sovereignty of my hands as freedom.

"What happened?" I ask, even though I know he won't tell me.

"Go back to sleep, Flowers."

"You can take the van," I offer. "Or I could drive you."

"I'm fine." His statement is firm, and I know there is no arguing. "What happens in my *life* can't involve you. Period."

I roll my eyes and wait, sitting up in bed, watching him leave. He starts out the door then comes back in, looking at me.

"Hey, listen…"

I wait.

"If I'm not back by morning, you can leave. Keep your mouth shut and go about your business like you never knew me. Okay?"

I stare at him, ice sluicing through my veins.

When I don't respond, he adds, "I mean it, Hannah. You never knew me. Never saw me. Nothing. Got it?"

He thinks there's a chance he might not come back. What does that mean? That he'll be dead? Or back in prison?

What in the hell is happening?

I'm suddenly terrified for him, but there's nothing to be said or done because he's already gone.

I sit in the lamp-light for a long time, my heart pounding for him. *Armando. Shit!*

Why does it feel like life or death for me, too? I don't want to care this much. He's not my boyfriend. He's not even a friend. He's not anything. And yet I'm already fully invested. Same as ever—falling too fast. Too hard. Too intensely.

But knowing that doesn't change this crashing sensation all around me. Armando is mixed up in something bad. And I really don't want him to die.

But this is my reality if there is to be anything with this man. He's in the mafia. I know this. I can't ignore this. He is who he is, and I'm just a girl who owns a flower shop.

There's a wall built around him made from bricks of traditions, rules, dictates from people more powerful than he. It's a den of sins he lives in, and no matter how much I'm enjoying this little game of playing house with him, I need to remember my reality.

What if he doesn't come back?

What if he *does* come back?

# CHAPTER TWENTY-EIGHT

*Armando*

Mother. *Fucker.*

My whole body's ice cold as I get out of the Uber in front of my apartment building. Four squad cars and an ambulance block the road, lights flashing. Cops crawl all over the place. I hold my hands in the air as I approach.

"I'm Armando Rossi, the guy whose apartment was shot up," I tell the first cop who spots me.

"All right." He speaks into his comm unit. "I've got the victim down here." He listens to the answer. "Yeah, I'll bring him up." He eyes me suspiciously. "You have any weapons on you?"

I keep my hands in the air. "No, sir."

He pats me down to be sure then says, "Come with me."

On my floor, I see Marco standing with an officer. His apartment is two flights up, next door to Leo's. I hope to God their places weren't involved in this shit too.

He lifts his chin at me. We pass the apartment manager, who points and snarls, "I want you out of this place by tomorrow. I never should've let a felon rent here."

"He stays," Marco's firm but raised voice cuts across the low conversations going on, making everyone look.

I ignore them both. I'm dead again. I taste ash on my tongue. My movements are mechanical. I see in shades of dark grey. Everything closes around me like the metal bars of my cell back in Joliet. I could easily kill or be killed right now without a single emotion.

A police officer meets me at my door. "You Armando Rossi?"

"Yes, sir."

He looks at the officer who brought me up. "Has he been patted down?"

"Yes, sir, he's clean."

"Can I see some ID?"

I produce my wallet and the ID card I got last week, since my license has been revoked. He pulls out a notepad and pencil and copies down my information. "Can you tell me what happened here?"

I shake my head. "No, sir. I was away."

"What do you think happened?" he snaps, obviously irritated by me. He's already made some judgement about me, and I'm sure it wasn't generous.

"I think..." I look around at my apartment. There are bullet holes in every wall. The glass in the artwork Marco had hung is shattered, covering the floors. The flat screen is busted all to hell. A giant spider web of cracks run through the window that overlooks the street, but the glass hasn't fallen in or out.

*Yet.*

Fluff from the sofa pushes from the upholstery. Marco already told me what he heard and saw, so it's easy to picture it. Some guys busted in and fired hundreds of rounds from a semi-automatic weapon into my place. "I think someone wants me dead."

"Who?"

I shake my head immediately. "No idea."

He narrows his eyes. "Who would you guess?"

I shrug. "No idea."

"Landlord said you're just out of prison."

I should say, *yes, sir,* but I'm suddenly done with the fucking conversation. I want everybody the hell out. I need to talk to Marco and Leo.

So I stare the asshole down. It wasn't technically a question, so I'm not going to deign to answer.

I clear my throat. "Can I look around?"

The cop narrows his eyes at me again. "You have anything worth stealing here?"

"No." I drop the *sir.* Like I said, I'm done.

He tucks his notebook and pencil back in his pocket. "Yeah. Look around, let me know if anything's missing."

I head into the bedroom. It looks just as bad as the living room. Bullet holes in the doors, the headboard. Feathers from the pillows strewn about the room. They probably started here. When they realized I wasn't home, they shot the place up anyway.

It's a message. They're coming for me.

This feels more like The Hermanos than the hit on Friday did.

I did stash some of that start-up cash the don gave me in the apartment, but I don't want to check with the cops here. I don't need to explain where I got seven large—what's left of the money after helping my ma and Hannah out. Marco wouldn't take any money for the deposit and rent he paid on this place nor for the furnishings he bought to fill it.

We stand around with our thumbs up our asses for another forty minutes before the boys in blue finally pack it up and leave. The landlord is still standing outside, waiting to confront me. Marco walks over to stand by my side.

"Listen," he says, spreading his hands in a conciliatory fashion. "I just can't have your type around here. My residents need to feel safe, and what happened tonight is going to kill my business."

There's a time I would've given shit back to him. I'm pretty fucking alpha dog, and I don't let anyone push me around. But at this moment, I just can't bring myself to give two fucks. I don't care if I stay in this apartment building or go. It's not like I've spent any time here to begin with since meeting Hannah.

I'm not even angry about what happened. There's no sense of vengeance ringing through me. No desire for retribution.

I'm just fucking dead again.

And that's really the only thing I find disturbing.

But then again, who gives a fuck? Because it's sort of an out-of-body experience.

But Marco, he gives all the fucks right now. He steps into the landlord's personal space, not touching, but getting right in his grill. "No, what would kill your business, friend, would be getting on the wrong side of the Pachino family. My cousin stays. I stay. My brother stays. And if you hassle any one of us again, I will fucking take this business down, along with you and everyone you care about." Marco steps back. "Believe it, old man."

The landlord believes it. He believes it so bad, his face turns white, and his goddamn teeth start chattering. And Leo, with impeccable timing, picks that moment to show up, his bulky mass adding to the threat.

"Now get out of our faces."

The landlord bolts.

Marco and Leo wait until he's gone before they push into my apartment. Marco's in his white undershirt and a pair of slacks, like he yanked them on when it happened. Leo looks like he took more time to get dressed. "Definitely the Hermanos," Marco says. "I saw the fuckers running to a car on the street. They wore ski masks and carried semis. I heard a cop say they shot out the cameras out front and the glass door. Then they just rode the fucking elevator up here and shot up your place. Did you tell Don G?"

"Not yet." I side-eye Leo because while he's also like a brother to me, the fewer people who know my shit, the better.

He produces a gun from his back waistband and ammo from his pocket. "I know you're not allowed to keep a gun but seems like you'd be safer with a piece on you at all times right now."

Maybe my soul hasn't completely shriveled because a thread of gratitude twirls through me. My family takes care of me. Through thick and thin.

I take the pistol and tuck it in the back waistband of my pants. "Yeah, thanks."

"I'm worried about your ma," Marco says. "If they didn't find you here, you think they'd look at her place for you?"

I scrub a hand across my face. "I had the same thought. I'll see if I can send her on a vacay."

I stalk to the bedroom to look for my cash under the bathroom sink. It's all still there. But I'm not surprised. This wasn't a robbery.

They were out for blood, for sure. And after making as much noise as they did, they had to get the fuck out fast. Frankly, I'm surprised they risked it in an apartment building like this one.

I pull a duffle bag out of the closet and start throwing my clothes and shoes and toiletries in it. Hannah's apartment is still the safest place for me. My instinct to stay there was dead on. But Marco's right, my mom could be in danger. And that thought does make me feel. I'd do anything for my mom. Growing up, it was just the two of us, and I'd kill or die for her in a second.

"I'll get my crew over here to clean shit up tomorrow," Marco offers.

"Thanks."

"What else can I do?"

"Nothing. I already owe you. I don't like being so out of balance with you, man." I give him one of those dude handshake hugs and thump him on the back.

He pulls back and meets my gaze. He's got light green eyes the color of cash. Total lady killer. "You'd do it for me." His expression is dead serious like he's swearing a vow.

I realize then that he's not just taking care of family. And it's not just pity. He feels guilty I got caught. I took the fall, and he didn't. Leo didn't. The rest of our crew that ran the car heist operation didn't. I just had the shit luck of getting pinched. And it goes without saying, I kept my mouth glued shut.

I want to say something to let him off the hook. Because it's the same story—he would've done the same thing in my shoes. Maybe he's eaten up because of how far I fell. I was at the top of my game then. I thought I was in love. Engaged to a beautiful woman. Making money hand over fist. I'd gained recognition and respect within the organization. I led my own crew—Marco and Leo worked for me. I was poised to become a leader and move up through the ranks as the older generation retired.

And then my fence got pinched, and I showed up at his garage driving a brand-new, stolen Mercedes Benz at the wrong time. I got out and ran, but they cornered me, and it was done. All I could do was ride it out. Serve my sentence and restart.

Since words are no longer my thing, I choke on any sentiment and settle for a fist bump. I bump Leo, too. "You still have a key to my place, right?"

"Yeah, we got it. You wanna stay at my place tonight?" Marco asks.

"Nah. I got a place." I pick up my duffel bag and head for the door.

Marco gives me a searching look but doesn't ask where I'm sleeping. In our line of business, the less you know, the safer you are. I know Marco and Leo would never roll over on me, but I wouldn't want them to be in the position of keeping secrets for me. They already keep enough.

"Lie low, then."

"Yeah. I will. Thanks again." I touch the pistol at my back and nod at Leo.

"Wait, no fucking way am I going to just let you walk out that door without some eyes. Especially if there is a girl in the picture now," Leo says.

"I got it under control," I say.

"Leo's right," Marco says. "At least let us put a man on guard. Back up just in case."

I open my mouth to argue but then think of Hannah. Though I'm trying to lay low, there is a chance whoever wants me dead now knows about her. If not for me, then I should most certainly make sure there are always eyes on her. Nodding, I say, "Yeah, not a bad idea. I want Hannah safe."

"So she has a name," Leo says with a smirk.

I walk over to the disaster of a kitchen and find a notepad and pen in the drawer. I jot down the address to her apartment and to the Garden of Eden and hand it to Leo.

He looks at the address. "That florist next to Rocco's?"

I nod again. "I'll text you the info on her friend and staff person who works there as well. I'd like to make sure she's kept safe during this. I don't want her caught in the crossfire."

Marco looks over Leo's shoulder at the note, and adds, "Consider it done."

"We'll figure out who's responsible and put an end to it. Guaranteed," Leo promises.

My younger cousin became a man while I was away. I see a maturity in Leo that didn't exist before I went to prison.

A million small things changed while I was away. The changes seem subtle, yet it's enough to feel like an entirely different world.

Or maybe it's just me who is entirely different.

And if I want to live to see next week, I'd better figure my shit out, fast.

What's going on. What to do about it.

Who I can trust.

Who do I have to kill to stop the hits from coming my way.

And yet, it's still hard to get interested in solving my problems.

The only thing that remotely interests me right now is Hannah. I want to be sleeping in her bed right now.

I'm a greedy bastard.

I know I should leave her alone. I should stay the fuck away from her, especially considering the danger I bring to anyone around me.

But I can't.

She's my lifeline.

The only road lit up is the one to her right now.

The only path I see to get home.

# CHAPTER TWENTY-NINE

*Hannah*

I stare down at Armando's sleeping form in my bed. He came in close to dawn and has been crashed ever since. He's sprawled on his back, the sheet tangled around his waist. His lean, sculpted muscles make him appear dangerous even in sleep. Shadow is curled up and purring against his waist, an unlikely bed partner.

I don't see any blood, scrapes, or bruises on him, and it makes me think that this could become my new normal—scanning his body for damage. If Armando and I continue with whatever it is this is, him leaving in the middle of the night, and me wondering if he's going to make it home unscathed, this will be our life.

But can I handle it?

Can I handle *him*?

When he came in and crawled up behind me, I pretended to be asleep. I didn't know what to say or do. It's not like I could ask him how his day at work went. I couldn't tell him I spent the night on the verge of puking and crying. I was terrified of what could happen to him, and what would happen if he never walked back through that door. But as he spooned his warm body up against mine, wrapping his heavy arm around my frame, I felt safe. In fact, I never felt safer. The feeling he gave me that very second made it all worth it. It made *him* worth it.

I debate whether to wake him or let him sleep. I have to get to the shop. I don't know why I feel like I need to ask his permission to leave. Just because he considers me a prisoner doesn't mean I am.

Except I like being his prisoner. That's the foolish truth. I don't actually want him to set me free and walk away. Because I'm already falling hard for this guy. Just like I always do when I start sleeping with someone.

I don't know how to contain my emotions. How to hold them back. I love big, and it's always messy. It always scares the guy away.

Maybe that's why being a prisoner appeals to me. Armando won't scare off. He's forcing himself on me, not the other way around. I can't really screw this up because there's nothing to screw. It's not a relationship. I didn't choose it. I can't even un-choose it other than refusing to have sex with him—which I epically fail at doing.

And why would I do that? It's the best part of this situation. Although it's not just the sex I enjoy. I love the excitement. The edge of danger offset by a level of trust. Also, I like how he takes care of me in micro ways—like buying me food and taking out the trash. Cleaning up after meals. My life seems a little more manageable with someone looking out for me. Contributing. I'm so used to being the one worrying about everyone else, it's nice to have someone paying attention to me for a change.

I touch his hard biceps. "Armando?"

He sucks in a sharp breath, sitting bolt upright with a gun in his hand... aimed at me.

I yelp in surprise and freeze. I don't even know where the pistol came from—I have to replay the scene to realize he pulled it out from under his pillow.

*My* pillow. Where there definitely wasn't a gun before.

He blinks, lowers the gun. Says nothing.

"Jesus, Armando," I let out on a shaky breath. When he still doesn't speak, I say, "Listen, I have to go to the shop. It's cool for you to stay here and slee—"

But he's already up, swinging his legs over the side of the bed and sending Shadow leaping to the floor and arching his little back.

"You don't have to come. I think we've established now that I'm not going to talk, right? So I just need my phone, and I'll get out of here. You're welcome to stay."

Armando ignores me, pulling on a t-shirt he produces from a duffel bag under my bed.

Okay. So I guess he's moving in.

It shouldn't make me happy, but it sort of does.

He dresses in seconds, strapping the gun to his leg before he pulls his pants on. He produces my purse and phone and the keys to the van —this time from the oven. He still hasn't said a word when we walk out my front door.

When we get down to the sidewalk, Armando lifts his chin in the direction of the Starbucks on the corner. "You eat?" His voice is gruff and gravelly from sleep. Grumpy, even.

I don't know why I find it sexy.

"No." I'm sort of an erratic eater. I stress-eat at night but usually get too busy and behind for regular meals. Too bad missing meals hasn't resulted in a Hollywood figure. But screw Hollywood. I'm curvy in all the right places. A fact that Armando seems to enjoy with abandon.

He cuts into the Starbucks and pulls out his wallet. His eyes are dead this morning. I've seen them dead like this before, but there's a particular lights-out quality to them today. Or maybe it's the empath in me picking up on the complete lack of emotion on him.

I keep thinking about that gun he pointed at me this morning. The menace on his face before he saw it was me. I felt emotion from him then —it was deadly. Like a trapped animal about to kill for his freedom. What kind of life has he led that makes him wake up and point a gun first thing? What happened last night? I want to ask, but I know he won't answer.

Armando orders an egg sandwich and double espresso and turns to me. I order oatmeal and a latte. He pays again.

It's stupid—it's not that much money, but I like being out with Armando. Having him buy my meals and groceries. I like his take-chargeness. The way he didn't ask or discuss fixing the van with me, he just took it to a shop and got it done.

It might annoy some women, but I find it hot.

There's a sexy daddy element to him, and though I never knew that kink to be my jam, I'm starting to realize it is.

We take the food to go, and Armando drives again. I appreciate that, too. I don't care if it's my van, I hate driving in the city. I like someone else being in charge. I can simply eat my oatmeal, sip my latte, and stare out the window without a care in the world—if only momentarily.

He's still completely non-communicative, and I don't attempt conversation. I know lots of people who don't like to talk in the morning, even if they did get adequate sleep and weren't dealing with some kind of crisis all night. I'll wait until he warms up again.

At my shop, we enter through the back door. Armando stalks through the place and opens the blinds on the front windows. Then turns around my open sign with the hours.

"What the fuck, Hannah?" he snarls.

I freeze. The menace is back—I sense it all the way across the room and it scares me. "What?"

He points at the sign. "You're not supposed to be open on Sundays. What in the hell are you trying to pull?" He turns sideways, looking up and down the sidewalk through the front window.

Christ. Does he think I set him up? Like the cops are going to show up and bust him now? Or whoever's trying to kill him?

# CHAPTER THIRTY

*Hannah*

I march over to him, partly to conquer my own visceral fear of him in this state and partly because I'm pissed that he doesn't trust me. And pissed he scared me. "In case you didn't notice, Armando, I can't pay my rent. I have to stay open every minute I can, and that means working Sundays, too. I work *every* day. *Every* hour. It's the only way I can survive."

He blinks at me, some of the hardness in his expression falling away.

I stare back. "Don't yell at me like that again. You're scary when you're mean."

I expect him to be sorry. I want him to call me *baby girl*, pet my hair, hold me close, and promise to never be scary again, but instead he scowls. "Yeah, you should be scared of me, Flowers."

Offense cuts swift and deep, straight through my chest. I thrust my chin up. "That right? Well why don't you just say it then? Say whatever it is we're not coming back from. Make your threats and be done with it. Then you can leave. It would be a whole lot easier for both of us."

He stands there a minute, conflict dancing over his face. I swear the room spins around us, like in those movies. And then his hand snaps out and captures the back of my head. His lips crash over mine. It's a juicy, lusty kiss because I give it right back.

This is what we do best. Our relationship may be a sham, communication is a joke, but we know this dance. I assume that's why he went for it. Just like I kissed him that first time when he was wondering what to do with me.

Do this.

This is what we do.

He breaks the kiss but doesn't release my head. "Is that what you want, Hannah? You want me to go?" Misery seeps out of him. A hint of desperation. He's holding my gaze like my answer will make the moon orbit.

"No," I admit. That's the last thing I want.

He pulls my mouth to his again and consumes me in a searing kiss. I kiss him back, my lips opening and closing against his, tugging on his.

"I'm sorry," he croaks when our lips part. "Someone shot up my place last night, and I'm paranoid as shit right now. I shouldn't have yelled. Especially at you."

My eyes round even though I suspected it was something awful like that.

"I *don't* want you scared." He shifts the hand behind my head to cradle the side of my face and runs his thumb across my lower lip. "I want these kisses like it's the end of the world. Fucking you like our lives depend on it."

A wave of heat crashes through me.

"You're the only thing keeping me sane right now. I'm on the verge of losing my fucking mind. But it's you holding the key to my sanity, Hannah. You."

I freaking love the way he rasps my name. I initiate the kiss this time, pressing my breasts against his hard muscles. "Like our lives depend on it, huh?" I murmur when I come up for air.

He pushes me back against glass doors and closes the shades again. His hands are everywhere, stroking down my sides, squeezing my ass. I lift one leg to wrap around his waist, and when he shifts to put his forearm under my butt, the other one wraps too. He presses me against the window, knocking the blinds to thrust the bulge of his cock between my legs.

He dances his lips across my collarbone, and then stops to find my ear with his teeth, catching me with a shorter, sharper nip than before. I feel it all the way to my core. His voice is low and throaty, his words sending a sexy vibration through my ear. "You're so fucking gorgeous. And kissable. And fuckable. I want to bend you over right here, right now. I want to shove you up against this window and fuck you until you scream."

I'm too breathless to answer. I can't think of anything to say. "Do it, now, I need you."

His hand moves from my ass to my hip, and then around to my stomach, his fingertips pressing hard into my skin. "I want to watch you come from behind. I want to watch your sweet little pussy take my cock. I want to fuck you for hours."

"I want it," I tell him, my throat feeling tight and dry. I want it, but I don't want it to end. I want to stay here. I want to stay in this moment forever.

He kisses me again, and it's not gentle this time but urgent, and then he spins and carries me behind the counter to my desk. My ass touches down on the surface. The coolness shocking me back to reality.

Reality.

We're in the shop. My business. Reality.

"Wait," I pant. "We can't keep doing this."

It's too much. He's too much. I'm definitely feeling way too much.

He stiffens. Pulls back. I register the loss of his touch like a shock of cold water. "Yeah."

I'm immediately sorry for putting on the brakes. I reach for him. "Wait."

He steps back between my legs and strokes his palm up my bare thigh. His fingers reach the hem of my short t-shirt dress and slip under. Our foreheads touch. "Talk to me, Hannah."

Talk to him. This is the moment where I show my true colors, and he runs. But maybe that's for the best. That's what I need.

"I just..." I draw in a fortifying breath. "I don't do casual sex. I feel too much, you know? And I get attached too quickly..."

Worst thing ever to say to a guy.

But it's the truth.

"Does this feel casual to you?" Armando's voice sounds scratchy.

"No," I admit.

He picks up a swath of my hair and winds it around his fist, staring at the bleached curls mixing with the dark ones. "It doesn't feel casual to me. It feels desperate and life-giving. Like a starving baby's first pull of milk."

Oh, God. My heart tumbles. I freaking love knowing I'm giving him something he can't find anywhere else. Maybe even changing him. It brings significance to our dance. To who I am and what my life means. I lift my lips for a kiss, but he pulls back a half an inch and leaves me hanging.

"But if you need a breath, I'll step back. I don't force women."

Swoon. "Don't forget..." I breathe, looking up at him from under my lashes. "I like to be forced."

His sharp intake of breath is everything.

So is the way he slowly captures my wrist and tugs me off the desk then turns me around and bends me over. He pins my arm behind my back and slaps my ass. "So you do." His voice has that froggy sound again. He slowly takes my other wrist and twists it behind my back as well. My face presses against the smooth surface of the desk, the scent of ink and paper mingles with his masculine scent. He tugs up the hem of my dress, pushing the fabric up over the mounds of my ass. Then he peels down my panties just enough to stroke a hand over my ass. "You sore from that spanking I gave you before?"

My pussy contracts at the mention of what he did to me. Or maybe it's clenching at what he's doing now. I shake my head.

"You took it like a good girl, didn't you?"

Oh God.

So hot.

He slaps one cheek, catching the underside and making it reverberate right in my core. He strokes his hand over the sting. "Yeah, keep pushing me, Flowers, because I'm always gonna want to spank this ass pink."

I waggle my ass back and forth to tempt him again, and he spanks me. Rubs away the sting. "You are the hottest woman I've ever been with. By far." He spanks me again.

I close my eyes, soaking in both the sensations and his words. He doesn't usually talk much, so his verbal expression now is a balm to my frayed nerves.

"And I like how much you feel." He smacks a little harder. "I like you attached." Another slap. "Because the only time I feel anything is when I'm with you."

Tears sting my eyes. For once, it seems like the guy I'm falling for is on the same page as me. It's a freaking miracle.

"Oh, fuck," he growls, his mouth on my neck. "You like when Daddy punishes you?" He spanks my ass again, and I mewl as I press against his palm.

He lifts me a little, and the rough fabric of his pants scrapes over the heated and ready flesh of my ass. I shudder, my hips rising to meet his touch.

"Y-Yes. I want it. I want it... *Daddy*." The word feels so fucking right rolling off my tongue.

"What do you want, Flowers?" he growls, his lips traveling up my neck to kiss me. "Tell me what you want."

"I want you to fuck me," I whisper, panting. "I want you to fuck me here, with my ass in the air and your cock inside me."

His hand grinds against my clit, and I whimper, my brain floating in a hazy sea of pleasure that's so much more intense than anything I've ever felt.

He presses a finger inside me. I'm so wet that it slides in easily, and my knees almost buckle. He slides in a second one and starts to stroke in and out while the tip of his thumb grinds over my aching clit.

I press my face against the desk, and my muffled cries of need echo in the room. The cool wood is against my cheek and his lips are on my back, whispering filthy things that go straight to my head.

"I'm going to fuck you like this, baby," he growls in my ear. "I'm going to make you come so hard with my cock in your sweet little pussy. But first, there's something you're going to do for me."

He slides his fingers out of me, and I whimper at the empty feeling.

He pulls the desk chair up behind him and sinks into it, freeing his erection. I turn to face him and drop to my knees. His gaze turns intent. Tortured, even. I totally owe him oral after how many times he's given me intense pleasure. He's always in charge, and I'm... well, I've been his prisoner. A role I seem to love.

But I want him to order me to suck him off. I want him to guide my head with my hair, commanding every move. I want to suck his dick because he demands it.

As if reading my mind, he says, "Put those lips of yours around my cock."

I wrap my hand around the base of his cock and swirl my tongue around the head. His erection juts out, suddenly thickening and lengthening in my hand.

"Oh fuck." he mutters, nostrils flaring, breath coming in sharply.

He fists my hair and tugs my head back, so my eyes lock with his. Heat floods between my legs. I'm turned on by the power I have over him and how much he has over me. I'm excited by how much pleasure I'm going to give him.

I hold his gaze as I slowly tighten my lips around his head and sink them lower.

His groan sounds pained. "Aw, Hannah." His fingers tangle in my hair and ball into a fist. "You—" he chokes as he pulls my head forward to take him in again.

It's another show of sexual domination. If you'd asked me before if I'd like it, I would've said no fricking way, but I do. Even as I'm slightly offended by the seeming lack of gratitude, by having my mouth used like nothing more than a fuck-hole, my pussy runs with arousal, my tightened nipples tingle, and I swirl my tongue around the underside of his cock with enthusiasm.

"Good girl, Hannah," he chants. "That's so fucking good. You're such a good girl." It's the third time he's called me *good girl*. Again, low-key offensive but so hot. His fist is tighter in my hair, pulling me over his length faster. I suck hard and use my hand to milk him, doing my best to give him pleasure.

His hips roll, and his cock slaps against my tongue. I wrap my lips around him and draw him into my mouth, my cheeks so hollowed his strokes slide with a wet sound from my lips to his balls. He's breathing faster, and I feel his biceps tense. I know he's close. I want to make him come.

I want the saltiness in my mouth.

His cock hardens and twitches. He groans and thrusts deeper, and I take him as greedily as I can.

I flex my hand around his length and massage the underside of his head with my tongue. His hand tightens in my hair, and I take him even deeper into my mouth, using my hand to stroke his length the way I know he likes.

He's still so hard it's almost impossible to fit him entirely in my mouth, and my jaw aches as I try to suck him.

I'm swallowing him; sucking him down as fast as I can. Fighting the gag reflex, my eyes water as I feel his cock swelling to an impossible size. He's getting ready to come, and when he does, I want it to be in my mouth. I want to taste him. I want to feel him shooting his cum on my tongue. I want to swallow him.

I start to run my tongue up and down his shaft and he tenses.

"Oh," he gasps. "Shit." He pulls me off, panting as he stares down at me with glassy eyes. "I wanted that to go on forever, but I wasn't gonna last." He shoves his hand in his pocket and pulls out a condom. "Climb on, Flowers. I'll give you a ride." His voice is a deep, sexy rumble. His dirty talk is on point today.

I ditch the panties still tangled around my thighs and straddle his waist while he rolls on the rubber.

"Oh God." A shudder of pleasure runs through him when I lower onto his dick. "Hannah. You're a fucking goddess. The flower goddess. Is there one?"

I've never heard this many unnecessary words come out of him. Something freed his tongue, and I absolutely love it. He palms my ass and controls my movements, even though he's on bottom. I take him deep when he thrusts up to meet me at the same time he yanks me in.

He kneads my ass. "I fucking love this ass, Hannah. It's so hot." He's losing his breath, sounding winded. I love watching his control slip. "Fucking flower goddess. Or wood nymph. You're like that fairy on your shoulder... but so much more. You're *carnal.*" His fingers dig into my flesh. I'm seconds away from orgasming.

So is he, judging from the intensity of his thrusts, his gritted teeth and the wild look in his eyes. He bounces me over him, my legs dangling around his hips, my hair falling over the right side of my face.

"You're beautiful, so beautiful." He peers through heavy lids. "Are you close?" He adjusts his hands to bring his thumb to my clit.

"Yes! I'm ready!" I gasp. I'm past ready because the moment he rubs my clit, I go off, my muscles spasming around his cock.

"Oh *fuck,*" he roars, forgetting my clit to grab my hips and yank me up and down over his cock.

He comes, lifting us both into the air as he thrusts so deep in me he leaves the chair. He puts the edge of my butt on the desk and pounds into me as he comes and comes.

I fall back on my elbows, panting, watching the guy who was made of stone this morning come unglued.

In the best possible way.

"*Cristo,*" he mutters when he opens his eyes and takes me in. He loops his arm behind my back and pulls me up against his chest. "Are you good?"

"Yes." I bite his chest and squeeze his cock with my core. I let out a breathy laugh. And then I'm suddenly crying.

Not sad tears—just a release. But I hate when I do this.

Armando's arm tightens around me. I expect him to freak out, thinking he hurt me or something. Or worse, to pull way back because I got too intense. That's what usually happens. This is usually where the guy freaks out and bails.

He doesn't say a word, though. Doesn't ask me what's wrong. Just holds me against his rock-solid chest and lets me cry into his shirt.

When it finally passes, he eases away and wipes my tears with his thumbs. "I fucking love your tears," he murmurs.

"What?"

He shakes his head. "Ugh, that sounded wrong. I didn't mean it like that."

I wait, but he doesn't elaborate. He's already distancing—doing the thing that always happens. But his words—those were different.

I catch his hand. "Say it again. What did you mean?"

He cradles the side of my face with his calloused palm. "You're okay, right? That was just... you? Or did I fuck up again?"

The *again* makes my stomach twist. In a good sort of way. Because he cares about screwing up with me.

I shake my head. "Yeah, just me being... too much. As usual." I say it in a defeated tone, not because he's made me feel defeated but from the accumulation of a lifetime of feeling everything too much.

He lowers his head to catch my eyes. "Nah. Not too much. I fucking loved it. You're like... some wild mythical creature—" he stops, looking up like he's searching for words. "I don't want to say *unicorn* because that's dumb. But something like that."

My heart spills over, coming out my mouth, filling my chest. A couple fresh tears come out of my eyes. Armando thumbs them away again.

"I don't know, Flowers. You're wide open. You take it all. You just fucking *receive* from me. And I think it's beautiful. And if I'm supposed to say *sorry* now, I will. But it would be a lie because I love seeing you crack apart and bleed your essence all over the place then gather it up and start over again."

I stare into Armando's hazel eyes, drinking up his praise. Expanding. Expanding into myself. Who I really am. The person I am with Armando—that's the real me. I'm more myself with him than anyone else. Possibly even including myself. He celebrates the parts of me I don't even like.

And knowing that, believing that he thinks I'm special, changes me. Makes me stronger. More whole.

He glances around the shop and smirks. "Something about the Garden of Eden. It makes me want to sin. Over and over." He kisses me. "And over again."

# CHAPTER THIRTY-ONE

*Armando*

Coming down from post-orgasmic euphoria, I decide it's time to discuss something that's been weighing heavy on me since I woke up.

I lean my forehead against Hannah's. "Am I bad for you? Do you want me to go? Honestly?"

She rolls her head against mine in a negative. "No," she whispers. "I never wanted you to go. This is what I was afraid of—what I was trying to avoid. But it's already here."

"It's already here," I repeat. I understand logically, but I have no idea what she feels. I'm empty, and she's too full. Maybe that's why we fit. What works for us.

There's no comprehending Hannah because she's so different from me and the people I've known. That's why she seems mythical. Her capacity for acceptance is monumental.

I stroke her unruly curls then scrunch them when I find them not so strokable. They were made for fisting, for sure. "So, am I forgiven? I'm sorry I was a dick."

She lets out a puff of air like a laugh. "We're good."

I ease out of her and dispose of the condom in the trash beside the desk. "What can I do around here to help?" I put my dick away and zip up my pants. Retrieve her panties from the floor and squat down to thread them over her ankles.

"Um..." She looks afraid to ask me something.

"Yeah? What? Name it, Flowers."

"Wanna help me clean out the cooler? That's what I usually do on Sundays before I open."

"I'll clean it. You do whatever else you need to do."

Her face lights with guilty surprise. She drops off the desk and pulls her panties up. "Really? It's kind of a shitty job although it will be easier for you because you're strong."

I scrunch up my forehead, trying to figure out what takes strength.

"You have to move all the heavy buckets of flowers around to mop up underneath. I usually end up slopping so much water around I get drenched. In the winter, I take my pants off before I go in, so they don't get soaked."

My dick sprouts a semi. "Making a note. Be here on Sundays in the winter."

Her smile is a sweet reward. Hell, I'd clean out a room full of dogshit for that smile.

I already know where her cleaning supplies are since I had to bleach the hell out of her floor. I pull them out and head into the cooler and move all the buckets of flowers to the hallway to sweep and mop.

I'm at it for a while before I realize something: I'm awake. Alive. That hollow-man deadness that settled in hard last night has dissipated. In fact, my whole body's buzzing. Not just that, but there's something there I haven't felt in years.

A thread of happiness.

I'm one week out of the pen with a gang trying to kill me, and I'm buzzing with a newfound contentment.

Hannah makes me happy. That's the only explanation for it. I like being around her. Things make more sense when she's around. And of course, the sex is off the charts good.

I hear a scream from the kitchenette, and all that happiness flips to furious purpose.

*No one fucks with my girl.*

Gun drawn and pointed, I'm there in a flash, readying to fucking kill whoever's in there. Ready to give up my life if it will save hers.

I whip around the corner and skid to a stop, pointing the gun right and left.

Um...

No one's in there with her. She's frozen in the middle of the tiny break room, her eyes wide and terrified.

Because of me. The gun.

I quickly lower it. "You screamed."

She lets out a shaky laugh and points toward the floor in the corner. "There's a mouse."

"A mouse." I will my heartbeat to slow. Try to take the death grip off the pistol. I flip it to the side and cock my head. "Want me to shoot it?" I deadpan.

She smiles at me and walks forward until her soft breasts press against my ribs. "A joke. I think that was your first."

Was it?

Damn.

I *am* coming back to life.

"You looked really scary when you came in here." She purrs it like it turned her on.

I shove the pistol in the back of my waistband and loop an arm around her. "I wondered."

"What?"

"What made you kiss me that first time? You like the tough guy?"

"I like *you*," she confesses, her hands sliding up my pecs. "I always did."

"Yeah?" That surprises me. I remember her from before, but she was young. And off-limits. Plus, I was engaged. I thought she was cute but didn't pay much more attention. Now I marvel at how much I missed. I wanna go back in time and review all my visits to the shop to put her in full focus.

"And, yes, I like that you're dangerous. It's a total turn-on."

"You're something, Flowers." I stroke her cheek with my thumb.

She backs up. "So can you be dangerous to my mice?"

I chuckle. "Yeah, sure. You got traps?"

"Um, yes. I bought some, but I couldn't bring myself to use them because I can't face cleaning up dead mice. Same reason I haven't used poison."

My lips twitch. Holy shit. I may actually smile. Didn't know my mouth remembered how. "So you're just putting up with the mice instead."

She nods. "Exactly."

"I'll take care of it for you, doll. I'm your guy. You won't have to worry about them again."

And as I go back to cleaning out the cooler, I notice it again: that lightness around me suddenly.

Like there's a reason to go on living.

I dare say I'm starting to feel normal again. If that's even possible.

"Hey, Flowers!" I call out from the cooler, feeling it's time to face something else I've been avoiding since getting out of prison. I thought it would be a long time until I'd be in the mood again for it, but I'm suddenly feeling now's as good a time as any.

She opens up the cooler and leans against the frame. "You rang?" Her smile is so damn big on her face. I could stare at it all day.

"It's Sunday."

She nods. "We've established that already."

"Take the day off."

"I can't. I told you—"

I reach into my wallet, pull out a hundred-dollar bill, and place it into her hand. "Take this as paid time off and come with me to church."

I need to expunge my sins. To make myself clean to be worthy of this treasure of a woman. I don't know if that shit is real, but my ma believes in it. She lights a candle for me every time she goes to mass—twice a week.

It may not be real, but it seems like a nod in that direction is warranted. For Hannah.

Her eyes widen. "Church?"

"It's Sunday. Church."

"Now?"

I nod. "Mass is already over, but the doors will be open."

She looks down at her clothing. "I need to go home and change."

I take her by the hand and lead her away from the cooler. "Trust me. After the secrets and confessions this church has heard, the last thing we'll be judged over is our clothing. Besides," I press my lips to her forehead, "you're beautiful."

"I didn't figure you for a church man."

"I used to be," I confess. "It's been a long time. But it's long overdue. Plus, I promised Father Fantoni I'd come by, and I haven't yet. I may be a sinner, but I'm a man of my word."

She gives me a soft smile. "Okay, let me go make sure we're locked in the front." She hurries to the front door and freezes with a gasp. I instantly reach for my gun but then realize it's probably just another mouse.

"Armando," she whispers, fear lacing her voice.

Pulling my gun, I rush towards her.

She points through a crack of the blinds and the door. "There's a man outside."

I release the safety, ready to defend the woman I— I see *Marco* on the other side.

Releasing the breath I'd been holding, putting away the gun, opening the door, and punching my cousin playfully in the arm, I say, "I could have shot you right there, man."

"Leo and I told you we'd have extra eyes stationed." Marco scans Hannah from head to toe, and I see approval in the devilish smile he offers.

"Why you? Not one of your men?"

Marco shrugs. "It's Sunday. Most of the men are with their families today. I have nothing better to do. Besides, if you want something done right, do it yourself."

Hannah clears her throat behind me, reminding me of my manners. "Marco, this is Hannah. Hannah, this is my cousin Marco."

She extends her hand, and with the sweetest voice says, "Nice to meet you, officially. I remember your face from you shopping on occasion in the store."

"You're the owner now, right?" Marco asks.

"Yes."

"We were just leaving. Going to St. Andrews. Care to come?" I ask him.

Marco chuckles. "If I step foot in that church, I'll be struck down. It's been so long since I've confessed that I wouldn't even know where to begin."

"Perfect," I say. "Then we can be struck down together."

Marco's eyes dart back to Hannah then to me. "Church, huh?"

"It's Sunday," I state.

"Yeah, I know what day it is." Marco smiles. "Well then, church it is." He directs his next comment to Hannah. "But I'm warning you, Hannah. Don't stand too close to us. It may not be a pretty sight if we burst into flames."

# CHAPTER THIRTY-TWO

*Hannah*

"Good girls get ice cream after church," Armando says as he leads me down the street hand in hand.

We just said our goodbyes to Marco. It took Armando practically threatening the man to leave us alone for a few hours. Armando promised that we'd head back to my apartment and stay put, so I'm confused as to why we aren't heading home.

"Growing up, my mother used to always reward me with ice cream if I was good during church service," he adds. He looks down at me and winks. "You were good."

My body lights up, feeling warm and fuzzy. We're holding hands like a couple, walking under the sunlight to go get ice cream. It's like we're on an official date. We're spending a leisurely Sunday together. Everything feels so normal and so right.

The ice cream shop is only a block away, and the minute I see it, I'm in love with the charm. The little shop is painted a pastel pink and white, with a giant ice cream cone sign hanging over the entrance. The air inside is cool and sweet, and I can hear the gentle chime of the bell above the door as we walk in.

The quaint space has a vintage feel to it, and the aroma of freshly made waffle cones hits us the moment we enter. The place is bustling with people, but we manage to find a free table in the corner. The sound of a guitar being played fills the air, and I notice a young man sitting in the corner, strumming away on his instrument.

"What's your favorite flavor?" he asks.

"Whatever you have," I answer. When it comes to ice cream, there is no such thing as a bad flavor.

Armando goes to order, leaving me to enjoy the music. As he waits in line, he turns around and waves at me, a grin spreading across his face. My heart flutters as I wave back, feeling a warm sensation in my chest. When he returns to the table, he has two cones in his hand.

"Two scoops. One is caramel chocolate, and the other is cookie dough." I see pride on his face that he's picked the best two flavors there are.

"Perfect."

We sit there, enjoying our ice cream and listening to the music. It's simple. Relaxed.

"You grow up in Chicago?" Armando asks, studying me over the top of his ice cream cone.

"Yep. Born and raised."

"Do your parents live here?"

I nod. "Yes. My mom's a nurse, and my dad works in construction."

It's crazy to have this casual conversation with Armando. Nothing about Armando and me up to this point has been simply casual. It's like we're the only two people in the world right now, and nothing else matters.

"You?"

He nods. "Born and bred. It was just my ma and me, but we're Italian, so I have a huge extended family. Twenty-some cousins. I'm closest with Marco and his brother Leo. They're like brothers to me, really. Oh, how we used to hell around." A warmth comes into his normally dead gaze. The light in his eyes makes me feel more alive than I've felt in a long time. He's actually sharing. He's opening up when I wasn't sure that was a possibility with this man.

"Thanks for this," I say when we finish our treat. "I haven't had a real day off in a long time," I admit. "And even when I tried, my mind was always so full of worry. So this is a rare day for me."

"We're going to have to fix that."

"*We?*"

He smirks. "You're stuck with me, Flowers." His face grows serious, his eyes darken. "You work too hard. You take on too much on those perfect shoulders of yours. It's time you have someone help with the heavy lifting."

I've always been an independent woman. Someone who wants to stand on my own two feet, but damn if it doesn't feel good to have a man sitting across from me... protecting and looking out for my well-being.

I finish my cone and wipe my mouth with a napkin. "Thank you," I say, not wanting the moment to end.

"Of course," he replies, taking my hand in his again. "We should do this more often."

I nod, feeling a smile spread across my face. "I'd like that."

As we leave the shop, I realize that this is the happiest I've been in a long time. I don't know what the future holds, but I know that I want him by my side. I want to hold his hand and walk under the sunlight every day. I want to listen to him talk and figure out how to make him laugh, but I also don't mind his darkness and the shadows that haunt his eyes.

I want to taste more ice cream with him and explore more charming little shops, but I also want to be there for him when the scars of his past come back or his demons conquer the day. I want to fall in love with him, and I want him to fall in love with me.

We stroll down the street, enjoying the warm breeze and each other's company. It doesn't seem like we have a destination in mind, but that doesn't matter. We're content just being together.

Suddenly, he stops in front of a small boutique. It's filled with vintage clothes and accessories. He turns to me, his eyes shining with excitement. "Let's go in."

I follow him inside, feeling like a kid in a candy store. The boutique is even more charming than the ice cream shop. The walls are covered in bright wallpaper, and the clothes on the racks are like nothing I've ever seen before. It's like stepping back in time, but also so trendy.

He starts picking out clothes for me to try on, and I can't help but laugh. He has a great sense of style, and everything he chooses would look amazing on me. As we browse through the racks, I feel a sense of closeness with him that I've never felt before. It's like we're in our own little world, and nothing can bring us down.

After trying on a few outfits due to his urging, I settle on a vintage floral dress. He pays for it without hesitation, insisting that I look beautiful in it. I'm noticing that he likes to take care of me, and I need to allow him to do it. I need to resist the urge to fight him on money and to constantly worry over every little cent.

As we leave the shop, he says, "I suppose we should head home. If Marco or one of his men get there to stand guard before we arrive, my cousin is going to kill me."

"We wouldn't want that," I say with a smile.

"You haven't seen Marco mad," he says with the hint of a smile.

Happiness on Armando is a good look. He's so fucking hot right now.

I lean forward, so close I can feel his warm breath on his face and smell the sugary sweetness from the ice cream.

"Kiss me," I say. "Kiss me like a boyfriend kisses a girlfriend."

He looks at me with a mix of surprise and hesitation, as if trying to read my mind. I sense his heart racing, and I know that I am pushing him way beyond his comfort zone. I said *boyfriend* and *girlfriend*. But I don't care. I want him to kiss me, to claim me as his own, to make me forget about everything else in the world.

He leans in slowly, his lips hovering just inches from mine. His hand drops to my waist, pulling me closer to him. I close my eyes and take a deep breath, trying to calm my racing heart. And then, finally, his lips meet mine in a tender, almost hesitant kiss.

At first, it's gentle and tentative, as if he's afraid of hurting me. But then, as I respond eagerly, he deepens the kiss, his tongue probing my lips. I moan softly, my hands clutching his shoulders, urging him on. He presses me against the wall of the boutique, his body hard against mine, and I feel a surge of desire like nothing I have ever felt before.

I wrap my arms around his neck, my fingers tangling in the short hair at the nape of his neck. I feel the strength in his arms as he holds me close. With a groan, he breaks the kiss, pulling back to look at me. "What are we doing?" His voice is husky.

"We're kissing," I say, a smile playing at the corners of my lips.

"Like boyfriend and girlfriend?"

"Exactly," I say simply, before pulling him in for another kiss. This time, he responds with even more passion, his hands roaming over my body as he kisses me deeply.

As our mouths move in perfect harmony, I realize that this is what I've been missing. Passion, desire, and the thrill of the unknown. I don't know where this will lead, but for now, all that matters is the heat between us, the hunger in our kiss and the promise of more to come.

# CHAPTER THIRTY-THREE

*Armando*

We enter her tiny apartment, kissing, surrounded in a hurricane of lust and desire. I need this woman more than I need to breathe.

As we stumble through the door, our lips pressed together in a frenzied passion, a sense of relief washes over me. Finally, I'm here, with her, and nothing else in the world matters. Her apartment is small, cramped even, but I don't care. All I need is her. We're two animals returning to our den. Our den of sins.

My hands roam over her body, tracing the curves and dips of her figure. Heat radiates off her skin, and it only fuels my desire further. I need to be inside her. Now.

I lift her off the ground, her legs wrapping around my waist as we stumble towards the bed. Her scent fills my nostrils, intoxicating me further.

As we collapse onto the bed, I break our kiss for just a moment to look into her eyes. They're dark, filled with a hunger that matches my own. I need her, all of her, and I know she needs the same from me.

"I'm going to fuck you like a boyfriend fucks a girlfriend," I say, remembering her request earlier and how she wanted me to kiss her.

Her hands are in my hair, pulling me closer. I feel her urgency, her need for me. "No. Fuck me like an animal would fuck his prey."

This girl... she's fucking everything. Everything.

I dip my head down to kiss her again, my tongue slipping into her mouth as she moans in pleasure. Our bodies are pressed together, my hardening cock aching to be inside her. Sliding my hand down between her legs, I stroke into her wetness and know that she's ready for me, and it only spurs me on further. I need to be inside her. I need to make her mine.

With one hand, I undo the buttons of her blouse, revealing the soft skin underneath. My lips leave hers, trailing down her neck and chest, leaving a trail of kisses in their wake. My other hand reaches for her skirt, pulling it down her body until it falls to the floor.

My hands roam everywhere, seeking out every inch of her skin. She moans and writhes beneath me, her own fingers gripping my hair and pulling me closer as if scared I'll leave her alone.

My mouth finds her nipple, and I begin to suck on it, teasing it with my tongue while the other hand finds and begins to tease the other one.

Her body trembles beneath mine, her breathing growing ragged. I slide my hand down her body, my fingers desperate to find her wetness.

She lifts her legs and wraps them around my waist, pulling me closer to her, desperate for me to enter her. When my fingers find the edge of her panties, I hook a finger in the side and pull them down with ease.

I slide one finger inside her, taking it out and sliding it back in again as she moans in pleasure. I tease her, torturing her with my touch. I want her to beg for me. I want her to know my power over her.

"Please," she breathes out. "Please, I need you. Fuck me."

My fingers are moving faster now, sliding in and out of her, my thumb rubbing her clit in quick little circles.

She throws her head back and moans, her voice filled with desire.

It's the most erotic sound I've ever heard. All I want is to have her screaming beneath me, moaning my name for the rest of my life.

She claws at my clothes, desperately ridding me of them and tossing them to the floor.

I need to be inside her, now.

With a quickness, I undo my pants, sliding them off and tossing them to the floor. I tear off my boxers as she reaches down to wrap her hand around my cock. I moan in pleasure, knowing what's coming next.

My cock throbs, precum oozing from the tip as it waits to be inside her. Her fingers slide up and down my shaft, teasing the head with her thumb. I groan as she plays with me, my body tense as I wait for what's to come.

I slide two fingers into her welcoming channel. She twitches and tenses with the slightest touch, like she's already close to climaxing.

I need to be inside her, now.

The tip of my cock finds her wet entrance, and she thrusts her hips up, desperate to take me inside her. She is dripping wet, and it makes my cock slip in effortlessly, the heat of her folds embracing my cock, taking me inside her. Her body shudders as I enter her, and I can tell she's desperate for me to move.

I pull out my cock until just the tip is inside her, before plunging back in. My hands grip her hips as I take her in pure animalistic bliss. I'm not being gentle, and with each aggressive push, she meets me with just as much force. She arches her back, meeting each thrust with her own. The look of pure pleasure on her face is indescribable. I'm taking her, and she loves every second of it.

I pull out, and she whimpers. I want her to need me.

"Beg for me," I growl. "Beg for me to fuck you."

"Please," she replies. "I need you. Please, fuck me."

Her voice is desperate, and I need to hear more.

I slide deep inside her, her legs wrapping around me, pulling me closer to her. "Fuck me," she says. "Fuck me like an animal."

I pull out, but she's ready for me. She's desperate for me, and I know she wants to be filled with me.

"Please, baby. Fill me. Let me come. Make me come," she cries out. "I need it. I need you. Fuck me. Please."

It's the most beautiful sound I've ever heard. I plunge my cock into her again and again, my pace quickening with each thrust, each movement.

As we move together, we're moaning, panting, and whispering. I sense her getting closer, her body tensing beneath mine. Her fingernails dig into my back as she tries to hold on.

My cock throbs as she thrusts her hips up, meeting each thrust with a moan of pleasure. The pleasure grows so great that I feel my own orgasm building.

It's the most intense feeling I've ever had. My cock throbs and pulses as I plunge in and out of her. She whimpers, begging me to make her come over and over again.

She's getting closer now. I can tell as her moans grow louder, and her body begins to writhe beneath mine.

"Come with me," I growl. "Come now."

I plunge my cock deep inside her, filling her and pushing her over the edge as she shudders beneath me. Her pussy clenches my cock, her juices flowing out of her as she screams.

Her body shakes, and she bucks her hips against mine, her orgasm shaking her to the core. My balls pump once, twice, four times as I bury myself deep inside her, releasing my seed into her.

I don't know how long we lay there, sticky, hot, and complete. Our breaths feel as if they morph to one, our heartbeat finds the same cadence. And for the first time in my entire life, I feel like I'm home.

# CHAPTER THIRTY-FOUR

*Hannah*

"So he's living with you now?" Josie asks. "Don't you think things are moving a little fast?"

I shrug. "In a way, yes. I don't know. It's not the normal situation between us. The way we hooked up sort of amplified things."

"Is he the reason there's a goon following me to and from work now?"

"He's making sure we're safe," I defend. "It's just while things settle with a situation with his work."

"Are we in danger?" Her eyes widen. "I didn't sign on for this shit."

"He's just being overly protective. It comes with the territory of what he does."

"Is this all worth it? Is he good?" Josie asks in a teasing voice as she pulls a tired bouquet out of the cooler and dumps the water in my industrial sink.

I have the usual anxious feeling in the pit of my stomach that I always have when she's working, but even so, I'm relieved to hash through the details of Armando with her.

My eyelids flutter. "So good. Like three times yesterday and once this morning good."

"Oh damn. That's so hot. So is it like... an arrangement? Like you pimped yourself out for the rent? Or what?"

I hurl a dead rose at her head. "Bitch, I did not whore myself out. He just offered to pay the rent. And I accepted the offer."

"Mmm hmm. And how did that go down, exactly?"

Okay, crap. I can't tell her the real story. "All right, yeah, I pimped myself out," I mumble, like I'm coming clean.

Josie's eyes pop. "Oh, that's hot. I think that's so hot. And he just ponied up the money and said *get in my bed, bitch?*"

I snort-laugh. "Yeah, just like that."

Josie eyes me with unveiled curiosity. She's as tall as I am short—six foot one, and the shortest of all her siblings. And yes, they all played basketball. Her family immigrated from Brazil when she was four. Dark-skinned like me, she's beautiful, with bleached-blonde hair blooming in a halo around her head. She's the reason I bleached the ends of my curls although I didn't go quite as light as she did.

She cocks her head. "I can't decide what I think about all this."

"What do you mean?" I may sound slightly defensive.

"I don't know. You look happy. Happier than you have in a while. But this is so out of character for you, I feel like I might need to call an intervention or something."

My face grows warm. "I like him, Jos."

She points a stern finger at me. "Don't tell him that. And do not cry! Please tell me you haven't already cried."

I cringe a little. Josie knows how relationships always end for me. We've been friends since high school—and there's definitely a pattern. I get attached too quickly—assign too much meaning to things. Then I blurt, "I love you!" or some other such clingy thing. Or I burst into tears or somehow over-emote about something, and then it's over. The guy hightails it away from me. I'm way too much for him.

"Well, I did cry," I admit. "—It was after sex, though!" I add quickly when Josie shoots me the *It's all over* look.

"Uh huh. And how did that go?"

"Um." I consider. "Actually not horrible. He rolled with it. Like he didn't seem to think it was that big a deal." Now that I'm saying it, I'm surprised. Why didn't he get uncomfortable or try to fix it or think I was nuts? "I don't know…maybe women routinely cry after sex with him," I joke, but thinking of him having sex with other women makes the words turn sour in my mouth. "He is that good."

Josie puts her hands on her hips. "When was this?"

The cringey feeling returns. "Yesterday… maybe the day before that too." And this morning, he abruptly ended our joined-at-the-hip thing.

He left while I was still asleep in bed. Just kissed my forehead and said he had to go to work. Like it was no big deal, and I hadn't just been his prisoner for days. He told me a man would be outside the shop all day, and to not leave without someone with me. But he wasn't sitting on me anymore. He told me he'd check in later as a normal couple would do.

I'd been thinking it meant he finally trusted me, but maybe it was the crying. Or me. Being too much, as always. He was bailing.

The bells on the door jingle and Jack, the FedEx guy comes in. "Package for you, young lady." He beams at me in a fatherly way as he hands over a padded envelope. "You have to sign for this one."

Perplexed, I sign his electronic clipboard and examine the package. I haven't ordered anything since I don't have any credit left on my credit card or cash in my bank account—unless I count the money Armando put there.

I tear open the packaging to find a tiny jewelry box. "Oh wow." My pulse quickens. He bought me a gift.

*A gift.*

That means something, doesn't it?

Josie makes an excited humming sound. "Somebody likes you."

"Oh wow," I murmur again, prying open the small lid with trembling fingers. "Wow." It seems to be the only word I remember how to say. I crack open the box. Inside is a gold nose ring with a diamond on the end.

Josie snatches up the certificate that came with it. "Eighteen carat gold with a conflict-free VVS diamond." She looks up at me. "*Dayum.* He definitely likes you."

I can't stop the stupid smile that plasters my face.

*He likes me.*

It's a thoughtful gift. It fits me. It's not some stupid diamond heart necklace or other cliché jewelry. He bought something that I'd like and wear. I slip out my plain gold ring and put in the diamond. "How's it look?"

Josie grins. "It's perfect."

"Yeah, it is." Of course he would've ordered this a couple days ago if it arrived today, so it's no guarantee he's still into me, but I suddenly feel much more hopeful that we have a chance.

I definitely want us to have a chance.

But I shouldn't start assigning meaning to things. This is how every relationship goes wrong for me.

I look over at Josie, thinking this would be a good time to talk to her about how her working here could use some adjustment. Now, while we're comfortable and close.

"Listen, Josie..."

"Hm?"

"Um, I was wondering... how do you like working here?"

She peers at me, a touch of alarm on her face. Butterflies flap their wings wildly in my belly. Up my esophagus. Into my throat.

"I like it, why?" Is it me, or does she sound nervous?

"Oh, um, I..." Christ! I'm a stammering fool! "Good. I'm glad. Just checking." I turn and flee to the workshop.

Great. That went well. Gah. I'm so not cut out to run this business on my own!

I need a breath of fresh air and step outside into the alley. I see Marco leaning against the wall, scrolling through his phone.

"Hey, Marco," I say, feeling both odd and protected that he is here. "Armando told me one of your men would be here today. I wasn't expecting you."

"I don't mind." He glances up from his phone and smiles. Marco looks a lot like Armando—the bloodline visibly thick between the two. So much so that I'm missing him already and hoping he'll call me soon. "I like feeling out the situation first."

"Oh yeah?" I lift an eyebrow and ask, "What do you *feel* about the situation?"

"My cousin likes you. A lot."

My heart flutters, and my breath hitches. "He does?"

"He does." Marco tilts his head and seems to scrutinize every inch of my face. "He's never taken anyone to church before."

I didn't know that, but I like hearing it.

"I'm assuming the feeling is mutual?" he asks.

My face feels as if it's a hundred degrees. My palms are sweaty, and I suddenly wish I had a cigarette. I don't smoke, but at least I'd have something to do, so I wouldn't feel so awkward simply standing in the alley with a man I barely knew.

"It's mutual."

"And do you know what that means?"

I look up and lock eyes with him.

"You understand the life Armando leads, right?"

I nod and focus my stare on my worn Converse. "I do."

"It can't be changed."

"I have no desire to change him."

Marco takes a step toward me and uses his finger to tilt my chin up, so I have to look into his eyes. He opens his mouth to talk, but my phone rings, interrupting us.

"It could be Armando," I say, not recognizing the number, but hoping it's him.

Marco nods to the phone for me to answer it.

# CHAPTER THIRTY-FIVE

*Armando*

"Give Nonna a kiss for me, okay?"

My mom calls me on her way to the airport. I bought her a ticket to see my nonna in Arizona for a couple weeks, just so I didn't have to worry about anyone fucking with her.

"I will. I know there's some kind of trouble, and I know you can't tell me, but Mando?"

I suck in my breath. "Yeah, ma?"

"You take care of yourself." Her voice wobbles.

"I will, ma. I am. I just need to know you're safe."

"Are you staying at your apartment? Maybe that's not a good idea."

"I'm not. I'm lying low. Actually..."

I don't know why I have the urge to tell her. Only because she deserves something—anything—to brighten her thoughts about me.

"I met a girl. I'm crashing at her place until things cool off."

My mom makes a little sound of surprise. "That's great. You must like her if you're telling me about her."

"Yeah. I do."

"Does she make you happy?"

"She does. I didn't think it was possible. But she does."

"You deserve to be happy."

"I'm not sure what I deserve," I admit.

"You may have made mistakes, son. You may make many more to come. But the one thing I know is you deserve happiness. Don't resist it."

"I'm trying not to."

"What's her name?"

I hesitate because we're on the phone, but I doubt the guys looking for me are sophisticated enough to pull off some kind of tap. Besides, it's a burner I picked up on the day I got out of prison.

"Hannah."

"Hannah. Is she Catholic?"

Leave it to my ma to ask that question. "We went to church together yesterday."

"That's great. Did you confess?"

"I did."

It was the hardest and yet easiest thing I'd done in a long time. I did it for me. I did it for Hannah, and I did it to try to free my soul. I spoke the words I needed to and didn't hold back:

*Bless me father for I have sinned.*

*My soul is damaged beyond repair.*

*It's been five years since my last confession.*

*Five years since my mother wept as they led me out of court in handcuffs.*

*Three years since I killed a man in prison. Now there's a price on my head.*

*Three days out, and I commit another sin to stay alive.*

*And then another with her, my beautiful witness.*

*And another with her.*

*And another.*

*I'm not asking for absolution.*

*All I really want is her.*

"That makes me happy to hear," she says. "I'd like to meet her."

Something crowds my chest. Because I don't get to do normal. I probably won't get to introduce Hannah to my mom even though I'm sure they'd love each other. They're both warm, open-hearted women.

"Yeah, we'll see. Travel safe, ma."

"I will. Be careful, Mando. I'll be praying for you."

"I know you will. I love you." I say the words, but I think I might also have a glimmer of the feeling, too. Or just the memory of the feeling. Moms are powerful that way.

I end the call as I head to my new job. The don told me to call in sick but fuck it—I'm going. Fuck the Hermanos. They can come for me on the construction site if they want. I have a piece, and I'm ready for them.

I need to get a life going on the outside. Hiding at Hannah's forever is not an option, as much as I enjoy her. Yeah, *enjoy*.

That's a word I didn't think I'd be using any time soon.

I was balls deep in her again multiple times last night. One epic session involved me putting her on her knees on the bed and fucking her with my thumb in her ass. Then, before the sun even rose, I found my hand cupping her pussy when I woke, and it was on again. I rolled her to her belly and spread her legs wide. Held her down with my hand at her nape because she likes a little struggle.

She came twice—she's so damn responsive. So brave.

I realized that at some point last night. The level of vulnerability she displays can only be born from immense courage. Her example is the only thing showing me the way back to being human again.

Not that I think there can be many humans like her.

It's so funny to me how normal she seems—like an ordinary twenty-something-year-old. She'd fit in anywhere. But she's anything but.

I can't get her out of my mind. I can't get the smell of her out of my nose. I can't make the vision of her lying in bed staring up at me to go away. She's everywhere I look. She's consuming.

Before I get out of the van of hers I'm borrowing, I decide I need to give her a call. I know Marco is standing guard, but it will put my mind at ease to hear her voice.

"Hello, Flowers," I say when she answers the phone.

"I was hoping it was you." I hear the smile in her voice.

"How has the morning been so far?"

"Good. Josie arrived on time, and we've been talking."

"Did Marco arrive? He said he would."

"Yes, in fact, I'm standing outside right now talking to him."

Just as I'm getting ready to tell her to get back inside where it's safe, I hear the worst noise imaginable. It's a loud *pop, pop, pop*, followed by an ear-piercing scream.

"Hannah!"

The scream doesn't stop.

"Hannah!"

And then there is silence...

———

Thank you for reading *Den of Sins*! *Rooted in Sin, the conclusion to Hannah and Armando's story is available for order here.* If you enjoyed this book, please consider leaving a review—they make a huge difference for indie authors.

# ROOTED IN SIN

A Dark Mafia Romance

# CHAPTER ONE

*Hannah*

A car screeches into the alleyway behind Garden of Eden, my flower shop.

Armando's cousin, Marco, who was stationed in the alleyway to protect me, whirls, hand reaching for the gun strapped to his side.

I instinctively flinch, my heart stopping. A guy leans out of the open window, gun raised and aimed directly at us. Time seems to slow as Marco's eyes widen with realization. "Get down!" He lunges toward me, throwing me to the cold concrete ground behind the garbage dumpster.

Marco's body shields mine as the deafening sound of gunfire fills the alleyway. He lifts his gun to return fire, but before he can, he's hit.

Pain flares in his eyes. His body jerks.

I scream. Blood splatters everywhere, and some of it pools on my legs, hot and sticky.

"Marco!" My voice is barely audible over the cacophony of gunfire hitting the metal dumpster.

My hands tremble as I reach out to touch him, the reality of the situation sinking in. This is no random act of violence—we were targeted.

"Stay down," he grits through clenched teeth, his body trembling from shock or adrenaline.

Even as his blood pools between us, he never takes his eyes off me, as if determined to protect me at all costs.

*Oh God.*

I've already seen one man die in the last week. Already been exposed to the violence of Armando's life. But that death felt surreal. Like watching a movie. Marco is a man I know. Armando's cousin. If he dies—

No, I can't even think it. He's still breathing. He seems alert.

Voices shout from the car, "That's not him" and "Go! Go! Go! Go!" It speeds away, leaving a cloud of dust and the sound of squealing tires as the only evidence of the drive-by.

*That's not him.*

They were trying to kill Armando, and they came to my shop. To the alleyway behind it. Does that mean they've connected me to him?

Is he no longer safe in my apartment?

That thought chokes me.

Marco's blood keeps draining, staining my clothes and skin. He groans and rolls partway off me, trying to push himself up.

"Take it easy. I'll call for help."

I search for my phone and see it cast to the side. *Armando.* I was speaking to Armando before this all happened.

"Armando!" I cry out, trying to pull my legs out from under Marco's. "Armando, Marco's hit!" Maybe he can still hear what's happening and now knows we are both alive but in danger.

Almost as if summoned by my voice, Armando appears at the mouth of the alleyway, his eyes wide with panic. He takes in the scene before him—Marco injured and me covered in blood and shaking uncontrollably.

"Hannah!" He runs to us, but his gaze is only on me.

"I'm okay, but Marco's hit."

"*Madonna mia,* what the fuck happened?" He crouches beside us, his hands hovering over Marco, like he's unsure where to touch or how to help. Fear is etched on his pale face, a vulnerability I've never seen from him before.

"Your buddies," Marco groans, shifting to sit up and gritting his teeth against the pain. "They came out of nowhere."

"Did you get a chance to see who they were?" Armando demands. I can see the gears turning in his head, already planning retaliation.

"I-I don't know," I stammer, still in shock. "I didn't see their faces."

"Fuck." Armando's gaze shifts between Marco and me, his concern palpable. "We need to get you both somewhere safe. Can you walk?"

"Of course I can walk," Marco scoffs, trying to climb to his feet. His face contorts with pain, and he collapses back onto the ground. Armando's jaw clenches, and he picks up Marco's arm to wrap around his shoulder, heaving him to his feet.

"Yeah, you're not walking anywhere like this."

I move to the other side of Marco to help. Together, we manage to hoist Marco to his feet, each of us taking one of his arms over our shoulders.

"Mando," Marco says quietly, his voice strained. "I didn't see it coming."

"We'll worry about that later," Armando clips. "Right now, we need to focus on getting you both out of here."

As we half-carry, half-drag Marco out of the alleyway toward my shop, my thoughts whirl with a gut-wrenching realization: my life has become irrevocably intertwined with this dangerous world and the man who brought me into it. Not that witnessing him kill a man with his bare hands hadn't already bound us together.

Blood soaks the back of Marco's leg, and I see Armando take it in, his nostrils flaring. "We need to get you to the hospital," he says.

"I'm fine," Marco insists through gritted teeth as I try to steady him on his feet. "Just get one of the guys to dig the bullet out."

"Shut up," Armando snaps. "I'm taking you to the hospital. Give me your keys." He props his cousin up against the brick wall by my back door.

"Dude, I don't want blood on the seats of the Beamer."

"You'd rather go in an ambulance?"

He makes a growling sound in his throat. "Fine." Marco reluctantly gives up his keys.

"Can you hold him up for a minute, Flowers? I'll pull the car around."

"Of course." My voice breaks. I'm still shaking all over, in total shock.

Armando must catch the fear in my voice because he pauses, gaze roaming over me again, as if he's still searching for any sign of injury.

"I'm okay," I promise. "Go get the car."

Worry clouds his dark eyes. "Are you sure?"

I nod, trying to ignore the lingering fear that clings to me like a second skin. "I'm fine. Really. Go!"

He gives a jerky nod and jogs away.

A few minutes later, a BMW zips into the alleyway and stops. Armando throws open the passenger door, then climbs out to help me get Marco into it. I climb into the back seat.

"You should just dump me in the front," Marco says when Armando takes off. "I wouldn't want this to affect your parole."

Armando's jaw tightens. "This is my fucking fault," he snaps.

"Quit your pity party, *stronzo*. I'm the one who got shot. You're gonna drop me in front and drive away. Call Leo and make sure he keeps it from our ma then come in with him when he arrives, like you just found out."

Armando looks grim, but nods. I see him checking the rear view mirror at me.

"I'll go in with him," I say. "I'm not on parole."

"No," Armando says immediately. "I don't want you tied to this in any way. *Capito?*"

At the hospital, Armando speeds up to the curb of the Emergency area. "Hey, *caging*," Marco rasps. "Don't worry about me. Just a flesh wound." He throws open his door and tumbles out, somehow managing to stagger toward the entry.

"I should go with him."

"Stay," Armando growls, his gaze on his cousin for a moment longer before he guns the car and peels out.

He circles the hospital then pulls into the parking area and shuts off the car. Armando's hands shake as he pulls out his phone. "I need to call Leo," he mutters, gaze darting around the parking lot as if expecting another attack at any moment.

"Leo, it's me." Armando's voice is thick with urgency when Marco's brother answers. "Marco's been shot.... In the alleyway at Garden of Eden. He was protecting Hannah. It was meant for me. Yeah, we're at Cook County now. Meet me here. And Marco said to keep this from your ma."

The conversation ends quickly, and Armando slips his phone back into his pocket.

When we get out of the car, he's still scanning me for injuries, like he thinks I secretly got shot and didn't tell him.

"Are you hurt?"

I shake my head.

"Let me see," he insists.

He wraps an arm around my waist, guiding me closer to him. His touch sends shivers down my spine, but it's exactly what I need to quiet the shaking in my limbs. It grounds me.

Armando's hands move gently over my body, checking for any injuries. He growls at the scrapes on my knees from the pavement. "Fuck, Hannah. Thank God you weren't hit." He drops his forehead against mine.

"Armando..." I begin, unsure of what to say or do.

"I'm sorry, Hannah." Armando's arm remains wrapped around me, his breathing ragged as he surveys our surroundings, his gaze darting from one shadowy corner to the next. I sense the tension building in him. "Sorry you're caught in my web."

"I'm not," I say softly. And it's true.

If Armando hadn't killed a man in my shop last week, I wouldn't have the privilege of knowing him. Of knowing what it means to be possessed by a man like him.

And I wouldn't give that up for anything.

But his expression is blank, like the shooting tweaked his PTSD. He just shakes his head. "I wanted you safe from all of this."

"Hey." I place my hand on his cheek, forcing him to look at me. "I am safe. And Marco will be okay too, Armando."

His dark eyes meet mine, and for a moment, I see something raw and vulnerable there. "I don't know what I'd do if that had been you, Hannah." He swallows hard. "I can't stand the thought of you getting hurt because of me."

"Everything's going to be fine. I'm fine. Marco soon will be."

Armando shakes his head. "Nothing is fine right now. But I'm going to make damn sure it will be."

# CHAPTER TWO

*Armando*

Hannah's colorful platform heels click against the sterile floors, echoing in the emergency room as she paces.

Leo sits with his ankle across his knee, his foot jiggling. "Have you told the don?" he asks.

I shake my head. "Not yet."

There was a time when I would go to Don G in a heartbeat. About everything. But I feel so disconnected from *La Famiglia* now.

Of course, I have to report this. I have to tell him what's happening. But I want to be able to tell him that I have it figured out when I do. That I have it in hand.

The trouble is, I'm so fucking far from having it in hand. I need answers, so I can finish this shit.

Especially because Hannah's involved now.

I can't have her hurt.

I glance at the clock. It's been hours since Marco was brought in, and the silence in this cold, white room is deafening.

"God, when will they tell us something?" I mutter under my breath, trying to contain my frustration and fear.

I brood in the corner of the room, apart from Hannah, fighting the urge to slam my fist into the wall. I imagine the scene of Marco taking the bullet meant for me over and over in my mind, a constant reminder that I am to blame. What if it had struck his heart? His head? Right now I'd be explaining to my aunt how her son died.

The thought makes me sick.

I wanted to feel something—anything—but not this.

Thank fuck Hannah wasn't hit.

"Damn it." I clench my fists. My gaze drifts to Hannah, her beautiful face etched with worry, and my chest tightens even more. If only I hadn't brought her into this world, into the chaos of my past, she wouldn't be here facing this danger.

"Armando." She walks over to me. "He's going to be okay. And it's not your fault."

I look away, unable to meet her eyes. How can she still be so fucking sweet after all this? After I've brought her nothing but trouble and pain?

"Stop blaming yourself," she pleads, her voice breaking as tears well up in her eyes. "You couldn't have known this would happen."

I stare down at her. I don't know how the fuck she can cry for me. I'm the walking dead, and she's an ocean of emotion.

"Couldn't I?" I ask bitterly, images of my past flashing before me. Every failed deal, every vengeful enemy—they all led to this moment. "You need to be safe."

"What I need is you," she whispers, reaching out to touch my hand.

"Need me?" I scoff, pulling my hand away as if her touch is scalding. "You don't know what you're asking for."

I catch the hurt in her gaze, and my guilt grows.

"Maybe not." She looks down at her feet before raising her eyes to meet mine again. "But I know that my feelings don't change for you just because of what happened in that alley."

Fuck. This girl. She's so much more than I deserve.

A nurse comes into the waiting room and addresses Leo and me. "He's out of surgery," she tells us. "We removed the bullet from his—"

I surge to my feet and head straight to the room without asking if we can see him. Hannah follows right behind me. Leo stays to listen to the nurse's report.

I just need to see with my own eyes that he's okay.

"Hey, guys," Marco calls out weakly from his hospital bed. "Apparently it was just a bullet to my ass. I always knew my ass looked good but never thought it'd be a literal target!" He chuckles as best he can, given the pain he's in.

I force a smile, appreciating his attempt to lighten the mood despite his own suffering. The sound of his laughter is like a balm to the heaviness in my chest. Though he tries to hide it, I see the strain on his face. It's evident that he's putting on a brave front for our sake.

"Nice one, *cugino*," I say with a half-smile.

"Come on, Hannah, you may not laugh at my jokes, but at least give me a smile." Marco gazes at her expectantly.

"Only because you're injured." Her smile could brighten the darkest prison cell.

"Hey, I'll take what I can get," he teases, wincing as he shifts on the bed.

"Thank you, Marco. For taking the bullet," I say sincerely.

"Yes, thank you," Hannah adds. "I know it could have hit me. You saved my life."

"Anytime." He shrugs. "I've been in this life long enough to know the risks. I'm not some innocent bystander who got caught up in your mess, Armando. I made my choices."

Despite Marco's words, guilt gnaws at me like a ravenous wolf. I clench my fists at my sides and look away from them, trying to fight the urge to rage and kill someone.

"Marco shouldn't have been there," I say, my voice strained. "It should've been me in that alley. The bullet was meant for me."

"Armando, you can't—" Hannah begins, but she's cut off by the sudden entrance of Marco's brother, Leo.

"What the hell happened?" Leo saunters into the hospital room.

"I got shot in the butt."

"So I heard." Leo barks out a laugh. "Well, at least it wasn't something important."

"Ha, very funny." Marco gives a rueful grin. "I did what I had to do."

"So now you have two holes in your ass?" Leo continues. "So you are a double asshole now."

"Keep it up, little brother," Marco growls.

"Listen," I interject, addressing Leo. "This is my mess. I'll make it right. I promise." The weight of responsibility settles even more heavily on my shoulders. I glance over at Hannah, who studies me like she can feel it. I'm sure she can. The girl feels everything.

I can't read her thoughts.

Leo stops joking with Marco and turns toward me. "Count me in, on finding the fuckers who scarred my brother's lily-white ass." Leo's face is serious. "We'll make sure they regret ever crossing our family."

As we discuss plans for retribution, Marco interjects, wincing as he adjusts his position on the bed.

"Before you guys go all vigilante on their asses, there's something we need to consider." He tips his head in Hannah's direction. "Maybe it's best if she gets out of town for a while, too. Like your mom."

"Absolutely not," Hannah responds immediately, her voice unwavering.

Fuck. Marco's right. If anyone connects me to Hannah, she'll be a target. The *stronzos* who want me dead were in the alleyway behind her shop today. They may have already tied me to her.

Then again, it could be they thought I'd be there because of Rocco's. Because it's where they found me last time.

Hannah puts her hands on her hips. "No. I have a business to run. I'm not going anywhere."

I'm a double-asshole because the truth is, I don't want her to leave. I don't want to stop hiding out at her place. I don't want to let her go. She's the only color in my black and white life.

"I don't think she's a target. Just me."

"True. I heard them yelling 'that's not him' after they shot me," Marco says.

A small sliver of relief worms its way through my chest. "That's good. Hannah stays, then."

She steps in close to me, and I wrap my arms around her, pulling her close, inhaling the scent of her hair—a mixture of fresh flowers and warm vanilla.

"You stay, but we'll need to take extra precautions."

"Okay," she murmurs, her arms tightening around me.

"All right, then," Leo chimes in, his expression still serious. "We'll make sure to keep her safe while you deal with this. And I'll help you handle the retribution, Armando."

"Hey, don't forget about me," Marco calls out, attempting a grin despite the pain etched on his face. "I might be down, but I'm not out. I'll be back on my feet soon. The retribution should be mine." He yawns. "But right now, I need to close my eyes and enjoy the high from all these pain meds."

Leo leans against the wall as he crosses his arms over his chest. "Yeah, man, and now you're gonna have all the nurses here fighting over who gets to change your bandages."

"Maybe I should get shot more often, huh?" Marco chuckles, wincing slightly from the effort.

"Maybe not in the butt next time, though. Takes the cool factor out of the equation," I quip, earning a laugh from everyone in the room.

"All right, All right, enough with the jokes," Marco says, catching his breath. "But seriously, Mando, promise me you won't go off on your own for this one. We're a team, remember?"

"Yeah." The room falls silent as I nod, holding Marco's gaze. "I promise." I take Hannah's hand and lead her out of the hospital room. "Let's go home."

# CHAPTER THREE

*Armando*

"We need to get you in the shower." I nudge Hannah to the bathroom in her apartment.

When my hand reaches the small of her back, I feel a tremble. Fuck. She's probably still in shock.

I hate seeing the blood on her. Though it isn't hers, it still makes me sick to my stomach imagining what could have been if Marco wasn't there to take the bullet.

I guide her into the shower, turning on the water and adjusting the temperature until it's warm but not too hot. She stands there, eyes closed, steam rising around her as the water cascades down her body. I can see the tension in her shoulders start to ease as she relaxes, and for a moment, I allow myself to let go of the dread that's been gripping me since I found her and Marco in the alley.

She closes her eyes and tilts her head back, letting the water soak into her hair. I reach for the body wash and lather it up in my hands before gently massaging it along her bare flesh.

"Are you okay?" I croak. "Really okay?"

She nods, the tension leaving her body. She's safe, at least for now. I know I can't stay in her life much longer. Not when I'm putting her through this kind of shit.

"It's okay," I murmur, "I won't let you be involved in anything else. I promise."

Twenty-four hours ago, there would be no way possible I could simply bathe this woman and not want to thrust my cock up inside of her. Soapy water streaming down her dark skin has my dick hardening, but I focus on my goal. Right now, all I want to do is soothe her. Wrap her in a fluffy blanket and chase away all her monsters.

Once she's clean, I help her out of the shower and wrap her in a towel. I lead her to the bedroom and help her into a fresh pair of pajamas before tucking her into bed.

"I'm fine, Armando," she insists again.

I sit beside her, unable to think of anything but the shooting. The blood pooling under Marco. He took a bullet for Hannah. I know he'd do it again in a heartbeat.

She shouldn't be involved in any of this. Shouldn't have seen me choke the life out of a man on her shop floor. Shouldn't have been shot at in the alleyway.

She's an innocent, and we don't involve innocents. Especially not women.

Fuck. I stand. "Get some sleep," I say gruffly.

She grabs my hand to stop me. "Don't go. Come to bed with me."

Oh, the temptation. She's looking at me with those big, brown eyes. So beautiful in her bed.

But she doesn't need sex right now. She needs comfort.

I kick off my pants and climb into bed beside her, and she snuggles into my chest, her hand resting on my heart. The rise and fall of her breaths are soothing.

I lie there and stare up at the ceiling, my mind chewing on the day's events.

I shouldn't have let myself get close to this girl. I feel I'm signing her death certificate.

Being with me is the same as walking toward the Reaper himself.

Fuck, I should leave...

"What happens now?"

I don't have the answer to that. All I know is that I can't keep putting her in danger. I can't keep this up forever. "I don't know," I admit. "But I'll figure it out. I won't let anything happen to you. Whoever shot at you and Marco is going to die. I'm going to tear his head off with my bare hands."

I feel her tense.

"Sorry." I should definitely spare her the details of my revenge plan. "What I mean is, what happened today will never happen again."

She gives a wobbly nod. Her gaze doesn't reveal any fear or revulsion for me. No, this is the girl who watched me kill a man with my bare hands and still kissed me.

I lean in and taste her mouth.

As her lips part, I deepen the kiss, exploring the sweet depths of her mouth with my tongue. She responds to me, her body pressing against mine with increasing urgency. Our breathing becomes ragged as we continue to kiss, lost in the intoxicating sensation of each other's touch.

I slide my hands down her back, pulling her in closer to me. Her breasts press against my chest, and a moan escapes her lips.

I pull away for a moment to catch my breath, looking into her eyes as I run my hand through her hair. We're lost in each other, and the world outside of this moment doesn't exist. I lean in to kiss her again, and I climb on top, my hands roaming over her body as I kiss her deeply. She responds with fervor, her hips grinding against mine. I can feel her wetness through her panties and makes my cock rock hard.

We both slowly remove the rest of our clothing, not wanting anything to prevent our skins from merging as one.

I trail kisses down her body, starting with her neck, continuing down to her breasts and then further down to the soft patch of dark hair between her thighs. I kiss her softly at first, and then I part her lips with my tongue and plunge in, tasting her.

She lets out a gasp, her hands grabbing onto my head as she arches her back. I continue exploring, my tongue darting with quick flicks as I lap up her juices. She gasps again, letting out a high pitched moan as she claws at my hair.

I part her thighs wider with my hands, running my tongue slowly through her folds. She shudders in response.

"Oh God." She lets out a shaky breath.

I slide my arms underneath her thighs, pulling her legs up to my shoulders. Her breathing quickens as my tongue flicks against her clit. She digs her nails into my back, arching as I lick her slowly, my tongue brushing over her sensitive nub. Her body tenses up as I flick faster, her muscles tightening as I push her closer and closer to the edge.

I continue my assault on her clit, running my tongue around it in tight circles. Alternating between licking and sucking as I hear her breathing deepen and grow shaky.

"I'm going to come," she mumbles. Her entire body is trembling now, her muscles tensing up and releasing in a powerful orgasm. Her juices flow into my mouth as she moans loudly.

I continue until she's done, finally sitting up and looking at her. She's breathing heavily, her chest rising and falling quickly. She wraps her arms around my neck, pulling me into a kiss.

I grab a condom from the bedside table. I tear the wrapping open with my teeth and slide the condom on. I lift her legs back up to my shoulders, looking deep into her eyes as I enter her with a single thrust. We both gasp, lost in the sensation of our bodies joining together. I pull out and thrust into her again. I pull back and thrust a third time, each thrust growing more and more powerful.

She pulls my head to her and kisses me, her lips meeting mine in a powerful, soulful kiss as we continue to make love to each other.

Not just fucking. Making love. My penance for all I've put her through.

She breaks the kiss, pressing her forehead against mine, and we continue to move together in unison. Her breath is hot against my face. My own desire builds, and I start to thrust harder and deeper into her. I begin to feel the familiar tingling sensation in my groin as she continues to moan and whimper, her breath getting more and more ragged. We're both nearing the edge now, and she tightens her legs around my waist as her breath quickens. I thrust into her one last time. We explode in a series of moans and groans, riding the wave together until it breaks. I slowly slide out of her, lying beside her in the bed. We're both trying to catch our breaths.

She turns to me, snuggling up to my heated body. I wrap my arm around her, holding her close to me. Despite the shitshow of the day, this feels right.

Being here, with Hannah. This connection.

Yet, this is the exact thing I need to give up if I care about this girl.

As she rests her head on my chest again, I can feel her body relax and her breathing grow slow and steady. Her eyes close, and I know that she's finally given in to the exhaustion that's threatened to overwhelm her since I found her in the alley.

I lie here, holding her close, and I can't help but think of how ironic it is that the one woman I should keep at arm's length is the one woman I can't bring myself to let go of.

# CHAPTER FOUR

*Hannah*

I wake in Armando's arms. The room is dark, his heavy breathing tells me he's been asleep for awhile.

I should be scared of this man. Terrified of the situation I am in. I don't even know how to define my relationship with Armando. Am I still his prisoner? His girlfriend?

Is he only here because he needs a place to hide out? Is he still making sure I won't rat him out?

Or does he want to be here? With me?

The foolish part of me likes to believe I'm doing something for him. A shock absorber in his messy, criminal life.

I know that's totally fucked up, but there it is. I want to be important to him. I want to know he needs me like I'm starting to need him.

His arms tighten around me. His grip is possessive, as if he's still afraid I'll run.

It feels like a lifetime since he literally crashed into my shop.

So much fear. Unknown. Pleasure. Lust. Even tenderness.

Yes, tenderness from the killer in my bed.

Now, as I lie here in his arms, I can't help but feel a strange sense of comfort. It's as if I'm finally safe from the world outside. The world that would judge me for being here. The world that doesn't understand the bond that has formed between us.

Do I even understand the bond?

I turn to look at him, and he stirs in his sleep. His eyes open, and he smiles when he sees me looking at him. I feel a warmth spread through my body. It's crazy, I know. But I can't help how I feel. I love him. I know I shouldn't, but I do.

"Can't sleep?" he murmurs, pulling me closer.

I shake my head, unable to find the words to express what I feel. I just stare at him, and he stares back, his eyes searching my face for something. He leans in and brushes his lips against mine, sending shivers down my spine. I respond eagerly, pressing my body against his.

In that moment, I forget everything that surrounds us. The hit out on Armando. The shooting in the alley. The threat of Armando breaking parole and ending back in prison.

I break the kiss, pulling back just enough so my fingers can trace light circles on his chest. "Just thinking," I whisper back, unwilling to break the spell of the moment.

He nods, his eyes searching mine. "About what?"

"About how close I feel to you. And what's going to happen."

He's silent for a moment, his expression inscrutable. "I don't have the answers, Flowers. I don't know."

"I know," I say quickly. "Of course you don't. Nevermind."

"I do know one thing..." His hand moves towards my thigh.

My breath catches in my throat when I feel his fingers brush against my leg. My skin is covered with goose bumps, my body responding to his touch.

I open my legs wider in an attempt to get his fingers closer to my pussy.

He lowers his hand to the edge of my panties. "You're a gift."

Every cell in my body celebrates his admission. Confirmation that I do mean something. That I am a contribution to his life. That he does need me.

"You're a fucking gift, and I want you more than I've ever wanted you before." His fingers slide under the fabric and find my swollen clit. I gasp, his touch sending a jolt through my body.

My whole body quivers in anticipation as he slides a finger inside of me. He pushes it deep inside, pumping it in and out in a rhythmic motion. My body knows what to do. It knows how to respond to his touch. It's been like this since the moment I met him.

"Thank you for accepting me." He strokes my inner walls. "I love the way you surrender to me. It's intoxicating. I can never get enough of you." He inhales the scent of my hair. "Never."

I've come to realize that Armando and I may struggle for words as we are just learning how to communicate. But one thing is for certain.

Our bodies know how to speak.

More so than words.

I let out a soft moan as his finger slides in and out of my pussy, "More," I whisper, my eyes never leaving his.

"More?" His lips curl into a smile.

"I want more than this. I want you inside of me. I need you," I admit, my voice catching in my throat.

I've never been one who could easily express my sexual needs and desires. But when I'm around him, he brings out a side of me that I never knew existed.

A side that craves his touch.

"I know what you need, Flowers." He rolls me to my back and pins my forearms by my sides.

"Yes," I breathe, thrilled by his dominance.

"You need me to fuck you?"

"Yes," I answer immediately.

"You need me to fuck you hard, baby girl?"

"Yes, please."

"You're asking for it." He reaches down to grab my panties and pulls them down my legs. He tosses them on the floor, then grabs my ankles and lifts my legs towards the headboard. I squirm in plea-sure as he spreads my legs apart, exposing my pussy to his hungry gaze.

"You're so fucking wet for me," he growls as he lowers his head, pressing his lips against my thigh, then moving towards my pussy. "So wet and ready for me, aren't you?"

He doesn't wait for an answer. His lips land on my clit, and he sucks it between his lips. His warm tongue flicks over my clit, torturing it in a most delicious way.

I squeeze my eyes shut, warmth spreading through my body as a bolt of electricity shoots up my spine. I gasp as he pushes his tongue deep inside of me, groaning as it slides against my swollen clit. His tongue pushes inside of me, and my pussy contracts, quivering against his mouth.

He pushes two fingers inside of me, and my pussy contracts around them. I'm so close. "Put it in me," I breathe, struggling to find my voice.

"Put what in you?" His fingers plunge even deeper, driving me wild. He's making me beg.

I oblige. "Your cock. I want it. I need it."

"Nice and slow?" he asks.

"Yes," I nod.

"Are you sure? Or do you want it rough and hard?" he teases.

"However you want. I just want you to fuck me." My heart pounds in my chest. The blood sizzles through my veins.

I've never had an addictive personality. I don't drink. I don't smoke. Nothing has ever taken hold of my senses.

Until Armando.

I'm completely addicted to him.

And I'm terrified he's going to break my heart.

# CHAPTER FIVE

*Hannah*

The sun spills through the thin curtains of my small apartment, casting a soft glow on the room.

I hear water running in the shower, and knowing Armando is still here calms me.

I get up and flit aimlessly around the bedroom, picking up strewn clothing without thinking. No, that's not true. I'm *trying* not to think, but yesterday's events are playing on loop in my mind. The sudden screech of tires, the sharp crack of gunfire, and Marco's pained eyes haunt me.

Someone wants Armando dead.

That thought terrifies me. I stare at the floor, searching for answers that aren't there.

As if on cue, the bathroom door creaks open, and Armando strides out, his damp hair slicked back from his face. He's dressed impeccably in a tailored suit, looking every bit the powerful and dangerous man he is. It's as if last night never happened, like he's untouchable. As always, his presence is both reassuring and intimidating.

"Morning, Flowers," he says coolly, eyes scanning me from head to toe. His voice is like velvet, soothing some of the anxiety that has been gnawing at me since I woke up. But his stoic demeanor also serves as a reminder that this kind of violence isn't new to him—it's part of his life.

"Morning," I reply, trying to steady my voice. "How's Marco?"

"Alive," he answers simply, his expression still as calm and collected as ever. "He'll be fine. It's not the first time he's been shot." There's a hint of bitterness in his words, daring me to question him further. But I can't help myself.

"Did he say how long he'll be in the hospital? I was thinking of sending him some flowers."

"Don't. I don't want you to be seen with him. Or me. I don't want that connection made for anyone. Okay?"

"Is this what your life will always be like? Are we constantly going to be in danger?"

His eyes flash with something dark, almost vulnerable, before he turns away. "There is no *we*, Hannah," he says quietly, his back to me. "*Because* of the danger. I'm sorry you got dragged into this, but I'm going to try to keep you out of anything else."

Right. No *we*.

Armando turns, and he must see my hurt because he moves to me, wraps his arms around me, and pulls me close. My face presses against his chest, the steady rhythm of his heart beating beneath my ear. It's comforting, grounding me in this moment.

"I'm sorry I got you into this." His voice is tense, but his fingers trace my back gently.

"I think the adrenaline of last night is wearing off. I feel... scared," I confess, my hands gripping the fabric of his suit jacket. "Not for me, but for you."

He lets out a shocked chuff. "Me? Don't worry about me, baby girl. The outfit... it's a part of me. Danger is woven into every day for me. That won't change. I can't give it up, even if I wanted to." His voice cracks slightly, betraying the pain he feels in admitting this truth.

"Is this who you are then? A man constantly surrounded by violence and fear?" I ask, trying to understand the depth of his involvement in the mafia but also hoping I don't sound judgey.

"Unfortunately, yes," he admits, his grip on me tightening. "I was born into this life, and I've done things I'm not proud of. But I don't want it to touch you any more than it already has, Hannah. You deserve better."

My eyes swim with tears.

I know he's saying he cares about me, but he's also pushing me away. Shutting me out. Telling me we have no future.

"Just because I'm scared—" I stop. I'm not sure what to say. "Armando, I don't care about your past or what you are."

He seems to stop breathing. "You should." His voice is hard. Dark.

"I know what I deserve. And right now, that's you."

My chest tightens at the thought of a future filled with violence and fear, but I can't imagine my life without him in it. I know it's not his fault that he was born into this world, and I don't want to ask him to change who he is. However, I can't ignore the fact that by being with him, I'm accepting a life that may never be free from danger.

Facing that reality doesn't mean I have to flee from it.

"I promise you, I'll do everything in my power to keep you safe. What happened yesterday will not go unpunished. I'll make damn sure none of this touches you again." Armando's jaw tightens, and I see the fierce protectiveness rising within him.

He looks at me for a long moment, the weight of his past heavy in his gaze. His breath warm against my skin. Something shifts in his expression then, a spark igniting behind his eyes.

---

*Armando*

I take the L to the construction site and check in with the foreman, Larry. He gives me the up and down. I dressed in a suit and tie, which I know is overdressed for a construction site. But it's not overdressed for a lieutenant of the mafia, and I need to establish who the fuck I am.

"Yeah. Okay. So on the books you're listed as a supervisor. If anyone ever shows up here to inspect, just look official. You dressed the part, so that's good. Other than that—you do what you want. I'm sure you know that already."

I nod. "Yeah. Definitely. So am I supposed to be your supervisor?"

His nostrils flare. "That's right. Real supervisor manages eight other sites. I handle everything here on my own."

I shove my hands in my pockets to look less threatening. Not a look I've perfected, but somewhere in me, there used to be a guy who knew how to do casual. "So maybe I'll just tag along with you... learn the ropes."

What else am I gonna do? I spent four and a half years bored. Now that I'm out, I don't want to lounge around and do nothing. Plus, I need something to keep my mind off the thought of Hannah almost getting shot. That and our night and morning of epic fucking.

Of course, Larry doesn't like that. Not one fucking bit. I know because he kinda goes stiff and freezes for a couple seconds before he lets out a choked, "Yeah, okay."

He has to say *okay*. No one's gonna fuck with me here. The Pachino family runs the union.

I follow him around and pay attention, introducing myself to the guys when Larry doesn't bother. It's not that I suddenly feel friendly. Fuck no. But I force myself to at least go through the motions.

"He's the union-provided supervisor," Larry inserts meaningfully each time, letting them all know exactly what that means.

I'm a mobster there to milk their employer for a paycheck while doing nothing.

Well, they might be surprised. I might end up doing more than texting my buddies all day. Or I might not. Who the fuck knows? All I know is I'm hungry to work. I had to hold myself back from inserting myself into Hannah's business. Telling her all the ideas I had for it.

That would be wrong. Hannah doesn't need me to bust in and tell her how to do anything. She's gotta figure that shit out on her own, or else she'll never take full ownership over there. But damn, I want to help.

A big black guy in his fifties comes over to talk to Larry. When I introduce myself, I find out his name is Harold, and he's an electrician.

I can tell he doesn't want to say what he is about to. "Listen, I've been a little short of breath lately, and my wife got me an appointment this afternoon with one of her doctors at the hospital. I know it's short notice, and we're on a deadline, but—"

"No way, Harold. Absolutely not. You know we have to get the wiring up today or the inspection won't pass."

I don't know if I'm dicking with Larry or just want to throw my weight around, but I interject. Afterall, I'm technically his boss, right? "Let him finish," I say. "Maybe he has a plan to make sure it all gets done." I turn my gaze on Harold. "Do you?"

"Yeah," he says. I can hear the piss-off in his voice. "I was going to say that I should be finished by lunch time, and if anything comes up in the inspection, Chad can handle it."

"Chad can't handle something this important. No way," Larry splutters. It's possible he's just pissed that I inserted myself. Or maybe he's always a dick. Larry's in his late thirties. Good looking. Probably has a pretty wife and kid at home.

I already want to bust his teeth in, and I'm sure he feels the same way about me for sticking my nose in the business.

"Short of breath sounds serious," I say. "You'd better keep that appointment."

*Eat my shit, Larry.*

Larry's face turns deep red.

"If something comes up during the inspection that Chad can't handle, can we call your cell?" I pull out my phone.

Harold appears relieved. "Of course." He gives me his number while Larry shifts from foot to foot, looking like he's getting anally fisted.

Probably not my brightest move pissing off the foreman on my first day. Then again, these fuckers can't touch me. Not that I need the organization's back in this situation, but the Pachino's have instilled enough fear in Local 352 over the past 30 years that no one in his right mind would even say *boo* to me.

And I'm already a shred closer to enjoying myself. I guess the alpha male in me needed to piss on someone. Plus, I know I'm right. Why the fuck would a foreman deny a guy short of breath from a semi-emergency doctor's visit? That's fucked up.

"Show me who Chad is," I instruct Harold and follow him further into the building.

I'm gonna make this job my bitch. Because right now, it's the only thing I have.

Unless I count Hannah. I mean, I definitely count Hannah, but I can't really consider her mine. Yeah, I claimed her right from the fucking start. And she definitely went with it.

But I have jack shit to offer her. I can't be her boyfriend. Not when there's a gang shooting up my apartment, a murder attempt on my cousin, and I'm an emotional carcass.

She deserves better than that.

Which means... fuck. I probably should leave her the hell alone. Make a clean break before she gets hurt.

Only I'm way too fucking selfish right now to do that.

Because that girl is about the only thing that brings me light right now.

# CHAPTER SIX



*Hannah*

At 5:30 pm, I clean up. I actually told Josie to leave early because there was nothing to do, and having her around made me anxious.

I'm still anxious even with her gone. A different feeling though. This one doesn't have that Josie signature on it.

It has Armando's.

Because I'm trying to figure out what to do. Do I call him to ask when he'll be home? I actually don't even think I have his phone number, which is lame. Will he be at my house when I return? He should be. He left a duffel bag of clothes there.

But what if he's not?

Why did he leave this morning? He said he had to work, but I don't even know what he does. He is the least forthcoming person I've ever known.

Probably because he has the most to hide.

Not that I think he was off robbing banks this morning or anything, but you never know. He's in the mafia. It could be anything.

The memory of him grappling with the guy trying to kill him flashes through my mind. His calm but deadly offensive. He was magnificent. Is it weird that I'm not overly bothered by his career or what he's done? And there was a shooting yesterday that, yes, rattled me, but oddly, I'm already over it. I should be terrified, but I'm not. It could be due to the suited men standing outside my shop all day, but the fear I had this morning has mostly dissipated.

The only true emotion I've had all day is longing. I miss Armando.

To me, the danger just makes Armando all the more appealing. He's the bad boy who lives by a code. There's honor to him. He's killed, yes, but it was in battle. Like a soldier.

Only his army is a Sicilian family, not a government troop.

Maybe I'm trying to rationalize it all, but the fact remains—I can't muster many misgivings about it. Because I like the way it feels to be consumed by him.

And that's when he walks in my front door.

My heart skips to the jingle of the bells. He looks sharp in a suit jacket and slacks, one hand shoved casually in his pocket.

I freeze, breath caught at having him in here again. He strides right over to me without a word, grips the back of my head and stares down.

"Hey," I breathe.

His gaze roves over my face, examining the nose jewelry he gave me as a gift right before Marco was shot. I forgot to thank him for it with all that happened.

"Pretty." A man of few words.

And then he kisses me. It's not the desperate sort of kiss we've engaged in—the kind where he consumes me, and I burst into flames. This kiss is more sensual. Like a Hollywood movie kiss. The kind at the end of the film where the guy gets the girl, the music swells and the camera circles around them.

I don't lift my arms, I just leave them dangling at my sides, loving the feeling of receiving what he's delivering. Letting him take what he wants without trying for more.

When he breaks the kiss, the shop spins in that panning camera feel, and he looks down at me and at the nose ring. "You like it?"

I find my breath. "I love it." And then, stupid me, my eyes fill with tears. Because, as usual, I make the gift mean way more than it probably does. "I meant to thank you before. But with everything that happened to Marco, I—"

He kisses me again. Hard. Claiming.

He's unmoved by the tears. Not in a bad way, but he doesn't react at all, just keeps looking down at me like he's trying to peer into my soul.

"What are you thinking?" I ask. Because I desperately need to get into his head right now.

"I'm trying to figure out if I should take you home to wear out your bed or take you to dinner." My expression must reveal my pleasure because he says, "You want dinner, huh?"

I actually don't care which he picks, I'm just looking forward to being with him, but a date does sound nice. I reach for him, looping my arms around his neck and initiating a kiss.

And then it's on. His dark hunger rears again, and his kiss and touch turn aggressive. He slides his hands up my dress, squeezing my ass, and his fingers are in my panties in the next breath.

I'm already wet. Maybe I was the moment he walked in that door. My body seems to belong to him. He commands it, and all I want to do is give it over to him.

But this is all so dangerous. I'm in way over my head. Any day now I'm going to figure out that he has no intention of continuing with me.

And dammit—isn't that just the insanity of relationships? You don't get a guarantee the other person wants the same thing you do. You just hope and wish and do your best as you fumble through. And yeah, it's messy. Yeah, it usually ends with a broken dream.

This probably will too. I try to remind myself at every breath, and it creates a riot of anxiety mingled with the pleasure that he hasn't left yet, which sadly only heightens the experience.

He's still dangerous to me, only now, it's in a far worse way.

I'm going to lose my heart to him.

He drags his open mouth along my neck and bites me. "You gonna let me fuck you in your shop again?" His voice is rough, a low growl. "Let off steam, so I can make it through dinner?"

Like he would have blue balls if we don't have sex first. Like he needs me that badly. It's a powerful feeling to be that wanted—I've never experienced it before.

"What do you think?" I want more words out of this guy. Find out if his thoughts match the feelings I absorb from him.

"I think you are." He steps back and unbuckles his belt.

My eyes track the movement, finding it slightly threatening and extremely hot.

"Oh, you want the belt?"

Shit! Do I? Definitely not. Only... heat floods between my legs.

He loops the belt around my waist and uses it to pull my hips against his body. "Tell me, *bella*, how do you want my belt?"

A shiver runs through my body at the thought of him using it to spank me. Do I want *that*? I don't think so, but my body disagrees, my excitement level ratcheting even higher.

He continues talking as he backs me toward the door and locks it, turning my *Open* sign to *Closed*. "You want it around your throat while I fuck you from behind? Hmm?" His breath is hot on my ear. "Or should I use it to bind your wrists behind your back?"

Oh, damn. I hadn't considered either of those possibilities. And they both freak me out and turn me on in equal measures.

"Or did you just want to feel it across your ass?"

This time the shiver that runs through me is big enough for him to sense.

"Don't worry, Flowers. I'll make sure you like it."

He shifts the belt to loop under my ass and pulls up to pin our bodies together. My core is molten right now. We've barely gotten started, and I'm already losing my sanity. Close to orgasm.

This is what this man does to me.

It's crazy.

He spins me around and backs me into the break room. "I wanted you on your bed. On your forearms and knees with those thighs spread wide. Will you do that for me later, beautiful?"

"Yes," I swear. I'd promise him just about anything right now. I'm drunk with lust. Drunk on him.

He turns me around and pulls up the hem of my short cotton dress. "You always wear these short fucking dresses. They make me crazy, Flowers. Make it so easy for me to bare your ass and spank this pretty skin purple." The most this guy talks is when we're having sex. No wonder that's the place I feel like we connect best. He yanks my panties down and delivers four slaps to my ass, then rubs out the sting. "You're so hot. So beautiful."

*Keep talking, boss man.* His words are a balm to my ears. Maybe I *am* needy. Clingy. Whatever. Because I drink his praise right now like it's an elixir. But this guy doesn't talk much, so when he does, it feels significant.

"Spread," he commands, shoving my panties down until they drop to the floor. His voice is so deep and sure. I can't imagine anyone ever argues with him.

I widen my stance and hollow my back, emboldened by all his praise. He slides his belt between my legs and brings the leather over my core.

"Mmm," I moan.

He pulls it back out and flicks just the end of it between my legs, spanking my pussy.

I gasp. It stings, but he went lightly. It's not painful. Just a little hurty.

"You like getting your pussy spanked, little girl?"

Oh damn. Now he's calling me *little girl*. Why do I love that so much?

"N-no," I lie.

He replaces the belt with his fingers and rubs over my slit. I'm sopping wet. "I think you do. You want me to spank your ass with it?"

My breath is audible. Not quite a gasp, but a rasping between us. I don't answer.

"Hmm? I think you want to try it, don't you? Are you scared, Flowers?"

I nod my head up and down. I'm facing the Formica table, the grey speckled surface swimming in front of my eyes.

He steps right up to me, kicks my legs wider, and cages my throat, pulling my torso up until my back meets his front. His hardened cock presses against my ass through his pants. "You like a little pain with your pleasure, don't you, Hannah? Or is it fear?"

Hot prickles skitter across my skin. I can already tell I'm going to bawl when this is over because there's pressure in my face, tears in my throat. His hand there amplifies the feeling. He's not squeezing, but he easily could. If those fingers tightened, he could end my life, just like that.

He's done it before, I'll bet.

Yeah, it's the danger. "Fear," I whisper. I feel things so intensely. When sex combines with danger, it amplifies everything.

He bites my ear. Not a nip, but a punishing bite that's almost too hard. "Are you afraid of what I'm going to do to you now?" He's wicked, taunting me like the devil teases his prey.

"Yeah."

"Three strokes," he murmurs and pushes my torso back down to the table.

I let out a whimper. I *am* scared. Scared it will hurt. Scared I'll embarrass myself with my reaction. Scared of being so vulnerable with this man who is quickly becoming so much to me.

"Then I'm going to fuck you good. And after I'm gonna treat you like a princess. *Capito?*"

Do I understand? Not even remotely.

But I am totally on board. A rush of adrenaline floods my veins as he steps back and winds one end of his belt around his fist.

Oh God. What am I getting myself into? This is crazy. Crazier than kissing a killer.

He whips the belt through the air. It lands across the lower portion of my buttocks leaving a line of fire. I gasp, clenching my cheeks together.

"Oh God." I try to straighten, but he holds me down.

"More?" He's letting me know I can stop this even though he's holding me down. I can't bring myself to ask for more. I'm not sure I want it. But I don't tell him to stop, either.

I leave it up to him.

And of course, he understands that. Despite how emotionally unavailable Armando may seem, he's pretty perceptive when it comes to my emotions. He does pay attention.

He whips me again, and I jump and let out a cry this time. He rubs over the two stripes, kneading the pain into a more generalized burning.

I moan softly.

"I said three. You gonna take the last one like a good girl?"

Checking in again.

"Yes." I bob my head, like promising to be good will make it any easier.

He slides his hand down and strokes between my legs. "Yes, you are a good girl, aren't you? Always so good."

I'm trembling all over. Feverish.

He plays with my clit, and I arch back, moaning. He grips my hips and leans over to kiss one of my burning buttcheeks. "One more," he says firmly as he rises.

Damn.

He swings, and I gasp, and then it's over. Armando's clothing rustles, and I hear the crackle of the condom wrapper. He drags the head of his cock through my juices. Finding me so ready, he feeds himself in.

I'm not sure penetration has ever been so satisfying as it is right now. The rightness of him filling me couldn't be more plain. Like my body was made to accept his. Like this is its purpose.

Armando groans. "You're perfect, Hannah. So perfect." He eases in, inch by inch, then slowly backs out, teasing me with his length.

He may require the warm-up, but I don't. I'm ready for him to pound hard. Bruise my hips again or pull my hair. Instead, he slides his hands up my sides, inside my dress and dips his fingers into my bra to pinch one nipple.

I press my hands flat on the table and arch up, lifting my head. "Don't tease me," I tell him. Need's made me cranky now. "I need to finish."

He answers with a hard slam home. "That what you want, beautiful? Nice hard fuck? 'Cause that always suits me."

He bands an arm around my waist, careful to protect my hips from the table this time, and starts jackhammering into me.

"Yes," I moan, satisfaction looming close.

He plants one hand beside mine for leverage and plows into me, his loins slapping my ass, grinding in the burn from his belt, smoothing it out, satisfying it.

"I love you."

Oh shit. Why the fuck did I say that? I definitely didn't mean to. These things always come out of my mouth! I mean, it's true. In this moment, the love is flowing, *but Jesus!*

Why did I have to say it?

He falters, breaking rhythm, and I'm sure this is going to end badly.

Like maybe the worst of all endings because this time I'm freaking head over heels for this guy.

But instead of getting awkward and weird, he gets more aggressive. He fists my hair and pulls my head back sharply, sending a thousand tiny prickles of pain across my scalp.

"You love it when I fuck you hard, don't you, *bella*?" he growls, like he's mad at me. Like he's saying the words between clenched teeth.

"Yes!" I cry out, relieved at how he twisted my words. How he ran with it.

"You're going to like it when I fuck this ass, too."

Oh God. I almost laugh out loud. Maybe that's what love means to him. Anal.

"Harder," I urge him on, wanting to get to my finish, but maybe also trying to rush past my mistake.

He keeps pounding into me, giving it the way I like. Loving me back with that big cock of his.

"I need you."

Oh my God, my mouth won't stop.

He pulls tighter on my hair. "I'll give it to you," he growls. And he does. Even harder. Hard enough I'm getting sore. Wonderfully brutal. Like a beast released from his cage.

And then I scream. I come hard as he gets rougher and rougher with me.

He comes, and when he's done, reaches around to rub my clit and gets a second orgasm out of me.

And now that it's over, I wish we were in bed where I could collapse my face into a pillow and pretend I fell asleep.

# CHAPTER SEVEN

*Armando*

*She loves me.* It's another of those moments where I'm sure I should feel more than I do. But I'm blank.

I mean, I'm not stupid enough to believe all the babble that comes out of a girl's mouth when she's about to orgasm, but I also know Hannah's an open book. She felt love for me in that moment and couldn't keep the secret.

And despite my lack of reaction to the words, I am changed by them.

Only problem is, I can tell she's embarrassed and wishing she hadn't said it.

She's also trembly as hell. I feel her legs wobbling where our thighs meet. I clean us both up and help her get back into her panties.

She avoids eye contact. "Hey, I hope you don't listen to all the crazy stuff I say during sex," she says in a rush.

"Nah, I'm taking it," I tell her, leading her out of the break room and shutting off the lights. "It's been a long time since I've heard that shit."

I shouldn't call it *shit*—that was a poor choice of words. But I'm trying to minimize the importance of it while still appreciating.

She shoots me a slightly tortured look that takes me aback. "Are you upset over her? Your fiancée?"

Oh.

She's jealous. *That* I experience viscerally. Like pleasure straight through my chest.

Hannah's claiming me.

Except I shouldn't like it. Because I can't be her boyfriend. Even if I didn't have an entire gang trying to kill me, I'm not boyfriend material. I'm the walking dead. I have nothing to offer a girl like Hannah—except for great sex. She's bright, vibrant. Has the whole world in front of her. She deserves everything.

I don't want to have this conversation. Like I'd rather pry off a toenail with pliers than talk about Grace, but Hannah's hanging out in the wind, vulnerability making her lick her lips and dart her gaze around.

So I stop in the darkened hallway and face her. "Grace is a cunt. No loyalty whatsoever. When I went to jail, she replaced me in weeks—fucking weeks—with another wiseguy. Didn't have the nerve to tell me for months, though."

Hannah cocks her head. "Does *wiseguy* mean another... guy in the organization?"

"Yeah. Emilio. He's like a cousin. Not a real fucking cousin but like one, you know?"

She stops breathing. I sound a little angry, which pisses me off. I want to go back to feeling nothing about it.

"When I got out last week, everyone thought there would be trouble. Me and him, you know? I used to be..." I don't even want to say it. What I used to be. Cocky. Self-assured. Proud. I don't even know that guy any more. "I don't know. Really fucking alpha dog. And I could be brutal. But you've seen that." I wince a little, thinking of what she saw here at her shop. I'm still amazed she showed no signs of trauma from it.

"The don warned me first thing not to touch it."

Hannah's worry has only increased. I swear to fuck, I'm catching her empath thing because even though I have no emotions of my own, I register hers clearly.

"But the thing they don't know is… I'm not that guy anymore. None of them fucking know me anymore. And I don't give a rat's ass about either of them. I mean, I'm disgusted by that shit—their lack of honor and loyalty—but it means nothing to me. Honestly, you know what would've been worse?"

"What?" Hannah whispers, eyes round.

I draw a breath, only just now realizing what I'm about to say. "If she'd waited for me."

It's true. If I'd had to get out and be expected to be the perfect boyfriend again—to live with Grace and plan our wedding together—I'd be cracking into pieces.

"I can't imagine having to marry her when I got out. Because I'm not the same guy who put the ring on her finger."

"But you would have?" Hannah asks.

I'm not sure what she's getting at or why she keeps picking this scab, but I answer honestly. "Yeah. I mean, I'd give her an out if she wanted it, but I don't break my commitments." I shrug. "I'm a man of my word."

She studies me with those warm brown eyes that see everything and never seem to judge. "You're loyal," she says.

I nod. "Always." I lead her out the alleyway door to the van. I open the passenger side and help her in. "Aw, hey. I forgot to check the mousetraps. You get any visitors?"

She cringes. "Yes."

"Are they still there? Need me to take care of them?"

More cringing. "Yes, please."

I give her a quick nod and go back inside to take care of it. Simple fucking thing for me to do for her. I'm glad there's something.

When I get back, I start the van. "Where do you want to go to dinner?"

"It's up to you, you're buying." She gives me an impish look. She likes when I pay. I used to be rolling in dough before I got picked up. If I still had that kind of money, I would flash it all over for her.

As it is, I'm doing okay. I have half the startup cash the don gave me, and I'll get a paycheck for a couple grand every two weeks. I'm not rich, but I can take a girl out for a nice dinner, for sure.

"You pick." I can't go anywhere I used to go. Hannah's place is still my safest hideout.

"Okay, um... I know a place."

Before I pull out, I pause and look at her. Really look at her. I don't want to just push her jealousy or concern about Grace aside, but I also don't want to discuss Grace anymore. "You're beautiful, you know that?"

Her eyes widen, her smile grows, and I can see she appreciates the compliment. I'm not good with words, but for her, I'll try. Every fucking day, I'll try.

"I've never had the privilege of being with a more beautiful woman before. Truly stunning," I add.

# CHAPTER EIGHT

*Armando*

Hannah directs me to an artsy cafe. Not fancy but not a dive either. Industrial look with the no-ceiling thing where you can see all the ductwork above your head and the one hundred-year-old bricks in the walls. They don't have hard liquor, but the waiter brings us a bottle of wine to share.

I order a burger that comes with sweet potato fries instead of regular ones. She orders a fancy salad—beet pistachio or some shit like that. I watch her pleasure digging in and want to take her out to eat every night. She deserves to be treated way more than she treats herself.

"So what work did you have to do today?" she asks after the waiter disappears.

My instinct is to just clam up and not talk. Go silent on her, but I took her to dinner. We're on a goddamn date, so I shake my head. "Don't ask about my work."

The words are too hard. Too harsh. I can tell they didn't land right by how stiff she gets.

"It's for your safety, Hannah," I try to explain. "We don't talk business, not even with our women."

She studies me for a beat. "Am I your woman?"

I drain my glass of wine and refill it. Fuck. I am so not up for relationship talk. "I don't have a label for you, Flowers."

She fidgets, going silent, and a twinge of something moves around in my chest. What is it? Guilt? For being such a bad fucking date?

I search my brain for something to say and finally land on, "How was your day?"

Her mouth turns down. "Slow. But Tuesdays are always slow." She butters one of the mini muffins they brought in a bread basket. "I'm still working on what you said. Just trying new things." She takes a sip of wine.

"Yeah?" I encourage.

"Yeah. I have some ideas."

I lean forward. "Good. That's good. Like what?"

She shrugs, flushing a little. "A lot of ideas. I don't know which ones are good or where to start."

"You never do."

"I finally started an Instagram account and posted some of my favorite creations on it. Josie's been telling me forever to get on there."

Instagram. There's all this new social media shit out since I went in the pen. I guess I'd heard of Instagram before I went in, but I haven't been on it. I nod, making a mental note to check it out and check out her account. "That's great."

"There's this competition in a couple months. An arrangement contest. Mary Alice got second place in it once. I mean, I don't think it would directly translate to business, but it might help build my reputation. For people who don't trust the business with Mary Alice gone."

"Or people who have just never heard of Garden of Eden. That's a great idea. So you're going to enter?"

She nibbles her lower lip. "Maybe. I don't know. It's an idea."

"It's a great idea." I try to figure out why she even hesitates. Seems like a no-brainer to me. "Is there an entry fee?"

"Um, yeah, but it's not horrible. Like one-seventy-five or something."

"I'll pay it," I offer right away. Not like charity but just to take money out of the equation. If that's part of her deliberation.

She brightens, a faint smile appearing. "Thanks. You really think I should?"

"You're doing it," I say firmly. "What are your other ideas?"

"Well, this is weird, but... do you have any connections with mortuaries?"

"What for?"

"Weddings are big money, but they're also a lot of work. Casket flowers are easy money. I need to get in with some mortuaries, so they recommend me or automatically use me when they're making the arrangements."

I nod. "I'll find out. I might have a hookup. Let me see." Seems to me that every funeral I'd been to for the Family had been out of the same funeral home. I just had to ask my ma about it. "What else?"

"Weddings. I stopped at Hotel Casper, but I need to go visit all the event centers around, so they'll think of me for meetings or weddings or whatever they're hosting."

"That's good."

"The thing is, I hate that part. I like arranging flowers, but the networking part freaks me out."

I shake my head. "Nah. You got this. Like I told you when you stopped at that first hotel, you're beautiful, inside and out. Your flowers are beautiful. Everyone's gonna want to do business with you."

She searches my face like she's looking for any clue I'm blowing smoke up her ass.

"I promise, Flowers."

Our food comes, and I pick up my burger and take a big bite. It's good—better than I expected. "Any other ideas?" I prompt.

It seems I do remember how to have a conversation once I get myself into it.

Hannah's shoulders tighten. "I don't know." She uses one of those doubtful tones.

"Yeah, you do know. What is it?"

She sighs. "I was thinking about seeing if Mary Alice would renegotiate my payments. It seems to me like she'd rather get less than get nothing, right? Like if I go out of business, she's either going to have to come back here and run the place herself or lose her retirement money from me."

"That's right. She's as invested in your success as you are. She's gonna want to make this work for you."

Hannah blinks rapidly. "I really hope so."

"Text her right now and tell her you need to talk."

Hannah's eyes widen. "What?"

"Get it over with. The sooner the better. Text her now."

Hannah slowly reaches for her purse. "You sure this is a good idea?"

"Positive. Get it done."

She glances back at me a few times as she does it, like she's still not sure.

We just finish eating when her phone rings. She looks at it and flips big eyes at me. "It's her."

"Take it."

She hesitates. "No. I'll call her tomorrow." She stares at the screen. "Should I?"

"Take it," I repeat.

"Crap." Hannah swipes across her screen and puts the phone to her ear. "Hi." She stands from the table, plugging her other ear with her finger to hear. "Yeah." She looks at me and points outside then picks up her purse and hustles out the front door.

Oh fuck no. I'm not letting her stand outside on the sidewalk at night by herself. Beautiful girl like her? She's gonna get hassled.

I flag down the waitress for the check and pay it, then exit to find Hannah out front, pacing the sidewalk, her head bent like she's listening intently.

I look around, checking for anything off. Guys loitering, cars running on the curb. I don't like standing out here like I have a target on my forehead, but protecting Hannah is more important. A car drives by slowly, and I keep my eye on it until it turns the corner.

"Right. Yes. For sure. That would definitely help. It would help a lot. Thank you." She looks up at me, her eyes shining with tears. "Thank you," she chokes. "Okay. Goodnight." She ends the call.

"She said yes?" I guess.

Hannah nods with a teary laugh. "Yes. She's going to give me three months off to get back on my feet, and then I'll just pay what I can from there." She falls against me with a sob.

I slide my arms around her and burrow my fingers into her hair to massage her scalp. "That's great."

She pushes away from me. "Sorry." She wipes her eyes. "This is so embarrassing."

"No." I catch her hand and thumb a tear away for her. "I like it when you cry."

She scrunches up her forehead. "Um. That's weird." She slaps my chest. "Sick-o."

I shrug. "I don't feel. I mean, nothing at all. But you—your emotions are so big. I don't know—maybe I'll find my way back through you."

Hannah's expression goes soft and then passionate. She throws her arms around my neck and kisses me. It's one of our crazy, frantic kisses, and my dick gets hard even though I already had her at the shop.

I loop one arm around her waist and slide my hand around to roughly squeeze her ass. "Careful," I say thickly when she pulls back for air. "You're gonna get yourself fucked in the back of your van."

Her pupils are already blown, but they get even bigger, like she loves the idea. I turn her toward the van. "Not tonight." I slap her ass. "I have plans for you that involve the bed."

# CHAPTER NINE

*Hannah*

I drink in the warmth of Armando's hands on my cheeks as his lips lightly graze against mine. His fingers tangle in my hair, and the smell of his cologne fills my senses. His lips are so soft, and he kisses me with a passionate fierceness that leaves me breathless.

The intensity of the kiss is building, the electricity sparking between us. We finally break apart, and I see the fire in his eyes. He looks at me with an intensity that makes my heart flutter. I could get lost in those eyes forever.

He takes my hand in his, and we make our way up the stairs to my apartment. My heart races as we enter through the front door.

"How can I thank you for everything you've done for me?" I ask between our kissing.

He breaks away with a smirk and devilish glimmer in his eyes. "Oh I can think of many ways."

Lust surges. I'm in a frenzy to unbutton his shirt and push down his pants. I need to feel his skin against me. I want to feel his mouth on mine. I can't wait another second. I need him inside me, now.

Our lips meet in an embrace of pure passion. Our tongues lock and stroke one another. His erection presses against my thigh. I have to have it inside me. I have to have him. I drop to my knees ready to please this man in whichever way he chooses.

He listens. He cares. He doesn't mind my overblown emotions.

And for that, he should be rewarded.

I pull down his pants the rest of the way, and his erection springs out, hard and thick, begging for my attention. My own body is filled with a deep need to please him, a craving that can only be satisfied by his pleasure.

I take him into my mouth, savoring the taste of him as I work him deeper and harder. His groans fill the room, spurring me on to take him to new heights of pleasure. He lets out a deep moan and burrows his fingers into my hair, gently guiding me. I use my hand to stroke what I can't take into my mouth, and I feel him lengthening and thickening in response.

A familiar wetness forms between my legs as I continue to work him. I feel him drawing near, and I move my tongue harder, deeper onto him. I can feel his pleasure mounting, can feel his muscles tightening. I want to take him to the edge, want to make him feel the way he makes me feel.

As my hand and mouth work together to bring him to the edge, he strokes my cheek, looking me in the eyes. The lust and desire in them is almost overwhelming. Pushing his pants further down his legs, I take all of him into my mouth and down my throat. I gag around the thickness, and I love the thrill from struggling to breathe. The sensual sacrifice has me doing it again, deeper this time.

"Fuck yeah," he murmurs between a moan. "Deep throat me, Flowers. Just like that."

Armando's praise spurs me to do it again and again. Each time my gagging reflex tightens around his thick cock. I continue to work him. I can feel him drawing near, and I move my tongue harder, deeper onto him.

He lets out a deep moan and tightens his grip in my hair, pulling my mouth deeper onto him. He is so close, so close that I can taste the precum. His breath catches, then he lets out a deep, rumbling moan as he comes down my throat. I swallow him down then lick him clean.

He lifts me to my feet, hands running along the curves of my body, shedding me of my clothes. Once I'm nude, he cups my breasts. Taking a nipple in his mouth, he gently teases it, sending a shockwave of pleasure through me. With hands exploring my body, feeling the curves of my waist, my hips and the wetness between my legs. I don't feel an ounce of self-consciousness when I'm with him. He clearly is turned on by every curve, every swell, and every inch of my body.

He drops to his knees and pulls me towards him. "Sit on the edge of the bed," he commands.

I oblige, and he spreads my legs and buries his face in my wetness. I throw my head back and moan as he works his tongue inside me, stroking my inner walls.

"I'm going to fuck you tonight where you've never been fucked," he warns then delves his tongue deep inside me.

I moan in response, unable to form words.

Armando continues to pleasure me with his tongue, rubbing my clit with his thumb. He pushes his tongue inside me, and the world melts away. His tongue is unrelenting, pleasure raking through me.

He spreads my legs wider, and the heat of his mouth zeroes in on my clit. He licks and teases, igniting a burn deep in my core. The feeling builds and builds, and I find myself grinding my hips into his face.

"I want you," I gasp.

He pays no attention, keeps licking, sucking and stroking me. I grab his hair, pulling him closer, needing to feel the intensity just a little bit longer. I feel the spiral, the chain of pleasure, and I'm almost there. I'm so close I can't take it anymore.

Armando stops and looks up at me with those deep dark eyes. "I'm going to fuck you in the ass. Would you like that, Flowers?"

I nod quietly, not trusting my voice.

"Good girl."

Armando gives me a reassuring smile and guides me to the middle of the bed and lies down next to me. He leans in close and whispers in my ear, "I'm going to make you come. I'm going to make you feel so good. But you're going to have to relax. You're going to have to let me in."

"Is it going to hurt?"

"A little. But you are going to love every biting bit of it."

His lips drag across my neck, nibbling on my ear. He slides one hand down my body. I arch my back, and push my breast into his hand. He squeezes it, working my nipple between his fingers.

I feel the hardness of him against my hip, and I am overwhelmed with the desire to have him inside me—inside my ass.

He grabs me by the ankles and pulls me towards him. Spreading my legs and positioning his body between them, he places his cock at my tight back entrance.

"It's going to stretch, baby. Are you ready?"

"I'm ready," I say, taking a deep breath.

He teases my ass with the head of his penis, working it only on the outside, as if warning me of what's to come. I let out a deep breath and relax, knowing that the more I let go of any tension, the more I am going to enjoy this.

Just as he pushes the tip of himself into me, I feel the tightness and stretching. It's not bad. It actually feels good.

He begins to push into me, working his way in.

"Breathe and relax, Flowers," he whispers, as I feel him push past the tightness.

"Ow," I gasp. "It hurts."

"You're doing so good, baby. Just a little more."

Panic sets in. He may be too big for me to take this.

"Oh, it hurts," I plead.

"Just breathe, baby. Don't tense. Relax and take me."

It feels like a shock of electricity rushing through me, my body stiffens, and a shiver runs through me.

As he works himself deeper, I begin to relax. I find myself sliding into a sort of trance, feeling him slide deeper and deeper into me. He is all consuming, his flesh warming me, his cock filling a part of me that's never been touched this way before.

"Are you okay?" he asks.

I nod. "Keep going," I whisper.

Armando groans and slides deeper. He is so deep and so thick that I can't breathe. He holds himself there, deep inside me, and I feel the pleasure, the tightness begins to build inside me. It keeps growing, so full, so hot.

"You're so fucking tight," Armando moans as he pushes my legs together and strokes deeper. I feel the blood rush inside me, his length filling me.

It hurts again as he thrusts deeper. But like Armando warned—the pain feels so fucking good.

Armando begins to grind into me, sweat drops from his body onto mine. The heat of his passion melts me, our flesh on fire for one another.

He thrusts in and out of me like a man possessed. His hands stroke my breasts. His lips are on my neck, kissing and sucking. He pulls out and works the head of his cock in circles around my tight hole. The pleasure is almost too much to bear. He guides his cock back into me, and a twinge of pain erupts in my ass. My body trembles as he thrusts into me again. Suddenly, the pleasure returns, and the pain is replaced. He pulls back and pushes in again, each time with a little more force, a little more depth. He hits my walls, over and over again—harder, faster.

I take him from every angle, the pleasure of his cock moving inside me pushes me to the brink of an orgasm. I tighten up, squeezing him. He pulls out, my ass tightening around him. He thrusts back in, and I scream in pleasure. My body erupts in fire. Each thrust is like a shockwave of carnal sensations.

He buries himself into me, as far as he can go, as deep as he can go.

"I'm close," I moan.

Armando holds his hand against my mouth, "I want to hear you. I want to hear you come for me. I want to hear you make that sweet little moaning sound."

My whole body is trembling. I push myself into him, filling myself completely with his cock. My hand reaches down, and I grab my clit, stroking it with my fingers.

"I love the way your ass feels on my cock, baby," he moans in my ear.

Armando grabs my hips, holding me onto him.

My body explodes in a mixture of orgasmic pleasure and a sharp, stinging pain. He continues to thrust in and out of me as the waves of pleasure crash over me.

I feel him explode inside of me, filling me. Each thrust pushes another wave of electricity inside of me. He thrusts once more, holding himself deep inside. He pulses and fills me, forcing me to come with him again.

Armando quickly turns me onto my side, spooning me from behind. He wraps his strong arms around my waist, pulling me closer. He kisses my shoulder and wraps his leg around mine.

"That was incredible," I say, my voice breathless.

Armando kisses my shoulder. "Are you all right?"

I nod. "I am."

"Good," he says, wiping the sweat from his brow. "Because I'm not done with you yet."

# CHAPTER TEN

*Armando*

"Mando."

It's Arturo, calling me during the day while I'm at the job. Non-job. Lame place I have to go to earn a paycheck for doing nothing. I walk away from the construction area, phone at my ear. "Yeah?"

"Heard you're pissing people off down there." He chuckles.

I bristle, even though he's not wrong. Larry, the foreman, fucking hates me. I've been tailing him all week, watching what he does, asking questions. Throwing my weight around when I feel like it. Which generally comes off as questioning his decisions in front of his men. Because I don't like him and because I can.

I've been a cocksucker, but he's definitely a *stronzo*, too. None of the workers like him, and I think that's telling. But none of the workers like me either. No one wants to be my enemy; that's a given. But no one wants to be my friend either. Even the man with the doctor's appointment whom I stood up for steers clear of me. Can't say I blame any of them. It's best to avoid men like me.

"What'd you hear?" I growl.

"Don G got a call from the union guy. Asking real nice if you could work less on your no-work job." Arturo's low laugh carries across the line. "You giving 'em hell down there?"

"What the fuck else am I going to do?"

I shouldn't complain. I sound like a spoiled bitch when I have this cush job for doing jack. Trouble is, I did jack for five years. I'm sick of that shit.

"You calling to tell me to stop?"

"Nah, you do whatever the hell you want. It's your show, Mando. The don was just passing the message along. You do what you see fit with it." He pauses. "You know you don't have to even go there, right? It's all for show."

"I need to be here," is all I say.

Picking up on what I'm saying, Arturo adds, "Whatever makes you happy, man."

I should say thanks now, but I don't feel like it. I've been irritable and restless all fucking week. I got no info on who wants me dead or what they're planning next. Marco's out of the hospital, but my guilt over the incident hasn't eased. And though I'm coming to work every day, the only thing I want to do is rush home and fuck Hannah. The woman has a grip on my dick so hard that I can't explain it. I have nothing to offer her but my cock, and though she doesn't seem to mind, I have to figure out a way to give her more. She deserves so much more. But I have to force myself to leave her and come here. I have to show up and spend all day with these *stronzos*, and I keep waiting for my life to start again, but it hasn't.

It won't.

All that time in prison waiting to get out and live again, and now it's impossible. I took the prison with me.

And now I got these pussies crying to the don like the bitches they are. My mood is growing more foul by the second.

"Listen, Mando—it's my grandson's baptism on Sunday. We're having a party at my house after. I'm sorry, my daughter didn't get you an invite because she made the list before you got out. No hard feelings, eh?"

"Yeah. No. It's fine."

"So you'll be there? St. Angela's at 10 a.m.."

Fuck.

"Yeah. 'Course. I'll be there."

"Good. I'll see you then. *Ciao*."

"*Ciao*."

I hang up the phone, more irritable than ever. I dial Luis, who's given me jack shit since we spoke five days ago. "Yeah, what'dya got?"

"Inconclusive. What I know is that, yeah, the Hermanos have it out for you. But I suspect I'm the guy who tipped them off that you're out. Which means they didn't send the first hit, but pro'ly were the ones who blew up shit at your apartment."

I curse in Italian.

So now I have two fucking hits on my head.

Fucking great.

"I need more," I say.

"Working on it."

# CHAPTER ELEVEN

*Hannah*

It's 6:30 pm, and he hasn't shown up. Every evening this week, Armando appeared at closing time to drive me home in the van. We ate dinner together. Had sex. Watched TV. I knew it was dangerous getting used to him being around.

I knew all along he wasn't staying. This isn't permanent.

But even so, I let myself sink into it. Enjoy the false domesticity. Cooking. Eating. Doing dishes. Him taking the trash bag or recycling box out of my hands and telling me he'd do it. Dying a little when he returned from the dumpster with empty boxes for Shadow to play in. It's obvious he has grown a fondness for my kitten, and my heart pitter-patters at the thought.

But tonight he's a no-show. I stalled. I worked late, making more arrangements than we need around here, hoping he'd show up, but he hasn't come.

My stomach tightens.

I have a phone number for him, but when I called it, there was just a generic voicemail, and he didn't answer my text. For all I know, he's changed phones by now. I'm not sure what the mafioso do. Get new burner phones every other week?

I'm not even sure that texting and calling him is appropriate. He's hiding at my house because someone's trying to kill him, and he wants to keep me safe. And we also happen to be having sex. Lots of it. But that doesn't make him my boyfriend, no matter how much it feels that way.

He already made that clear.

No matter that this deranged unlikely scenario might actually be my healthiest relationship. Because Armando sees me and doesn't flinch. And that's the most terrifying thing of all.

I get in the van and drive home, my fingers tight on the steering wheel as I navigate city traffic. It takes me forever to find a parking spot because I came home so late, but eventually, I catch someone pulling out, and I back-and-forth it thirty or forty times to fit the giant van in the small spot.

When I get up to my apartment, I hesitate outside the door.

I hear the TV.

My stomach somersaults in a weird mix of elated and pissed off. I push open the door to find Armando on my couch, feet on the coffee table, watching TV. I thunk my purse down on the table and shut the door. "You're here."

"Hey." He wears his expressionless mask that right now makes me want to kick him in the shin.

I head into the kitchen. He has boxes of Chinese takeout open on the counter, and it looks like he's already eaten.

It's one of those moments where I know I'm overreacting—I know I'm doing clingy and weird, but I can't stop the trainwreck of petty emotions coursing through me. I dump some of the food into a bowl and pick up a fork then turn around, eating standing up.

"So, I never agreed to just having a permanent roommate," I say.

He's acting casual, uncaring. It seems like a legitimate statement.

He picks up the remote and mutes the television then unfolds his large body to stand. His relaxed position on the couch was deceptive. Now he's suddenly imposing, both in size and his don't-fuck-with-me demeanor.

He walks toward me, a frown on his face.

I have to work to hold my ground and not shrink from his intensity.

"You want me to find another place to go?"

My stomach bottoms out. This is the ironic behavior of relationships—where you push away when you actually want more. I set the bowl of food on the table. Thrust my chin forward and shrug.

He gets closer, towering over me, but not touching. I *want* him to touch me—to handle me in that rough, insistent way he has, but doesn't. "Yes or no?" His tone is total authority, demanding my answer.

I swallow and shake my head, turning away.

He catches my arm and pulls me back. "What's this about?"

"Nothing," I snap, annoyed now.

"Tell me."

Maybe I don't want to be handled because I'd definitely prefer to turn away from him now. My neck and chest flush with heat. I shake my head again and look away. "I don't know."

*"Bullshit."*

Armando has a way of saying *bullshit* that hits like a punch. It's an assault on my senses, and I feel it everywhere. When I flinch, he pulls me even tighter, right up against his body. "Don't say you don't know when you do. Why are you pissed at me?"

I blink back the tears. Damn them! Damn him! Damn me. I'm so ridiculous!

He circles one arm around my back and brushes my curls back from my face with his free hand. "What'd I do?" he asks it softer, now.

"I'm sorry," I gulp then berate myself for apologizing. "I'm being stupid. Let's drop it."

He doesn't move, just stares down at me. "We're not dropping it. Just say it."

I shrug, defeated. It's so freaking embarrassing, but I admit it. "You could communicate a little more. You know—call to let me know you're coming here instead of the shop?"

Yep, I sound clingy. His expression turns vacant, and he releases me and steps back, just as I expected.

"I told you—I'm being stupid. You're not my boyfriend." I throw my arms in the air. "I don't know what the hell you are, but you're not that." I pick up my bowl of food again and walk around Armando, who's just standing there like a stone statue. I flop down on the sofa and turn the volume back up.

Armando doesn't move. I see nothing on the TV screen, even though my gaze steadily fixes on it. All I can do is force myself to swallow down the emotion in my throat. He's going to leave now, and that's fine. That's what needs to happen. Because the sooner I get him out of here, the sooner I can stop caring.

He walks to the door but stops and stands there, facing it. When he turns back, I dart a glance at him. "I can't be your boyfriend, Hannah." He sounds ancient. Exhausted.

I cringe. I don't want to hear this. I definitely don't want to hear this.

"I got nothing to offer. I'm fucking empty and dead and apparently one inch from having someone blow off my head."

"I know," I rush to agree, wanting to end this conversation. "Can we forget it?"

"I'm an asshole for staying here. I know I'm a dick for taking from you when I have nothing to give." He gives me a long, unfathomable look. "But I don't want to leave." He shoves his hands in his pockets.

My stomach's up in my throat, and I can't breathe. I don't know what to say.

He shrugs. "You want me to go, I'll go. That's all you gotta say. Your choice."

Like a fool, I get up and rush to him, wrapping my arms around his middle and pressing my face against his chest. His arms band around me, strong and protective. This guy would kill for me in a heartbeat. I know that already. Loyalty is his gig, and I'm under his protection.

"I don't want you to go," I admit. My belly shudders trying to hold in a sob.

He slides his hand into my curls and massages the back of my head. "Cry for me, Flowers," he murmurs, resting his chin on top of my head.

I sob a little into his shirt. "That's so wrong."

"Maybe I'll wake up," he murmurs. "Maybe I'll wake up and be your prince."

My prince. He already is my prince. Maybe that's not saying much, maybe that's just proof that I haven't dated any men of quality. Or maybe I just desperately *want* him to be my prince. I want to believe there's a happily-ever-after for the two of us. Love will conquer all and all that sap.

But for now, it's enough. Knowing he *wants* to wake up and be my prince is everything.

And I also love him for accepting my tears. Never once has this guy told me not to cry, and I've been told that my whole damn life by nearly everyone in it.

Armando tells me to cry more. To cry for him. Cry his tears.

It makes them like a tribute. Gives them meaning. Makes them pass through me more easily. I dry my cheeks with my fingers. "What are you watching?" I say to bring things back to normal.

"Old *Parks 'n Rec* episodes. Come here." He takes my hand and my bowl of food and pulls me to the couch. "What do you want to watch?"

I curl up beside him, and he puts his arm around me, tucking me into his side as he opens Netflix and scrolls through my recommendations.

*"Married to the Mob,"* I blurt then regret it because now he's going to think I want to marry him. I'm sure my subconscious produced it because I've been mulling over the consequences of dating someone in the mafia.

"Oh Christ," he mutters but looks it up.

"We don't have to watch it," I backpedal.

"Nah, it's funny. And Michelle Pfeiffer's hot. Just don't ask me if anything's realistic."

"I won't," I promise, but I want to. I want to know everything there is to know.

Even more because he won't tell me. But I also love that he keeps the lines so clear.

Shadow mews and jumps up on the couch then promptly curls up in Armando's lap as he pulls up the movie. He sets the remote down and rubs under Shadow's chin.

"Hi, buddy," he says as Shadow starts purring loudly. "You are the coolest cat, you know that?"

I smile and join in on petting Shadow. "Sorry I was bitchy."

"Don't apologize." He kisses the top of my head like a real boyfriend. "I fucked your life up, I know." He lowers his head and brushes his lips across mine. "I appreciate you letting me stay here."

And just like that, I forgive him for everything.

# CHAPTER TWELVE

*Armando*

The next few days, I'm better about communicating with Hannah. I text her at the end of the day to tell her when and where I'll see her. Or what's for dinner. I was a dick that night she called me out, and I deserved a tongue-lashing. But Hannah gave me grace, and for that, I appreciate her even more.

It doesn't kill me to treat her like the queen she is. At least for now, while we're doing this. It's not a relationship because there's a deadline on it. I find out who wants me dead, get rid of them, and I can move back into my own place.

I wish I had something more to offer her, but I don't. I got nothing for anybody at this point. I'm not fit for any kind of relationship.

I stop at the mortuary on my way to Hannah's. I'd called my mom in Arizona to ask, and she gave me the name—Angel's Wings, run by a guy named Angelo. Of course he's Italian. Don G wouldn't give business elsewhere if there was a *compaesano* available. Plus, I imagine there are advantages to having a mortician in your pocket. Hiding evidence or whatever.

I push my way into the quiet lounge. There are candles burning in front of a cross and pamphlets on grieving. A thirty-something woman in a tasteful blue dress comes out to greet me. I wonder if she's related to Angelo. This doesn't seem like the kind of business you hire outsiders for. No one wants to work in a mortuary, right?

"Welcome." Her voice is hushed and respectful, like we're in a church. "How may I help you?"

"I'm here to see Angelo. Tell him it's Mando, Don Pachino's nephew."

I see recognition and curiosity glint in her eyes. Definitely a family business. She's not just some receptionist—she knows the organization.

"Of course," she says smoothly. "I'll let him know you're here."

A few moments later, a short balding man in his sixties comes out from a room down the hall, tugging the lapels of his suit jacket closed around his protruding belly. He holds out his hand like I'm an old friend. "Mando, what can I do for you?"

"Yeah. Can I go back?" I lift my chin toward his office.

He only falters for a second. He's a little nervous, but I doubt he's done anything to warrant fear of the Family. The greeting was warm, just perplexed. "Of course, come on back."

I follow him back and sit down across from his desk as he straightens a pile of papers. "I know you're the mortuary of choice for my family, so thank you for your service over the years." I'm fucking rusty at greasing wheels—real rusty. But this is for Hannah, so I'm gonna make it work.

Angelo bobs his head, still concerned. "Of course, anything for Don Pachino and his family members."

"I'll get right to the point. You order flowers for the caskets? When people don't have their own florist or don't want to do it themselves?"

"Yes." The word holds a question.

I push a stack of Hannah's cards across the desk. "I'd like you to order through this business—as a favor to me." I tap the stack. This is how deals get done in *La Famiglia*. I don't ask—I tell. But then I call it a favor.

Up to him if he wants to question whether he has to do it or if it's a polite request.

Nah, fuck that. Even polite requests get followed when you're dealing with the Pachinos.

Do I wonder if Don G would be pissed I'm throwing around his name to help the girl I'm fucking? Only a little. If he gets pissed, I'll take the heat. I didn't think it merited begging permission before I went in. I'm not killing anyone here. Just making a business deal.

Angelo picks up one of the cards and looks it over. "I'd be happy to."

There. Easy as that.

I stand up. "Appreciate it." I stand up and shake his head. "I'll show myself out. *Buona giornata.*"

"*Buona giornata,*" Angelo says to my back.

I don't look back.

When I get home—well, to Hannah's home, but it feels way more like mine now than that empty fucking apartment with all my old shit that I can't go back to—I find her in the shower.

I strip out of my clothes and join her for another fuck-fest.

Because putting my dick in Hannah is pretty much the only thing worth living for at this point.

"Hey," she says, welcoming me to join her.

I'm not in the mood to talk. I've spoken more words today than I care to. Right now, I have one goal in mind. I flip Hannah around, placing her palms on the shower tile.

"Stick your ass out," I demand.

Hannah does as she's told, knowing that I like it when she's submissive like this.

She's so wet that my cock slides into her with ease.

The heat from the water turns us on, and we fuck with reckless abandon. She's making these little mewing noises, and her moans are loud as I ram my cock into her.

"Fuck yeah," I growl. "Just like that."

The water pelts down on our entwined bodies, her hair matted down on her face, my hands holding onto her hips tightly.

"Harder," she demands. "Give it to me harder."

I oblige her, and her moans are loud enough that they may as well be screams.

I'm slamming into her, and it's so fucking hot.

I want to come all over her ass. I slide my hand around to explore between her legs and play with her clit.

"Fuck. Oh, fuck. Oh, fuck," she cries, louder than ever.

I spank her ass as I drive deeper with each thrust.

It's animalistic. It's primal. And I fucking love it.

"Do you like when I spank you, naughty girl?"

She pushes out her ass and wiggles it. "I do."

I spank her again and again. "That's what I like to hear."

"It stings with the water," she says with a moan.

I swat her harder. "Good."

I reach around her body and spank her pussy. She squeals, and I feel her pussy tighten around my cock.

"Who's pussy is this?" I ask as I spank her pussy again.

She mewls out, "Yours. Yours."

I spank it again. "Don't ever forget it."

I push her hair from her face and lock eyes with her as I pump into her.

She's so hot.

Her face is tense. Her body is rigid from the pleasure I'm giving her.

I come deep inside of her, and she screams as she comes on my cock.

I pull out of her, and we both collapse against the shower wall.

The hot water is still beating down on us, and it feels so fucking good.

I pull away from her and smile.

"What's that look for?" she asks.

"You're mine," I tell her. At least for now. This very moment. And I'm going to enjoy every fucking minute of it.

She smiles and kisses me.

"Yeah. I'm yours."

# CHAPTER THIRTEEN

*Hannah*

"Yes, I will be there," I promise my mom as I put together a red, white and blue horse wreath. Mary Alice had this gig every Fourth of July making wreaths for the horses in the parade downtown. What sucks is she took their fifty percent deposit before she left, so by the time I pay for the cost of the flowers, I won't make a red cent off this deal. But hopefully, they'll book again next year.

"We missed you last week," my mom complains. She's miffed I didn't come over last Sunday night for dinner. I hate obligating myself to go this Sunday—I'd rather hang with Armando, and I doubt he'd go anywhere near my parents' place, but there's no putting my mom off.

"Your dad had some medical tests done. He has high cholesterol and blood pressure," she tells me. "They're doing stress tests on his heart."

"Anything I should worry about?"

"Well, he was getting short of breath. But I got him in to see a good specialist." My mom is a nurse at a pediatrician's office, so she knows all the best doctors in Chicago.

"Could just be because he's fifty-five and out of shape," I offer drily.

"He's not that out of shape. Your dad is still solid muscle."

"Solid muscle with a beer gut," I observe, but my mom is right. My dad works hard, and his body is in better shape than most guys his age.

"So what's new for you?" my mom prompts.

I nibble my lip, debating whether I should tell her about Armando. I hate keeping stuff from her, but what am I going to say? This mobster is hiding out at my apartment, and he can't leave because my life might also be in danger?

"Mary Alice is giving me a break on payments for a couple months, so I can get business boosted."

Thanks to Armando getting me to renegotiate.

"Are you having trouble?" My mom's voice gets tight and concerned. My parents were worried about me taking on the business. They helped me put together a down payment and wanted to help more, but my little sister, Kiana, is at SIU, and tuition is killing them.

"No, I think I'm going to be okay." I'm not sure if that's true or not, but it sure feels more true than it did a week ago. But then, everything seems easier with Armando around.

Screw it, I had to tell her. "I'm sort of dating this guy."

"You are? Bring him on Sunday!" my mom exclaims.

"Um, no, Mom. It's way too soon for that. And he's kind of anti-social at the moment."

"What do you mean, anti-social?" she asks suspiciously.

I exhale, weaving another flower through the mesh. "I don't know. He's got some PTSD going on. He says he doesn't feel anything."

"Is he military?" my mom asks.

"Not exactly. But it's kind of like that. I don't want to tell his story without his permission."

"Well," my mom says slowly. "Sounds like his brain chemistry is off. You should get him to get his neurotransmitter levels checked."

It's so obvious I wonder why I didn't put a scientific explanation to Armando's malaise. Of course it's a brain chemistry thing. Depression probably set in in prison, and the change in neurotransmitter levels wouldn't just instantly shift back because he's out. It makes perfect sense. I'm not sure he's the kind of guy I could convince to get tested or help, though.

Still, it made me feel better. It seems like Armando thinks he has some kind of fatal flaw. Soullessness. Like he's dead inside and nothing will bring him back. Maybe knowing it's just neurochemical would help him.

"Thanks, Mom, I will talk to him about it. That's a good idea."

"Well, if he wants to come Sunday, he's welcome. And we won't make a big deal about it."

"No chance, Mom. I'll see you then."

"All right, sweetheart. Love you."

"I love you, too."

I end the call as Josie breezes in late again. My stomach cinches up the way it always does when she's around these days. My beautiful best friend who's killing me as an employee. I think about Armando. What he would say. How he urged me to text Mary Alice as soon as I'd arrived at the decision. My mouth goes dry just thinking about what has to be done here.

"Josie," I start, my voice coming out like a bark.

"Yeah?" She tucks her purse behind the counter and comes over.

"Can we talk?" The flapping wings in my belly grow more wild.

I swear I see the same anxiety I feel on Josie's face.

Oh God. I don't know if I can do this.

"You know I love you, right?"

She goes still. She's wearing a bronze highlighter on the tops of her cheekbones and forehead that make her look like a model. I'm actually not sure why she isn't a model, come to think of it. She's got the beauty and the height.

"Yeah." Her voice is quiet. Almost scared.

Shit.

I'm scared too. That's why I've put off this talk for so long. I don't want to lose my best friend. I don't want to hurt or offend. But if I don't change things, I'm going to end up hating her. I think about Armando just forcing me to say why I was mad. It had been a good thing. Maybe this would be too.

"I don't know if you working here is the best thing for our friendship." I get it out all in one burst, like the air rushing out of a balloon.

Her eyes widen. "Yeah," she says, sounding sort of surprised.

I open my mouth, but nothing comes out, mainly because I'm taken aback by her *yeah*.

She runs her thumbnail over the workbench surface, eyes down. "I've been wanting to talk to you about it for a while." Her voice is low and sorry.

I blink. "You have?"

She nods. "Yeah. I just didn't want to leave you in the lurch, you know? This place is everything to you, and you're working so hard. I don't want to abandon you, but... the flower shop isn't really my gig. I want to get back to interior design, but I'm not going to put myself out there if I keep telling myself you need me."

Relief pours through me, mingled with a little hurt. "Right. You were just helping me out. Of course this isn't your gig."

"And you were helping me," she says firmly. She'd been depressed after getting laid off from her apprenticeship when I offered her the job. She was good at interior design. I figured she'd love flowers, too. We both wanted to help each other. But it makes sense that this job is holding her back from her dreams.

"So... you'll find something else?"

She nods. "If that's okay with you. I'm sorry—I've been meaning to talk to you about it for weeks, but it never seemed like the right time. My stomach's been in knots every time I was here."

"Oh my God," I let out a laugh. "That was yours!" I rub my own belly, and suddenly, now that I've identified its source, the nervous feeling is gone. "I was feeling it with you!"

Josie shakes her head. "You are so weird. Like sci-fi weird."

"I know. Star Trek—I'm Gem, the empath who steals other people's pain. Only I don't really take it out of them, I just feel it too. It's such a useless ability. Like why couldn't I be able to see ghosts or predict the future or something? Being an empath isn't a superpower, it's a handicap."

Josie pulls me in for a hug. "It's a superpower. You just haven't figured out how to use it yet. Now, what can I do to help today?"

"Casket flowers. I think Armando ordered this mortuary to give me business. The guy called and said he understood I'd be the flower shop he'd be dealing with from now on." I open my eyes wide and cover my exaggerated "O"-shaped mouth.

"Oh my God! Married to the mob has its advantages."

"I'm not married. But um, yeah. He makes things happen, that's for sure."

Josie clucks her tongue. "I never would've put you with a guy like that, but you know what? I can see how it works."

"You can?"

She shrugs. "Yeah. I mean, aren't Italians supposed to be so passionate? And you're Ms. Emotional. So that works."

I shake my head. "He's not emotional at all. He's the opposite—like flat-liner opposite. But you're right. Maybe that's why he doesn't mind my over-emoting. He's used to it."

"Or, maybe he's just really into you." Josie waggles her eyebrows.

My fingertip touches the diamond nose ring he bought me. "It doesn't seem like it. But I don't know. I guess it's hard to tell with a guy who's flatlining on emotions."

"If you've done your crying thing and he didn't bail, he's into you. Trust me."

I give her a stupid-happy smile, wanting to believe. And also so relieved that we got work things out in the open.

I hate to jinx anything, but it seems like my life is actually starting to work. I'm facing business stuff. Friend stuff. I'm having great sex. I'm in love with a guy who accepts me for who I am and also encourages me to be something more. There are problems to be worked through, for sure. But hope is soaking in through all the broken places.

# CHAPTER FOURTEEN

*Armando*

Hannah straddles my ass, her wet pussy sliding over my skin as her hands slide slowly up my oiled back as she gives me a massage.

It's hard as fuck to take. It isn't sex—I already thoroughly fucked her. I fucked her until the neighbors banged on the wall, and I had to yell some shit back at them to shut them up.

But this?

Almost torture. I don't like being touched.

Maybe I used to—hard to say. It's been too long to remember. I always liked being the one in charge—that's for sure. But now it's hard to take. But Hannah wants to give me this. She made a big deal about it—went and got the oil from the bathroom, looked so pleased with herself.

So I close my eyes and listen. I listen to her soft, breathy moans as she leans her weight into her thumbs, working up the ropes of my muscles. Like stroking my body turns her on. I soak in the attention she's paying to my body, the way she finds all the tight spots and works them until they soften.

And the whole time, I'm trying to figure out why she's doing this. Why she *wants* to do this.

"What did you miss most when you were in prison?" she asks. "I mean, apart from freedom?"

Oh Christ. Are we really gonna talk about prison right now?

All the work I'd done—the work she'd done—to unwind my muscles goes out the window. I feel my tone turn solid again. I'm tempted to shut her down. Just not answer or tell her I don't want to talk about it. But she's giving so much right now, it makes me feel like an asshole. So I think about the question.

"Sex would be the easy answer. I missed it most at first—before I..."

"Before you what?" she asks softly.

"Before I changed. Lost feeling. Stepped out of my body."

Hannah's hands continue to caress my back, smoothing away the ripples of discontent that come out as I speak.

"So what were you looking forward to most when you got out?"

I consider. It was mostly freedom. I didn't want to see anyone. Or anything. "Food, maybe," I admit. It's the only thing that even sounds remotely true. "My ma's baked ziti. Gio's calzones."

"You like your Italian food." I hear a smile in Hannah's voice. "All I know how to cook is spaghetti."

She says it like she wants to cook for me, which is really fucking sweet. Especially considering she's no cook, as far as I can tell. I don't even think she likes food much.

"Were those the calzones you ordered the first night you were here?"

"Yeah."

"What about the ziti? Have you had it yet?"

"No. I sent my mom out of town while things are hot for me here. I don't want her to get hurt." Now I'm talking business with Hannah—something I never should do.

But it feels right. Like she deserves these facts about me.

"Are you close to her?"

"I was before, yeah. She's the best. She'd do anything for me, you know? My dad walked out when I was eight, so it was always just me and her."

"And you got into the Outfit to help support her?" She slides her hands down my shoulders, massaging the muscles of my upper arms.

I wait a beat, knowing I shouldn't discuss any of this shit with her. "Yeah," I say finally. "Her sister is married to the don. So I was considered family, and the offer of a job was made to me. Me and Marco and Leo. They're cousins on my mother's side. We all came in together. They're like brothers to me now—as you know."

Hannah hums softly and continues kneading my muscles.

"Why are you doing this?"

"What?"

"The massage? The questions?"

She's quiet, and I figure it was a dick question, and she doesn't want to answer. Then she says, "I just want to make you feel good. That's what you do for me."

She wants to make me feel good. Not with any goal in mind beyond that. Not even an orgasm. It's not a transaction with her.

That knowledge does something to me. A fissure splits in the metal casing around my chest. Slowly, over a period of long minutes, I let go. I let her give to me in this way she wants to.

And then I roll over and stare up at her. She stares back, her oiled hands running over my pecs, down the fronts of my shoulders. And all the while, I stare right into her warm brown eyes.

"You're beautiful," I murmur.

It's deeper than sex. Way deeper. This... this is fucking intimacy. And I must feel something. It's nothing huge. Discomfort. A soft fuzzing. A fullness in my chest.

*Connection.*

That's what I feel.

I'm locked on and locked into Hannah. I reach for her face and mold my hand around her cheek. I grasp her head and flip her to her back, swapping our positions. My urge is to go hot and heavy, like we always do, but I rein it in. Keep up the staring. The connection. I kiss her like it matters. Not like I'm gonna die if I don't—which is how I usually feel when I'm touching her. This time, I go lighter. I listen to the space between us. Around us. In us. My lips slide over hers, and it's sensual. Erotic but not lustful. My tongue slides in her mouth, our lips twist.

I'm hard again, and I can't stand the thought of putting on a condom. It's like I want no barriers between us in this moment.

I nudge her legs apart and push in. "I'll pull out," I promise. "I want to feel you. Is that okay?"

There's so much trust in her gaze as she nods, eyes shining like I'm her whole world right now. I glide in and out of her slowly, not working on a rhythm, just relishing every single sensation. This must be love. If I could feel it—this must be what makes people believe they're in love.

Presence.

I kiss her again, like it's our first kiss. Like I'm the kind of guy who goes slow and shows a little finesse.

Eventually we do build to a crescendo, and I'm so locked into her gaze I almost forget to pull out and come on her belly.

And that seems wrong. Like I definitely should've come inside her. I rest on my forearms and keep staring down at her until those warm brown eyes fill with tears. She stares right back, letting them leak out the sides of her eyes and fall to the pillow beneath her, not hiding or shrinking.

Giving me those tears—offering them up to me.

If only I could figure out how to use them.

But it feels like I am. Like I'm closer.

Feels like something's changing in me. Some trapped piece of humanity is finding its way out.

Every night with Hannah brings me closer.

·············································

# CHAPTER FIFTEEN

·············································

*Hannah*

I can't help but feel cheerful as I plan the surprise date to the waterfall. My pulse skitters with anticipation, hoping the serene setting might be exactly what Armando needs to relax and open up to me. Plus, I desperately need a break from the constant grind of worrying about Garden of Eden. We both deserve this moment of respite.

"Armando." My voice trembles slightly with excitement. "I have a surprise for you."

He raises an eyebrow, his expression unreadable. "What is it?"

I step into him, my hand brushing down his rock hard abs. "If I told you, it wouldn't be a surprise."

He hesitates. "Surprises...might not be the best for me right now. Considering my situation."

I expected this kind of response. It doesn't deter me, though. I'm determined to bring some light into his life, even if it means chipping away at those walls he's built around himself.

"I understand your situation, but I promise this won't put us in danger. Here"—I toss him the keys—"You can drive." I hope giving him that measure of control will be enough to get him to come with me.

The corners of his lips tilt up slightly. "Okay, Flowers. If I'm driving." He reaches a hand out for me, and I take it as we leave the apartment and head out to the van.

He remains guarded, however, as we drive towards the unknown destination. I'm aware that the weight of his past and the dangers that still lurk in the shadows are never far from his mind. But I'm hell-bent on breaking through the wall he's built to protect himself.

"Are you going to give me any hints?" he finally asks, glancing over at me as he drives.

I'm practically bouncing in my seat, struggling to not blurt out what's coming. I've never been good at secrets. "Nope!" I giggle, shaking my head. "You'll just have to wait and see."

He lets out an almost imperceptible sigh. "Fine," he concedes, a small smile tugging at the corner of his lips. "But I'd better be impressed."

I can't contain my happiness as I notice Armando's smile. It's subtle, but it's there, and it feels like a victory. We're getting closer to the waterfall—a little hidden secret just outside Chicago's city limits, and my giddiness grows with every passing mile. I haven't been to this place in ages, and I'm questioning why as we get further and further from the city.

"Almost there." I practically bounce in my seat. "Less than thirty minutes, I promise."

Armando shakes his head, but there's amusement in his eyes. The sunshine is starting to break through his grumpy exterior. My plan may be working.

I direct him to the spot. The sound of cascading water fills the air when we finally step out of the van. The lush forest surrounding us feels like a secret world just waiting to be explored.

"Do I look like the hiking type?" he teases, but I can see he's happy.

"It's not far. Come on," I say, grabbing Armando's hand and leading him down the well-worn path towards the waterfall. "You're going to love it here."

As we walk closer to the roaring water, he scans our surroundings, taking in the vibrant greenery and the delicate wildflowers that line the trail. It feels like the perfect moment to share a piece of my past with him.

"I used to come here all the time when I was a kid," I confess, feeling a bit vulnerable as I open up to him. "It was a needed break from the loudness and the dullness of the city. This is where I first fell in love with flowers and foliage. I always knew I had to work around color and beautiful things."

"I've never been much of a nature man." He walks up and puts his arms around me. "But I am now." He kisses my jaw. "At least, I'm a huge fan of flowers."

I laugh.

"Yep, I have all the color and beautiful things I need simply by being around you."

My heart skips a beat with my victory. Armando is softening. Opening up. I can feel it in the steadiness of his embrace. I hear it in his words. And as he looks into my eyes, I see it.

He takes a deep breath. "Prison was... suffocating," he begins, his voice heavy with emotion. "Everything was gray, from the walls to the floors to the bars that kept me caged. It was hard to imagine anything else." He leans down and gives me a small peck to the lips. "Until now."

I can't even begin to comprehend what he must have gone through, but I appreciate his willingness to open up to me. I have so many questions about his time in prison, but I'll never ask. I'll simply wait for moments like this. When he willingly gives me little peeks into that time.

"I don't deserve you," he says.

"You do." I kiss him. "You're the best thing that has happened to me."

"My life..." He pauses and looks around. He motions to his surroundings. "This has never been my life. Flowers and nature and—this just wasn't my life."

"It is now." I tug him toward the final destination.

As I lead him along the riverbank, the sound of rushing water and delicate bird songs fill the air. The sun filters through the trees, casting dappled shadows on the ground beneath our feet.

As we continue our stroll, my foot slips on a particularly slick rock.

Instinctively, Armando reaches out and grabs my arm to steady me, ensuring I don't lose my balance. His watchful touch sends a thrilling jolt through me, but as much as I appreciate his protectiveness, I want to show him that I'm capable of taking care of myself too. Gently, I pull my hand away from his grasp and navigate the rocks on my own.

"Everything okay?" His voice is gruff. My tough guy. Everything is a growl or a grumble.

"Everything's fine," I assure him. "I just want to prove to myself, and to you, that I can do this on my own."

He nods, seemingly understanding my need for independence, though I can see the concern in his eyes.

"Just don't bust your ass, Flowers," he says, stepping back slightly but still watching me closely. "I've grown fond of it lately."

The sound of the waterfall grows louder as we make our way along the riverbank, its misty spray creating a refreshing coolness in the air. As we round a bend, the waterfall comes into full view, cascading down into a crystal-clear pool below.

"Wow," I breathe, struck by the beauty of the scene before us. "It's even more amazing than I remembered. It's been way too long since I've been here."

Armando takes in the serenity of the secluded spot. His gaze lingers on me for a moment, and I see the tension in his shoulders easing ever so slightly. He looks almost... relaxed.

"Close your eyes," I instruct gently, placing my hand on his chest. He hesitates but eventually complies, his eyelids fluttering shut. With my other hand, I pluck a wildflower from a nearby bush and bring it to his nose, letting him take in its delicate scent. "Smell that?" I ask softly. "That's what happiness smells like to me."

Slowly, he opens his eyes, and he leans toward my neck and inhales deeply. "This is what happiness smells like to me."

He pulls me close and captures my lips in a searing kiss. His hands tangle in my hair, anchoring me to him as we lose ourselves in each other's embrace. Scooping me into his arms, he lowers me onto a soft bed of moss near the waterfall's edge. Our lips meet again, the passion between us growing more intense by the second.

I run my hands down his chest, feeling the defined muscles ripple beneath his shirt. Armando's hands roam over my body, tracing the curves of my form. I arch my back into him, a low moan escaping my lips as he presses his body tightly against mine.

His lips leave mine, trailing soft kisses down my neck, sending shivers down my spine. His fingers hook into the waistband of my jeans, tugging them down my legs along with my panties. I moan as his fingers brush against my inner thigh, his warm breath tickling my skin.

"Hannah," I think I hear him say, over the sound of the waterfall.

He kisses his way back up my body, his lips meeting mine once again. I feel the heat emanating off his body, the bulge in his pants pressing against my thigh. I reach down to undo his pants, freeing his hardened length.

I pull him closer to me as our bodies become one. The heat between us is palpable, our desire igniting a fire that burns fiercely. I want him, need him, and he knows it. His hands travel down my body, finding the sweet spot between my legs. I gasp as he begins to stroke me, each touch sending shockwaves of pleasure through my body.

I don't think it's possible to ever tire of this man. I've never had so much sex in my life, and I'm greedy for more.

He groans as I wrap my hand around him, stroking him slowly. He kisses me deeply, his tongue tangling with mine as he positions himself at my entrance.

"I want you." His voice is gruff with desire. "I don't know if that was your intent by taking me here. But I can't resist any longer."

Slowly, he pushes himself inside of me, his hardness filling me completely. I moan loudly as he begins to thrust, each movement drawing me closer and closer to the edge. I dig my nails into his back, holding on to him as our bodies rock together.

I can feel myself getting closer to climax with each passing second. I tense my muscles and hold my breath, trying to hold back the ecstasy I know is on the horizon.

Armando's breath is ragged, his face and neck flushed with passion. I can tell he is getting close to release, but something is holding him back.

"Come with me," I whisper in his ear, squeezing my thighs against him as I press my lips to his.

My whispered words seem to spur him on. He slams into me harder than ever, burying himself deep inside me. I cry out as I feel a wave of pleasure crash over me. My muscles spasm as I feel Armando shoot his seed into me, shaking with pleasure as he climaxes.

He collapses onto me, stealing breath from my lungs. Our bodies are slick with sweat, but we don't move. We lie together for a few moments until Armando finally pulls out of me. He kisses me slowly on the lips.

We don't speak. We only breathe.

As the sun begins to dip below the horizon, casting the world around us in hues of gold and pink, Armando and I break apart for a moment, our gazes locked. The look in his eyes tells me everything I need to know—he's in this just as deeply as I am.

# CHAPTER SIXTEEN

*Armando*

I double park the van and throw the hazards on. We're downtown on Saturday because Hannah has to deliver a dozen horse wreaths for the Fourth of July Parade. It's a fucking zoo, which doesn't bother me. I like the energy of the city, or at least I used to, back when I felt.

Back when I wasn't looking over my shoulder every second.

Hannah's turned on by it, for sure. She's in this hot as hell white halter dress that makes her tits look edible but has me ready to slam my fist into the first guy who looks at them.

"What are you scowling about?" she asks lightly, piling a huge stack of wreaths into my waiting arms.

"Nothing," I mutter.

"Bullshit."

I look around the flowers because it's not like her to curse, and I realize she's mimicking me from the other night. She grins.

"Your fucking cleavage," I admit. "I'm gonna kill the first *stronzo* who looks at it. And then I'll have to go back to prison."

She smiles like I just told her something sweet. "No, you're not. You're going to strut your stuff because this"—she indicates her banging body with her hands—"is with *you*."

Aw, damn. I'm sort of surprised by the sensation that promise produces. Maybe I really am catching feelings because a sense of approval leaps up when she says it.

Like, *damn straight.*

I pin her with a gaze. "That"—I give her a sweeping once over—"is *mine.*"

Just want to get things straight.

She arches her brows. "Oh really?"

I shake my head in warning. "Don't give me shit. I will lose it. You know how little it would take for me to bust a guy's face in."

Her smile grows wider as she pulls out the rest of the wreaths to carry herself. She likes my asshole ways.

Lucky for me, I guess.

We make our way through the gathering crowds. The parade doesn't start for another two hours, but things are already jam-packed. We find the group that ordered the wreaths and leave them with the person in charge.

"Want to stay and hang around a little bit?" Hannah's face shines bright. Her crazy curtain of curls swing down her back as she walks, sweeping her butt with each rotation of her sexy hips. She's happy today—much lighter. She and her BFF Josie had a talk last week, and Josie quit. Or Hannah fired her. But it was on good terms, and Hannah's mood lifted a ton. I should have known that relationship was weighing on her with all the other problems at the shop.

"You don't have to get back to the shop?"

She left Josie in charge today—her last day of work, but I know her friend isn't completely reliable.

"I might as well enjoy the help while I've got it," she says. "I'm going to be working on my own for a few months while I get caught up. This is my last chance to *not* work on a Saturday."

I reach for her hand and lace my fingers through hers. I swear some of her joy is seeping in. We walk through the gathering crowd, the sun warm on the top of my head and my shoulders. I stop at a Jamba Juice to buy us smoothies because it's getting too hot. Music blares from speakers on the streets, people walk by in red, white and blue clothing and face paint.

And then we pass a few guys on the sidewalk. I recognize the tattoos, but I drop my head and keep walking. After a few paces, I steal a look backward.

*Fuck. Me.*

They stopped and are looking back at me.

I thrust the keys to the van in Hannah's hand. "Run. Get to the van and wait for me. If I don't show in twenty minutes, drive home. Forget you knew me."

"What?" Panic flares in her eyes, but I shove her into the thick of the crowd and take off running the other way—down an alley—praying they don't try to go for Hannah to get to me.

They don't. All three of them tear down the alleyway after me.

I run hard, but my cardio abilities suck at the moment. I may have been able to keep up my physique with push ups and crunches in the pen, but we weren't exactly running laps around the prison yard.

Still, my life fucking depends on it. I'm just praising baby Jesus they didn't have guns, or I'm pretty sure I'd already have a bullet in my back.

There's a decent chance I could take all three. Depends on if they have weapons. But we're in the middle of downtown with people everywhere, and I sure as hell don't want cops involved in this shit.

I run for the L station and manage to get in and pay before they come up the stairs. There's a security officer standing near the top, and I park my butt near him, stooping to pretend to tie my shoe.

They come up and look around, miss seeing me at first.

The train rumbles in and the doors open. I move too fast, catching their attention, and they dash over to get in the same car as me. I start running toward the end of the car, watching as they push through the throng of people to get to me. The moment the doors start to close, I leap back out.

One of them manages to get off to follow me. The other two point and shout through the window as the train speeds away.

My chest is tight from the running, and my heartbeat's out of control.

I stare at the guy who got off, and he stares back at me. It's just one guy. I could probably take him. He's not so brave without his friends.

Of course, I might have to kill him like I did the hitman in the flower shop. And we're in a public place, which means I'd go down for it.

I'd go down hard.

I remember Hannah.

She's the reason I ran in the first place. To draw them away from her.

She's the reason I didn't risk it. And she's waiting for me now.

I take off, racing down the steps two at a time and jumping the last four. I just have to lose this guy and get to Hannah. I can do this, even though my lungs already feel like they want to give out.

I tear down the streets. I think the gang member is following, but I push into a crowd and lose him.

I run eight blocks until I spot the van. I look around first. No way I'm going to let anyone see me get in it if I'm still being tailed. Hannah's behind the wheel, and she starts it up as she sees me coming. It looks clear. I jump in and slam the door.

"Drive, Flowers. Fast as you can."

She nods, nostrils flared, eyes wide. Her hands grip the steering wheel in a strangle-hold.

As we tear off down the street, I catch sight of the guy.

And I'm pretty sure he sees me, too. He sees the van. He fucking sees Hannah.

"Fuck!" I explode, slamming my palm down on the dashboard.

Hannah jumps. "What?"

I shake my head. I don't want to tell her—she's already scared enough. "It's okay. I'll take care of it," I promise, even though I have no fucking clue how I'm going to do that.

All I know is no one's going to fuck with Hannah. And I'm going to make sure I stay alive to keep that promise.

# CHAPTER SEVENTEEN

*Hannah*

My heart pounds the whole trip back to the apartment. Armando makes it worse by not saying a word, yet his body is a live wire, filling the van with tension that chokes me.

*It's not mine,* I remind myself, remembering how the anxiety I'd felt around Josie had actually been hers. *It's not mine. It's his.*

Still, the man I care deeply about, despite my desire not to, is being hunted down like prey, so dismissing the tension is impossible.

"Who's after you, Armando? Why?" I know I shouldn't ask. He doesn't talk business, but this is the second time I have felt like I could die. I have the right to know.

He rubs his face. "I killed a guy in prison. Self defense." He shoots a dark glance at me like he's worried about my reaction to his words.

I nod. I'm actually not shocked. I knew bad stuff had happened to him there.

"He was a member of a gang. Now they're trying to kill me."

*No!* a voice inside my head screams. Even though I knew someone was trying to kill Armando, hearing him explain it makes me want to rage for him. He's a good guy. He has a moral compass. He follows a code. He's been mixed up in dangerous business from a young age, but it isn't his fault. He's doing the best he can with what life dealt him.

And I really want life to give him a break for a change.

I find a parking place when my mom calls. I'm going there tomorrow for dinner, so I ignore it. As soon as it stops ringing, she calls again.

I throw the van in park and pick up.

"Hannah, it's your dad," she says in a tight voice. "I had to call an ambulance for him, and I'm following now."

"What?" A sob chokes my voice. Could this day get any worse? "What happened?"

Armando goes rigid at the terror in my voice, his eyes intent on my face.

"He had a heart attack, but I kept up chest compressions until the paramedics got there. I think he'll be okay, but we'll have to see."

"What hospital?" I manage to ask.

"Cook County."

"Okay," I choke out. "I'm coming now, too."

"Thanks, baby. Call me when you get here."

"What is it?" Armando demands the moment I end the call.

"My dad." Tears spill down my cheeks. "He had a heart attack."

"Okay," Armando says softly, pushing his door open. "I'll drive, *bambi*."

I have no idea why he called me Bambi, but I don't have the presence of mind to inquire. I tumble out of the driver's seat and let him catch me on the way down. He pulls me into a strong hug.

I soak it up—all his strength and power. His support.

We drive to the hospital in silence, me picking at a hangnail until it bleeds. Armando shooting me concerned glances. He's got someone trying to kill him, but he's more worried about me.

We find my mom in the waiting area, and I must introduce her to Armando, but it all blurs together. As we sit down to wait, I start to understand Armando's hollowness.

There's a numbness that sets in. I block out the fear, and in its place I find nothing. A total void of feeling.

I hear sounds—the television, people talking—but they mean nothing. I feel Armando's hand clasping my own but can't find any gratitude for it or even comfort.

I don't know how long we wait like that, me not breathing, barely living, waiting in the purgatory of the unknown. Of emptiness.

And then a doctor comes out. "Mrs. Munn?"

My mom surges to her feet, and Armando and I follow.

"You can come back now. Your husband suffered a mild heart attack. I'd like to keep him here under observation for the night, but he'll probably be ready to go home by tomorrow."

"Thank God," I breathe, falling into Armando. He holds me up with a strong arm around my back. His lips find the top of my head before we follow the doctor back.

As we walk in and I rush to give my dad a hug and kiss, I adjust to the shock of seeing my dad hooked up to monitors, so I don't notice that Armando's gone stiff.

"You," my dad spits, looking past me at Armando.

My mom and I gape in surprise to find him glaring at Armando.

"Why the hell are you here?"

I peer up at Armando, misgiving twisting in my gut. "You know my dad?"

"Oh no," my dad cuts in, decisively. "Not my daughter. You are not messing around with my daughter."

Armando holds his palms in the air and starts backing toward the door.

"*Armando*." I try to stop him with my voice.

"I don't want to upset anyone." He lifts his chin toward my dad.

It's good thinking, considering my dad just had a heart attack, but I'm too upset by the fact that I don't understand what's going on.

"Wait, how do you know my dad? What's going on?"

"We work together," Armando says, and my dad snorts. Armando's at the door now. "I'll wait for you in the lobby. Take your time."

I stare at the closed door, feeling more than a little abandoned. What. The actual. Fuck? I look at my dad. "How do you know him?"

My dad frowns at me. "Tell me you are not dating that guy."

"Not exactly." I'm screwing him on the regular, but we're not officially dating. Somehow I don't think that's going to endear my dad to Armando, so I don't explain.

"He's the one you told me about?" my mom asks. "With PTSD?"

I nod, still eyeing my dad. "Tell me how you know him."

My dad tries to push himself to sit up and winces.

"Take it easy." I lay a hand on his chest. My mom slips her hand in his and squeezes.

"Hannah, honey, I hate to tell you, but that guy is mafia."

I almost laugh. "Oh. Yeah, I know, Dad. Remember I told you the building where I have Garden of Eden is owned by the mafia? I've known Armando for years."

My dad's brows drop low, and he glowers at the door. "I do not want you involved with guys like him."

I bristle, but my dad's in a hospital bed, and I probably shouldn't upset him. "He's a decent guy, Dad. But we're not officially dating, so don't worry about it."

I look at the door again. Armando didn't even try with my dad. He just backed out and left. I know he's not my boyfriend, but it still hurts. Like he didn't fight for me.

"So wait, does he work in *construction*?" I ask, hardly believing it.

"He's dead weight," my dad says. "One of those guys the mafia forces the union to give a job to. He collects a paycheck for doing nothing. He's a real upstanding guy, your boyfriend," my dad sneers.

"He's not my boyfriend." I say it firmly, like I'm willing myself to finally accept it. I mean, how much more obvious do I need him to make it? We're not entering a relationship. He's hiding out at my apartment, and we're having sex.

End of story.

I'm all hot and flushed. Now that I've seen my dad is okay, I'm itchy to get out of there. I lean over and give him a kiss on the cheek. "I'm glad it was just a small heart attack, Dad. You really scared us."

"I'm okay, baby," he tells me, catching my hand and squeezing it. "You coming over tomorrow night?"

"If you're home, I'll be there. If not, I'll come see you here. Deal?"

"Deal," he says.

"Okay, feel better, Dad."

"Be careful with that guy, Hannah," my dad warns as I reach the door. "I don't want you mixed up in the kind of trouble he'll be into."

Armando may not have fought for me, but I don't feel the same way. I turn back, defensiveness creeping up my neck. "He's not into trouble. He literally just got out of prison and is trying to figure out how to live again."

My mom's eyes go soft, my dad's mouth tightens. "Bring him to dinner tomorrow, so we can get to know him," my mom suggests, and my dad shakes his head with that resigned sort of huff.

"I don't think so," I say, my heart sinking deeper into my belly. "But thanks. I'll see you both tomorrow."

I leave the room and find Armando standing with his hands stuffed in his pockets looking sexy as hell. His face is that blank mask he always wears. I'm ready to be pissed, but then he opens his arms and folds me into them, and I let out an involuntary sob.

He combs his fingers through my curls and rubs the back of my head, and I melt into him, letting his strength sustain me.

He's not my boyfriend, but in this moment, he's enough.

He's what I need him to be.

# CHAPTER EIGHTEEN

*Armando*

We drive back to the apartment in silence. I don't have to be a mind reader to know that Hannah is upset. This is one of those times where I don't know how to do the relationship shit. Do I push her to talk? Or do I allow her to be quiet and alone with her thoughts? Finally, as we pull into the nearest parking spot, I turn off the van and reach for her hand.

"I'm sure your father is going to be just fine," I try to comfort.

"He's tough," is all she says as she stares out the window, pulling her hand free from mine.

I take a deep breath. "Have I upset you?" It's a stupid question. It's clear that I have.

She shrugs. "Not really. Maybe. I don't know." She turns her head and locks her eyes with mine. "Are you going to make me ask how you know my dad, or are you going to just offer that little bit of information?"

"We work at the same construction site," I say.

"Construction? You go to work every day in a suit." Her eyes narrow as she says the words.

"I oversee." I'm trying to give her enough information to satisfy her, but I'm uncomfortable telling her anything at all. "I helped your dad get some time off to go to an appointment with his shithead boss, and we crossed paths that way." I can see she's analyzing every word I say. "It's not like we really work side by side or anything." I don't want her thinking her dad is mixed up with the mafia or is keeping secrets from her.

Feeling I've said enough, I get out of the van, rush over to her side, and lead her upstairs hoping we can end this shitty day on a higher note. Or at the very least, we can crash and pretend it never happened.

Shadow greets us at the door, and I pick up the little fur ball, happy that someone in this room isn't sour with me. I eye Hannah as she walks straight to the kitchen where she begins doing dishes right away. This isn't Hannah. Not my Hannah.

"Okay, spill it," I say, putting Shadow down after a couple scratches behind the ear. "Tell me what I need to do to cheer you up."

"Nothing," she says, running a wine glass under the water. "It's been a long day."

"Hannah," I give my best warning voice. "I don't like games."

She turns off the water and faces me. "I don't either." There's accusation oozing from her lips.

"I don't *play* games either."

She shakes her head. "I don't even know how to explain what we are to my parents."

And there it is... something was said in that hospital room. I'd be a fool to think that nothing was. It was very obvious that Hannah's father wasn't pleased when he saw me.

"What do you want me to say?"

She crosses her arms against her chest. "Nothing, I suppose."

"Are you unhappy?" I ask, hating to think I've truly upset this woman.

"No. I'm actually happier than I can ever remember being. But I'm also... confused."

"How so?"

"One minute you are using words like 'mine' and being overly protective and possessive, and the next minute I'm realizing I know absolutely nothing about you. And then when it comes to defining us,

I don't even know how to begin. And then we spend all our evenings together like we're a couple, and yet we aren't—"

My phone rings, and I think we're both grateful for the distraction.

"Go ahead," she tells me, motioning for me to pick it up.

It's Marco. "Hey," I say as I regain my composure. Hannah and I were about to go down a path that I wasn't ready for yet. I could tell she was going to start asking me questions I didn't have answers for. At least not the right ones.

"Meet me at *Sins* tonight. Leo is also coming—"

"I'm with Hannah," I interrupt, using her as my excuse to not attend the sex club that Marco loves to frequent.

"I know. Bring her. Leo and I are both bringing women as well. It can be one of those triple dates that the normal people do."

"We are far from normal," I say. "Hannah and I have had a long day—"

"Do I have to use the 'bullet in the ass' card to get you to do something with your cousin?" Marco cuts in. "Because I will. My ass will forever be scarred, and—"

"Marco wants us to go out with him and Leo tonight. They have dates," I say to Hannah.

Her eyebrow spikes, and she smiles. "That sounds like fun."

I shake my head and mouth the words 'no'.

"It would be nice to see them again," she continues, ignoring me.

"It's a sex club," I blurt out, knowing that will be enough to scare her away.

She tilts her head. "Really?"

"Stop trying to talk her out of it, dickhead," Marco chimes in from the other side of the phone. "Don't make her think it's all leather and orgies."

Hannah's smile grows. "We like sex." I can't tell if she's teasing me or not. But she genuinely doesn't seem afraid of the idea.

"My bullet ass will see you at *Sins* at nine," Marco says and hangs up before giving me an opportunity to argue any further.

"There's a sex club in Chicago?" Hannah asks.

"Several, but this one is tamer as far as sex clubs go. It's more of a high-end nightclub where there are no rules when it comes to public sex, nudity, sharing and so on."

"Will we have to have sex there?"

I choke on an unexpected laugh. "No, Flowers. We don't have to do anything."

"Will you want to?"

I pause to consider the idea. I've had sex at *Sins* before. But never with someone I considered mine. And Hannah is most definitely mine. I don't share. I don't even want anyone to look at her. I'd snap the neck of anyone at the club who even dared do a double take in her direction.

I take a step toward her and reach for her arm, tugging her against me. "What I want is sex *now*."

She looks up at me, her eyes meeting mine. A smirk spreads across her face as she runs her hands up my chest and around my neck, pulling me into a deep kiss. Our lips move in sync as she pushes me back onto the bed, straddling me.

"I'm sorry," she says. "For my... mood."

I shake my head. "Never apologize for your feelings, Flowers. I need them. I crave them."

"I don't do well with unstable," she says.

"I get it. I do."

My hands find their way to her waist, gripping her tightly as she grinds against me. I work my hands under her shirt, feeling the softness of her breasts, teasing her nipples into hard peaks. She arches her back, pressing her ass against my cock.

I give a firm squeeze, eliciting a gasp and moan from her full, pouty lips.

"I don't have the right answers to your questions. I'm not ever going to be that man. But what I can give you—" Tugging her shirt over her head, her breasts bounce with the motion, and I take a second to simply stare.

I then work a hand between her legs, rubbing her clit through her panties, drawing a moan from her. A sly grin splits her face, and she slides her panties and then her skirt off, revealing everything.

I unbuckle my belt and reach for my zipper. Hannah grabs my

hands and laces her fingers with mine. Our eyes lock as she unzips my pants and tugs my belt off. She holds my belt in her teeth, and she shakes her head back and forth. I chuckle at her, and she spits it out, licking her lips seductively. She reaches for my pants, pulling them off and tossing them to the side.

Her legs wrap around me as she pulls me close, grinding against me. I slip my hand under her, but she slaps my hand away. Instead, she reaches down between us, her delicate fingers searching for my cock. Her fingertips find the head, and she rubs against it, spreading my pre-cum over her pussy lips.

I reach into the nightstand and draw out a condom. I shudder when she grabs it and slides it on, groaning at the feeling of her hand moving over me. She straddles me again, sliding down over my rock hard cock.

"So what do we do at this sex club?" she asks, her voice husky.

"Whatever we want," I say, sucking her bottom lip.

She rolls her hips, grinding against me. "What if I want to have sex for all to see?" she mouths against my mouth.

"That's fine. Just know I go back to prison afterwards," I groan, lifting my hips.

She puts her hands on my chest, pinning me to the bed as she moves up and down, taking me deep into her. I feel her nails digging into my chest, and I wrap my arms around her, holding her tight as I thrust up into her.

"Why prison?" she asks, her voice breathy.

"I'd have to kill any man who saw you naked," I answer, pushing up harder.

I speed up my thrusts, my grip so tight it's almost painful. I can feel her tightening around me, her body ready to explode.

"Then we can watch? Will that keep you out of prison?"

"We can watch, Flowers. Maybe. I might kill the man you watch, however."

"Well then maybe I'm going to just have to keep you distracted," she says as she cries out as I thrust even harder.

"I'm counting on it. Keep me out of prison, baby girl. That's your task for the night."

"Deal," she moans, convulsing around me as I erupt inside her.

# CHAPTER NINETEEN

*Hannah*

The city lights dance on the black car's tinted windows as we pull up to Sins, Chicago's notorious erotic nightclub, and one of Marco's favorite stomping grounds, according to Armando. He insisted on hiring a town car to take us, and it is an indulgence I'm not used to. I glance at Armando, his chiseled jawline and piercing eyes making my heart race. His tailored suit hugs his muscular frame, radiating an air of dominance and mystery that has me captivated.

"Ready?" Armando asks, his voice low and commanding. I nod, tugging at the hem of my little black dress. The plunging neckline and daring slit up the side make me feel both vulnerable and powerful, and I'm eager to see what the night has in store for us.

I would never have pegged myself as someone who would willingly enter a sex club, but I'm excited. I also love the idea that I'm getting to enter on the arm of Armando as his date. Like a couple. Like boyfriend and girlfriend. Marco didn't just invite Armando. He invited his *woman* too.

As we approach the entrance, the pulsating beat of the music reverberates through the ground beneath us, drawing us into the seductive world that awaits inside. The velvet rope is unclipped by the imposing bouncer, and we descend down the dimly lit stairs, leaving the ordinary world behind.

The moment we enter the club, we're enveloped by its intoxicating atmosphere. The leaden lighting casts shadows on the writhing bodies around us, while the music sends vibrations echoing through my very core. My eyes are immediately drawn to the sultry performances taking place on the elaborate stage—dancers in barely-there outfits moving with hypnotic grace, their bodies entwined like serpents tempting their prey.

"Wow," I breathe, feeling Armando's hand on the small of my back as he guides me further into the club. "This place is... intense."

"Intense can be good, Hannah," he murmurs close to my ear, sending shivers down my neck.

I nod, my heart pounding in my chest as I take in the sights around me. Couples and groups indulge in various acts of pleasure, emboldened by the club's unapologetically sinful nature.

"Do I look?" I begin. "Or is it rude?" I don't know the rules. I don't want to look like the inexperienced sex club virgin I clearly am.

"Shh," he whispers, his fingers brushing against my cheek. "Don't overthink it. Just let the atmosphere guide you. You aren't going to do anything wrong."

I close my eyes for a moment, taking a deep breath and allowing myself to be carried away by the symphony of sensations that surround us. The heat of Armando's body pressed against mine, the taste of the anticipation on my lips, the sound of the music that sends shivers down my spine—all of it combines into an experience unlike anything I've ever felt before.

As we continue to explore the depths of Sins, my desire for Armando grows stronger with each passing moment. I can feel the electricity between us, our bodies drawn together like magnets as we navigate this seductive world that seems to exist solely to ignite our passion. My senses are heightened, every movement and sound feeling like an electric current running through my body.

"There they are," I say, motioning toward the VIP section where Leo, Marco, and their dates are seated. The ruby-red velvet ropes surrounding the exclusive area make it feel even more alluring.

"Ah," Armando's voice is smooth and confident, a stark contrast to the tightness in my chest as we approach the table. He leads me by the hand, his grip firm yet reassuring.

"Mando! Hannah!" Marco exclaims, his warm smile welcoming us as he rises from his seat. "Glad you could make it."

"Your *ass* didn't give me much of a choice," Armando replies, pulling me closer to him as if to remind everyone present that I am his.

"Let me introduce you to our lovely company for the night," Marco continues, gesturing to the two stunning women sitting beside him. "Isabella and Valentina."

"Nice to meet you both," I offer, doing my best to appear at ease in this unfamiliar environment. Both women appraise me with curiosity, likely wondering how someone like me ended up with a man like Armando.

"Likewise," Valentina purrs, her eyes flicking to Armando with interest before returning to me. I can't help but feel a twinge of jealousy, despite knowing it's unfounded.

"Let's get some drinks," Armando suggests, sensing the need to break the tension. "What's everyone having?"

"Champagne for Valentina and me," Isabella chimes in, batting her long, fake lashes.

"Whiskey on the rocks," Leo adds, his voice deep and commanding.

"Make it two," Marco agrees, his focus momentarily shifting from Valentina's barely-there dress.

Armando nods, glancing at me expectantly.

"Um, I'll have a glass of red wine, please," I say, feeling decidedly out of place among this group.

Armando brushes his thumb over my knuckles before turning to the waiter who has just arrived. "You heard the lady—one glass of your finest red wine, two whiskeys on the rocks, two champagnes, and for me... a scotch, neat."

The waiter scribbles down our orders before disappearing into the shadows.

"Here's to a night we won't soon forget," Leo proposes as soon as our drinks are delivered, raising his glass in anticipation.

"Cheers to that," Marco agrees, the clink of our glasses a sharp contrast to the pulsating music surrounding us. We drink deeply, the potent concoctions fueling the fire that's already burning within each of us.

As the alcohol courses through my veins, my inhibitions start to dissolve, replaced by a growing hunger for everything this night has to offer. There's so much to see. So much to feel.

"You okay?" Armando leans to my ear and asks.

I nod. "It's a lot to take in."

"Let's go for a walk. Take a look around." Armando takes my hand and leads me through the throng of bodies, his confidence and presence commanding the space around us. As we reach an open spot, he turns to face me, his eyes locked on mine with an intensity that sends shivers down my spine.

"You want to dance?" His voice is barely audible over the pounding beat, but I nod in response, eager to lose myself in the rhythm.

"You dance?"

"No. Not at all. But I will for you."

My chest warms. This guy. I'm addicted.

As the music swells, Armando and I move closer together, our bodies instinctively finding their own beat within the chaos. Our hips sway in sync as we dance, his strong hands guiding my movements with electric precision. The heat between us grows with every passing moment, and I'm lost in the delicious friction it creates.

"I'm never going to hear the end of this from Marco and Leo." Armando leans in close, shouting into my ear so I can hear him. "I feel like a brick wall gyrating."

I laugh loudly, appreciating that he's giving me something to help put me at ease even if it means he's out of his element. Armando may not be able to give me the right words all the time, but he certainly knows how to give me the right actions.

My body moves with newfound fluidity, uninhibited by doubt or restraint. Armando's gaze never leaves me, and I feel a surge of pleasure knowing that I am the sole object of his attention.

I become increasingly aware of the illicit activities taking place around us. Couples entwined in various sex acts, some concealed in shadowy corners while others brazenly display their passion for all to see. Kinky play unfolds before my eyes, a world I had only ever glimpsed in whispered conversations and late-night fantasies.

The sight of these unapologetic displays of desire only serves to fuel the fire growing within me. I feel a primal urge to explore this darker side of my own sexuality.

"Armando," I breathe, my voice barely audible above the music as I glance around at the debauchery surrounding us. "This is... no words to describe it."

"Is this place too much?" he asks, his dark eyes searching mine for any sign of discomfort.

"No," I reply, surprising even myself with the conviction in my voice. "I'm intrigued."

"Good," he grins, pulling me closer until our bodies are flush against one another.

The pulsating beat of the music seems to vibrate through my bones as Armando and I dance. The heat between us is palpable; the air around us crackles with electricity as we share heated glances and stolen touches.

"Your heart's racing," Armando murmurs huskily into my ear, his breath hot against my skin, sending shivers down my spine. "Is it the excitement, or is it me?"

"Maybe a little of both," I admit, feeling bold under the euphoria of the night. Our eyes lock, and for a moment, everything else fades away—the music, the people, our friends. It's just us, and the undeniable connection that's been growing stronger since the moment we met.

He watches me intently, his gaze dark and possessive, feeding the fire within me. I can feel his need for control, his desire to protect me, even in this chaotic world we've chosen to explore together.

As we dance, I catch sight of Marco and Leo at the edge of the dance floor, their laughter mingling with the music. Their dates have moved closer, body language open and inviting, as they engage in flirtatious banter. Leo brushes a strand of hair behind his date's ear, his smile all charm and mischief, while Marco leans in to whisper something that makes his date giggle and blush.

Every now and then, they glance over at Armando and me, their approving smiles telling me that they're happy to see us together.

I place my hand on his chest as the music continues to pound around us. "Let's take a break from dancing and explore more of Sins. I'm curious to see what else this place has to offer."

"Are you sure?" he asks, his dark eyes searching mine for any sign of hesitation.

"Absolutely," I reply with a smile, feeling a thrill race through me at the thought of venturing deeper into this mysterious world. "I want to experience everything tonight."

"Just don't put me back in prison," Armando says, his lips curving into a dangerous smirk as he takes my hand.

As we weave our way through the heated crowd, I notice how other patrons are drawn to Armando—both men and women alike. He exudes a raw power that is impossible to ignore, and I feel a surge of pride knowing that he's mine for the night.

We discover hidden rooms and secret corners where couples and groups engage in even more sinful activities than those taking place on the main floor. The scent of sweat and arousal fills the air, along with the low hum of moans and whispers carrying the secrets of the night.

"Look at them," I murmur into his ear, as I nod towards a couple entwined together on a velvet chaise lounge. "They're lost in their passion, completely unaware of the world around them."

"That's how I feel with you," Armando confesses. "Everything else is blocked out."

My heart pounds in my chest as I turn to face him. I pull him into one of the secluded alcoves that line the perimeter of the club. It's dimly lit and hidden from view, offering us a moment of privacy amidst the chaos.

He kisses me deeply, his hands slipping around my waist as he pulls me closer.

My fingers trail up his chest to cradle his jaw. His gaze never leaves mine as we stand on the precipice of surrender.

"I'd fuck you here," I whisper, closing the distance between us as our lips meet in a searing, passionate kiss. "But I want to keep you locked up with me. Nowhere else."

Our mouths move together, tongues exploring and tasting each other, as the heat between us grows more intense with each passing second. Armando grips my hips tightly, pulling me flush against him, so I feel his arousal pressing against my thigh.

"I can't share you, Flowers. At least not yet. I'm a greedy bastard that wants that hot piece of ass of yours to myself," he says, his voice rough with desire as he rests his forehead against mine. "But I promise that when I get you home, I'm going to have you screaming out my name."

"Promise?"

"Fucking count on it," he replies, his eyes dark and full of promise.

We emerge from the shadows, our hearts still racing from our passionate exchange, and make our way back to the VIP table. As we approach, I see Leo regaling everyone with a story, his hands animated as he narrates some wild experience. Marco, sitting beside him, nods along in agreement while their dates listen with rapt attention.

"Ah, there you two are!" Leo exclaims, spotting us. "We were just discussing the unique... entertainment Sins has to offer."

"Unique is certainly one word for it," Armando agrees, a wry smile playing on his lips as he pulls out a chair for me. I slide into the seat, feeling the buzz of excitement and anticipation still coursing through my veins.

As the conversation continues, laughter and teasing filling the air, I can't help but steal glances at Armando. The connection between us has only grown stronger tonight, and I can feel the heat of his gaze on me, even when I'm not looking directly at him. His strong hand rests on my thigh, a silent promise of what's to come.

But also a certain kind of... possession.

He's used the word 'mine' multiple times. Always in the heat of passion. But right now, sitting and laughing with his cousins, I actually feel like his. Truly his. And I love it.

Time seems to slip away as we share stories and jokes, each of us lost in the thrill of the night. But eventually, even the most magical of moments must come to an end.

"Looks like they're starting to close up," Leo observes, noting the staff beginning to clean up around the club.

"Guess it's time to call it a night," Marco agrees, standing and stretching his arms overhead.

"All right, let's get out of here," Armando says, rising from his seat and extending a hand to me.

"Goodnight, everyone." I wave to our friends as we make our way towards the exit.

"Good job getting Mando out of the house," Leo says to me. "You're good for him."

"She's a keeper," Marco adds, filling me with pride. Nothing is a better feeling than winning over the family of the man you... love.

Stepping out into the cool night air, the muffled sounds of *Sins* fading behind us, I squeeze Armando's hand, eager for whatever comes next.

"Tonight was fun," I say.

"It's just beginning. I made a promise to you, remember?" Armando says, his voice low and full of promise.

# CHAPTER TWENTY

*Hannah*

"What if I had insisted we have sex at Sins?" I ask as I strip down naked before Armando, not giving him any doubt what I have in mind for the remainder of the night. Seeing all those naked bodies ignited something inside me. Something darker. More primal.

"I would have fucked you," Armando answers, also removing his clothing. "But not like I plan on fucking you now."

I raise an eyebrow. "Oh yeah, and how is that?"

"Harder than you've ever been fucked before."

My heart double-pumps. My knees get weak. But I'm definitely having whatever he's offering. "I'm not afraid," I tell him, with a note of challenge. "I've taken it hard before."

"Yeah?" He saunters toward me, his eyes dark with intent. "Prove it." He sprawls onto the bed completely naked.

I smile and step up on the bed and crawl toward him, never taking my gaze from his. I circle my arms around his body. Deeply. Passionately. Wantonly.

He wraps me in his arms and flips me to my back, his tongue dancing with mine. He tastes like scotch, and it's a good scotch, I can tell. I like the way it tastes on his tongue and the way he tastes on mine.

"Tell me what you want." He lifts my chin, forcing me to look into his eyes.

"I want it... kinky. Dark. I want to feel... submissive to you," I confess, feeling safe to admit my darkest desires. "I don't want gentle. I don't want caresses. I want it dirty. The way you like to give it."

I don't know what got into me and why the request is coming so easily. But we just left Sins, and if there is ever a time to completely let go, now is it.

"You want me to fuck you hard?" he pushes. "Push you around a little? Fuck you like the dirty little slut you just admitted you want to be?"

"Yes," I whisper.

"I'm going to do all that to you and more." His smirk is dangerous.

"Don't hold back," I breathe.

"Roll over, I want to see your ass," he orders, releasing me and climbing off.

"Like this?" I roll to my belly.

"Up on your knees, Flowers."

I step up on my knees and bend over, then look over my shoulder at him.

"Exactly like that. Now spread your cheeks."

I do as I'm told, and he strokes his hand over my ass. I hear the snap of the tube of lubricant and his slickened fingers slide over my pussy, his thumb at my asshole. I shamelessly push back onto his fingers, begging for more.

"You want this?" He slaps my ass hard with his other hand, then rubs the hurt away.

"Yes. I want you to fuck my ass."

"What else, Flowers?"

"I want you to get rough with me. Fuck me so I can't walk straight. Until I can't even think anymore. All night long."

Armando growls and plunges his fingers inside my pussy.

"I want you to slap my ass until it's red and sore."

"Fuck, baby. You're getting me harder than stone. What else am I going to do to you?"

"I want you to..." I almost don't dare ask for this one. But it's a fantasy I've had since the day he showed up in my flower shop.

"What, Flowers?"

"Choke me."

"Yeah? I'll choke you, baby. You want a hand necklace while I fuck you hard?"

"Yes, please."

"You like a little fear with your sex? Want me to cut off your air? Or just pretend, baby?"

I grow dizzy, scarcely believing we're having this conversation. That my fantasy is actually going to come true. "I want you to cut off my air... make me feel like you're about to end me. Like I'm about to die for you."

The room spins. I'm terrified by my request, but I go on. "I want you to own me. Make me yours and only yours. Your slut. Your dirty girl. Yours."

I've never said any of these words aloud before. Never thought them. But Armando awakened something in me. He's shown me I can trust him with my body, even when there's a little violence involved. And after all the crazy things we saw tonight, it feels safe to ask for this. As I speak, I realize that's exactly what I'm doing. I'm letting him in, and more importantly, I'm letting myself out. I'm freeing myself from a lot of my fears and insecurities, and I'm hanging on to Armando's every word, waiting for him to tell me what to do next.

"That's so hot, Hannah. You are my dirty girl. I'm gonna give it to you good, Flowers."

He keeps working his fingers between my legs, sliding his thumb into my ass, all the while peppering my cheeks with slaps. A chaotic, exotic mix of stimulation that heightens everything I feel. I moan. I'm drowning in lust. So far beyond my normal inhibitions.

Mando puts a pillow beneath my hips and pushes me down over it then climbs between my legs. He rubs the head of his cock over my pussy as he grips my hair, twisting my head back, so I'm forced to look up at him.

"I'm the only one that's going to fuck this pussy," he commands at the same moment he pushes inside me.

"Oh God." My internal muscles squeeze around his cock. I'm already orgasming from just one stroke.

He goes slowly, arcing in, sliding out, teasing me. Torturing me.

"Spank me," I plead, wanting more intensity.

"Spank you?" He pulls out of me. "You need to earn that spanking."

"How?"

"Beg me for it." He slaps my ass a few times, and the pain is sharp and intense, but I love it.

"Please," I plead, needing to feel that heat radiating from my ass and spreading throughout my whole body. "Please, Armando. Please spank me harder. Please."

He does it again and again, until my ass is burning and stinging. It's exactly what I crave. What I need.

"Good girl." He pulls me around to sit me down on the edge of the bed. "Now spread your legs for me."

I do as he commands, and he gets on his knees in front of me, gripping my thighs and spreading them wide.

"Look at you," he says. "Your pussy is so fucking wet, and your pussy lips are swollen."

"Your cock made me that way," I say, reaching out and gripping his cock, stroking it hard.

"Show me how much you want my cock," he says, taking his cock and rubbing it up and down my pussy. "Suck my cock and show me how much you want it. I want you to taste how much your pussy loves this cock."

I watch his cock enter my mouth, and I swirl my tongue around it and lick it, paying extra attention to the head and the sensitive area underneath his cockhead.

"That's a good girl," he encourages while gripping my head and pushing his cock deeper into my mouth. "Take it all."

I do, and as I suck on his cock, I feel him take one of my hands and wrap it around the base of his cock, and he guides my hand up and down his cock while he fucks my mouth. I'm moaning so hard, I'm sure that my neighbors can hear me, but I don't care. I've never felt so free and so wild.

I want this every night. I want to be his dirty little whore. I want him to make me feel beautiful and wanted, opening my mouth wide and lifting my chin up so he can fuck my face however he wants.

I want everything he is willing to give me.

I want to be possessed by him.

He fucks my face harder, and I struggle to take it, but I take it. I take it all. I look into his eyes and see the intensity and the passion. I see his desire, and it's a beautiful thing.

I'm his beautiful, dirty girl, and I love it.

I love him.

"Make me come all over my dirty girl's face," he commands, and I pull my mouth off his cock, stroking it hard and fast. He starts to breathe hard, and I know he's close.

"Do it. Come all over my face."

He comes hard. Ribbons of his cum hit my face and splash against my cheeks, and I rub it in immediately, letting it drip down my face as I make sure to get it in my mouth.

"That's a good girl." He wipes away the cum from my face with a nearby towel. "Now get on the bed and wait for me."

I do as I'm told, and as I lie on the bed and look up at him, I'm in awe of what he is.

"Time for your spanking. You earned it. Roll over, ass in the air."

I do as I'm told, and I feel my body shaking with excitement.

"Spread your legs," he says, rubbing my ass with his hands.

I spread my legs, knowing that I belong to him and that he is slowly taking over my life.

And I'm fine with that.

I'm fine with being his dirty little whore forever.

He slaps my ass a few times, and then he lifts it up and squeezes it. He spanks my cheeks again, and I feel the sting in my ass, and it makes my pussy tingle even more. He spanks me until my ass is red and stinging and burning. It hurts, but it feels so good at the same time.

"Spread your ass apart," he commands. "I want to see all of that beautiful pussy."

I spread my ass apart and look back, eager to see what he's going to do to me.

He slaps my ass, and then he takes my hand and places it between my thighs, rubbing my pussy.

He slaps my pussy with my hand, and then he slaps my pussy again, and then he puts my fingers in my mouth and forces me to suck them.

"You're a dirty girl," he says. "Taste how dirty you are."

"I'm your dirty girl," I agree.

"And I'm your Daddy," he says, spanking me over and over, making me cry out loudly. "I'm the one who fucks this pussy, this beautiful pussy."

"Yes, Daddy," I agree, crying out in passion as he hits my pussy harder and harder.

"And this ass belongs to me," he says, slapping my ass so hard I feel the pain radiating and spreading.

"It belongs to you. Only you."

"That's right," he says. "Only me. You're mine."

"I'm all yours."

"Good girl." He slaps my ass again.

"And now I'm going to make you come with my tongue," he says, spreading my ass cheeks with his hands. He puts his tongue in my ass, and I moan loudly.

"My dirty girl likes that," he says. "You like when I rim this asshole of yours."

"I like it a lot," I agree, my pussy dripping wet.

He licks my ass, and I can't help but grind against his face.

"I'm going to make you come like you've never come before." He rubs my pussy and then slides his fingers inside me and pumps hard.

I start moaning, and it doesn't take long before my body is shaking.

"Come on my fingers, baby. Come all over them."

His words are dirty, and they're nasty, and they're exactly what I want to hear.

"Come for me, Flowers," he says, and I do, my body shaking and shuddering and convulsing.

He holds me close to him as my body comes down from the rawest, dirtiest orgasm ever.

We lie in the darkness together, our breath mingling. Our heartbeats slowing from a gallop.

"Thank you," I murmur softly.

Armando lets out a chuff. "You're thanking me? No, baby. You're fucking amazing, Hannah."

His words make my heart sing.

And that's the real danger. Not how this man handles my body.

But how he handles my heart.

God I hope he doesn't crush it.

What's even scarier is that he has the power to break my soul.

# CHAPTER TWENTY-ONE

*Armando*

*I'm running through the streets of Chicago, being chased by the Hermanos. I get knocked down and cornered by the entire gang, all of them pointing pistols at me. But then the faces turn familiar—one of the guys in my face is Emilio, another is Harold, Hannah's dad.*

*I climb to my feet and offer my chest as target. "Do it," I say, but then I hear Hannah calling my name.*

Armando.

*Hearing her voice changes my plan. I can't let her see me die. I can't die when she might need me. I decide to try to fight my way out of it or to escape. I grab the wrist of the nearest guy to wrest his gun away.*

"Armando!"

I gasp, sitting bolt upright in the bed, my fingers closed around Hannah's wrist in a crushing grasp.

"Oh, shit!" I drop her wrist like it's on fire then snatch it back up again, gently. I kiss her racing pulse. Her eyes are wide and horrified.

"I'm sorry, Flowers. I'm so sorry." I press her wrist to my lips again. "I hurt you. Fuck."

She's naked, her beautiful brown breasts shifting as she adjusts to sit up as well. "It's okay," she whispers, looping her arms around my neck in a strangling hug.

I don't deserve her forgiveness, and I suspect there's sympathy mixed in there, too, which makes me itchy and angry, but I can't reject her sweetness. She's the fucking reason I want to live if I analyze the damn nightmare.

Our sex we just had before we passed out was... fucking animalistic, and I now worry. Am I being too hard on her? Am I allowing the darker side to come out of me too quickly?

Fuck. Am I fucking this up? I called her a whore. A whore!

Hannah deserves better. She deserves a man who can give her flowers and candy and whisper sweet nothings. I'm not this man.

"Let me make you feel good," I beg because sex is pretty much the only thing I have to offer these days, and she fell asleep in the middle of last night.

She lets me push her to her back and crawl down between her legs, satisfying her with my tongue before I let myself sink my cock into her.

We finish and I roll out of bed and into the shower. It's Arturo's grandson's baptism, so I have to put on a suit and go to mass this morning.

When I come out, Hannah heads into the shower, and I get dressed and make us coffee.

I hand her a mug when she comes out with a towel wrapped around her luscious curves.

She sets it down without drinking any. "Thanks but my stomach's off this morning. Where are you going?" she asks. It kills me that she looks like she doesn't expect me to answer. Or like she doesn't deserve to ask. It kills me that I don't have more to give to Hannah Munn, the girl who offered up her whole world to me when I didn't ask nicely. When I didn't ask at all.

"A baptism. And the party afterward."

I see hurt flicker over her face and feel the knife in my chest twist deeper. I want to invite her. Hell, nothing would make me happier than having Hannah at my side. It would make dealing with

Emilio and Grace so much easier, it would stop all the stares and whispers of everyone wondering how I'm dealing with Emilio and Grace.

"I'm going to my parents for dinner. You're, um, welcome to come," she says, but her normal morning glee is void from her tone.

Fuck. I rub my shaved jaw. "I don't think that's a good idea, Curls. Your dad didn't exactly love the idea of me hanging around you."

Of all the men in the world, Hannah's dad had to be on the same job site as me. At least I have the very small satisfaction of having backed him up when he asked for the doctor visit.

Fuck, probably the doctor visit that should have prevented this heart attack.

"You working today?" I ask.

"Yeah."

"'Kay. I'll go there after the party. See if I can help you with anything."

She nods, but I still see the hurt in her face. I brush my lips across hers. "Be good, Flowers. I'll see you soon."

———

The baptism party is like any Family party. I've been to a thousand of them, but this one is excruciating. Almost as painful as my welcome home party.

Marco and Leo stick near me, and I do my best to not look like a sullen cunt although I probably don't succeed.

Fucking Grace has to come over again—I swear she must be suffering from more guilt than I gave her credit for. But then, there was a time when I thought we truly loved each other. Just because my heart is darker than night now doesn't mean she doesn't still feel the pull of what we once had.

She just doesn't know that guy is dead.

"Hi Mando," she says, all breathless. "Listen, um, this is awkward." She shoots a glance at Marco and Leo, who hold their ground.

I don't tell them to do anything different.

"I just wanted to say, um, that I have your invite to the wedding. I

just—I couldn't decide which was worse—to send it or not to send it."
Her eyes swim with real tears, which takes me by surprise.

"Aw, Grace." I'm suddenly so fucking tired. Too tired to deal with
any of this shit. What does she want me to say? That she's forgiven?

Eh. Maybe she is. I don't know.

Seeing her standing in front of me right now with her perfect
makeup and her fake nails, it just brings home how superficial our relationship was. We were together because we looked good together. We
fit, in terms of the Outfit and the circles we ran in. She wanted a guy
who flashed the money around. Who treated her nice and fucked her
good. Who played all the romantic gestures right out of the playbook.

I did that for her. She did what she was supposed to do for me—
look pretty on my arm. Say the right things at Family gatherings, do
what she was told.

It wasn't a relationship. It was two people playing at one. We did it
well. Until we didn't. Because prison didn't fit the role she wanted
from me.

Hannah wouldn't write me off when things went wrong. Hell,
everything with Hannah has already gone wrong. I've killed a man on
the floor of her shop. Tied her up and held her prisoner. Offered her
nothing of my dark, dead heart.

And still she cries for me. Still she wrapped those arms around my
neck when I had a bad dream, even when I nearly broke her wrist for
trying to wake me.

I love her.

The thought hits me like a bowling ball. Especially because I don't
know what to do with it. I can't be what Hannah deserves.

If I had any kind of decency, I'd move out and leave her out of my
mess right now.

I stare at Grace, my gut churning. "Yeah, Grace, I'd rather not
come, honestly. But thanks for asking. Listen, I have a question,
though."

"Yes?" She raises her manicured brows.

"You order your flowers already?"

Confusion flits over her face. "Um, no, but I'll be doing it this
week, why?"

"Make sure you get them from Garden of Eden. They're award-winning. They do all the best weddings." It's the old Mando talking. The one who cared about designer names and having the best of everything. Because I know Grace still cares about all that shit.

Her eyes widen. "Oh, okay. Is that the place you used when you sent me all those—" she breaks off and swallows.

"Yeah," I say softly. "They did a great job, right? They're even better now. Like best in town."

I notice Marco and Leo looking at me speculatively, but I ignore it.

If I can get Hannah some business out of Grace and Emilio's fucking wedding, I'm going to do it.

"Okay, I'll call them tomorrow. Thanks for the tip." She looks at me again, regret soft on her face.

I'm a bastard because I still don't feel like letting her off the hook. But when she turns away with slumped shoulders, I say her name, softly.

"Grace."

She turns back.

"Thanks for checking in with me," I say. It's the best I can offer her at the moment, but it seems to be what she needs. Relief floods her face and she nods, smiling sadly.

"Of course. Good luck, Mando. With everything."

"Yeah, you too."

I watch her walk away, and Marco waits until she's out of earshot to say, "She's still a cunt."

I've forgotten how to smile, but the corners of my mouth twitch. "Yeah, she is," I say, but there's nothing behind it. And not the dead, blank nothing I felt when I got out, but really nothing. An empty space, waiting to be filled.

Maybe I really am coming back to the living.

# CHAPTER TWENTY-TWO

*Hannah*

A week of feeling seasick.

Not being able to drink the wine Armando pours for me with dinner. I'd be stupid if I didn't consider the possibility.

We've been careful... sometimes, even most of the time. But fuck... not all the time.

I remember the odds from high school health class. They're not great.

I pick up a pregnancy test on my way home, rushing to get there before Armando does.

The queasiness in my belly grows, probably from nerves, and by the time I get home to my bathroom, I'm doubling over it and retching.

Ugh.

This shouldn't be happening.

I'm with a guy who doesn't even want to be my boyfriend. Being with Armando is like being on a rollercoaster of emotions. But this could throw us off the tracks, plunging toward the hard reality down below. An unplanned pregnancy is not going to help matters.

*Or maybe it will,* my stupid little voice of hope whispers.

No, it won't. I try to savage it with bared teeth.

Shadow meows and threads his soft little body around my ankles, purring. I ignore him and read the directions for the test. I should wait for my morning pee, when the hormones would be the strongest, but I'm too wound up. I've bought the damn thing, and I need to do it now. I sit on the toilet and aim the stick in my stream of pee. Then sit there and wait.

My belly flutters out of control when the results appear. A faint positive line.

Tears spear my eyes, but I'm not devastated.

Strangely, it's a mixture of excitement and fear that churn together.

And, of course, before I even have time to get my head on straight, I hear Armando walk into the apartment.

Shit! I don't know what makes me throw the test into the kitty litter box and cinch the bag up for the trash, but I do. I rush out of the bathroom, somewhat desperate to get rid of the evidence before he sees it.

"You want me to take that out?" He reaches for the knotted bag of dirty litter.

"*No*, I'll take it out." Dammit, I sound breathless. My strange behavior doesn't go unnoticed. Armando's eyes narrow, and he cocks his head.

"Be right back," I call as I sweep out the door.

Nausea hits me hard on the trip downstairs. I gag at the dumpster, the nasty smell pushing me over the edge. I run away from it, my belly heaving, but fortunately not pushing the contents of my stomach all the way up and out.

Ugh.

When I get upstairs, I find Armando in the kitchen holding the cardboard box the test came in, a stunned, unhappy expression on his face. "Fuck, Hannah."

It's hard to believe in the course of two minutes a mama bear energy could enter me and take hold, but it does. I'm instantly on the defensive, and protecting my baby is all that matters.

"Fuck!" he says louder, turning to face the wall and punching it. His knuckles break through my drywall, sending crumbles to the floor. "It's my fault. I didn't use a condom all the time. I let our passion take over, and... fuck!"

And with that, he finally crushes my hopeful pink Cinderella heart. There will be no happy ending for us. He's not a prince. He's not even a boyfriend.

He doesn't want me or this baby. And I'll be damned if I'll let him taint any part of this pregnancy. And suddenly, things become crystal clear. I have a tiny life growing inside me that I need to protect. Honor. I need to do for my baby what I couldn't do for myself.

Demand more.

Demand *a lot* more.

And Armando is not going to give that to me. He simply can't. He's made that abundantly clear.

"It was negative," I say loudly, suddenly grateful for my instinct to bury that evidence with the kitty litter. "I'm late, but I'm not pregnant. I just wanted to be sure."

Armando swivels back slowly and eyes me.

I'm not the best liar, so I hide it under bluster. "But this pregnancy scare brought it all home to me." I suck in a ragged breath. "It's time for you to leave, Armando. Things are getting too complicated." My eyes fill with tears, and for once, I'm not ashamed. They're honest tears and only serve to strengthen my resolve right now. "I don't want a broken heart. It's already cracking. I'm cracking. I can't do this anymore."

The color drains from Armando's face. I might've celebrated the fact that he had an emotional reaction to anything under different circumstances. But as it is, his shock and pain reverberate through me, shattering what little control I have left.

"You want me to leave?"

I nod.

"But I need to keep you safe."

"You can do that from afar. Keep your men on me," I suggest. "You and I both know you being around me is putting me in more danger than you staying. And you staying here—"

"Hannah..."

I start to cry in earnest. I'm sure the hormones aren't helping. "I need you to leave," I say through my tears.

Armando's eyes go dead. He launches into action, his movements jerky and mechanical. He moves through the apartment and packs his things into the duffel bag he brought over. He picks Shadow up from the floor where he's twining around his ankles. He brings him up to his face and kisses my kitten's head. "Take care of her, you hear me?"

He walks to the door. "I'm sorry, Hannah." His voice is tight and gruff.

I nod, closing my throat around my sobs.

It feels so wrong, but I know it's the right thing to do. I'm not saddling this baby with a father who doesn't want him. I'm not going to have the discussion with Armando about whether or not to keep it.

I'm keeping it. And he's got to go. That's all there is to it.

I don't have room in my life for a non-boyfriend. Not when this baby's going to need everything I have to give it.

He looks at me like he wants to say something else but then just nods and turns back to the door. He opens it, walks through and closes it without looking back.

And the moment he's gone, I drop to my knees and sob.

# CHAPTER TWENTY-THREE

*Armando*

The world dims the moment Hannah tells me to leave.

I know it's for the best. I've known all along I should leave because I'm fucking toxic to her. I have zero to offer, and on top of that, every minute I spend with her puts her life in danger with the people who want me dead.

And Christ, when I thought she was pregnant, I couldn't think of anything worse. Endangering a helpless infant? I'd have to leave her—never see her again, not even as a friend.

So her making the decision for me should've made it easier.

It should have.

But a grey haze descends around my vision as I stand out on the street with my duffel bag and try to figure out what the fuck I'm going to do.

And then, because I honestly didn't give a fuck if the Hermanos want to kill me now, I head to my apartment.

I take the L because I can't stand the thought of being cooped up with an Uber driver. At the apartment, I pass the landlord in the hall-way, and he gives me the stink eye.

I can't even bring myself to react. Not a look. Not a blink. Definitely not a grunt of hello.

*Go fuck yourself* is what I say in my head.

And then I find myself pounding on Marco's door. Not because I need a shoulder to cry on. Fuck that. But because I'd love somebody's face to pound, and chances are good Marco's got someone he needs to send a message to—from the don.

"Hey, what's up?" Marco asks, pulling the door wide and studying my face.

I don't say anything, just stalk in without seeing him or his place.

"You got anybody to send a message to?"

Marco gives me a wary look. "You need to put the hurt on someone?"

"Yeah."

Marco shoves his hands in his pockets and angles his body half away from mine, like he doesn't want to bear the full weight of my focus if it's directed at him. "Hannah?"

Some of the blur in my vision clears at having my problem named.

"I don't want to talk about her," I snarl because, like I said, I'm out for blood right now.

"You guys seemed super tight the other night. You've been inseparable. What happened?"

In a flash, I slam his back against a wall, my forearm choking off his windpipe. "Stop asking me about her."

I think he hisses something like *cocksucker* through his bared teeth.

"It's over, and you're never going to speak her name again."

He pinches his lips and grinds his teeth together while I continue to cut off his air flow. Finally he punches me in the ribs. Twice.

Hard.

I loosen my grip on the second punch because it knocks the wind out of me.

"Peace, Mando." Marco's hands are in the air when I lift my head. "Chill, man."

I want to punch his teeth out so badly, but I also love him too much to do it.

"What the fuck's going on?" Leo appears in the living room.

Marco side steps, keeping his shoulders squared to me like a boxer circling his opponent. "Mando wants to kill someone. I'm trying to keep that guy from being me."

Aw, fuck it. I take a swing at him. He ducks and plows into me, knocking me onto my back. In a moment, both he and Leo are sitting on me, holding me down.

"Girl problems," Marco says to Leo.

"Fuck you," I snarl, fighting to get free.

"Chill the fuck out, man. We're on your side. You want blood, we'll go get some. Just talk to me first," Marco says.

I lift my head and smack the back of it down on the wooden floorboard. Smack it again.

"She kick you out?"

I smack it harder. "When I tell you to not talk about her, I mean it," I rage. I can't seem to get free of my two cousins, who are determined to hold me down.

"What the fuck is going on?" Leo demands.

"His girl," Marco non-explains. He looks at me. "What happened? You piss her off?"

The rage seeps out of me, and I'm back to being the hollow man. Worse than ever, though. I try to swallow, trying to shuffle through the jumble of images in my mind.

The pregnancy test.

Hannah's pinched face. Her tears.

*I'm cracking. I can't do this anymore.*

"I pushed her away," I croak, sickened by the realization.

Marco's expression shows nothing. We both have perfected our masks. "You can't fix it?"

"No," I rasp. "I can't be what she needs. An entire gang wants me dead. I'm a goddamn danger to her."

Marco continues to look at me passively. "So we fix that."

I stare back. If that problem were gone, could I be what Hannah needed?

The sickness in my stomach resurfaces.

Not even fucking close.

I'm nothing. I've got nothing to offer. I don't even know who the fuck I am anymore. I have no life, nothing.

I close my eyes, all the remaining fight leaving my body. "No."

"No?" Marco demands, challenge in his voice.

"No," I say firmly. "I can't be that guy for her."

"I'll tell you one thing," Marco says, climbing off me. Leo follows. He clasps palms with me and hauls me to my feet. "The Mando I know figures shit out when he wants something."

I stare at him. Resentment burns in my gut. Now that I'm feeling emotions again, I'd like to set the whole fucking city on fire. "The Mando you know is dead," I tell him and walk out the door.

"Hold up, man. You still want to pound someone's face in?"

I stop. Crack my knuckles. "Fuck, yeah."

"Let's go. I have a visit to pay."

# CHAPTER TWENTY-FOUR

*Hannah*

I go to my parent's house for Sunday dinner. I thought about canceling, but I'm actually hoping my mom will somehow know the right thing to say to fix me. She's good like that sometimes.

I cried for five days straight. I can't stop the waterworks to save my life. I've always been a crier, and I know the hormones don't help, but it's ridiculous.

Last week, I tried to run my shop and interact with people and put arrangements together, and the whole time, I had tears falling down my face. Josie had to come in and take over the last two days, so I could stay home with my head under the covers.

I walk in without knocking. My mom stands at the counter, throwing together a salad. I sink down in a kitchen chair, too exhausted to even go over and give her a hug.

"Hannah? What's wrong, baby?" My mom rushes over and envelopes me in one of those mom hugs that usually makes everything better.

I cry into her shoulder. "I'm pregnant," I blurt. "And I broke up with Armando."

She squeezes me even tighter. "Oh, baby." Her hand rubs circles on my back.

"I'm sorry, Mom." She drilled it into me young to use birth control until I was married and ready to start a family, but I had to go and fuck it up.

"Don't you worry about me," she says. "Let's worry about you, sweetheart. This is a lot."

"It is." A fresh spate of sobs come on.

"Hey, *hey*." She gives me a little shake. "This is big. But you know you're going to be okay, don't you? No matter how things turn out?"

I sniff and nod into her shoulder. "I can't tell if I made a mistake," I say between sniffs and sobs.

"Ending things with Armando?"

"Yeah." I pull away and wipe beneath my eyes. "But he was breaking my heart, you know? He said he couldn't be my boyfriend because he was too messed up."

My mom studies me, concern etched in the lines of her face. "Well, you're allowed to change your mind."

Fresh tears gush down my cheeks.

"What's going on—" my dad says from the doorway, but my mom waves him away, and he quickly retreats.

"I don't know, Mom. It just hurts so bad. I thought I would feel strong by ending things. I did feel strong while I did it. But now, I'm just a mess."

"Yeah," my mom says softly. "Breakups are never easy, even when they're the right decision."

My head snaps up, stomach tightening into a cruel knot. "Do you think it was the right decision?"

"I didn't say that," she cautions. "I don't know what the right answer is. But I do know one thing. You're smart and strong. And you have a huge heart. And I know you're going to be able to figure this out successfully."

I stare at her in despair. I want to believe her, but success feels completely impossible right now. I would settle for being able to turn off the water works for five minutes.

"What do I do about Armando?" I whisper, even though I know my mom, and she's not going to give me the answer.

"Well, I'll tell you one thing. If you keep this baby, there'll be no getting rid of him. When you have a baby with a man, he's in your life for the rest of your days whether the two of you are together or apart. Unless he chooses to walk away from his responsibility."

"What if he never finds out?" I croak, knowing how wrong it is but still clinging to the idea.

"What?"

"I wasn't going to tell him about the baby," I admit in a whisper.

"Why not?" My mom's voice sharpens.

I suck in a terraced breath. "Well, when he saw the test box, he freaked out. So I know he really doesn't want it. That's when I told him to leave. And I just lied and said the test came out negative."

I sense the censure from my mom as she draws in a slow breath. "So let me get this straight. You broke up with him because he didn't react the way you wanted him to when he was surprised by the idea of a pregnancy?"

I pull my lower lip into my mouth and suck on it. It sounds a little extreme when she puts it that way. "He's emotionally unavailable," I assert.

My mom nods slowly. "That may very well be, but it sounds to me like he was experiencing *some* emotion. Stress, maybe? Which is healthy. Because having a pregnancy you didn't expect is a big deal."

Well, *yeah*.

I wipe some more tears. "What should I do?"

"Well, the better question is what do you think you should do?"

I freaking hate when she says things like that. I shake my head. "I don't know."

My mom nods. "I think you probably do."

My chest aches as I realize my mom calls bullshit on my *I don't knows,* same as Armando, only nicer.

All the ways he paid attention to me flood my mind. He may have claimed he had nothing to offer, but it wasn't true. He took care of me. He noticed when I was off or mad and didn't let it slide. He tried to fix things when they were broken.

And what had I done?

Run away from my problems, same as ever. Opted to not deal with them.

I bailed. On him. On us.

Maybe if I'd given him a chance, he would've risen to the occasion of being a dad. It's hard to imagine he would stop taking care of me.

And then I'm suddenly bone tired.

I scrub my hands over my cheeks and stand. "I don't think I can stay for dinner, Mom," I say. "Please don't tell Dad about what's going on with me yet. I need to figure stuff out."

My mom glances toward the living room and gives me a noncommittal shrug. "He may have already heard enough, but I'll leave it for you to share." She wraps me in another hug. "I love you, baby girl. Nothing's insurmountable. Remember that."

I nod. "Love you, Mom."

# CHAPTER TWENTY-FIVE

*Armando*

The evening sky is painted with hues of orange and pink as I trudge up the steps to my apartment, the weight of a long day pressing down on me like a heavy cloak. As soon as I unlock the door and step inside, my thoughts drift towards Hannah. Her laughter echoes in my mind like a melody, her presence soothing my weary soul. But the danger lurking beneath the surface—the darkness that threatens to consume us both—casts an unshakeable shadow over my heart.

I collapse onto the bed, not bothering to change out of my clothes and allow sleep to claim me. But instead of finding refuge in the warmth of slumber, I'm thrust into a nightmare that chills me to the core.

*I'm standing in the middle of an abandoned warehouse, the air thick with tension and fear. The walls loom high above me, like ancient guardians of some forsaken realm, while shadows dance across the cracked concrete floor. My heart races, each beat pounding against my chest as if trying to break free from its cage.*

*"Where am I?" I whisper, my voice barely audible above the eerie silence.*

*A sudden gust of wind sends shivers down my spine, and I wrap my arms around myself for comfort, but it's no use. I can't shake the feeling that some-*

*thing isn't right, that some malevolent force has trapped me here in this desolate place.*

*"Armando," a familiar voice calls out, echoing through the vast emptiness.*

*Hannah. The sound of her voice sets off a flare of panic within me, igniting every protective instinct I possess. I need to find her, to make sure she's safe from the dangers that have haunted my past and now threaten our future.*

*"Where are you?" I call out desperately, my voice cracking with the strain of emotion.*

*"Help me, Armando," she pleads, her voice distant and muffled by the oppressive darkness.*

*I grit my teeth, my resolve hardening like steel. No matter what it takes, I will find her and protect her from the shadows of my past that have come to claim us both. With each step I take, determination courses through my veins, fueling my need to save the woman who has captured my heart and awakened a fierce love within me.*

*Hannah's muffled cries grow louder, guiding me through the darkness. My heart hammers against my chest, my breath coming in ragged gasps as I navigate the maze-like structure of this forsaken warehouse. The air hangs heavy and oppressive around me, a tangible weight on my shoulders that I struggle to shake off.*

*"Armando!" she calls out again, her voice wavering with fear.*

*"Keep talking, Hannah," I shout back, my words dripping with desperation. "I'm coming for you."*

*"Please... hurry," she whispers, the sound barely reaching my ears.*

*I push myself harder, sprinting through the labyrinth of shadows and echoes, each turn revealing another dead end or empty corridor. But I refuse to give up, driven by the knowledge that Hannah's life depends on me finding her.*

*"Armando... I'm so scared," she admits, her voice cracking under the weight of her terror.*

*"Stay strong, Hannah," I plead, my own fear seeping into my words. "I'll find you. I promise."*

*Finally, after what feels like an eternity, I reach a dimly lit room at the heart of the warehouse. And there, tied to a chair in the center of the space, is Hannah. Naked, vulnerable, and trembling with fear, her eyes lock onto mine, wide and pleading.*

*"Armando," she gasps, tears streaming down her cheeks. "You found me."*

*"I'm here," I say, my voice strained with relief and determination. "I won't let anything happen to you."*

*As I move closer, I can see the ropes biting into her skin, leaving angry red welts across her wrists and ankles. My fingers fumble with the knots, my urgency making the task more difficult than it should be.*

*"Who did this to you?" I ask, trying to keep my voice steady as I work to free her.*

*"I don't know," she admits, her eyes darting around the room as if searching for answers. "They kept their faces hidden."*

*"Once I get you out of here, we'll make sure they never hurt you again," I promise, my hands shaking with anger and fear.*

*"Do you really think we can escape them?" Her voice is barely a whisper.*

*"Fuck yes," I reply, forcing confidence into my words even as doubt gnaws at the edges of my mind. "I won't let anyone or anything come between us. Not now, not ever."*

*A faint smile flickers across her lips, her eyes shining with love and trust despite the terror that still lingers in their depths. And in that moment, I vow to myself that no matter what it takes, I will protect this woman—the one who has brought light back into my darkened world and given me a reason to fight for a better future.*

*"Thank you," she whispers.*

*"Always, Flowers. Always," I reply, my heart swelling with determination as I finally untie the last knot, setting her free from her bonds.*

*As I step closer to Hannah, the air around us seems to thicken, as if charged with an impending storm. The hairs on the back of my neck rise, and a shiver of dread snakes down my spine. Without warning, the warehouse is filled with the low murmur of voices—voices that I recognize all too well.*

*"Armando," Hannah whispers, her eyes wide with fear. "Who are they?"*

*"Stay quiet," I urge her, my voice barely audible. I can feel their presence closing in around us, like vultures circling their prey.*

*"Long time no see, Mando," one of them sneers, stepping out from the shadows. His grin is cruel, his eyes cold and calculating. I recognize him as one of my former mafia associates, a man I had hoped never to cross paths with again.*

*"Leave her alone," I growl, positioning myself between Hannah and the menacing figures. My heart hammers against my ribcage, but I refuse to let them*

*see any signs of weakness. My dark world has found me, but I'll be damned if I let it take away the only person who truly matters to me.*

*"Ah, so this is the girl who's got you so whipped, huh?" another one chimes in, leering at Hannah. "You should have known we'd find you eventually, Armando."*

*I glance over my shoulder, locking eyes with Hannah. Her gaze is filled with terror, but there's also a flare of determination there. As if she's silently urging me to fight back.*

*"Get away from her," I snarl, my fists clenching at my sides. With every fiber of my being, I want to protect Hannah—to shield her from these monsters and the horrors that they represent.*

*As if sensing my resolve, the men lunge forward, their faces twisted with malice and vengeance. I throw myself into the fray, fists flying as I slam them into the first attacker. The impact jolts through my arm, but it only fuels my adrenaline.*

*"Armando!" Hannah cries out, her voice strangled with fear.*

*"Stay back!" I shout, desperation clawing at my insides as I struggle to keep the attackers at bay.*

*But they just keep coming—too many for me to handle alone. Their numbers give them an advantage that I can't overcome, no matter how fiercely I fight. Blow after blow rains down upon me, each one landing with brutal precision.*

*Pain flares through my body, but it's nothing compared to the agony of knowing that these men are here because of me—because of the life I led before I met Hannah. My past has caught up with me, and now she's the one who will pay the price.*

*"Armando," she whispers, her eyes filled with love and trust even as tears stream down her cheeks. "Tonight's the night I die."*

I wake up wanting to die. It's the fourth fucking night in a row I dreamt about Hannah. Nightmares. Always with her in danger because of me. About to be killed. Tortured, screaming my name. All to hurt me. This time it was at Lollipops. She was there but tied to a chair, naked.

Like it was the guys in the Outfit who wanted to hurt her and not some street gang.

She was screaming my name, begging—not for them to leave her alone but for them not to kill me.

I don't know where I was in the dream. There, but unable to help. My limbs wouldn't move. My mouth couldn't speak. I tried to shout, to fight, but nothing happened.

I roll off the bed. I'm still in my clothes from yesterday, soaked with sweat, reeking of whiskey.

Since the night Hannah broke up with me, I've drunk myself to sleep every night, but alcohol does little to numb the sensation of having my heart cut out with a chainsaw. Everything swirls around me like a fog.

I pull off my clothes and step into the shower. All week, I've tempted fate. I've been at my apartment. Gone to my job. Walk in broad daylight. Done everything I can to fucking dare the Hermanos to find me, but my deathwish isn't answered.

I just want to get things settled. Kill or be killed.

Then, maybe, I'll find my way out of the dark.

My phone rings while I'm in the shower, and I shut off the water and step out to get it.

"Luis."

"Hey, I talked to one of the Hermanos. It's not about the guy you ended in prison—they don't seem to care about that. Word is a few of them are working for hire. Nothing personal."

*Nothing personal.*

"You found out who hired it?"

"Nah. Guy I talked to didn't know. I'll keep trying, though."

"Yeah. Thanks."

"Uh huh. You good for this?"

"How much do I owe you?"

"Seven hundred."

It's seven hundred bucks for not a lot of info, but I don't complain. "I'll drop it by."

"Cool." He ends the call, and I stand there, dripping.

All I can think about is Hannah. I *have* to clear this fucking contract.

For her.

Even if she never wants to see me again.

Even if we never talk, never touch again.

# CHAPTER TWENTY-SIX

*Armando*

The dimly lit bar feels like an extension of the night outside as we push through the heavy doors. The air is thick with cigarette smoke and the low hum of murmured conversations.

"Scotch, neat," I order gruffly, my voice strained, betraying the turmoil I've been trying my damnedest to hide.

Marco and Leo exchange concerned glances.

"Make it three," Marco adds, his voice steady and strong.

The bartender nods in acknowledgment, placing three glasses before us. The amber liquid catches what little light filters through the smoky haze, casting a warm glow over the worn wooden table.

I waste no time, grabbing my drink and downing it in one swift motion. The clink of glass against wood punctuates the moment, and it occurs to me I'm seeking solace at the bottom of a glass. I've never been that man before.

Maybe I'm that man now.

"Are you all right, man?" Marco asks. "You look like shit."

"Fine," I reply tersely, but the way my hands grip the edge of the table tells a different story.

"Talk to us, man," Leo urges. "We're here for you."

"Like I said, I'm fine," I insist, but my voice wavers ever so slightly, revealing the cracks in my armor.

"How are you holding up after everything with Hannah?" Marco asks, his voice gentle and concerned. His gaze is steady and sincere, a softness in it that I've rarely seen.

I take a deep breath, knowing that I can't avoid this conversation any longer. "It's hard," I admit, my voice cracking slightly. "But it's for the best. She asked me to leave, and I can't blame her. I've been trying to get her out of my head since. And epically failing at it."

"Hey, don't be so hard on yourself," Marco replies, placing a reassuring hand on my shoulder.

"Enough about me," I say, trying to change the subject. "How's your ass, *cugino*?" It's a weak attempt at humor, but I'm desperate to steer the conversation away from my own pain.

Marco chuckles, shaking his head. "You're really gonna ask me about that now? Fine, it hurts like hell at times, but I'll live."

"You get asked about your ass on the daily now," Leo chimes in, rolling his eyes. "That ass of yours is becoming famous."

"Don't be jealous of my famous ass," Marco retorts with a smirk, before turning back to me. "But seriously, Mando, we're here for you, man. If you need to talk, just let us know."

"Thanks," I mumble, taking another swig of my drink. It burns going down, but I welcome the sensation—anything to help numb the ache inside me.

As the warmth of the alcohol spreads through my chest, I can't help but think of Hannah. Of her smile, her laughter, the way she made me feel alive again. But that life is gone now, and all that's left is the cold, hard reality of my past.

"I have to be frank with you, man," Leo says, leaning forward with a serious expression. "You're a fucking fighter. Always have been. You don't just give up on shit so easily, man. Why the fuck would you just walk away? You obviously care about this chick. So why the fuck are you here with us instead of demanding her back?"

I stare into my glass, the amber liquid swirling around as I contemplate his words. The truth is, walking away was the hardest thing I've ever done. But what choice did I have?

"I didn't want to walk away," I confess, the weight of my emotions threatening to overcome me. "But I can't risk hurting Hannah. Our life... it's dangerous. It'll catch up to us, and she'll be in the crosshairs. She deserves better than that."

"Deserves better?" Leo scoffs, clearly not buying my argument. "She deserves a man who loves her, and from what I've seen, that's you. Maybe it's time to stop running from your past and face it head-on. For her sake."

"Maybe you're right," I admit, my fingers tightening around my glass. "Maybe I need to confront my past if I want any shot at a future with Hannah. But where the fuck do I even begin?"

"You need to see her," Marco interjects. "Talk to her. Tell her everything you just told us—about your fears, your love, your willingness to fight for her. Then, together, you can figure out the best way to move forward."

"Maybe," I agree, my chest swelling with newfound determination and even hope. My cousins may be right. I can't let Hannah go without a fight. She means too much to me.

"By walking away without a fight, you've already lost her. You had something special with Hannah, and you just let it go," Marco says.

"Marco's right," Leo adds, leaning forward in the booth. "You didn't even put up a fight for your relationship. We all have our demons, but that doesn't mean we can't fight for love."

I look at both of them, their expressions a mixture of frustration and empathy. My chest feels tight, my thoughts consumed by the memory of Hannah's face when I walked out her door.

"Remember when we were kids?" I ask, trying to change the subject. "Alter boys, all three of us. Who would've thought we'd end up where we are now?"

"Definitely not me," Marco chuckles, the mood lightening a bit. "But that's life, right? It's unpredictable."

"Damn straight," Leo agrees. "And you know what else is unpredictable? Love. But that doesn't mean we shouldn't fight for it."

"You're lucky," Marco says, his voice filled with sincerity. "I'd give anything to have more than just a fuck here and there. You and Hannah have something real. Don't throw it away like it's nothing."

"Besides," Leo chimes in, smirking as he swirls the ice in his drink, "you've always been one stubborn bastard. Why give up so easily?"

I can't help but smile at their words, knowing they both have a point. They've been with me through thick and thin, and they've never steered me wrong.

"All right, all right," I concede, my resolve beginning to strengthen. "Maybe I did walk away too quickly. Maybe I should've fought harder."

"Damn right." Marco nods, his eyes meeting mine with determination. "Now it's up to you to fix it."

"Good man." Leo grins, raising his glass in a toast. "To fighting for love and finding our way back home."

"*Salute*," Marco and I echo, clinking our glasses together before drinking, the alcohol burning like liquid courage.

Despite the growing warmth in my chest, uncertainty still gnaws at me. I can't shake the feeling that I'm walking a tightrope between love and destruction. My cousins' words have given me hope, but they haven't fully convinced me.

"All right," I finally say, forcing myself to sound more confident than I feel. "I'll stop moping around. But I need to think this through before I take any action."

"Fair enough," Marco acknowledges, his eyes narrowing as he studies me. "Just don't wait too long, okay? We both know women like Hannah can be snatched up in seconds."

"Believe me, I know," I mutter, my thoughts turning from pity to rage. The thought of her being with another man sends homicidal thoughts through me. "I'll think on it."

"Good," Leo grins, his mood shifting as he claps his hands together. "Now, let's lighten up the atmosphere a bit, shall we?"

"Agreed," Marco chuckles, raising his glass. "To not having bullets in our asses!"

The absurdity of the toast pulls a half-hearted chuckle from me, and I hold my own glass up to join theirs. "Amen to that."

Our glasses clink together with a satisfying sound, and for a moment, I allow myself to forget about the weight on my shoulders. We drink to our shared camaraderie—three cousins bound by blood, loyalty, and the ghosts of our pasts.

As the night wears on, the conversation drifts away from Hannah and back to lighter subjects. I appreciate my cousins' attempts to distract me, but I can't help but feel the persistent tug of my thoughts pulling me back to her.

I let her go.

I fucked up.

But it wouldn't be the first time I sabotaged my life.

The question now is what will I do next? Continue to dig my grave, or fucking walk toward the light that is Hannah?

# CHAPTER TWENTY-SEVEN

*Hannah*

The next week, I drag myself back into work, but I'm wearing Armando's faded Cubs t-shirt—the one with a hole near the collar. It was in my hamper because I'd slipped it on after having sex one night, so he didn't pack it when he left.

I don't know why I put it on today—to torture myself? It really makes no sense.

I've really been thinking over what my mom said to me.

Maybe I was hasty in breaking up with Armando. Certainly not telling him about the baby was wrong. I knew that even before my mom let her judgment bleed through. But hearing it reflected back at me brought it home.

I've been feeling like the injured party, maybe because my heart's so damn sore, but really, I'm the one who caused this pain. For both of us, assuming Armando's also grieving.

I flip open the wedding arrangement album and price list and push it across the counter. I'm helping a couple order flowers for their wedding. It's only the third wedding order I've taken since I took over the shop, so despite my low spirits, I'm thankful. The somewhat bored groom-to-be looks familiar. I'm pretty sure he's one of the mafia guys who gets their hair cut next door. So it seems greasing that wheel is working.

Thank-fucking-god.

"I heard you're an award-winning florist," the bride-to-be says, looking around.

I flush, wondering if the place looks like an award-winning shop. Also, wondering where the hell she heard such a thing. But screw that, my arrangements are good—damn good. Better than Mary Alice's. And I have a decent shot at winning an award in that competition in a couple months. I square my shoulders.

"We like to keep things fresh and original here. I put a lot of thought into my arrangements to make them fit the individual—or the couple."

I kick myself for not updating the arrangement book with designs of my own—the photos are still Mary Alice's. But I go off-book and start offering what I can see this couple using. "What color are your bridesmaids wearing?"

"Black cocktail dresses of their own choosing," she says.

"Evening wedding?"

"Yes."

"So you could do almost anything with the flowers. Do you have favorites?"

Her eyes sweep around the place again. "Roses, I guess," she says.

"Roses are classic, of course. White or red would be the most formal, or you could do any other color that's a favorite."

The bride looks uncertain.

"Or you could do something totally unique. Mix something exotic in with roses. Like shades of pink and blush old fashioned roses with peonies. Or star-gazer lilies."

She brightens. "Yes, something unique sounds great. I'd love the peonies."

I talk her through the order, suggesting possibilities for table arrangements, altar, decorations, bridesmaids, groomsmen and, of course, her bouquet. At the end, we come up with a package close to $2500, which the guy doesn't seem to blink at.

"So how did you hear about us?" I ask, hoping I sound casual.

Forcing myself to make an attempt at being personable, even though I don't feel like it.

"Armando Rossi," the bride says.

When I start, she goes still, her eyes slowly traveling from my face down to my chest. No, to the t-shirt. "Wait, are you... *dating* Armando?" she asks incredulously.

Shock flashes through me, mirrored in both her eyes and—strangely—those of her fiancé.

I blink rapidly. Dammit. I made it all day without a tear. "Ah..." I don't even know what to say. My stomach turns queasy again.

Why I didn't realize that, of course, Armando was the one who told them I was award-winning. Who else?

And then further realization sinks in. I gasp. "Are you *Grace?*"

She stares at me with bald curiosity. "You're dating him. Wow. I didn't see that one coming."

Her fiancé frowns. "You and Armando?" he demands, wagging a finger from me to my cell phone.

"No. Well, we were. But it's..."

I don't know why it feels so wrong to say *no*. I want to claim Armando as mine in front of these people. In front of his ex-girlfriend and her new fiancé. Maybe it's to help restore Armando's pride, maybe mine. I'm not sure.

"It's complicated. But yes," I answer, lifting my chin.

"Whoa. Okay. Sorry, I didn't mean to make this awkward," Grace says. "Armando told me I should come here to order the flowers for my wedding, but he didn't let on that you two were an item. Congratulations. I mean, I'm really glad for him. For you both."

My stomach churns at the lie. At wishing we had something to be glad for.

Strangely, I think she means it.

Her boyfriend looks at me with a cool, assessing gaze that unnerves me. Like, what the heck is he trying to figure out?

My hand drops protectively to my abdomen, and his gaze tracks the movement.

I clear my throat. "The total on your deposit is $1348," I say.

"Sure, doll." Emilio pulls out a wad of cash with that swagger that

I'm used to seeing from my mafioso customers and peels off fourteen hundred dollar bills. "Keep the change and give my lady a nice bouquet, all right? Whatever she wants." He turns to Grace. "I'm gonna step outside and make a phone call, doll." He leans in to kiss her cheek.

I'm turned off by the fact that he calls us both *doll*. I sort of instantly hate him for hurting Armando although that's irrational. If he hadn't stolen Grace away, Armando might still be with her. And that would leave me without ever experiencing what it meant to be consumed by a man like him. To swim in his intensity.

"I'll make you something special," I tell Grace because there's no one else in the shop, and I can spare a few minutes to throw something together that she'll love. I'm still trying to impress her, despite the fact that she broke Armando's heart.

Despite the fact that I may have smashed what was left of it after she finished.

"I'll be right back."

I have the back door to the alley propped open to let the breeze through because it's cool for once, and I hear the boyfriend talking on his cell phone.

"Call it off. Yeah, I'm sure. I'm rescinding the job. It's off. No money will be paid."

A shiver sidles up my spine. I'm certain that's a conversation I shouldn't be overhearing. Not wanting to once again become a witness to something illegal, I hurry to finish the arrangement and rush back to the lobby with the vase in hand.

"Here you go." I force a smile, still fighting off the sense of foreboding from hearing that phone call and the ache of having all my feelings for Armando activated once more.

"Thank you." She studies me with curiosity. "Can I ask how you and—never mind." She shakes her head. "It's none of my business. I'm just happy for you guys."

If only happiness could be ours.

"Thanks." I watch her walk out before I pick up my phone and pull up an old text from Armando. He hasn't texted once since I kicked him out.

I don't know why I thought he would. But some part of me must've hoped because every day that goes by without hearing from him makes me die a little more.

My thumb hovers over my screen trying to decide if I should initiate communication. Finally, I settle for, *Thanks for recommending me to Grace.*

Then I delete the whole thing. If I send it, he might call and I'm not sure I can handle talking to him.

Still, I want to thank him. I can't imagine he enjoyed talking to her. I just can't picture him chatting her up in any way. So that fact that he stuck his neck out to make sure she got her flowers here means something. Whether it was before or after we broke up, I don't know, but either way, it was nice of him.

And that's when I'm sure.

I made a terrible mistake.

# CHAPTER TWENTY-EIGHT

*Armando*

Larry's happy, I'm finally doing what I was supposed to on this job —sit back and do nothing while the rest of them work.

I rub my swollen knuckles and stare at Hannah's dad, who's back on the job already. I was on edge, ready to fuck Larry in the ass with my boot if he gave Harold any shit about being out, but nothing happened.

Harold refuses to look at me, and Larry tries to pretend I'm not here anyway.

The last week has been a fucking blur. I go out every night with Marco and Leo delivering messages for the don then losing my mind in a bottle. The days are nothing. I don't even know how they pass. It's like being in prison again. One minute bleeds into an hour bleeds into a day. Nothing but violence and staying alive to fuel my existence.

At quarter 'til five o'clock, everyone starts moving in unison, packing their shit up to go. I stand and start to head out, but I see Harold looking over at me.

I wait because—fuck—I'm desperate for any kind of news about Hannah, any kind of connection to her. I've been so fucking lost without her. Dead.

He walks toward me like he's pissed. With intent. Like he's going to punch me in the gut.

And when he reaches me, he does.

I take it like a man, and I don't fight back because he's Hannah's fucking dad. If he thinks I deserve his wrath, he's probably right.

He hits me again, this time in the ribs. Then once more in the jaw.

"I don't care who the fuck you are. Or what family you work for. If you think you're gonna knock up my daughter and walk away, you'd better think again."

It takes a second for his words to sink in. *Knock up.* He said *knock. Up.*

I swipe the blood from my lip with the back of my hand. "Hannah's pregnant?" I demand.

The guy goes still, like he realized he might have fucked up. Like maybe I wasn't supposed to know.

I remember that pregnancy test box on the table. She told me it had been negative.

She lied?

Why?

A dozen scenarios run through my mind, but I don't stop to ask Harold, who obviously doesn't know what's going on in his daughter's head any more than I do. I leave him standing there and jog to the street. I need a fucking Uber.

Right fucking now!

For once in my goddamn life, things seem to go my way because a taxi pulls over when I flag it, and I throw myself inside, giving the address for Garden of Eden.

She lied and broke up with me rather than telling me she was pregnant. Why? *Why?*

Because she knew I'd be no good as a father and provider was the most obvious answer. That was the reason I'd freaked out when I saw the test box. And because I already had someone who wanted me dead, and I sure as hell didn't need to endanger a tiny innocent life with my fucked up drama.

Something uneasy twists in my gut as I replay my reaction. What if she lied because of how I acted? My sensitive, beautiful flower. She feels every emotion I should've been feeling. She's like a conduit for them. Maybe she felt my dismay and shut me out because of it. Maybe she thought I'd pressure her to get an abortion or some shit.

*Fanculo!* I failed her in every fucking way! I completely botched the pregnancy test in addition to my refusal to show up the way she needed me to. To be her man. To offer a genuine partnership.

Fuck! It's all I can do not to punch the hell out of the taxicab door, but I restrain myself. I can't get kicked out of the cab—not before I get to Garden of Eden.

And I don't even know what the hell I'm going to do or say to win her back. I still don't have a solution to my life-threatening shitshow. All I know is that I'm sure as hell going to fight for her.

For us.

I fucked things up big time, but that doesn't mean it's irreparable.

At least, I really fucking hope not.

# CHAPTER TWENTY-NINE

*Hannah*

The store is empty as usual when my phone rings at the shop. I pick it up where I'm putting together arrangements in the back.

When I see who's calling, I'm slightly alarmed. "Daddy?" He never calls me. It's always Mom who reaches out. I know my dad loves me, but he's definitely the strong, silent type.

Like Armando.

Dammit, why does everything remind me of Armando?

"Hey baby. Listen, I know you have something personal going that you aren't ready to tell me—"

"Daddy, please. I'm at work. I don't want to talk about it now." I blink quickly to clear my already smarting eyes and jockey an alstroemeria around in the bouquet until it sits right.

"I know, I know—that's okay," he says in a rush. "I heard enough when you came over to put together that you're pregnant and broke things off with that boyfriend of yours."

I stop arranging and hold my breath. Suck it in like I was punched in the gut, and it stays in, suspended. quivering.

"Well, I probably shouldn't have said anything to him..."

I gasp. Why hadn't I considered the fact that my dad and Armando still work together? "What'd you say?" I lay the rose in my fingers down on the counter, unable to continue.

"Hannah, you're not in any danger from that man, are you?" he asks sharply.

"From *Armando*?" I demand with exaggerated skepticism. "No. *He's* in danger from some gang, but no. He would never hurt me."

"Okay. But he doesn't know? I mean, he does now... I'm sorry, baby. It was pissing me off watching him show up hungover every day and not giving two fucks about the job when I knew you were crying your eyes out over this."

I swallow. "He was hung over?" That doesn't sound like him. It's stupid to think it might be because of me, but my foolish heart wants to.

"I'm pretty sure he's on his way over there now. I just wanted to give you a heads up."

"Okay, thanks," I whisper and close my eyes as I slowly lower the phone, my heart flopping wildly in my chest. Hope and anxiety over-lap, weave together, turn me inside out. Rational thought flees. I try to recount the reasons I didn't tell him. The reasons it was important to stay broken up, but they disappear.

I hear the bells I wrapped around the door handle to let me know when someone enters, jingle, and I step out to the front, my pulse racing. The moment I see his haggard face, I hiccup-sob and cover my mouth.

"Hannah." His voice is gruff as he crosses the floor of the shop in a few swift steps and comes around behind the counter. He's going to wrap me up in his arms. I sense his intent as strongly as I sense his angst, his strength, his determination.

"Don't," I plead, holding out a hand to stop him. Because once I'm in his arms again, I will never have the strength to push him away. I'll never have the will to end things. It will feel too right. I already know that. "I'm trying to get over you," I choke out.

"Please," he rasps. "I need to fucking hold you." His voice sounds like broken concrete and steel—wrecked but so damn strong.

And of course, there's no resisting him. I need him. I fall into his arms, and he pulls me against his muscled chest.

"I'm sorry, baby. I fucked everything up. Right from the start," he confesses to my hair, his lips moving the curls, his breath warm against my scalp. He doesn't ease the steel lockhold he has on my body, which is good because my legs stop working. "I didn't know going into this I was going to fall in love."

I stop breathing.

"I didn't know you'd become the fucking *heart* beating in my chest. All I knew was that you'd witnessed me kill a man and that made you a risk, but there was no way I could hurt you or even pretend I might hurt you. And all I could think to do was to take you home." His fingers slide under my hair, and he runs his thumb lightly over my nape. "Fuck, maybe I did know, even then. Because after that kiss, I never wanted to let you go. I wanted to tie you to my bedpost and keep you for-fucking-ever."

I realize I'm trembling all over. Incapable of speaking. I soak him in even though I resolved to be strong.

"Hannah." Now he eases the arm around me and pulls back, cupping my face. It's painful to look at him, but he waits until I do, and then I can't look away. I realize with a shock he has a bruise on his jaw and dark circles under his eyes.

"I fucked everything up, but if you give me a do-over, I swear to Christ you won't be sorry. I will figure out how to be your man." He leans his forehead against mine. "Please let me be your man."

I suck in a breath. "Are you here... because of what my dad told you?"

I don't know what I want him to say—there's so much packed into this, and it's all twisted together.

He hesitates like he wants to get the answer right but isn't sure how. "I want this baby—" he blurts suddenly, dropping his hands from my face and shoving them in his pockets. Giving me space. "I mean, if you do. I support you, no matter what. I'm sorry I freaked. It just scares the ever-loving shit out of me to think something might happen to either of you because of me. But I'm gonna solve that shit," he vows, his gaze steady. Firm. "I'm gonna solve it, and I will keep you safe. I promise you that."

It's the first time since he's been back I see that old confidence in him. The guy who sat on top of the world. Who knows what he wants and how to get it. Maybe Armando just needed a reason to give a damn about life on the outside.

Maybe I'm that reason.

"Hannah." His voice goes soft, and he steps in again, resting a hand lightly on my waist. "Give me another chance. Please. I'll get it right this time. I won't let you down." His other hand snakes around behind my head and tilts my face up. "And I want the baby. But no pressure."

His handsome face turns blurry from my tears. "I want the baby, too," I whisper. "She can come to work with me. I mean, I'm my own boss. I can totally make this work."

His eyes crinkle, and the corners of his lips tug up slightly. Leave it to our unborn baby to be the first thing to make him truly smile. A real, toothy, honest to God smile. "*She?*"

I shrug. "Feels like it."

His lips stretch wider. "She'll be beautiful. Like you." His gaze roves lovingly over my face. "May I kiss you?"

I let out a little puff of air because he sounds like we're on a first date. "You're asking permission now?"

His eyes crinkle again. "I told you, I'm gonna do it right this time. If you'll have me." He leans forward and stops with his lips millimeters from mine. "Say you'll have me."

"I'll have you," I whisper then push him away, right before his lips crash down on mine. "But you *can't* break my heart," I warn.

He shakes his head. "I'm all in, Hannah. And when I commit, I'm loyal as hell. This time will be good, I swear."

I close the distance between our lips and kiss-attack him. He gives it back to me, like he always does, devouring my mouth, his tongue plundering, his lips taking, drinking.

"I love you, Flowers," he murmurs when we come up for air.

My vision goes blurry. "I love you, too."

# CHAPTER THIRTY

*Armando*

The thing with love is that it makes you miss things you should've caught. My mind zeroed in on seeing Hannah. I knew it was Friday, and the guys were next door, but I didn't spare them any notice when I walked by. Nor did I pay attention to the guy loitering across the street.

I was too consumed with getting to Hannah and fixing that shit.

When the door bells jingle, we break apart, and I see Lorenzo, one of the old-timers come in.

"Mando," he says, like he's surprised to find me behind the counter in a liplock with Hannah.

"Lorenzo. How's it going?" For the first time since I got out, I don't hate everyone. I'm almost glad to see a familiar face. Proud to show off my relationship. My beautiful, pregnant girlfriend.

"What's going on here? You and ah..." His curious gaze shifts between the two of us.

"Hannah," I fill in, guessing he doesn't know or remember her name. "Yeah. This is my girl. Hannah, this is Lorenzo."

"I know Lorenzo," Hannah says with a laugh. "Two bouquets for you today?"

Lorenzo grins at her. "That's right. One for the wife and one for the *goomba*." He winks at me.

Hannah heads to the cooler. I realize she's wearing my Cubs shirt over her red short-shorts, and it floods my chest with warmth.

Feelings.

Feelings are fucking breaking through all over the place.

But that's when the shit hits the fan.

Gunshots ring out, and the front windows and glass doors shatter.

"Get down," I shout, lunging for Hannah and dragging her to the floor. Lorenzo draws a weapon but stays on the floor, crawling across the floor to where we are, behind the counter.

I'm usually cool as fuck in an emergency, but Hannah's here, with my unborn child. When the shots stop, I say to Lorenzo, "Get her out the back. Please." I take the gun from his hand because I don't have a weapon on me.

Lorenzo doesn't hesitate. He's a soldier, like me. He grabs Hannah's arm, hauls her up and books it for the back door. Glass from the windows falls in the eerie silence after the deafening shots.

"Lorenzo," I call out, and he turns at the door. "Make *sure* she's taken care of... if I don't make it out."

"No!" Hannah screams, and Lorenzo has to wrap his arms around her to keep her from running back to me.

"And my mom. Promise me." I cock the gun.

"You have my word."

"*Lorenzo*" —It seems so fucking important to say—"She's pregnant."

"*Lo prometo*," Lorenzo says in Italian with the reverence of swearing an oath, and then he hauls Hannah out the back door.

I suck in a breath and flatten my back against the wall just behind the counter.

More glass breaks, and I hear the crunch of footsteps over glass.

"Armando," someone sings. "Come out, come out, wherever you are."

This is it.

This is where I die. Right when I found a reason to live. When I'm needed. To think I could leave Hannah and our child before we even got a chance rips my goddamn lungs out.

But I also can't go on hiding. I can't have her or our baby in danger because I have a price on my head. This ends now. Tonight.

I check the magazine of the pistol to count how many shots I have then swallow back the bile in my throat. In the reflection of the cooler door, I see three of them. I can take them all.

"Drop your fucking weapons, or we'll mop the motherfucking floor with your blood."

My heart double pumps. *Arturo.* Many footsteps. The guys would've been next door for Friday haircuts. *La famiglia. My* family.

I step away from the wall, my own gun leveled at the guy closest to me. Arturo, Marco, Leo and Emilio are all there, guns leveled at the backs of the three gang members' heads.

"Nice and slow," Arturo says. "I don't know what the fuck you think you're doing, but no one messes with a Pachino. You touch one hair on his head, Don Pachino will erase the existence of every one of you—every gang member, your mothers, your brothers, your sisters, and your fucking dogs—from the streets of this city."

"Easy man." I recognize the voice of the guy who called my name when he came in. He holds his gun out by the handle and slowly lowers it to the ground. His two friends do the same. "You don't know what you're talking about, man. The order came from Don Pachino. He hired us for this shit."

My body flushes with ice. The fuck?

"Bullshit," Arturo says immediately.

The guy slowly turns around. "Tell them." He lifts his chin at Emilio, whose eyes dart all over the fucking place.

Arturo sends a quick look at Emilio. *"Tell us what, Emilio?"* His voice is deadly. It makes goosebumps stand up on my arms.

"He hired us," the guy says.

"I called it off, asshole," Emilio grits through clenched teeth. Sweat beads at his forehead. He's as pale as a fucking Swede.

The ripple of shock that runs through the wise guys is palpable.

"I called it off today." Emilio shifts from foot to foot.

The guy shrugs. "I didn't get no memo."

"I called it off!" Emilio shouts, like he's losing his fucking head.

"You heard him," Arturo says, picking up the thread. "And that fucking order didn't come from the don. So if you don't want your entire gang obliterated, I suggest you walk out of here and never come near any of us again. *Capito?*"

"Yeah, okay." The guy tries to sound cool, but he and his two buddies exit swiftly.

The sound of sirens approaching fills the air, and Arturo curses. "Give me the fucking gun," he says to me because if I get caught with the thing, I'm gonna get another five years in the pen, just like that.

But I'm not about to give up my weapon. Not when there's a fucking traitor in our midst. I point it at Emilio's head. Marco and Leo do the same.

Emilio holds both hands in the air, his gun dangling on his trigger finger. Slowly, he drops to his knees and places the Walther PPK on the floor. "I thought you were going to kill me, Mando," he croaks. "Because of Grace." His hands visibly shake, but he holds eye contact with me, which is pretty fucking ballsy, considering he's admitting to putting a hit on me.

"You fucking bastard," Marco spits.

"I was afraid of you. Everyone thought you'd do something to me. Everyone, right?" He looks around for support, but no one says a fucking word. The cops screech up, lights flashing.

"Enough," Arturo snaps. "The don will settle this. Not any of you," he says fiercely, throwing his warning glance at me, Marco and Leo. "I mean it. He's a made man. You can't touch him. Don G. will decide his fate. Now give me that fucking gun, Mando, before you land your ass back in the can. Everyone else, put your goddamn pieces away. I'll handle the cops."

I put the safety on the gun and toss it to him as the cops advance. The rest of the guys put theirs away, and everyone raises their hands in the air. Emilio climbs awkwardly to his feet, never taking his gaze off me. He still thinks I'm going to kill him.

"They're gone," Arturo hollers to the cops. "It was some kind of gang hit, but they ran when we came out of the barbershop with our own weapons." He slowly walks outside, hands loosely held in the air. Don Pachino has some boys in blue on the payroll, and chances are good Artie knows who they are and vice versa. I can only fucking hope he can talk us out of this shit show.

I expect them to order us all face down, but they don't. They definitely know Artie. They let him approach and give them his story about what happened.

Marco purposely knocks into Emilio as he walks out, and Leo shoots him a look that swears death. I should be thinking about killing the bastard, but I don't. Because as I step outside, I see Hannah standing in front of Rocco's, tears streaming down her face. Lorenzo stands protectively by her side and nods to me when I lift my chin.

"Armando!" she cries out.

"It's okay, Flowers." I hold open my arms, and she runs into them. Her soft body collides with mine, she presses all those curves against me, buries her face in my chest. "It's over now. Forever."

She blinks up at me, and I stroke my thumb down her smooth brown skin. "It's over," I repeat, realizing it might be true.

Emilio revoked the hit. Arturo warned off the Hermanos who hadn't heard the message. That means other than the shit that needs to be resolved between me and Emilio, my life's safe for the moment.

My girl and our baby are safe.

I slide my fingers in her curls to cup the back of her head and meld my lips to hers. "Marry me?" I ask.

Her lips part in surprise. "Are you serious?"

"Dead serious, Flowers. You're the reason I want to live. The reason I'm glad I'm free. Even without the baby, I'd want to move you into my place and keep you forever."

She lets out a watery laugh. "Wow. I don't know."

My heart stutters. I put a knuckle under her chin to lift her gaze to mine. "You don't know?"

"What about—" she flutters a hand at her ruined shop, the glass shattered from bullets.

I draw a breath and nod. "It's solved. I'm not a target anymore. And I swear to Christ I will not let anything like this touch you or our baby again."

She throws her arms around my waist and hugs me fiercely. "It's solved? Oh my God, Armando, that was horrible. I thought you were going to die."

"I know, beautiful. But it's over now, I promise."

She pulls away and lifts her face. *"Yes."*

I don't breathe. Is she saying *yes* to my proposal?

"Yes!" She nods vigorously as tears stream down her beautiful face.

"I love you." I look into her warm brown eyes when I say it. Hold her gaze, so she knows it's the goddamn truth. I'm her man, and I'm going to stand by her for life. Loyalty is my gig.

I look over to where Marco and Leo stand, sandwiching Emilio between them, like prison guards.

When Marco sees me looking, he mutters something and comes over, his curious gaze sweeping Hannah.

She swipes at her tears, wipes them on my shirt, letting out an embarrassed laugh.

"I hope you took him back. He's been a big baby since you kicked him out."

I don't even punch him because I'm too fucking happy. "Hannah just agreed to marry me."

Marco's face stretches into a grin. "That right? Congratulations!"

I hear Leo growl something like, "If you fucking run, I will hunt you down and eat your goddamn liver," to Emilio before he comes over and holds his hand out. "Did I just hear that right?"

"Yes," Hannah says with a watery laugh.

"She's now my fiancée," I fill in. "And she's having my baby."

"Whoa!" Marco grins.

Leo's brows wing up. "Way to lock it in, Mando."

There are smiles all around. Hell, I may even be smiling—that would be new.

"Mando." Hannah looks up at me under her curled lashes. "That's what they call you?"

I nod. "Yeah. Childhood nickname."

"I like it."

"I like you." I pull her against me and kiss the bridge of her nose.

Emilio stands and watches us, shoulders slouched, misery and fear lining his face. Frankly, I'm surprised he hasn't made a run for it, but he probably knows Leo told the truth. We would hunt him to the ends of the earth if he ran. Besides, he has a fiancée waiting at home for him.

Maybe he thinks he'll still make it out of this alive.

Arturo yells to Lorenzo in Italian to watch him, and I feel somewhat vindicated. It's not just Marco and Leo on my side. It's everyone.

I don't know what the don will do, but that current of loyalty, the strength of family that's been missing since I got out, turns back on. All but one of these men have my back.

It takes most of the sting away from knowing one of our own tried to buy my death.

## CHAPTER THIRTY-ONE

*Hannah*

"This is my place," Armando murmurs, opening the door to his apartment and flipping on the lights. His cousins, Marco and Leo both have apartments in the same building. I know because we all took the same elevator up.

After Armando called some friends in to clean the glass up at my place, he left someone in charge of staying all night to watch over the place until we can get the windows and door replaced tomorrow.

"It's nice," I say. It's way nicer than mine in terms of size and location although devoid of any personality.

"We could live here, if you want, because it's bigger. You can do whatever you want with it—make it colorful, like you."

I peer up at him. "You think I'm colorful?"

He turns to fully face me and wraps both arms around me. "Yeah." He brushes his lips over my nose. "Beautiful. Vibrant. Full of life." He glances at my belly, and his lips turn up. "Literally."

I love seeing the smile on his face. There are signs of fatigue around his eyes, but he looks more relaxed and happy than I've ever seen him. He told me on the way home that everything had been solved—there was no longer a hit out on him, and that it had been

Emilio who put the contract out and hired the gang to execute it after Armando killed the first hitman. I told him about the phone call I overheard—how he must've canceled it after he learned we were a couple. I'm not saying that makes it all right—and I won't forgive Emilio for what he did—but it counts for something, I guess.

He leads me to the bedroom and gently pulls his shirt over my head. "I love seeing you in my clothes, Flowers," he rumbles, working the button on my shorts. He drops to a crouch, sliding his hands down my thighs as he pulls them down and off my legs. Then he stands and walks around me, trailing his fingertips lightly over my skin. It's so different from the rough way he usually takes me. He kisses across my shoulder, along the lines of my tattoo. "So beautiful," he murmurs.

Warmth floods my chest, making my breasts grow heavy, my nipples taut. I don't know if I'm sensing his emotions or my own— they're so intertwined. All the hard edges, the walls between us are gone now.

He moves behind me and unhooks my bra then cups my breasts, strumming my nipples with his thumbs. His teeth graze my neck. "That goomba shit with Lorenzo?" he says. "That's not me. I won't ever do that to you. I make a vow to you, Flowers, I'll keep it."

My heart picks up speed. This man is going to be my husband. Daddy to our child. I hadn't doubted him, but it's nice to hear him swear to be faithful. I lean my head back against his shoulder and cover his hands with my fingers. He catches my wrists and pulls them above my head caged in one of his hands, lifting and spreading my breasts. With his other hand, he pinches my nipples, which are already hard as diamonds.

I moan softly. "They're tender," I complain.

He immediately stops. "Sorry, angel." He nuzzles his mouth against my jaw.

"No, don't stop. I like the way you touch me."

"Come here." He walks us both backward until we hit the bed and tumble to the springy mattress. After he pushes me to my back, his mouth descends on mine. The tenderness vanishes as raw hunger takes over. I tear his shirt off over his head. He knees my thighs apart. I unbutton his pants. He pulls off my panties. We are a wild tangle of lips and hands and melding bodies. I stroke my hands over his hard muscles, greedily touching everywhere I can—the bulging muscles of his arms, the ridges of his abdominals, the hard curve of his ass. He shucks his pants and slides into me unsheathed, his teeth sinking into the flesh of my neck.

I arch to take him deeper. "Yes."

"Yes," he echoes. He rocks into me with powerful surges. "Mine." He braces my shoulder to keep my head from hitting the headboard, but strokes my cheek with his thumb, a shred of tenderness still there. "You're mine now."

My lids flutter with the effort of keeping my eyes from rolling back with pleasure, but I lock my gaze with his. "I was yours from the beginning," I confess.

It's true. He didn't need to kidnap me and hold me captive. I would've gone with him anywhere. He had me with the first commanding touch.

"I love you," I tell him, never having to hold back those words again. He must know, though, because I'm incapable of hiding feelings.

Armando throws his head back, almost like he's in pain. He bares his teeth and roars, slamming into me hard, harder.

"Yes," I gasp. "Please."

Armando stills, his face taut with strain, his hands gouging my hips into the mattress as his cock swells inside me. He groans, his head falling forward, his arms coming around me to keep me close. "I love you," he whispers.

He thrusts deeper, and I gasp, loving the feeling of his enormous cock filling me to the brim and aching with need for more.

I lift my hand to stroke his cheek. His eyes close as he leans into my touch and kisses my palm.

"Forever mine," he whispers.

My heart swells.

He thrusts his cock even deeper. A tear leaks out of the corner of my eye, and Armando licks it away.

"Forever," I whisper.

"And always," he says, his thrusts slow and deep and perfect.

His cock throbs, the girth increases, and the heat intensifies.

The pleasure is so intense I can barely breathe. I'm being consumed. Consumed by his unending love. Is this solely my feelings, or am I also feeling his?

"Oh, Armando," I moan, the ecstasy so intense it feels like pain.

He moves faster, his cock slamming into me with such fervor I cry out. I don't know what's happening to me, but I can feel every ounce of raw, unadulterated emotion that courses through his body. It's like I can feel every emotion he has ever felt in his lifetime.

I can feel every old wound he has suffered, every time someone he cared about hurt him, every time someone he trusted betrayed him. I can feel everything inside this man.

His fingers dig into the tender flesh of my hips, and he slams into me once more.

"Jesus, you feel so fucking good," he declares as he pounds into me. His lips move to my neck, and he nips at my throat.

I feel every inch of him inside me, and I want nothing more than to relish this feeling. I know that this moment is fleeting, but I want it to stay with me. I'm falling into oblivion. I'm not sure what I'm falling into, but I know this is peaceful. This is how I want to forever feel in this world. Nothing can touch me. Nothing can hurt me. Nothing can make me feel this good.

My lips touch his, his body trembles against me, and I feel his soul in my soul. My legs begin to tremble, my toes curling as I scream out. I'm so close. So damn close.

"Oh Christ, *now, Hannah*—come now," he shouts and plunges deep, filling me with his hot essence.

Because he does command my body, it responds immediately, the walls of my channel clenching and squeezing around his cock in the most satisfying—emotionally and physically—orgasm of my life.

Armando slows his rocking and showers kisses on my cheeks, eyelids, across the bridge of my nose. "I love you, beautiful girl."

"I love you, too," I croak, fighting my way back from the other galaxy where I'd been shot by my pleasure. I wrap my legs around his back and pull his hips in even tighter. "So much."

# CHAPTER THIRTY-TWO

*Armando*

The scent of dirt, metal and blood hits my nose the minute I'm let into the warehouse.

It's three in the goddamn morning. I had to leave Hannah in my bed for this, which nearly killed me. But the don called me himself and told me to get down here. And when the don calls, you come. No questions. No complaints.

He could've dragged it out and made Emilio sweat his judgment, but instead the don chose to mete out the punishment tonight.

There are two parts of me now. The dead part. And the part Hannah made feel. The dead part doesn't give a shit what goes down tonight. Not if they bury Emilio at the bottom of Lake Michigan with a pair of cement shoes. Not even if they make me pull the trigger.

But the other part—the Hannah part—*fuck*. I can't stomach it. Like it physically makes me ill to think of Emilio getting whacked. Gracie being widowed before she even gets married. Not having her big wedding.

I don't like it.

It's not that I forgive the guy. He hired a hit on me just to save his own ass after stealing my girl.

The thing is, Grace isn't my girl anymore. Right now it feels like she never was. We were pretending. Going through the motions of what Made Men and their pretty, gold-digging girlfriends did.

I am in one of the don's warehouses in Little Italy, not far from Garden of Eden.

Emilio's curled up in the fetal position, bleeding and crying like a baby. The guys have already worked him over pretty good.

Everyone important is here. All the old-timers. Alex, Don G's son-in-law. Marco and Leo.

Don Pachino glances my way and lifts his chin to summon me. I walk over like the scene means nothing to me.

Which is only half true.

I've seen enough violence to harden me to the sight of it. Hell, I perpetrated enough violence to make Emilio think I was going to kill him when I got out. So the sight of him bruised and bleeding does nothing to me.

But knowing he might die soon? That makes me itchy.

"Emilio violated his oath." The room goes quiet when Don G speaks. This is it: Emilio's sentencing.

Looking around, I can tell I'm not the only guy who isn't entirely comfortable. Everyone looks grim. Hands stuffed in pockets, no hint of pleasure in any of it. Emilio may have fucked me, but he's still one of our own. He's Family. A brother-in-arms.

And he's been a favorite of the don's.

"He betrayed us all when he attempted to kill a member of La Famiglia."

Emilio lets out a sob, but he doesn't beg. He knows better.

Don G crosses his arms over his chest and lets his words settle over all of us. Lets the tension grow. "Armando, you are the injured party. What justice do you seek?"

Fuck.

I hoped the decision would be made for me.

"I'm not the only injured party," I say, looking toward Marco. "He got shot in the ass."

"And he's a bloody mess because of it," Marco says. "Don't worry. I got mine."

"You sure?" I ask. "You want to shoot him in the ass too. Seems only fair."

"I considered it," Marco says with a smirk.

Emilio peers up at me through the swollen slits his eyes have become. There's pleading in his gaze. Apology. "I'm sorry, Mando. I tried to cancel it, I swear to Christ, I did."

Of course, that reminds me of Hannah, which makes me feel again. "Yeah, I know."

The room is silent. I don't think anyone even breathes.

"Hannah heard you calling it off."

I watch hope bloom on Emilio's face. He drags himself up on his forearms, then sits up with a wince, holding his ribs, which are undoubtedly broken.

I shove my hands in my pockets like the other men. Consider Emilio, the sorry *stronzo* at my feet. "You're such a fucking pansy, you couldn't even try to kill me yourself."

Tears fall down Emilio's face. He spreads his hands. "I'm sorry, Mando. I just love her so much. I always loved her. Even before you went in the can. I just wanted to live to marry her."

"How's that working out for you?"

I sense the agitation in the room at my dry threat. The implication that he wouldn't live to marry Grace.

I meet his pleading gaze. "Offer me restitution," I demand, throwing it out like a challenge. Like I might not accept his offer.

Relief and eagerness spread across his face. "Anything. I'll pay it. Name your price."

"How much is that wedding worth to you?"

"Anything," Emilio begs.

"Fifty thousand." I throw out the first number that pops in my head.

"One hundred," Don G interjects firmly.

Emilio nods eagerly, dragging himself slowly to his knees. "I'll pay it. Yes, of course. I'll pay it."

"Bring it to him tomorrow, and we'll put this to bed." He looks at me. "No retributions."

I hold my hands up. "I never threatened him in the first place. You told me to leave it, and I did." I lift my shoulders. "I follow orders. I'm loyal."

*Unlike some other* stronzo *fucks*. I don't say it, but I know everyone there's thinking the same thing.

Emilio will have to live with his shame for the rest of his life. He may still be in the Family, but he lost all respect tonight.

"Yes." Don G's glance slides back to Emilio with distaste. "I misjudged which direction the conflict would come from."

Fuck it. Hannah's love made me generous. Or maybe she's just working through me. That infinite abundance of non-judgment she seems to carry. I close the distance between me and Emilio and hold out my hand.

He looks at me doubtfully, like he still expects me to pull out a gun and shoot him through the teeth, but I wait with my palm extended, steady.

When he finally takes it, I haul him to his feet. "Dumber things have been done to keep a woman. You be good to Grace." I pull him in for a bro-hug, and he grips my shoulder tightly, like I'm the only thing keeping him alive. Which I guess is sort of true.

The tension in the room releases all at once, grunts of approval going around.

"Don't—don't tell her," he begs when I release him.

I shake my head, totally cool. "Never. Nobody here will." It's probably true, but I look around to be sure, making it a warning.

Everyone nods his agreement.

Don G. turns and walks away, like he's not going to dignify Emilio with any more of his attention. He stops at the door. "Settle it by tomorrow. Mando, tell me when it's done. And then I don't ever want to hear of this shit again."

"*Capito, Capito,*" Emilio says, but Don G gives him his back again.

Marco saunters to my side, eying Emilio with disdain. "Well, I'd be worried, too, if I took your girl. You are a fucking badass."

It's a joke, and it lightens some of the tension in the room. Guys start moving around, talking to each other.

"My girl's waiting for me at home, so no offense, but I got better places to be."

"Go. Go home." Lorenzo makes a shooing motion. "Take care of that pregnant girl of yours."

Some of the guys grunt in surprise to hear my news.

I suspect Lorenzo's invested in me and Hannah and the baby since I entrusted him with their lives earlier. I might think about making him godfather. Although Marco would be a wiser choice, not just because he's younger.

That guy would saw off his own hand for me.

I clasp his hand, and we smack each other's shoulders.

"See you tomorrow, Emilio," I say without any taunt in my voice. I don't know how the guy is going to come up with a hundred grand by tomorrow, but it's not my problem.

Even if I offered to give him some time to pull it together, Don G would never stand for it.

He made his ruling. His will be done.

———

*Hannah*

Armando comes in at six in the morning.

I remember him getting a phone call and leaving. It must have been around three.

I sit up in bed, scared. Searching his face for bruises or blood, but apart from looking tired, he seems whole.

"Is everything okay?"

I don't ask where he's been. I know he can't tell me.

He nods. "It's good. Shit got resolved with Emilio."

Emilio. It's not like me to hold a grudge, but he put a hit on Armando, so I'm not sure I'll ever forgive him for that.

Still, I don't really want to hear he's dead, either. Not that Armando would share that with me if he was.

"Will there... still be a wedding for him and Grace?"

Armando shucks his clothing and comes to the bed. "Yeah. He's paying me restitution. Do you know what that means, Flowers?" He crawls toward me and pushes me back down, covering my body with his own.

I have absolutely no clue. "No?"

"It means I have money to invest in Garden of Eden. Our family business."

My eyes fill with tears.

*Family business.*

I don't think I realized how alone I've felt running Garden of Eden until this moment. I brought Josie on to try to lessen that burden, but she wasn't invested in it like I am.

But now I have Armando. And I already know this man can do anything. Which means, the business is saved. I know he'll help me straighten it out. Fix everything.

That's the kind of guy he is.

"That's it, baby. Cry me those tears. Are they happy ones?"

"Yes." I nod. "I'm happy."

He grins. It's a rare occurrence to see a smile on him, and it takes my breath away. "What are you happy about?"

"That we're a family."

His smile grows wider.

"You're my family, Flowers. You and that baby are everything to me."

I reach for him and pull him down.

After a searing kiss, he lifts his head. "You're mine, Hannah," he says, his voice low and possessive. "You're mine, and I'll do everything in my power to make you happy."

A shiver runs down my spine at the conviction in his words, but I don't shy away from them. Instead, I welcome them, wrapping my arms around his neck and pressing my lips to his. We kiss deeply, passionately, the world around us fading away as we lose ourselves in each other.

There's something about him that makes me feel safe, secure, like nothing can touch me as long as he's by my side.

I moan softly into his mouth as he nudges my legs apart.

He kisses every inch of my skin, starting with my neck and moving down my shoulders then to my breasts. I arch my back as his lips close around my nipple, his fingers slipping between my legs. I gasp as he enters me, his movements slow and deliberate.

But I want more than his fingers. I want his dick buried deep inside me. "More," I moan. "More."

I don't even realize what I'm doing until I'm on top of him after shedding him of his pants, my legs straddling his hips. I position myself, his dick pressing against my sex. The thick tip of his cock slips into me, and I gasp, my body momentarily stilling.

He's so fucking big, and this angle almost hurts.

But I like the pain. I love it.

I start to move, sliding up his length, the feeling of his thickness stretching me so much more intense than his fingers.

I'm impaling myself on his cock, my moans loud and throaty. His hands grip my hips, forcing me to ride his cock, his hips rising to meet mine, driving his cock deep inside me.

I throw my head back, throwing my hair behind me as I let myself go, my orgasm exploding through my body like fireworks in the night sky.

I ride him harder and faster, my body desperate for more, needing more. My nails dig into his shoulders, my hips bucking wildly against him. I'm moaning louder and louder, my cries of pleasure echoing through the room.

I slow to a stop, straddling him and staring him in the eye as I move myself up and down his cock. He looks at me like I'm the most beautiful woman in the world as I ride him, my movements slow and rhythmic.

My eyes flutter closed as I near my next orgasm.

"That's right," he whispers, his words soft and full of need. "Come for me, Hannah. Come for me."

His words push me into my orgasm, his words and his cock. I throw my head back and scream his name, my body quivering as I come again.

He flips me over on the bed and positions himself behind me, his cock sliding into me once more. His hands grip my hips, and he thrusts deep into me.

His cock pulses inside me, his body growing tense and tight. He thrusts a few more times before growing still. He moans deeply as his cock twitches inside me, his hot seed filling me.

He pulls out and lies beside me on the bed, pulling me against his body.

"I love you, Flowers."

I tuck my face against his neck, basking in the power of his words. In his love. His attention. His promise.

"I love you so much," I tell him.

"You brought me back from the dead. You gave me a reason to live. I owe you everything. I want you to know, I will never let you down again."

Tears spear my eyes once more. "I know you won't," I whisper against his skin.

I trust this man with my life. With our child. With our future.

He's my everything.

# EPILOGUE

*Hannah*

"The judges have viewed all the entries and picked four finalists to compete. Will the following florists step forward..."

Armando's arm tightens around my thickened waist from behind. "It's gonna be you," he murmurs in my ear.

Marco and Leo both thump me on the back. I'm touched they came along. It's really true that Armando's family looks after one another. And that now includes me.

My heart taps a staccato beat against my ribs, but the truth is—I don't care if I don't make it to the finals. What's more important to me is this feeling in my chest now.

The pouring flow of love, of support from him. The pleasure of having the person I care about most in this world at my side for the moments that matter.

As he promised, Armando used Emilio's restitution payment to invest in Garden of Eden. He bought a new van and hired two part-time guys to make my deliveries. He's thrown himself into building the business—our *family business,* he calls it—and in the last two months, revenue has already tripled. He talked the don into making physical upgrades and is looking into a second location. All the stuff that used to terrify me, he's taken over, and he makes it look so easy. I can focus on what I'm good at—the artistic side, and we do the networking together, so it's less intimidating.

"Hannah Munn," the announcer says, and I gasp. I really didn't expect to make it to the finals.

"Told you," Armando rumbles in my ear before releasing me to go up on stage.

I draw in a shaky breath, shake out my hands and bend over to pick up my bucket of flowers.

"Stop," Armando scoffs. "I'll carry them up there."

He doesn't let me pick up anything heavy. Or stay on my feet for too long. Or work too hard. He treats me like a princess, except for in his bed. There, he still turns animal on me, even with my growing baby bump.

I make my way up there, and he follows, carrying my bucket full of flowers and setting it beside me on the floor. "Knock 'em dead, Flowers," he murmurs and squeezes my hand before he slips away, leaving me with the other contestants. The next step is to design an arrangement for them with flowers we provide while everyone watches. Then to make one with flowers they provide.

I wait for the timer then put together my arrangement. It's an artistic spiral of multi-colored roses interwoven with freesia and silver wicker wisps. When I finish and step back for the judges to view, I don't let myself look at the other three contestants' arrangements— I'm too nervous and doubt wants to creep in, hard. Instead, I find Armando in the audience. We lock gazes, and immediately, I sense his strength. His confidence in me. It pours into me, washing away the nerves. I attempt a small smile, and he grins back.

Full-on grin. Nothing makes me happier than seeing his face crack a smile like that. Knowing I'm the one who helped revive him.

Last week was Grace and Emilio's wedding. I did my very best on the flowers—not because Emilio deserved it but because it's Armando's family, and I'm a part of it now. We attended the wedding as guests, as well. It was Armando's decision. He said he was too happy with me to hold a grudge with either of them.

The organizers bring us their buckets of flowers, and the next round begins. I don't think, just let my fingers pluck the flowers and arrange them, no plan in mind. I know if I start trying to figure out the right thing, I'll get it wrong. My creative genius happens when I don't edit, don't worry, don't think.

So I ride the bliss of Armando's love. The pleasure of wearing his ring and building a life, family and business with him. And the arrangement creates itself—a simple but striking multi-tiered arrangement of peonies and star-gazer lilies.

The timer dings. We step back. I catch Armando's eye, and he winks. Hope starts to leak in. I made it this far, it sure would be amazing to win. But no, I shouldn't let myself go there because what if I'm disappointed?

The judges confer, and I get a little dizzy waiting. The pregnancy's doing a number on my blood volume, or so my mom has told me. She's overjoyed with my pregnancy now that I'm happy. I think my dad is even starting to accept Armando although he doesn't like the fact that he's part of the mafia.

Armando says that's something he can't change, but he promises to shield me and our family from any of its negative effects. I know there are no guarantees. He could end up in prison again. Or be killed. But for the moment, the don is letting him stay out of the business to run mine. And it's hard not to feel invincible with his love wrapped so tightly around me.

"The judges have made their decision. In third place, Jaya Lowe." The crowd claps. I pretend I'm breathing. "In second place, Eric Diamond."

Crap. That probably means I didn't get it.

"In first place, the winner of this year's competition is... Hannah Munn, of Garden of Eden."

I hear Armando shout. I try to stop the waterworks already spewing from my eyes, but it's impossible. There will be no elegance and poise for me as I accept the trophy. But it doesn't matter.

I won.

I carry the trophy back to Armando on shaking legs, and he sweeps me off my feet into a spin. "You did it! I knew you would, Flowers."

"I can't stop crying." I say the obvious.

He sets me gently on my feet and kisses away the tears. "Keep crying, Flowers. It only gets better from here."

# TASTE OF SIN

## A Chicago Sin Bonus Story

# CHAPTER ONE

*Taylor*

My feet are killing me, my ears ring, and I'm dying of thirst.

Pretty normal after a seven-hour cocktail shift at Sins.

I wince as I walk out to my car in the dark parking lot, balancing two plastic cups of ice water in one hand, along with my purse and keys. I can't believe I forgot my water bottle—not that there's ever a free moment to drink it.

I'm in a pair of high heeled stilettos. Yeah, they bring the tips in, but damn, do they hurt!

You would think for someone pursuing an education in physical therapy I would take better care of my body. But then I wouldn't bring in the big bucks. And Lord knows, I need the money. I'm still paying down the loans from my undergraduate education, living on ramen and mac and cheese. If I didn't have the job at Sins to supplement my student loans, I wouldn't be able to afford the gas in my car.

The club closed an hour ago, but there are still a smattering of cars in the parking lot, including a slick BMW that can't possibly belong to any of my co-workers.

Must be one of the customer's then.

Probably mafia-owned.

My lips quirk as I think about the hundred dollar tip in my pocket from one of them.

Marco. He and his brother Leo come in here with different women on their arms every freaking weekend.

Tonight he had the nerve to ask me if I'm ever tempted to come on my nights off.

"Never."

He flashed that cocky smile. "Never, ever?"

"No," I told him. "I don't like pain."

"Do you like pleasure, angel?" He arched a sexy brow.

I roll my eyes as I open my car door. I would've told him I'm not his angel, except I like his money way too much to draw that line in the sand.

I groan when I drop to the driver's seat and take the weight off my feet. I set the water cups down on the center console and lean down to unbuckle the ankle straps on my heels. "Ow, ow, ow," I mutter. I can't stand another minute with these torture devices affixed to my poor throbbing feet.

As soon as I get them off, I start my old Honda Accord and back out.

When I turn to drive out of the lot, one of the water cups careens off the center console and dumps ice and liquid into my lap.

"Ack!" I accidentally twist the wheel when I grab for it and try to shake the ice from my already-soaked dress. One of my heels tumbles under the brake pedal.

Fuck.

I try to kick it out as the second cup of water tumbles all over me.

I reach down to grab the shoe, but my foot jams onto the gas pedal and the car lurches forward.

I plow straight into a parked car.

I scream. There's a sickening crunch of metal and plastic, and I still can't get the shoe out from under the brake! The engine revs as I continue to shove against—oh God.

It's the BMW. Of course it is.

Fuck, fuck, fuck!

I kick the shoe out and press the brake, gripping the steering wheel so hard my knuckles crack.

What do I do? I'm in a total panic. There's no logic running through my brain at all.

Or very little, anyway.

I look around quickly for the crowd of observers, but no one's here.

That's when I make the dumbest mistake of my life.

I throw the car in reverse and hit the gas. After a few excruciating moments of engine grinding and breaking parts, my car pulls free of the wreckage.

I straighten the wheel and flatten the accelerator pedal to the floor.

There's a screech of rubber on asphalt as I tear out of there.

Away from the scene of the crime.

Straight toward consequences I'm not even remotely equipped to face.

———

*Marco*

What. *The fuck?*

I reach for a piece, but I'm not wearing one.

Weapons aren't allowed on premises at Sins.

"What is it?" Leo's instantly at my side, moving his body protectively in front of his date for the evening.

"Some asshole just smashed into my car."

My brand new BMW.

"Did you get a look at him?"

The club bouncer beside us clears his throat.

"What?" I snap. "Do you know who that was?"

He rubs his nose, looking uncomfortable. "I, uh, think it was just an accident."

I fist his shirt and push him back against the wall, even though he's bigger and brawnier than I am. "Who was it?" I snarl. "What do you know?"

He doesn't resist, because he knows I'm fucking dangerous. He lifts his hands in surrender. "It was a *her,* not a *him.*"

I loosen my grip.

Maybe it was just an accident.

Some drunken club-goer?

She's still going to have to answer to me.

"Do you know her?" I demand.

"What are you going to do?"

Okay, he definitely knows her.

"I don't hurt women," I assure him, then glance over my shoulder where our dates for the night are standing, looking glassy-eyed and thoroughly pleasured. "Except when they like it."

"It was Taylor," the bouncer admits. "The cocktail waitress?"

I release him, completely relaxed now.

Taylor. The adorable little blonde who looks far too innocent and wholesome to work here.

"Text me her address."

"What are you going to do?"

I glance in the direction she sped off.

"Tomorrow, I'm going to pay her a little visit."

# CHAPTER TWO

*Taylor*

The next morning I pace through my one-room apartment, gnawing on the inside of my cheek.

What I did last night was unbelievably stupid.

Not only did I break the law, but the car I hit is probably owned by someone dangerous. They only have to ask the owner of Sins, Jack Lindstrom, to pull the security video feed from the parking lot last night to get my name and address.

Which means, instead of facing a possible ticket and jacked up insurance rates, I'm probably now going to be wearing cement shoes in Lake Michigan.

I wipe the clammy sweat from my palms on my pajama shorts.

I should preemptively call Jack and confess. Maybe he can tell me who owns the car and I can try to make things right. That's what a sane person would do.

Of course, a sane person wouldn't have sped away like a coward.

That's where I really screwed myself.

Okay, I need to call Jack right away. It's the only answer. I hunt down my phone, which is still in my purse from last night. Of course, it's dead. When I plug it in, it dings showing fourteen text messages. The knot in my stomach tightens.

Before I can open the messages to read them, a heavy pounding sounds on my door.

The tight band around my temples cinches, sending blinding pain between my eyes.

This is it. I'm a dead woman.

For one stupid moment, I consider climbing through the window and down the fire escape, but that would be making the same choice I did last night. That kind of cowardice is what got me into this in the first place. No, I need to just face this head on.

I walk to the door, square my shoulders, and throw it open, pretending I'm not terrified of what I will find on the other side.

My belly flips at what I see, but not entirely from fear. Because the man on the other side of the door is my heavy tipper.

Marco.

The very hot mafia player who was hitting on me last night. He leans against the doorframe in a deceptively casual pose, his hands shoved in the pockets of his thousand dollar Italian suit pants.

"Hello, Taylor." There's a smirk on his face and a *Gotcha* look that makes my tummy flutter even more. Heat floods between my legs—even more when he takes a slow perusal of my body.

I realize I answered the door in nothing more than a flimsy, spaghetti strap bralette and thin pajama shorts. My nipples bead up under the top.

"You don't look surprised to see me."

"Marco, I'm so sorry. I panicked last night after I hit your car. But I was about to try to make it right this morning, I swear."

He arches a brow. "Were you, Angel?"

"I swear," I repeat, backing up as he advances through my threshold and shuts the door.

He makes a tsking sound. "Leaving the scene of an accident is a crime, Taylor."

"Are you going to turn me in?" I hope my voice sounds more flirtatious than dry.

We both know he's not going to call the police.

He's mafia. They handle their problems personally. Usually with violence, not that I've ever seen that from him.

His lips quirk. "Nah, I'm not here to turn you in. I'm here to give you a spanking."

I blink, trying to figure out if he means metaphorically or literally.

For some reason, my body takes him at his word and my ass clenches. I grow hot and tingly everywhere. A slow pulse starts up between my legs.

As if he somehow realizes the effect of his words on me, his smirk grows. He advances another step, invading my personal space. His hand settles lightly on my waist. I have to work to lift my eyes and meet his gaze.

Very gently, without insisting, he tugs me forward until my body is flush against his. He brings a knuckle under my chin and lifts my face even more. "Are you ready for your punishment?"

I attempt to swallow and fail. "M-my insurance will cover it."

His grin widens. He has one dimple on his left that melts my panties. "I saw your car out there, angel, and I see the size of your apartment. I'm guessing you can't afford the insurance hike."

My heartbeat is wild and irregular. I think I know where he's going with this and I'm not sure I mind.

"What are you suggesting?" I attempt to keep the wobble out of my voice.

"I'm not suggesting anything." His hand drifts from my waist southward. His tone holds notes of black velvet and Scotch. "I'm here to take you to task for leaving without making things right." His palm lightly molds around the curve of my ass. "And then we're going to talk about *how* you're going to square things up with me." My core clenches.

His fingers close and he squeezes my ass.

"Do I have a choice here?"

Why does my voice sound so husky?

"Do you *want* a choice?"

I stare up at him, trying to decode that reply. It's hard when he's kneading and massaging my butt. I'm not wearing panties under the pajama shorts, and my own arousal is leaking onto my thighs.

"Or is it better to pretend you don't?" He shifts his knuckles from under my chin to brushing across my cheek.

I'm still not sure what he means. But he said pretend. So that means I *do* actually have a choice. Right?

"I've seen you watching the scenes at Sins. You say it's not for you, but your expression tells me something different."

I'm trembling now. Not from fear.

From anticipation.

Arousal.

The possibility of something dark and dirty happening between us.

I'm also stunned to hear he's watched me. Especially considering he always has a gorgeous woman on his arm.

"What about your girlfriend?" I ask.

He shakes his head. "You know I don't have a girlfriend."

He's right. I do know. Because he never brings the same woman to Sins twice.

"Enough stalling." He walks me backward, toward my bed. "It's time for your punishment."

When my thighs hit the bed, he stops. Holding my gaze, he slowly pulls the bralette over my head.

"What are you going to do?" The question comes out as little more than a whisper.

"I told you what I was going to do." His response is a warm rumble. More like a purr.

I catch his hand when his thumb tucks into the waistband of my shorts and he stops. He doesn't say anything, just waits.

He just proved my consent matters. He's waiting for me to decide.

And that's when I throw reason to the wind.

I release his hand. "Okay."

# CHAPTER THREE

*Marco*

Oh damn.

My dick is so hard right now at the prospect of spanking Taylor.

She's beyond adorable in her miniscule pajamas—the ones presently dropping to the floor at our feet.

Her body is small and she's fit, like a lean athlete. I think she told me once she's studying to become a physical therapist.

"You have a beautiful body, Taylor."

She steadies herself as she steps out of her shorts by catching my forearms, and I feel the tremble in her limbs.

I suddenly get the idea she's not all that experienced. Not like a virgin, but more like she hasn't had many partners.

She doesn't play the field.

That thought produces a surge of protectiveness in me. This may be punishment, but I'm going to make damn sure it's good for Taylor.

Show her what she's been missing out on at Sins.

"Come here, pretty girl." I sit on the bed and tug her hips until she stands between my legs. "Were you drinking last night? Is that why you ran?"

She covers her breasts with her hands, and I allow it for now.

"No," she groans. "I ran because I was stupid and panicked. And the accident happened because I spilled my water and my shoe got caught under the brake pedal and then my foot accidentally hit the gas. It was a total calamity."

I nod, rubbing her back and tracing soothing circles on her skin. She's actually...cute. Sexy as fuck, but she also has this endearing innocence to her. It's clear she simply panicked and didn't act out maliciously at all.

Her big eyes connect with mine. "Are you really going to sp--spank me? Like... over your knee?"

I reach behind her and pinch her pretty tight ass. "What do you think?"

She gasps.

Her skin is warm against my thigh and I breathe her in, letting the scent of her shampoo and perfume wash over me. Her pussy is pink and bare, and I love that I don't have to avoid staring at it.

I'm a fucking goner.

I settle a hand on her lower back and tilt her forward over my lap.

"Is this your first spanking?" I ask.

She nods.

I pat her ass and she instantly jerks forward. I reach around her tense body and pinch her nipple, and I'm rewarded with her sharp intake of breath. "You need to be a good girl and take it."

I give her five hard swats right off the bat. She cries out and then goes still, like I've effectively rendered her motionless. It's a sight to behold, her skin pinkening, her breast still protruding, and her body bending to my will.

My hand rubs over her, soothing her, teasing her, making her believe the pain will all go away. I'm a bastard, because I know the next smack will sting more.

"Oh, god," she cries.

I spank her harder.

"Marco, please, I'm sor--"

I cut her off with a quick smack to her ass, and then another. I spank her harder this time, making a point to cover the entire bottom half of her ass cheeks.

I'm hard as fuck, my cock pressing against my pants—so fucking hard, it hurts. I want to do more than spank her. I want to thrust deep inside her pussy and just pound her until she screams, but when I have a mission, I stick to it.

She whimpers, but I know the tears will be coming soon. I can't wait to see them. I want to see her release those tears, the ones she is trying so hard to hide from me.

I rub her ass and then deliver another, harder spank, again and again.

Her noises are soft, but when I run my fingers down the seam of her ass and find her wet pussy, she not only moans, she also releases a sob at the same time. The breath releases from her lungs in a whoosh.

She's so fucking wet, and I know she wants this. Her body can't hide the fact from me. I rub her clit and then press a finger into her pussy.

"Oh, fuck," she groans.

Her pussy is tight, and I find a spot that makes her cry out again, only louder this time.

"Oh my god," she moans. Her body shudders.

"You're going to be a good girl now, aren't you, Taylor?"

"Yes. Yes, I'll be a good girl." Her voice is raw.

I pump my finger in and out of her, driving her closer and closer to the edge. "*My* good girl. You are only going to be good for me."

"Yes."

As much as I want to fuck her, I need to stick to my plan. She's going to learn a lesson, a lesson that will make her see how fucking sexy she is and she should never resist her true desires.

I won't let her refuse them again.

And after this, I won't let her fuck anyone else again.

I'll make sure she's mine.

I've never been possessive like this before.

And never had a girl get under my skin in such a short amount of time, in such a powerful way. Not by simply spanking her ass. There's something about Taylor. Maybe it's knowing she doesn't belong in my world. She doesn't even belong in the world of Sins. And yet, that's where I found her. An innocent, ripe for my corruption.

Something shiny in a world of darkness.

And I don't want to tarnish her shine. I just want her to discover what drew her to Sins. What drew her to me—because I know she's turned on by me. She flirts with me. I'm sure she told herself it was for tips, but her nipples got hard every time I held her gaze for longer than I should.

The fact that I finally have her where I've wanted her for the last six months? Fuck me, this girl has me by the dick right now.

I pull her up to standing, back between my legs where she was before the spanking.

"Oh, god," she cries out, and it's the cutest fucking thing I've ever seen.

She collapses forward, her face buried in my shirt.

She's breathing hard, her body full of tension, but she's fully relaxed, too. I stroke her hair and then run my hand down her back.

"Are you okay?" I ask.

She nods against me and stays where she is.

Naked.

Vulnerable.

Submissive.

I smell her arousal, and I know I'm leaving her on edge. But I have a plan. I have to wait.

"That was your punishment for leaving last night without making things right with me," I say as I kiss the top of her head. "And now we have to discuss the repair of both our cars."

She pulls away, her face flushed, her eyes dilated. "Okay." She pushes her hair from her face.

"I will cover the cost. We don't need to involve the insurance. And in exchange, I want you for a night at Sins. For one night, you will be mine. You'll be protected by the rules of the club, of course, but other than that, you are to do whatever I ask."

"I--I can't," she says. "I have work every night and--"

"I'll take care of that." I slide my hand from her back to her neck, my thumb tracing circles on her skin. "You'll have the time off. And don't worry about the money, I'll pay you. A lot. More than you'd make." I smile at her horrified expression. "I'm not asking you to do anything you don't want to do, angel. You're free to say no. But I know you won't. And every night we play, you could say no... but I also know you won't."

I squeeze her heated ass and move her to the side, ignoring my cock that is demanding to be inside her. I've never been a patient man, but right now, I'm going to be.

"This is crazy," she whispers.

The look of panic and confusion in her eyes makes me hard. I want to fuck her, but this is more important. I need her to understand that.

"Tell me you want me to spank you again," I say. "That you want more. That you want to see what Sins is truly all about."

She shakes her head, but her eyes are full of lust.

I grab her chin and tip it up. "Tell me."

I lean toward her, my mouth inches from hers.

"Maybe... yes. I want you to spank me again. I want more." Her voice is raspy and honest, and it makes me throb for her.

I grip her hair and tug her head back, giving me an amazing view of her breasts. I want to suck on them, bite them, but I need to leave.

I release her and then turn and head for the door with her eyes burning into my back. I open the door and stare back at her. She's so fucking hot right now—naked and punished—and I want her so fucking bad.

"Meet me at Sins tonight at eight," I say. "I'll be waiting for you."

She swallows.

"Don't worry—I promise I'll make it good for you."

She licks her lips, her gaze dropping to my tented pants.

Fuck.

But no, I'm going to make her wait for it. I need to ensure she doesn't chicken out tonight.

"I know you've got an ache between those sweet thighs right now, angel," I tell her. "Show up tonight like a good girl, and I'll take good care of you."

# CHAPTER FOUR

*Taylor*

For a moment after Marco leaves, I just stand naked in my living room, trembling.

What just happened?

That was crazy.

Seriously.

Insane.

I go to the bathroom and twist to look at my heated, tingling ass in the mirror. Marco's handprints are still all over my lower cheeks.

Wow.

I'm wet—*beyond* wet—and slightly delirious, almost as if I have a fever. This must be the female equivalent of blue balls.

I feel needy and impatient and a little pissed off that Marco left without getting me off. But I'm sure that was his intention.

He's making sure I don't chicken out tonight. Making sure I actually show up.

I will. I don't want the huge insurance hike from reporting the accident, and I don't even have coverage on my own car, so I'd be out the full cost of a repair on that.

But who am I kidding? It's not even about the money.

After what just happened, I *want* to go tonight.

Yeah, I want to pretend he's making me, pretend he forced me into this, but that's because I don't want to admit the effect it had on me. How addictive I found Marco's attention. I definitely want more of what he's dishing out.

I turn on the shower and step under the spray.

Maybe this is the perfect excuse. I get to try out the dark and dirty things I've seen at Sins without admitting this might be what I really like. If I'm super honest with myself, it might be the reason I took the job at Sins. Yeah, the money is great, but I also was fascinated by what I saw there—from the safety of my position. I could hide behind the cocktail apron and tray and know I never had to try anything myself.

I take my time in the shower, shaving everywhere, shivering when I realize my body will be on display tonight. Not for everyone—unless Marco chooses that. But Marco will see me again.

*You have a beautiful body, Taylor.*

He made me feel beautiful. He made me feel free—like I could explore my body and sexuality in a complete judgement-free zone.

I mean, I guess that's what Sins is supposed to be, but I never gave myself permission to try anything there. I just needed to be coerced.

And I'm definitely not sorry that Marco is the one pushing me. I always had a fascination for dark villains—not that Marco is so villainous. He's usually a gentleman.

He always tips me well and treats me with respect. Although there is also always the uncurrent of sex. He gives me the appreciative up-and-down sweep of his gaze when I approach. Speaks in a sexy, low rumble, and lets his lids drop to half-mast when he smiles or flirts. You might say he is respectfully disrespectful toward women.

I finish my shower and step out, wrapping a towel around my body.

Marco and the guys he comes in with are mafia, though, for sure, so that makes him the villain. But it's not his Family ties that bother me.

What bothers me is knowing I will be one of at least three dozen different women he's scened with at Sins this year.

The guy is a total player.

Which, I guess, is fine. It means he's experienced. He will know what he's doing. I believe him when he said he would make it good for me.

Anyway, it's not like I'm thinking this will go anywhere.

It's not like I'm going to date the guy.

I just have to show up and let him do depraved things to my body.

It's not a bad trade, so long as I prevent myself from wanting more.

Because with Marco, that's an impossibility.

---

*Marco*

That afternoon Don Pachino leans back in his chair and considers me, my brother, Leo, and my cousin, Armando.

We're on the outside patio of Tony's, the sidewalk cafe with the best calzones in Chicago. This is where the don likes to conduct business.

"I need you guys to take care of something."

"Of course," Armando says, but then his phone buzzes on the table where he laid it facedown. He jerks and looks at it guiltily, but doesn't move to pick it up.

"Am I interrupting something?" The don doesn't like to be disrespected, and he especially doesn't like anyone touching a phone while he's talking.

Armando's throat bobs. It appears to be taking all his effort not to flip the phone over and take the call. I don't know what he was thinking, leaving it out on the table. He's usually smarter than that. Lately, his head isn't in the game though because—*Oh.*

"Could that be about Hannah?" I ask, trying to have his back.

"Oh, yeah," Leo catches on.

"Yeah." Armando flips his phone over so fast Don G instinctively reaches for his gun.

The moment Armando reads his screen he shoots to his feet. "It's time! Her water broke. I have to go." Then, collecting himself, he looks to the don. "I'm sorry, Don G. No disrespect."

The don waves a dismissive hand. "Go. Be with your wife. Let us know how it goes."

He waits until Armando is out of earshot before he chuckles and shakes his head. "I remember when Summer was born. It's not a fast process for first babies. I doubt that baby will be born before sunrise."

"Yeah?" I say. What do I know about babies?

"But, of course, he needs to be there for Hannah." He steeples his fingers together. "I can't rely on Armando having any focus for the next year. I need you two to stay sharp."

"Of course, Don G."

"Absolutely," Leo says.

He sits back and pulls a cigar from his inner pocket. "As soon as a guy gets married and has kids, he goes soft. Suddenly, all they can think about is how precious life is." He snips the end off his cigar.

"Well, we have no plans to marry any time soon," I say.

"True story," Leo agrees. "You probably don't ever have to worry about Marco in that department. He hasn't dated the same girl twice since third grade."

The don chuckles.

I smile, but I'm thinking about Taylor. How she surrendered to me this morning. How much I fucking loved it.

She's the kind of girl I would date twice. She's the kind who would be worth keeping.

*Forever.*

I can't wait until tonight when I get to reward her for her submission. Get to show her everything she's been missing while she skirted around the BDSM scenes at Sins and pretended she wasn't into it.

And now I'm thinking about sex in front of the don.

I clear my throat. "So what do you need us to take care of?"

"I need a message sent to the *stronzos* moving in on my Saturday card game."

"Who is it? The Russians?" There's been a tentative peace between the Chicago bratva, the Pachinos and the Tacone Family for the last ten years, but everyone knows those kind of truces can easily go south.

Just a few years ago Junior Tacone, head of the other Italian mafia family, single-handedly wiped out an entire bratva cell at an Italian deli. There were no complaints from Ravil Baranov, the boss of the opposing bratva cell.

"No, the Russians can have their game. This is a couple of drug dealers looking to supplement their income." He shows me the Instagram page of a guy posing with a flashy Corvette. "Find out where the game is this weekend. End it. I want them out of my fucking town."

"Consider it done."

Leo cracks his knuckles. "The guy is toast."

Don G slaps a meaty hand down on Leo's shoulder and stands. "Good. Let me know when it's done."

"Absolutely," I say, also getting to my feet.

Acting as enforcer for the boss is our regular job. This won't be a problem. I'm just relieved it can wait until Saturday, because I wouldn't want anything to interfere with my plans tonight with Taylor.

Of course, Leo reads my mind. He knew where I was headed this morning when I went to Taylor's.

"How did it go with the cocktail waitress?"

For some reason, I'm annoyed by the question, even though we usually banter about our latest conquests without filters.

It's because Taylor doesn't feel like a conquest and I don't like Leo even talking about her.

"Her name is Taylor. And I took care of it."

Leo's brows rise at my business-like tone. "It sounds like you didn't enjoy it."

"Oh, I enjoyed it. I just don't want you disrespecting her."

"Huh. It's like that." Leo looks at me like I'm a new person.

Hell, maybe I am. Taylor's someone special.

"Like what?"

Leo's lips quirk, but being my younger brother, he's smart enough not to poke the bear. "Nothing." He holds his hands up in surrender. "Nevermind. I'm glad you took care of it."

The image of Taylor standing naked before me pops into my mind and my nostrils flare at the reminder of how incredible she looked bared to me. How much I loved the feel of her skin, the sound of her little cries when I punished her.

I can't fucking wait until tonight.

By the end of the night, *Taylor will be mine.*

*Taylor*

I'm trembling when I arrive at Sins. I sit in my semi-wrecked car and try to work up the nerve to go in.

I'm wearing black thigh-highs with the seam up the back and little satin bows at the top, a short black skirt, and an asymmetrical top that's sleeveless on one side and strappy on the other. I'm not sure how to play this. My co-workers will think I'm coming in for my shift. When they see me with Marco, I will never hear the end of it. Everyone is going to want to know how he broke down my resolve to never play at my workplace.

A light tapping at my window makes me scream.

"Oh! Marco!" I struggle to open my door with trembling fingers, but he gets it open first.

He's in dom mode, wearing one of those commanding, unforgiving masks the doms put on for their submissive. It's different from the indulgent charm he uses when ordering drinks from me.

Whatever he sees in my face makes his expression soften.

"Hi." He cradles my cheek with his hand—like a lover, not a master—and slowly lowers his face to mine.

His lips brush over my open mouth, then he tastes me. The kiss grows, starting soft, ending with his tongue deep in my mouth, his teeth scraping over my lips and me soaking my panties.

"You look beautiful, Taylor," he murmurs, still cradling my face with one hand.

I'm breathless. "Thank you."

"Thank you, Sir," he corrects but his lips quirk at the corners. "Tonight you'll follow protocol. You'll address me as *Sir* or *Master.* You'll do nothing without permission or my command. Any hesitation or disobedience will be punished. Are we clear?"

My palms are sweaty and my heart hammers against my ribs. My head bobs my agreement.

"Yes, Sir," he corrects.

"Yes, Sir." It sounds like I've just run a hundred yard dash.

He kisses my forehead. It seems like an oddly tender gesture and I try to remember if I've seen him do it with his submissives before. "Good girl."

I'm not working for his tips tonight, but it seems I still love to earn his approval, because the words enter my chest and send warmth cascading down to my toes. I relax and allow him to usher me out of the parking lot and through the back door.

"I've arranged for a private room upstairs," he says, guiding me to the back staircase.

I'm instantly relieved. He seems to understand that I don't want to be observed by my co-workers while we scene. The private rooms upstairs cost five grand a night. I'm sure Marco can afford it, but he usually chooses a more public play area downstairs, so I'm gratified he was willing to make this consideration for me.

His hand rests lightly at my lower back as I hike the stairs in my stilettos, distinctly aware of everything around me—the deep, grinding pulse of the music, the shimmer of red and blue light, the distant crack of a paddle and a resulting scream.

Landon, one of Sins' dungeon masters stands in the hallway, monitoring.

Even the private rooms are supervised at Sins with black curtains instead of doors and a one-way mirror in each area for observation. My boss wants to ensure everything remains safe, sane, and consensual.

I know that if I said "Red" and Marco didn't respect it, Landon would step in. He and I once had a conversation about the fact that Marco and his buddies were probably mafia but that wouldn't stop him from protecting a submissive from one of them if he had to. He also said that the guys had never once given him any trouble, which has been my experience, too. In fact, I feel like they're more respectful than a lot of the guys who come to Sins.

Landon points us to our reserved room and Marco holds the curtain back for me to enter.

It has a leather loveseat, a spanking bench and a small table with an array of implements neatly arranged. I see a paddle, hairbrush, leather slapper, cat o'nine tails, and soft red ribbon.

My knees buckle.

Marco loops an arm around me from behind and pulls me against his body. "Don't be scared, angel." His breath feathers hot against the shell of my ear. "I won't use the wicked ones unless you misbehave."

My pussy clenches.

"But you're not going to misbehave, are you?"

"No, Sir."

"Good girl." His hand slides lower, down my thigh to the edge of my skirt, then back up the inside. He traces the top of my thigh-high with a light touch. "I like these." He turns me to face him. "Let me see them, properly." His voice takes on the deeper tenor of a command.

My hands fly to the waistband of my skirt, but then I hesitate. Does that mean take off my skirt? Is this like Simon Says? He told me I shouldn't do anything without permission or command.

Amusement flickers over his face. I see the trace of indulgence that he wears that makes him so sexy to me when he flirts.

"Take off your skirt, angel." His tone is milder now.

I'm grateful he's not going full dom on me right now. I'm way too nervous to handle it.

I shimmy out of my skirt.

Marco's lids droop as he takes in my see-through lace panties that match the black thigh-highs.

"Fucking gorgeous. Lose the top."

I pull off my top. I'm not wearing a bra, so I'm now in nothing but my panties, hose, and heels.

"Good girl. You're perfect. Absolutely perfect." He takes my upper arm and leads me to the side of the sofa, where he bends me over the overstuffed arm. "Let's see how your ass fared from this morning's spanking."

He runs a hand over my skin. He left marks this morning—nothing terrible. Some red blotchy marks. They don't hurt anymore except for a twinge or two when I squeeze them.

He gives my ass a couple of light slaps, then strokes a slow circle around the globes of my ass. "I think a submissive should always have a red, hot ass while we scene. It helps focus you, reminds you who is in charge and that there are consequences for disobedience."

"I'm not going to disobey," I say tartly.

Seriously.

There's no way I'd disobey. I have no interest in experiencing a spanking from anything other than his hand.

He delivers three hard spanks and I yelp. "You just did, angel."

Moisture leaks between my legs. My mind races to understand what I did wrong so I don't repeat it.

"I'm not going to disobey, *Sir*," I correct. "I mean, I won't disobey again, Sir."

Apparently, he's not mollified, because he holds my hip with one hand and starts spanking me steadily.

Already sore from this morning, I squirm and try to dodge his hand, but he doesn't relent until my ass is burning and I'm whimpering from the sensation.

"Mmm." He strokes his palm over my heated skin. "That's better." He leans down and kisses one cheek. "You're going to be my good girl?"

"Yes, Sir."

He helps me to stand upright and turns me to face him. "Do you want to use the standard safe words of *red, yellow,* and *green?*"

I nod. "Yes, Sir. I mean, whatever you want."

This earns me a sexy smile. "Good girl. On your knees, Taylor," Marco commands as he takes a handful of my hair and lowers me to where I'm at eye level with his hard cock.

I want to taste, swirl my tongue, devour his length, but I wait for his command as he has taught me to do.

He pulls my hair back. His hold is firm.

"Open your mouth," he says.

I do as he says... slightly.

His cock slides between my parted lips, and he rubs it over my tongue.

He pulls my hair back and thrusts his cock deeper and deeper, sliding it into my mouth, and I suck him all the way down, cutting off my air supply.

His dick pulses, and he groans as I lick the underside of his smooth skin.

"So good, Taylor. Lick it. Swirl it." He guides my mouth up and down his shaft. "Now tighten those lips around me."

I do as I'm told, hollowing my cheeks to suck, squeezing and releasing as I bob up and down on his cock, trying to suck him as hard as I can.

"That's it. You're such an eager little cock sucker," he groans. "Such a good girl."

I'm consuming his cock, pushing through my throat, taking as much as I can.

"Good, girl," Marco praises me more as he yanks on my hair again. "I am going to teach you to be the best submissive you can be."

My body trembles as my orgasm builds simply from his praise and knowing I'm pleasing him.

"Enough." He pulls his cock out of my mouth, and it is glistening with my saliva.

He rubs the head over my lips, and I simply look up into his eyes and wait for my next command.

"Stand up. Then go bend over and put your hands on the couch."

I obey, my head a little dizzy, as I rise to my tiptoes and bend over.

"Spread your legs."

I widen my stance, biting my lip when I feel his hand on my ass.

He reaches around my body, and I gasp when he slaps my pussy, the sting sending shivers down my spine.

"I didn't give you permission to bite your lip."

"I'm sorry, Sir," I apologize quickly, enjoying the feel of the word *Sir* and how it flows from my mouth with ease.

He rubs his hand over my ass, and then spanks me hard. I lower my head and try to calm my nerves. My mind screams *no*, my body demands *yes,* and the confusion nearly buckles my knees.

"Open your legs wider."

I do as I'm told, and then feel his hand on my ass. He spreads my ass cheeks with his thumbs.

"Has anyone fucked this ass before?"

I shake my head. "No, Sir."

"Good." He then lowers his hand to my pussy and spanks it again. "Is this *my* pussy?"

I nod again.

"Say it."

"This is your pussy, Sir."

"Good girl. If you continue being a good girl, then I might fuck this needy pussy tonight, my cock stretching your tight, little hole. And tomorrow night... I may just fuck this ass of yours too."

I'm trembling even more now, so turned on by it all. "Yes, Sir," I moan.

"Put your finger in your pussy, Taylor. I want to see you make it nice and wet for me. Stretch it for my cock."

Holy hell, the way this man speaks to me is... everything. So demanding. So powerful. And so damn sexy.

I place my finger in my pussy, slowly moving it in and out, knowing he's watching every move I make. I like putting on a show for him, knowing his eyes are watching my every move.

"Such a pretty, pink pussy," he says as I continue to finger fuck myself in front of him.

I've never done anything like this before. I've never been so bold, so free, and so absolutely turned on. I don't even try to hold back the moans. I know better than to try to hide my emotions from this man.

"Is your pussy wet, Taylor? Add another finger."

I slide in a second finger and push deep inside, gasping as I do. "Yes, Sir."

I keep fucking myself with my fingers, knowing that it's not going to take much to push me over the edge.

"When you're ready to come... stop."

Whimpering as I quickly pull my fingers away in fear of coming without his permission, I await his next command.

"Does my angel want to come?"

"Yes, Sir. So much, Sir."

———

*Marco*

I have always been a fan of edging. Taking someone to the final point of a cliff and delightfully hanging her over, only having me to hang on to. But with Taylor... I am losing control. I have never wanted to be buried balls deep inside a person in my life as badly as I do now.

I need her.

I need her now.

"Taylor, say it out loud. Tell me."

"I want to come, Sir. I want your cock. Please fuck me," Taylor whimpers.

God, she is a natural submissive. How did I not see this before? Her body is so responsive and my body reacts to every mewl, every cry, and every pant she gives.

I kneel down beside her, watching her intently as I rub the side of my thumb over her pussy lips, her legs still spread wide in front of me.

"You're so wet, Taylor. You are so fucking beautiful. Perfect. I think I'm going to come just from the sight of you."

I place my other hand on her pussy and begin to rub her clit in circles while I still rub her pussy. "So swollen, Taylor. So wet."

I love saying her name. It feels right.

"Oh, fuck, Sir," she moans as she grinds her pussy into my hand. "I'm gonna come. Fuck, I'm gonna come!"

When she reaches the edge and is ready to fall off, I stop touching her and watch her back arch.

I'm a fucking asshole, a tease, a tormenter, and she's going to learn to love that about me.

"No, please, Sir. Please let me come."

I reach for my pants and pull out a condom from the pocket. I can't torture her anymore, because I'm damn near killing myself. I rip open the foil, roll the condom down my shaft, and then stand behind her, rubbing up and down her slit with the head of my cock.

"Is this what you want, Taylor? You want my cock, huh? You want me to fuck this tight pussy?"

"Yes, Sir. I want that so badly," she says as she rocks her hips back and forth.

"You are so fucking wet," I grunt as I impale her with my cock. She gasps, and the sound sends a shot of lust straight to my cock.

I begin to fuck her slowly at first, holding her hips as I thrust deep inside her. All I can see is her ass and her pussy, and I can't imagine going another minute not being inside her. I don't ever want this to end. I can't get enough.

"Does my angel want me to fuck her?"

"Yes, please, Sir. Fuck me, Sir," she begs as she pushes her ass back against me.

I spank her ass, and she gasps, arching in the perfect most fuckable pose. Her pussy tightens around my cock and I'm nearly undone, but I'm a man on a fucking mission.

I squeeze my eyes shut, trying to hold on to my release just a little bit longer.

"Do you want to come, my angel?"

She whimpers as she claws at the couch, a clear indicator she's close. "Y-yes, Sir."

"Beg me to let you come."

"Please, Sir. Please let me come. Fuck me. Spank me. Anything. Just allow me to--"

I reach back and give her ass a hard slap, and she cries out.

"Such a good girl. I'm going to let you come now."

"Thank you, Sir. Oh, fuck, thank you, Sir."

I pump in and out of her as fast and hard as I can, giving her exactly what she's so desperate to take.

I thrust into her a few more times before I tighten my hand on her hips and release inside the most perfect pussy I've ever experienced. Her cunt tightens even more around my cock, and I know she's going to come again.

I hear her cries and watch the orgasm roll over her body, and I know that I'm, without a doubt, lost to her.

For the first time—ever—I wish I were somewhere more intimate. More private. Like in my bedroom, not a BDSM club.

I suddenly hate all the structure that allows a safe distance between partners. Allows for exits and endings. I don't want to walk Taylor back to her car at the end of the night, give her a kiss and tell her to send me the bill for her car.

"I changed my mind," I say, attempting to sound in control when my body feels anything but. "One night is not enough to cover what you owe me."

"What?"

"I need more of you."

I'm telling her. There's no choice. No option. And as her body collapses beneath me, her breath escaping her pouty lips in gasps, I don't believe she's going to argue.

# CHAPTER SIX

*Taylor*

"Don't even think about getting dressed," Marco growls at me from his bed. He's naked and glorious—all cut muscle with a tattoo of a snake and flowers winding around one shoulder.

After declaring he needed more of me last night at Sins, he brought me home where we had a second round of the hottest sex of my life.

Now we've just finished round three and I'm coming back from using the bathroom.

I drop his T-shirt back on the floor. "Yes, Sir."

"Mmm," he rumbles, reaching for me. "You are such a good little submissive, aren't you?" He tugs me over his body.

I fall on top of him, laughing. My body is buzzing—warm, and sated from all the attention he's given it.

He holds the back of my head and thrusts his tongue in my mouth as I squirm over him seeking pleasure when my clit finds the root of his cock. Marco's phone buzzes from the nightstand. He ignores it, kissing me, deeply, but it buzzes again and then again.

"Sorry, angel." He reaches for the phone. "I just need to check this." After quickly scanning the screen, he exclaims, "Oh, damn!" but there's a ring of joy in it.

"What?"

"My cousin had his baby!" He quirks a boyish grin at me and my heart squeezes. He's no longer the powerful and dangerous mafia boss, but a three dimensional person with cousins and babies and ordinary joy.

"Your *cousin* had the baby?" I tease.

"Well, his wife did." Marco's grin is infectious. "I'm so fucking happy for him. The last five years of Armando's life have been pure misery and then he meets this girl—under terrible circumstances—and knocks her up, and suddenly... well, she changed him. It's amazing to see what love can do to a man."

I sit up on the bed, leaning on one hand and drinking in the sight of him in his naked beauty. "I love that," I say.

Marco's eyes lock on mine, and for a moment, I wonder if he's thinking the same thing I am—whether love could change him, too.

"Hey, do you want to come with me to the hospital to welcome the new baby? Her name is Daisy Jane."

My heart skips a beat. He's asking me to do something that isn't just about sex. It's not even somewhere you would take a new date. It's the kind of activity reserved for a steady girlfriend or partner.

I hop off the bed. "I would love to meet Daisy Jane!" I throw on a pair of jeans and a top.

Marco puts on his clothes from last night, minus the jacket and we head out to his car. It's a rental he's using while his is getting fixed–a sweet convertible Mercedes.

"So why were the last five years so bad for Armando?" I ask after we hit a drive-thru coffee shop for bagels and coffee.

Marco gives me a sidelong glance, like he's deciding whether to tell me the truth or not. "He was in prison," he says after a moment's hesitation.

"Oh, wow."

"And when he got out, there was a hit out on him. He holed up at Hannah's place until he straightened things out."

I don't ask how things were straightened out. I have a feeling that even if Marco told me,  I wouldn't want to know. I'm just honored he's being real with me. I like him as the demanding dominant, but I like this glimpse into his ordinary life even more.

We get to the hospital and Marco buys a huge flower arrangement from the on-site florist.

"Hannah's going to kill me for this," he says.

"Why? Is she allergic?"

He grins. "No, she's an award-winning florist. She's going to be insulted I brought her flowers."

He laces his fingers with mine on the elevator ride up. "Thanks for coming with me."

I step closer to him so he can wrap an arm around me. "I'm actually surprised you asked me."

"Why?"

"I thought you'd be the type to leave my place before dawn."

The elevator doors open on Armando and Hannah's floor but Marco prevents me from getting off. "Hold up, angel. What do you mean?"

I shrug. The elevator doors close and we start to ascend further. "I mean you're a player. I work at Sins—I know you have a different girl every weekend. So you don't strike me as the *let's-get-breakfast-together* on the morning after type."

"You're right, I'm not."

A sick feeling starts in the pit of my stomach and I suddenly wish I hadn't come along. I'm starting to really fall for this guy and he's clearly not a safe choice for me. I hit the button for our floor again, over and over again.

"Hey." Marco catches my arm and pulls me back against him. "I don't usually spend the night." He looks down at me, his warm brown gaze searching mine like he wants to be sure I catch his meaning.

I want to be sure, too. "Why did you spend it with me?"

He lowers his head and nuzzles his nose along mine. "You're special, Taylor."

The elevator dings and this time, Marco moves to exit. His words ricochet around my head as we walk down the sterile hallway to find Armando and Hannah's room.

*I'm special.*

I'm almost afraid to admit how much I hoped that was true.

————

*Marco*

"I hope I look that good after being in labor for sixteen hours," Taylor says as we leave the hospital room and head to the elevator. "She was simply glowing."

Pulling Taylor against my side, I kiss the top of her head. "I can't imagine you ever looking anything but stunning."

The thought of her pregnant with a baby–*my* baby–has my cock hardening. I don't want a baby *yet*, but I sure as fuck want to practice in the baby making. And the idea of Taylor having *my* baby–

Jesus. Who the fuck am I? Soft kisses, loving compliments, and feeling as if I can't get enough of this woman is just not me. Never has been, and yet, here I am.

The surprised look on both Armando and Hannah's face when I entered the room with a *girlfriend*, reminded me of the fact that I was acting completely out of the norm for me. Luckily for me, they were both so wrapped up in the baby that I didn't get interrogated, but I'm pretty sure it's just a matter of time until I do.

But fuck it. I like it. And I really like her.

The elevator opens and the don steps out with Leo by his side. They are both carrying a bouquet of pink and yellow flowers and look as out of place in the hospital hallway as I'm sure I do.

I immediately disentangle myself from Taylor. Leo knows I didn't spend the night at home, but the don doesn't need to find out.

"Oh hey. You coming from Mando's room? How's the mama?" Leo asks.

Trying to avoid the narrow-eyed scrutiny the don is giving Taylor, I answer, "Great. I've never seen her so happy. And wait until you see our cousin. He's grinning from ear to ear. Fatherhood looks good on him."

"The delivery went well? The baby?" the don asks.

"Everything went smoothly. They're also enjoying the larger suite you arranged for them. Armando is very appreciative."

Don G's gaze is still locked on Taylor, and without thinking about it, I take a step away, opening the space between us. It's probably too late to give off the appearance that we aren't anything more than friends, but I'd rather avoid a conversation about it.

"Who's this?" the don asks.

So much for avoiding the conversation.

He isn't exactly being rude, but he isn't being friendly either. I know the don well enough to know he's not happy to see me with a girl after I just promised I'd never have a girlfriend and would keep my head in the game.

I distance myself a little more. "My car's in the shop, and I needed a ride," I say. "She works at Sins."

Taylor's eyes dart to me, and I see a flash of pain, but then it's quickly replaced with anger. She then plasters a smile on her face, turns to the don, reaches her hand out to his, and says, "My name is Taylor." She then glares at me again and adds, "We should get going. I need to get back *to work.*"

Fuck.

I totally fucked up.

"Yeah, definitely." To the don and Leo, I say, "You both should get in there. Visiting hours are almost over."

Seemingly satisfied with my answer, the don and Leo head to the hospital room, and I silently hit the elevator button trying to think of a way to soothe the stormy waters that I obviously caused.

"I can explain," I begin.

Taylor raises her hand as the ding of the elevator fills the silence. "No need. I'm just a girl who works at Sins."

Her words ooze from her lips like venom, and I know I just fucked myself.

"Taylor—"

She steps into the elevator, not saying another word.

# CHAPTER SEVEN



*Taylor*

I shouldn't be mad. We had one night together. That was my only commitment to Marco.

He made absolutely none to me.

We're not a couple. We technically haven't even had a date. I traded my body for car repairs.

Ugh. It sounds horrible when I put it that way.

No wonder I feel sick to my stomach right now. I walk quickly through the parking lot, wanting to leave this all behind me as fast as possible. In fact, maybe I'll just Uber home.

Yeah. I should definitely–

"Taylor, hold up." Marco catches my arm to stop me.

"Don't touch me," I snap and I'm gratified when he immediately drops my arm. I turn to continue.

"Hey." His voice is coaxing. He keeps pace with me, trying to catch my eye from the side. "Taylor, listen. I fucked up. I need to see your face right now. Please."

I stop and whirl. *"What?"*

He jerks his thumb in the direction of the hospital. "That was the don. My boss."

I raise my brows and fold my arms over my chest. I don't care if it was the freaking pope. What matters is that the truth came out. Marco pulled a *one-and-done* with me and now it's over.

"He just made me promise I wouldn't get a girlfriend and lose focus like my cousin has. So I panicked when he saw you here."

It takes great effort for me to force some breath out of my chest.

"But you're *not* just some girl who works at Sins to me." He reaches for my hand and squeezes it. "Last night was special. I don't usually go home with women."

I purse my lips.

"I don't. Leo can attest to that. But last night, when we were through, I didn't want it to end. And I still don't."

I look up at him, my throat closing.

"Taylor, I was going to ask if I could see you again." He picks up my other hand and holds both of them between us, like we're a bride and groom at the altar.

Damn my eyes for getting wet.

"You were?"

"Definitely. You weren't just a good lay to me—excuse the expression. You're smart, you're hot. You're ambitious. I know you're getting your PhD in physical therapy. You're going places, Taylor. I'm probably not the kind of guy you were looking to date, but damn, if I don't want to be."

He remembered what I'm studying. And he thinks I'm hot.

"Okay," I say softly.

"Yeah? You'll let me take you out? It will be on a proper date, with dinner and flowers, and the whole thing."

I smile. "That sounds nice," I manage to say. "I would like that."

He pulls me closer, tugging our joined hands right up to his chest. When he lets my hands go, I slide them up over his pectorals and around to the back of his neck.

"I want more of you, Taylor. *A lot* more."

I tip my face up to his and rise up on my toes to mate his mouth with mine.

He smiles against the kiss, then takes over, catching the back of my head with his hand, and sweeping his tongue between my lips.

We kiss in the parking lot for a solid two minutes before Marco breaks the kiss, and picks me up with his forearm beneath my ass to straddle his waist.

"What are you doing?" I laugh as he walks toward the car.

"Claiming you."

I glance up at the hospital windows. "What if the don sees you?"

Marco sets me down beside the car and kisses me again. "Well, I'll just have to prove to him I can have a woman in my life and still stay focused."

My heart thuds against my chest. Marco really does want more.

With me.

I don't know what it means, or what it would look like, but I know one thing for sure—

I want it, too.

Last night Marco rocked my world. More than that, I love the way I feel with him. Safe. Excited. Sexy and smart. Respected and objectified all at once.

Yes, I want more than just a taste of what he has to offer.

I want the whole thing.

Would you like more than just a Taste of Sin from Renee Rose and Alta Hensley? Be sure to read DEN OF SINS and meet not only Marco, but Armando, Hannah, Leo, and more. This is a mafia romance you won't want to miss.

# WANT FREE BOOKS?

**Receive a slew of free Renee Rose books:** Go to **http:// subscribepage.com/alphastemp** to sign up for Renee Rose's newsletter and receive free books. In addition to the free stories and bonus material, you will also get special pricing, exclusive previews and news of new releases.

**Download a free Lee Savino book** from www.leesavino.com

# ALSO BY ALTA HENSLEY

<u>Gods Among Men Series:</u>

Villains Are Made

Monsters Are Hidden

Vipers Are Forbidden

———

<u>Secret Bride Trilogy:</u>

Captive Bride

Kept Bride

Taken Bride

———

<u>Wonderland Trilogy:</u>

King of Spades

Queen of Hearts

Ace of Diamonds

———

<u>Dark Pen Series:</u>

Devil's Contract

Dirty Ledger

Dangerous Notes

———

<u>Spiked Roses Billionaires' Club:</u>

Bastards & Whiskey

Villains & Vodka

Scoundrels & Scotch

Devils & Rye

Beasts & Bourbon

Sinners & Gin

———

Evil Lies Series:

The Truth About Cinder

The Truth About Alice

———

Breaking Belles Series:

Elegant Sins

Beautiful Lies

Opulent Obsession

Inherited Malice

Delicate Revenge

Lavish Corruption

———

Gold In Locks

Sick Crush

Secret Bride

Captive Vow

Ruin Me

Delicate Scars

# OTHER TITLES BY RENEE ROSE

**Contemporary**

**Chicago Sin**

*Den of Sins*

*Rooted in Sin*

*Taste of Sin*

**Yacht Kings**

*Revenge*

**Made Men Series**

*Don't Tease Me*

*Don't Tempt Me*

*Don't Make Me*

**Chicago Bratva**

*"Prelude" in Black Light: Roulette War*

*The Director*

*The Fixer*

*"Owned" in Black Light: Roulette Rematch*

*The Enforcer*

*The Soldier*

*The Hacker*

*The Bookie*

*The Cleaner*

*The Player*

*The Gatekeeper*

**Bratva Heirs**

*Prince of Control*

**Alpha Mountain**

*Hero*

*Rebel*

*Warrior*

**Vegas Underground Mafia Romance**

*King of Diamonds*

*Mafia Daddy*

*Jack of Spades*

*Ace of Hearts*

*Joker's Wild*

*His Queen of Clubs*

*Dead Man's Hand*

*Wild Card*

***Master Me Series***

*Her Royal Master*

*Yes, Doctor*

*Her Russian Master*

*Her Marine Master*

Her Fire Master

Her Hollywood Master

Her Stepbrother Master

***Double Doms Series***

*Theirs to Punish*

*Theirs to Protect*

***Holiday Feel-Good***

*Scoring with Santa*

*Saved*

### ***Other Contemporary***

*Black Light: Valentine Roulette*

*Black Light: Roulette Redux*

*Black Light: Celebrity Roulette*

*Black Light: Roulette War*

*Black Light: Roulette Rematch*

*Punishing Portia (written as Darling Adams)*

*The Professor's Girl*

*Safe in his Arms*

### **Paranormal**

### **Wolf Ridge High Series**

*Alpha Bully*

*Alpha Knight*

*Step Alpha*

*Alpha King*

*Alpha Varsity*

### **Bad Boy Alphas Series**

*Alpha's Temptation*

*Alpha's Danger*

*Alpha's Prize*

*Alpha's Challenge*

*Alpha's Obsession*

*Alpha's Desire*

*Alpha's War*

*Alpha's Mission*

*Alpha's Bane*

*Alpha's Secret*

*Alpha's Prey*

*Alpha's Sun*

### *Shifter Ops*

*Alpha's Moon*

*Alpha's Vow*

*Alpha's Revenge*

*Alpha's Fire*

*Alpha's Rescue*

*Alpha's Command*

### *Werewolves of Wall Street*

*Big Bad Boss: Midnight*

*Big Bad Boss: Moon Mad*

*Big Bad Boss: Marked*

*Big Bad Boss: Mated*

*Big Bad Bully*

### *Alpha Doms Series*

*The Alpha's Hunger*

*The Alpha's Punishment*

*The Alpha's Promise*

*The Alpha's Protection*

### Two Marks Series

*Untamed*

*Tempted*

*Desired*

*Enticed*

### Wolf Ranch Series

*Rough*

*Wild*

*Feral*

*Savage*

*Fierce*

*Ruthless*

Primal

Rugged

Ravenous

## Sci-Fi

## Zandian Masters Series

*His Human Slave*

*His Human Prisoner*

*Training His Human*

*His Human Rebel*

*His Human Vessel*

*His Mate and Master*

*Zandian Pet*

*Their Zandian Mate*

*His Human Possession*

## Zandian Brides

*Night of the Zandians*

*Bought by the Zandians*

*Mastered by the Zandians*

*Zandian Lights*

*Kept by the Zandian*

*Claimed by the Zandian*

*Stolen by the Zandian*

# ABOUT ALTA HENSLEY

Alta Hensley is a USA TODAY bestselling author of hot, dark and dirty romance. She is also an Amazon Top 10 bestselling author. Being a multi-published author in the romance genre, Alta is known for her dark, gritty alpha heroes, sometimes sweet love stories, hot eroticism, and engaging tales of the constant struggle between dominance and submission.

She lives in a log cabin in the woods with her husband, two daughters, and an Australian Shepherd. When she isn't battling the bats, and watching the deer, she is writing about villains who always get their love story and happily ever after.

Facebook: https://www.facebook.com/AltaHensleyAuthor/
Amazon: https://www.amazon.com/Alta-Hensley/e/B004G5A6LI
Website: www.altahensley.com
Instagram: https://instagram.com/altahensley
Bookbub: https://www.bookbub.com/authors/alta-hensley
TikTok: https://www.tiktok.com/@altahensley
Join her mailing list: https://landing.mailerlite.com/webforms/landing/c9b6n3

# ABOUT RENEE ROSE

**USA TODAY BESTSELLING AUTHOR RENEE ROSE** loves a dominant, dirty-talking alpha hero! She's sold over five million copies of steamy romance with varying levels of kink. Her books have been featured in USA Today's *Happily Ever After* and *Popsugar*. Named Eroticon USA's Next Top Erotic Author in 2013, she has also won *Spunky and Sassy's* Favorite Sci-Fi and Anthology author, *The Romance Reviews* Best Historical Romance, and has hit the *USA Today* list fifteen times with her Bad Boy Alphas, Chicago Bratva, and Wolf Ranch series.

*Renee loves to connect with readers!*
www.reneeroseromance.com
reneeroseauthor@gmail.com

facebook.com/reneeroseromance
instagram.com/reneeroseromance
bookbub.com/authors/renee-rose
goodreads.com/Renee_Rose
tiktok.com/@reneeroseromance